FIDDLER ON THE MAKE

FIDDLER ON THE MAKE

Peter Kerr

ISIS
LARGE PRINT
Oxford

First published in Great Britain 2007
by
Accent Press Ltd.

Published in Large Print 2008 by ISIS Publishing Ltd.,
7 Centremead, Osney Mead, Oxford OX2 0ES
by arrangement with
Accent Press Ltd. c/o Pollnger Ltd.

British Library Cataloguing in Publication Data
Kerr, Peter, 1940–
    Fiddler on the make. – Large print ed.
    1. Villages – Scotland – Fiction
    2. Real estate developers – Scotland – Fiction
    3. Large type books
    I. Title
    823.9'2 [F]

ISBN 978–0–7531–8138–6 (hb)
ISBN 978–0–7531–8139–3 (pb)

Printed and bound in Great Britain by
T. J. International Ltd., Padstow, Cornwall

CHAPTER
ONE

One Man and His Dog

Jigger McCloud had never lived in a street in the entire forty years of his life, yet he was as streetwise as an alleycat, and with morals to match. Or so it had been said . . .

Bert, Jigger's dog and regular companion, had probably been a wire-haired fox terrier in his younger days, when his amorous exploits had been rumoured to rival those of his master. But now he was merely an ageing, shaggy mutt with a touch of arthritis in the leg joints, partial deafness in one ear and total silence in the other. And, as if that weren't enough, he'd developed a fat behind, resulting from too much sitting about in Jigger's truck eating Yorkie Bars. This latter pastime had also contributed to the rotting of his teeth, which, in turn, had rendered his doggy breath as sweet as the contents of a fishmonger's trashcan on a warm summer's evening.

Yet Bert's eyes were still as bright and alert as a pup's, and his libido could also still be rated (for his age) as Don Juan Class A. For even if he wasn't as fast on his feet as he used to be, he had never lost his uncanny knack of knowing in advance when any lady dog within a five-mile radius was due to come on heat — probably even before the lady herself did. So, Bert would always be at the relevant back door, all spruced up and ready for action, well before any of the neighbourhood competition had even had a long-distance sniff of the pleasures that were about to come on offer.

"He must keep a secret diary somewhere," was all Jigger could offer by way of explanation for this phenomenon, which had turned Bert into something of a legend in his own twelve-year lifetime. Also, it had made him the proud father of legions of little springer spaniels, beagles and Border collies — all of a semi-wire-haired strain, of course. Bert's choice of female companionship, it should be noted, had been limited to these few locally-popular, if unexotic, breeds following a nasty experience he'd had while attempting to mount a particularly attractive Afghan Hound damsel while still in his prime. His well-thought-out technique for overcoming the problem of the obvious height difference between himself and the leggy temptress was to jump down on her from the henhouse roof. So far so good. But, as we know, the best-laid plans (or, in this case, best-planned lays) of dogs and men gang aft a-gley. In Bert's case, disaster struck when he missed the target and became stuck with his dangly bits rammed up the rusty spout of a long-discarded watering-can.

The pain and embarrassment of that one misguided act of over-ambition had never left Bert, and prudence eventually prompted him to avoid romantic encounters with even those moderately-statured spaniels, beagles and collies. Nowadays, he preferred to play it smart and concentrate solely on Yorkshire terriers. Their diminutive height was just right for the bent-leg coital technique that the arthritis obliged him to employ — particularly in damp weather.

"I worry about you, Bert," said Jigger, stopping at a set of traffic lights and lobbing his pal another chunk of chocolate. Jigger gazed admiringly through the truck windscreen at the parade of pretty girls stepping smartly over the pedestrian crossing in front of him. "You've got a one-track mind, Bert," he grinned. "That's your trouble."

Bert effortlessly intercepted the piece of Yorkie Bar in mid-air. Then he stuck his nose out of the passenger window to take in a lungful of the aroma of a passing hamburger, this latter treat being gobbled by a schoolboy creeping, like a snail, unwillingly to school.

"See what I'm saying?" Jigger added. "A one-track mind."

He stuck his own head out of the driver's window to take in an uninterrupted eyeful of a pair of passing legs attached to a mini-skirted girl strutting along the opposite pavement. "Hmm. Tidy pair o' pins!" He liked driving through the centre of Edinburgh early on warm spring days like this.

Whatever the attractions to Jigger of sunny city mornings, it was the smell of hamburgers that really turned Bert on to the urban environment, at all times and in all weathers. You see, he had never had a hamburger — not even a tiny scrap of one. The fact

3

was, as Bert had come to realise over the years, you just didn't come upon any dropped hamburger remnants lying about in the gutters where he came from. More's the pity, but that was one of the great disadvantages of living on a farm — no gutters. Still, maybe someday. A dribble of saliva dropped from his hoary whiskers as the smell of the schoolboy and his burger faded along the street.

"You're disgusting, Bert," laughed Jigger. "A bloody glutton."

Bert wagged his tail and gave Jigger a little panting smile. He didn't know what his master had just said, but it sounded nice and friendly, and that was all that mattered. Being a dog, Bert didn't really know many words at all, although everyone thought he did. "Clever wee bugger, that," they would smile, shaking their heads in amazement. "Knows every word you say."

In reality, though, Bert only knew words like "Bert", "biscuits", "Yorkie Bars" and "Pedigree Chum". For all that, people credited him with recognising complicated verbal compositions such as: "Going for a ride in the truck today, Bert?" But he didn't. He only perked up and looked happy on such occasions because, like all dogs of reasonable wit, he could read his master's mind. Extrasensory perceptionists don't need words to know when a jaunt with the boss is imminent.

The traffic lights changed to green, and Jigger set the truck rolling again. Flashing a grin, he raised his baseball cap to a gaggle of giggling office girls scurrying up the steps from Waverley Station. "Good morning, ladies," he called out. "Have a nice day, eh! Yeah, and keep yer hands on yer ha'pennies!"

The giggles, like the hamburger whiffs before them, receded along Princes Street as the truck picked up speed and headed out of town.

Jigger had been making one of his regular deliveries of hay to the stables of the Edinburgh police. With only a small troop of horses, this particular outlet generated what Jigger considered to be a ludicrously modest income for his hay. He could, and did, charge three times as much for the same stuff to the horse-and-pony types who now frequented, in ever-increasing numbers, his farmyard in their trendy 4×4 off-roaders. But it was an outlet on which Jigger placed considerable importance, nonetheless. Not only did selling it to the police bestow a mark of unquestionable quality upon his hay (the very mark which rendered it possible for him to sock the aforementioned triple whack to the off-roader brigade), but it also provided him with an invaluable "in" with the Chief Constable. This stern and yeomanly Highlander took great pride in his small mounted division, and he always made it his policy to be at the stables on delivery mornings to inspect the hay with his super-sensitive police nostrils. Jigger McCloud's hand-picked bales of sweet, mould-free horse fodder never failed to meet with the Chief's scowled approval.

"Fine that then, Mr McCloud," he would boom cheerlessly after his educated nose had rummaged through handfuls of dried grass drawn at thoughtful random from the bales. "I take it ye'll be submitting yer

5

bill in the appropriate manner at the appropriate time as usual. Aye, and I'll be checking it myself, as is appropriate in such cases." He would then nod towards Jigger's rig and grunt, "Have ye got a licence for yon dog in yer wee vee-hicle there?"

"He's a farm dog, Chief," Jigger would reply, pointing to the *Acredales of Cuddyford* address painted on the side of his truck. "Don't need a licence for him." Jigger thought it wise never to remind the Chief Constable that the law requiring *any* dog to have a license had been abandoned years ago.

It was always the same routine, the Chief displaying the keen sense of observation and sharp memory for legal detail commensurate with his career climb to the very pinnacle of the "polis".

He *had* observed one detail entirely accurately, however. Jigger's wagon was, indeed, a wee one. It was only a little Mitsubishi pickup truck, and so it was debatable whether Jigger and Bert were even entitled to be sitting in there downing lumps of chocolate like the macho juggernaut jockeys in those old Yorkie Bar TV ads that Jigger admired so much.

But Jigger didn't care. He was happy with his little rig. It suited his purposes fine. And, after all, he told himself, size wasn't everything — well, not in relation to trucks at any rate. And Bert cared even less. He was happy with the little Mitsubishi too, simply because it had a forward-control cab. This meant that it had no view-impairing bonnet sticking out in front, so a small dog could sit high in the saddle and miss nothing of the passing show. This type of detail is important to a little fellow who spends his life at little more than ankle height to the rest of the world. Given his way, Bert would have spent every waking moment in that truck — except, naturally, for those moments when it was necessary for him to attend to "extramural" activities with those little Yorkshire terrier ladies of his.

Yet all the chunks of chocolate on Earth wouldn't tempt him into Jigger's car. And the fact that it was a 1959 vintage Humber Super Snipe with two-tone paintwork, white-wall tyres and real leather upholstery mattered not a monkey's to him. An invitation to ride in that car meant only one thing to Bert — the humiliation of being relegated to the back seat, while Jigger's wife was elevated to the co-pilot's position that was rightfully his. Plus, there was the inescapable and pride-crushing fact that he was too small to see out of the rear window without clambering up and lying on the shelf. That, in his firm opinion, was a decidedly poncy feat performed only by namby-pamby lapdogs, but NOT, under any circumstances, by a trucker's mate like him. Besides, he reluctantly conceded, the arthritis had put the mockers on such agile manoeuvres years ago. So, they could go stuff their car, hide-upholstered seats and all. For Bert, it was the wee, forward-control truck, or nothing.

But all thoughts of the hated Humber were far from his mind as the little Mitsubishi pickup bowled along the open highway. The noisy rumble and nose-nipping fumes of the city had been left far behind, replaced now by the sound of Jigger whistling a merry tune, while the inspiring pong of horse manure swept in through the cab's open windows.

"More valuable than a dozen police hay cheques, that dung," remarked Jigger, pausing in mid-whistle to glance back at the steaming heap piled high on the little truck's deck.

Bert woofed on cue, clueless as to the meaning of this latest verbal composition, but keen to show interest all the same.

"Yes, it may be only a load of horse shite to you, boy, but it's bread and butter to me." (Jigger liked to keep Bert up to date with the finer complexities of business while on these trips).

The little dog cocked an enquiring ear and tried to look intelligent, his expression suggesting a request of "Tell me more, boss" to Jigger's highly creative sense of imagination.

"That dung's got 'Green' and 'Organic' stamped on every dollop, Bert. Yeah, and these days that means dosh. Get the message?"

The horse manure was something of a bonus for Jigger. It was magnanimously proffered by the Chief Constable at the conclusion of every hay delivery, accompanied by a benediction of: "Take yon stuff with my compliments, Mr McCloud. Aye, there's enough bullshit in the force without getting ourselves buried under a mountain of the equine variety, would ye no agree?"

Jigger made it his business always to regard that final question as being purely rhetorical. He never quite knew whether there was, in fact, a glint of humour emanating from those tiny, heather-pelmetted eyes set deep beneath the peak of the Chief's chequered cap, or whether he was just being shiftily pumped for a potentially self-damning critique of the Edinburgh Constabulary. "You're very generous, sir," was all he would counter, tapping the peak of his own cap and saving the airing of his opinions of the "polis" for less suicidal locations. He forked the dung on board and got the hell out of there.

The sight of a truckload of horse manure speeding along the main road was nothing particularly exceptional in these parts, but a topping of a cast iron Victorian bath flanked by three solid pine Georgian doors did cause the occasional head to turn in eye-blinking curiosity. But these dung-mounted items were only the result of another aspect of Jigger's abiding interest in passing through Edinburgh early in the morning. In addition to being afforded the opportunity to eye up pretty girls hurrying to work, he could survey, from the modest loftiness of his truck, the contents of any rubbish skip that had been filled the previous night. Very often, these would contain potentially saleable household fixtures, dumped by apprentices doing "el cheapo" homes for unenlightened new residents. Edinburgh's burgeoning financial sector had become an employment mecca for upwardly mobile young people, many having sold a modest pad in the stratospherically-priced south for enough money to buy an elegant Georgian residence in the city's "New Town". Then, occasionally (and just to give the old place a trendy feel), in would come the moulded plastic turbo-bath and some wood-effect, pressed-hardboard doors from B&Q, and out would go the original period fittings.

With a bit of luck, Jigger would light upon such gems of architectural salvage and have them away before any zealous member of the local conservation committee had made the shocking discovery in the skip. Such a find would have resulted in firm action being taken by the committee to encourage the culprits to return the ripped-out items to their original positions forthwith. But, as was often the case, Jigger had got there first this morning. Also, to his quiet self-satisfaction, he knew a man who might be only too pleased to convert these particular spoils into a few hundred smackers, and with no more effort on Jigger's part than giving the underside of the bath a fresh coat of paint, and dip-stripping the doors in his handy acid-bath behind the cowshed.

The man he had in mind was the mysterious Babu Ng, an eastern multi-millionaire who had recently bought the rambling and long-neglected old manse on the outskirts of Cuddyford village, not five minutes from Jigger's farm. Oh, yes indeed, Jigger liked passing through the city early on a sunny morning like this.

"Tidy haul," he grinned, congratulating himself on his day's work so far, "and all one hundred per cent honest and above board. You have to admit it, Bert," he chuckled, "you can't get anything much more legal than a load of police horse droppings freely given by the Chief Constable himself." He smiled at the thought for a moment, then went on: "Yeah, and I doubt if any member of the New Town conservation lot would want to soil their nice, clean hands grabbing the bath and doors back from where they are now, even if they were entitled to. Which they aren't." He patted Bert's head. "No, no, boy — finders keepers — that's the only rule of the early morning skip-harvesting game."

Bert sniffed the truck's ambient aroma approvingly and settled back to enjoy the rest of the journey home to Cuddyford.

April can be a capricious month in that quarter of southern Scotland — some days mild and seasonably showery, others wild and wintry, with north-east gales firing hailstones like shotgun pellets at the cowering populace. Yet, often enough, like today, the weather could be warm, sunny and fairly oozing the magical charms of spring.

It was the sort of day on which Jigger's native county revealed in all its understated beauty just why it had become known as the Garden of Scotland. Jigger cherished every square inch of it. Heading along the new motorway, he was surrounded by lush, gently-undulating fields that stretched away towards the county town of Horseburgh, lying snug in its hidden valley just a few miles ahead. From there, wooded banks and grassy braes flanked the Cuddy Burn as it meandered its unhurried way to the sea, still barely visible through a shroud of morning mist on the far horizon.

Looking to his right, Jigger couldn't help but marvel, as ever, at the serenity of the landscape that rolled almost imperceptibly upwards through wood and field to the Lambsfoot Hills, their soft shoulders caped in cloaks of heather and whin, their pastured slopes ribboned with wind-soothing plantations of pine.

For so long, this wonderfully peaceful little corner, the very antithesis of the popular image of a rugged, mountainous Scotland, had been known to relatively few tourists. Other than occasional packs of plaid-trousered Americans on pilgrimages to the area's renowned coastal golf links, the only visitors had been those who came to soak up the gentle ambience of the countryside and the timeless peace of its villages. So, Jigger's cherished home county had remained quite unspoiled by time and the disruptive hands of external influence.

But progress, in the form of that very new road on which Jigger was now speeding homeward, had changed all that for ever. The capital city was now only a twenty-minute drive away from the very heart of the county. Sleepy Horseburghshire had been "discovered", opened up and exposed to weekend waves of motorised invaders, and to summer coaches full of rubber-necked package tourists from around the globe. But, worst of all, its charms had been laid bare to the most insidious infiltrator of all . . . the commuter!

Not that Jigger was too bothered. Why get your knickers in a twist about something you can't stop? Let as many locals who wanted to moan and groan about the hordes of incomers living in newly-built clumps of executive brick boxes on the perimeters of the villages. These were the same "white settlers" who roared along the narrow lanes like loonies in their four-wheel-drive off-roaders — trendy gas-guzzlers that were never exposed to anything further off-road than a paved, executive driveway. But those locals who complained had no imagination. That was Jigger's view. Opportunity, in the form of incomers, was welcome to knock on *his* door any time. And besides, these people had provided Bert with an ever-growing harem of Yorkshire terriers. Jigger savoured the notion, and, equally contentedly, the scenery.

Away to his left, he could see the wide waters of the Forrit Firth. For once, the sea was flat calm and mirror-like, perfectly reflecting the white-dappled blue of the spring sky, in which seagulls circled lazily on the upcurrents of air rising from the shore. Twenty crow's miles away on the far side of the Firth, the hilly outline of the ancient "Kingdom" of Drummy lay shimmering, its patchwork of fields rising from the coast through folds of mellow green and brown. Blessed as the area was with such views, Jigger understood why it now seemed as though the world and his wife wanted to come and live here. And he was happy to share what was his, with them all. Well, *some* of what was his — *and* at a tidy price, of course!

CHAPTER
TWO

Playing Chicken

Jigger lifted his arthritic old pal down from the truck cab in the cobbled yard behind the Acredales of Cuddyford farmhouse. "Breakfast time, Bert," he said. "Time to get yer morning fix o' Pedigree Chum, eh?"

The words struck a recognisable chord, and Bert shuffled off stiffly into the house, where Jigger's wife Agnes — or Nessie, his little Loch Ness Monster, as he had always called her — was already placing Bert's brimming bowl next to his basket beside the ancient black range that occupied almost half a wall of the kitchen.

Jigger gave Nessie a peck on the cheek and a simultaneous pinch on the bottom. "Must get that dirty old range hauled out and a tidy new Aga put in," he said.

"That'll be the day," Nessie laughed, shooing away Jigger's wandering hands as she bent over the hot stove to arrange two neat ranks of bacon rashers on the hissing griddle. "You always say that."

And so he did. But both Jigger and Nessie knew, and were content to accept, that the old black range would continue to beat as the warm heart of the Acredales farmhouse for as long as Jigger's old granny was alive. She had lived with them for the ten years since her husband, old Tam, passed away. Or, to be absolutely correct, Jigger's family had lived with *her*, moving in, on the old woman's insistence, from their cottage up the road near the old rubble-stone steading. Jigger had since converted those redundant farm buildings into a cosy little community of a dozen roses-round-the-door country abodes, and had flogged them for a handsome profit to members of the incoming *nouveau rustique* set.

It wasn't that Granny McCloud didn't like change. Indeed, she was all for it — as long as it didn't come into the house. Mind you, as she was quick to concede, washing machines and dishwashers and fridges and freezers and even microwave ovens and central heating were OK. She liked them fine now, every bit as much as the TV, and the wireless before that. But the old range — well, that was different.

It wasn't just a fire to heat the kitchen, or a stove to cook on, or an oven to bake in. It was also grand for drying your wellies, for taking the chill off your hurdies when you came inside, or for warming your boots before you ventured outdoors on a nippy winter's morning. In snowy weather, it was ideal for thawing out frosted logs, and it got your circulation going first thing in the morning as you raked it, stoked it and polished it with black lead. More than that, it was where you hung the washing to dry on rainy days, and its mantel shelf was a handy place to park your teeth overnight in a nice mug of Steradent. Sometimes, it even served as a foster mother that could save the life of a shivering orphan lamb. But most importantly of all, to Granny, it had been the place where she sat at night beside her Tam, watching the homely glow flickering in the grate, while they listened to their favourite programmes on the wireless, safe in the knowledge that the bairns were sleeping snugly upstairs. The old range was her friend.

That a clean, oil-fired Aga could boast all of the range's practical qualities (minus the need for raking, stoking and black-leading it!) was gladly ignored by Jigger and Nessie. They would never get rid of the old range as long as Granny was still around. And they hoped that she'd be around for a long while yet. Even inflated offers, received from tradition-besotted incomers, plenty of whom were falling over themselves to replace their new Agas with just such a bothersome old relic as this, would have to wait. That range was as much a part of Granny's memory-filled life as the country blood that still flowed strongly through her veins, so Jigger's ever-alert commercial ears were willingly rendered deaf to all such overvalued overtures, no matter how tempting.

Truth to tell, there was nothing Jigger wouldn't do for Granny. After all, she'd been like a mother to him — literally all the mother he had ever known — since her daughter Nell died giving birth to him all those forty years ago.

Of his father, nothing had ever been said to Jigger, other than that he'd gone away before Jigger was born. Moreover, as Jigger hadn't got round to marrying Nessie yet, he'd never had reason to see his own birth certificate, so he didn't even know his father's name. It was a subject that his grandparents had chosen not to talk about, and that was good enough for him. In Jigger's eyes, Old Tam and Granny were his real parents in any case.

He sat down at the big kitchen table and flicked through the morning newspaper while Nessie got on with making breakfast.

"Two eggs or one?" she asked.

"Three, please. All that hay and muck-flinging this morning has got me fair Lee Marvin." Then, without looking up from his paper, he casually enquired, "Where's Granny, by the way? Out checking her snares, is she?"

"No, she's given that up for the spring season."

"Giving the rabbits and hares a chance to breed in peace so she can catch even more of them later on, eh?"

Nessie cracked the eggs into the pan. "Something like that."

"So, where is she?"

"She just popped down to the village on her moped to get some milk from the shop. We're down to the last carton, and you know how much milk the kids scoff in the morning."

"Tell me about it," Jigger mumbled, suddenly engrossed in an article about a proposed change in EU agricultural hand-outs. "Got her crash helmet on, has she?"

"You must be joking!" Nessie nodded towards the far side of the room. "That's it over there on the window sill with the daffodils in it. Best thing for it, she says —

her reason being that she can't hear the car horns honking behind her when she's wearing it."

Jigger shook his head and chuckled. "If she'd only drive on the left like everybody else, she wouldn't need to bother about horns honking behind her."

"Maybe so, but she reckons that, with eyesight as poor as hers, you need something to aim for, so the white line up the middle of the road it is."

"Unbelievable," said Jigger, folding his newspaper. He got up to lift Bert's now-empty bowl, its owner having already retired to his basket for his first forty winks of the new day. "A woman of her age shouldn't be roaring about on a moped, anyway. She's a menace to other road users." He put Bert's bowl in the sink. "And a danger to herself. It's just a pity the police wouldn't arrest her for dangerous driving and ban her for life."

"Have a word with Sergeant Brown, then."

Jigger sat down again at the table and contemplated his cuticles. "Already have," he shrugged.

"And?"

"He said the last time he stopped her and cautioned her for driving in the middle of the road, she set about him with her handbag and threatened to run him down if he ever got in her way again. Accused him of interfering with a defenceless old lady in the course of her travels."

"Then what?"

"She called him a dictatorial Nazi bastard and whizzed off in a cloud of two-stroke smoke." Jigger gave a little laugh. "Sergeant Brown says her moped's like a motorised broomstick." A little smile of admiration sparkled in Jigger's eyes.

A fusillade of spitting and crackling burst from the recess of the range as Nessie turned some sausages on the griddle. "So what's he going to do about her?"

Jigger raised his shoulders. "Nothing. He says that, by getting in the way of everything behind her, she has what they call — in current police parlance — a traffic-calming effect on the road into the village." Jigger smiled at the notion for a few moments, then said: "Matter of fact, he's come round to thinking that every built-up area should have a biker granny like her scooting up and down the middle of the approach roads. Better than speed cameras any day," he says.

Nessie began loading the breakfast plates with bacon, sausages and eggs from the stove. She turned and gave Jigger an impish wink. "I only hope I'm still able to ride a motorbike like her when I'm that age, right?"

There wouldn't be much doubt that she would, Jigger thought, his eyes twinkling as he approved of how fit and youthful Nessie still looked. Tidy! Yeah, and her nearly forty, an' all! Still the slim, supple body with first-class bumps in all the right places. Still the flowing auburn tresses framing that pretty face with the laughing green eyes. Still that bewitching mix of femininity and tomboyishness that had knocked him for six when he first set eyes on her.

That had been on a Saturday evening in April, and all of twenty-three years ago. Sixteen she was. Jigger had a good memory for details like that. It was at the end of a beautiful spring day, he recalled. A day just like this one was shaping up to be. He'd gone along to Edinburgh's motorbike speedway track to lend a hand to his pal Camshaft McClung, son of the owner of the Cuddyford Garage. Camshaft was still only an apprentice, but he was nuts about speedway, and had managed to talk himself into a spare-time job as one of the home team's mechanics, when they were pushed. It had been a fairly lacklustre race meeting, as far as Jigger could remember — until the very last event of the night, that is.

"Just look at that kid go!" Camshaft shouted at the start of the novices' race. He beckoned Jigger over to the pits gate to get a close-up view of the svelte young figure in crimson leathers, effortlessly broadsiding his bike round the banked curves. He was already half a lap ahead of the three other rookies, who were struggling to control their machines on the slick dirt track. Camshaft was enthralled. "Look at the style, the speed, the control! That's a future champ, if ever I saw one." He elbowed Jigger in the ribs. "Who is he?" he yelled above the roar of the engines, never taking his eyes off the rider for a single moment.

Pulling a race programme from his pocket, Jigger turned his back on the spray of shale shooting out from the rear wheel of the leader's bike as it sped past in a spectacular sideways slide. "All it says here is his name's Red Stenton. No more details."

"Well, that's a name to remember," shouted Camshaft. "A future champion, that. Mark my words."

20

A cheer rose up from the crowd to acclaim this exciting new talent at the end of the race, in which the only other finisher had been lapped twice, the other two greenhorns having ended their participation by kissing the dirt on the very first bend.

Camshaft was the first man forward when the victorious youngster cruised back into the pits. "That was fantastic, mate," he beamed, slapping the lad's back. "You're a natural, and if there's anything I can do to . . ."

Camshaft's and Jigger's jaws dropped in unison as young Red Stenton's crash helmet was removed. A mane of glorious auburn locks tumbled out, and the dirt-smeared face grinning up at the two astonished lads didn't have the grease-monkey features of a loopy boy biker, but those of a stunningly attractive young woman. She looked, Jigger reckoned, just like she'd stepped out of one of those glossy magazines that advertise female beauty products. Max Factor and Avon and all that other film star stuff.

"Christ!" wheezed Camshaft, poleaxed. "You're a —"

"A girl," Jigger dreamily interjected. "Oh, yeah," he drooled. "Tidy!" Young Jigger was smitten.

"The name's Agnes," chirped Red. "Agnes Stenton. I only used the name Red to get into that race." She shook her head to untangle her hair, sending the Titian tresses billowing over her shoulders.

Jigger and Camshaft gulped in unison.

"Did it for a dare," she revealed, apparently oblivious to the effect she was having on the pulse-rate of her gawping audience. "Wouldn't have been allowed to enter if the management here knew I was a girl, see."

"But where did you learn to handle a bike like that?" Camshaft gasped.

"Oh, my dad's got a wee hill farm over the water there in Drummy. Us kids have been on motorbikes since before we could walk. We use them to round up the sheep."

"A girl," Jigger repeated glassy-eyed, his smitten count rising towards overload.

At that, the white-coated track manager stormed onto the scene, mauve-faced and patently not best pleased. "So it's right enough," he spluttered, giving Red the once-over. "You're a bloody girl!"

"They don't get much past you, do they, pal?" smirked Agnes the Red.

"I had my suspicions earlier," the manager stormed, "when you arrived wearing your goggles and crash helmet in the van." He ignored Red's "so what's the big deal?" shrug. "Anyway," he went on, "it's for me to tell you that girls do *not* get licences to ride at this speedway track."

"And why not? I licked those three blokes fair and square, didn't I? And I can ride a bike as well as any of the guys in *your* team, that's for sure."

"That's hardly the point. It's for your own good."

"Oh yeah? Meaning what?"

"Well, put it this way — if I was to let a bonnie wee lassie like you go into the changing rooms and showers with all the horny, oily gits that ride bikes for a living at places like this . . ." He paused and looked her straight in the eye. "So, away you go home to your mother, and don't let me see you around here again!"

And that was the end of the brief career of the mystery novice whose meteoric debut race was the talk of Edinburgh speedway fans for weeks to come. But it was only the beginning of the whirlwind romance that was to sweep both Nessie and Jigger off their feet, and still had them mutually swept these twenty-three years later.

"Come here and let me give you a great big cuddle," Jigger growled, grabbing Nessie as she carried the first two brimful plates to the breakfast table. "Come and sit on my knee and give me a nice handful of your vital statistics, eh!"

"Jigger McCloud, you're a sex maniac!" squealed Nessie. She thumped the plates on the table and let out a blood-curdling giggle as Jigger's fingers found her tickly bits with expert ease.

"At it again, you two?" yawned Davie, their fifteen year-old son, drawn tottering and sleepy-eyed into the kitchen on the end of an almost visible current of fried bacon smells. "You're worse than a pair of rabbits."

Jigger resisted the temptation to say that this was rich, coming from someone who was already known as Bugs at Horseburgh High School, and not because of any tendency towards the buck-toothed appearance of the cartoon bunny. No, nature had bestowed upon young McCloud the same roguish good looks as his father, valuable assets that he had already learned to use extremely effectively on contemporary members of the opposite sex. So, Jigger merely acknowledged his son's observation with a gratified smirk and a well-timed: "All the world loves a lover."

Nessie greeted that remark with a deliberately deadpan expression. "And that, Davie," she said, "is why your father is so well regarded in every corner of the community." Disentangling herself from Jigger's clutches, she shot him a mischievous look and added, "Or so they say!"

Jigger chortled, winked at Davie, gave Nessie a final squeeze, then released her to her breakfastly chores.

The sound of car horns blaring down on the main road indicated that Granny McCloud was homeward bound. This was confirmed by Maggie, Davie's sister and four years his senior, striding businesslike into the kitchen, immaculate in her long-skirted grey suit, white, buttoned-to-the-neck blouse, and sensible black lace-up shoes.

"The old witch almost caused another multi-vehicle pile-up just then," she said, staring aghast at the breakfast fare being heaped on the table by her mother. "I was watching from the upstairs bathroom window, and if it hadn't been for some pretty clever evasive action by a bus driver, little Granny dear would only be fit for use as a bookmark by now."

The bookmark reference related directly, though perhaps subconsciously, to Maggie's love of things literary and to her life's calling — assistant to the head librarian at the Horseburghshire County Library. Always a good-natured, pretty little thing as a child, since leaving school and embarking upon her chosen career, Maggie had developed into what her younger brother called "a right stuck-up bitch, who looked like the headmistress of a Victorian borstal."

Nor could it be denied that young Maggie seemed to have gone to considerable lengths to disguise the visual attributes with which she had been generously blessed. Gone were the billowing auburn locks inherited from her mother. Her hair was now hauled severely back and crammed into a tightly braided arrangement, which, according to Davie, gave the back of her head the appearance of an old-style, lace-up rugby ball. And her heart-melting emerald eyes were almost completely hidden behind horn-rimmed, tinted spectacles, worn, not to correct any myopic condition, but (in her brother's opinion at any rate) simply to give herself "that genuine librarian look."

It had worked. While not quite matching the sinister picture so eloquently composed by her junior sibling, young Maggie was certainly no longer the flirtatious, mini-skirted little turn-on who'd had the boys at Horseburgh High swooning in her wake just a few months earlier. Maggie was going places, upwardly mobile places, and she had convinced herself that the "right" appearance was an essential passport to such desirable destinations.

"And just look at those charred remains of dead animals you're all about to devour," she scoffed. (Maggie, you see, had also converted to vegetarianism and animal welfare causes since seeing the light at the other end of the social ladder). "Yuck!"

"A lot healthier than eating pages out of the dictionary like you do," Davie parried, ramming a thick wad of sausage, bacon and egg into his mouth. "You should get your guts drenched for bookworms. And anyway," he continued, a valid point coming suddenly to mind, "eggs aren't bits of dead animals, smarty pants."

"Precisely, young brother. The poor creatures that they were created to produce have had their life expectancy negated in pre-embryonic state by man's criminal interference with the sacrosanct course of nature."

"And what does that mouthful of rubbish mean?"

"It means, David, that eating an egg is tantamount to murdering a chicken."

"BOLLOCKS!" It was Granny, safely home from the shop, and standing four-square in the kitchen doorway with a litre carton of milk in her hand. She looked like a cross between Margaret Rutherford's portrayal of Miss Marple and an escapee from a Giles cartoon. "And I could only get this semi-skimmed muck," she huffed. "No *real* milk 'til the next delivery!"

Maggie clicked her tongue derisively. "She can't even recognise the healthy alternative," she muttered into her muesli, "not even when it hits her between the eyes."

"Don't you mumble at me, young lady!" Granny snapped. "If ye've got anything worthwhile to say, speak up — otherwise button yer lip. *And* I don't need any of *that* from you," she added in response to a testy sniff from Maggie. "I've had enough unnecessary aggro from those bampot drivers on the road down there." She swatted the air. "Inconsiderate arseholes! How any of them ever passed a driving test beats me!"

Conveniently ignoring the fact that, in her day, you didn't even need to *sit* a driving test, far less pass one, she took her place at the table and surveyed her heaped plate of charred remains of dead animals with undisguised relish. "And," she declared with a contemptuous glance in Maggie's direction, "you can take your new-fangled healthy alternatives and stick them where the squirrel stuck his —"

Nessie diplomatically cleared her throat. "Granny's quite right, Maggie." She directed a sympathetic little smile towards her daughter. "We all look pretty well on this so-called unhealthy food we eat, don't you think?"

"That's right," said Jigger. "And, eh, on the subject of food, we were just saying, Granny, that it's high time we got rid of that old range for cooking on."

Granny grunted into her mug of tea, but otherwise made no sign of taking Jigger's bait. If he thought he was being funny, his clumsy attempt certainly did *not* amuse her.

"Come on now, Granny," he persisted, "you've gotta admit we'd be better off with a tidy new Aga, eh?" He gave Nessie a surreptitious wink. Pulling Granny's leg about the range was usually a good way of changing the subject when she was in one of her grumpy moods.

Granny speared a sausage with her fork and cast Jigger a withering glance. A distinctly wan smile quickly replaced the cocky grin on his face. After a suitably dramatic pause, Granny pointed at the impaled banger with her knife. "Lay one finger on that bloody range, young Jigger McCloud," she growled, "and I'll put paid to your favourite fun and games — for *good!*"

There was a glint of stainless steel, and her knife sliced through the speared sausage in what young Maggie might have described as an impromptu show of primitive symbolism. Although interpreting her action in less verbose terms, the main drift of what Granny was driving at was still painfully obvious to Jigger.

At that very moment, a peal of excited cackling erupted outside, suggesting that a further supply of eggs had arrived. To Jigger, however, the sudden poultry chorus denoted only that a customer was approaching his little farm shop in the old converted stable at the other side of the yard. He excused himself from the tense atmosphere of the breakfast table and set course for the stable.

Waiting there was one of his regular 4×4-driving customers, a mousey little creature in her late twenties whom he knew to be Tabetha Spriggs, wife of Nigel Spriggs. Nigel claimed to have been head-hunted in London to do his "creative thing" for an up-and-coming Edinburgh advertising agency. He now resided with Tabetha, their two-year-old son Toby and a recently-purchased Yorkshire terrier bitch, answering (sometimes) to the name Heather, in one of the bijou maisonettes in Jigger's steading conversion up the road.

"Morning, Mr McCloud," she warbled as she alighted breathless from her dinky, pink Suzuki Vitara with a struggling Toby in tow. "I — I hope I haven't called at an inconvenient moment. Only I — I —"

"No time would ever be inconvenient for me to serve you, Mrs Spriggs," Jigger interrupted in a well-practiced Sean Connery drone. "And please, it's Jigger, not Mr McCloud. OK?"

Tabetha Spriggs trembled ever so slightly as Jigger ambled forward. He paused deliberately close to her side while he proceeded to unlock the shop door with what she thought was almost insolent calm. Insolent . . . but hunky. She trembled again — not quite so slightly this time. What was it about this, this *farmer* that made her come over so wobbly and useless every time he came near? Yes, that was it — it was his raw, *manly* smell. God, she could smell it even now. The smell of honest, hard toil; the smell of new-mown hay, of trouser legs damp with morning dew (or something); that trace of freshly fried bacon on his breath, mixed with the scent of Lynx aftershave. And was it? Could it be? Yes, it was there, too — the merest hint of that spellbinding aroma that turns the legs of even the most urbane of adopted countrywomen to jelly. The thigh-quivering aroma of horses!

A light zephyr was wafting over from Jigger's pickup truck and caressing Tabetha's eagerly receptive nostrils.

"You all right, Mrs Spriggs? You look a bit pale."

"Ooh . . . yes. I — I was only thinking —"

"Sorry I'm taking so long to open the door, Mrs Spriggs." Jigger looked down into her eyes, which were now darting from side to side like those of a cornered hare looking for a bolt hole. "There, that's done it. My, my, I was trying to put the key into the wrong hole. Not like me, eh?"

Tabetha Spriggs brushed quickly past him, all a-flutter, cheeks flushed, fingers fumbling with her cardigan buttons.

Jigger was revelling in the fun. He followed her into the shop. "One thing's for sure," he thought to himself, "the nearest thing to wildly erotic excitement she must ever experience is reading those books with cover pictures of big hairy pirates towering over fainting, half-naked women. And little wonder, being married to that wimpy little Nigel, with his pink-framed specs, his pigtail, and his crushed linen shirt-tail hanging out. Hell's bells, he looks more like Granny Clampett, than a man."

Toby started to whine.

Jigger looked askance at the scrawny, pink-spectacled, pigtailed toddler, who was trying hard to work himself into a tantrum over by a crate of spring cabbages. "A real chip off the old block," Jigger silently mused.

"There, there, Toby darling," Tabetha flustered. "Don't cry — there's a good boy. Mummy won't be long now."

Toby pouted, frowned and took a swipe at a cabbage with his green-wellied foot.

Tabetha was in a flap. "Oh, listen to Mr McCloud's chickens!" she gushed in a flash of embarrassed inspiration. "Aren't they singing loudly?" She touched the top of Toby's head, hesitantly, as you would a live electric cable. "If you ask nicely, perhaps nice Mr McCloud will take you to see them."

"'Fraid not," Jigger stated flatly. "Against government health regulations, you see." He shook his head. "Nope, top quality, free-range hens like mine have to be kept in strict quarantine conditions. Their paddock's out of bounds to members of the public."

"*Ree-lee?*" said Tabetha, her face a picture of bamboozlement. "Oh well, I suppose it's worth it to get eggs like yours. So much nicer than those battery-produced ones, aren't they?" She allowed herself a shy little smile, pleasantly surprised at how knowledgeable about country matters she had just sounded. Jigger *would* be impressed! "Yes," she added with uncharacteristic confidence, "it's worth paying the extra for the free-range quality, I always say."

"I always say so, too," Jigger readily concurred.

"You can tell by the taste that they've been laid by happy chickens, can't you?"

"I always say that, too."

"Just a dozen today please, Mr . . . er, Jigger." Tabetha blushed. "The brown ones, as usual, if you've —"

"They're all brown ones, Mrs Spriggs. My clients rightly feel it's worth paying the premium over the white ones. Can't beat the flavour of a Rhode Island Red, I always say."

"*Ree-lee?*" Tabetha was bamboozled again. "I don't think I've ever tasted a red egg."

From outside, the happy sound of cackling hens was augmented by the clarion call of a cockerel.

"Oo-oo!" squeaked Tabetha. "I thought roosters only crowed at dawn."

"Not if they're happy, free-range ones," said Jigger, smiling reassuringly. "My cock is at it all day long," he continued, with but the slightest arching of a suggestive eyebrow. "So, that says it all, doesn't it, Mrs Spriggs?"

Tabetha blushed again, violently this time, then fumbled the bottom button right off her cardigan.

Jigger was enjoying himself. While he placed eggs into a cosily-traditional papier-mâché tray for the visibly trembling Tabetha Spriggs, he reflected on just what a nice little earner this free-range, brown egg caper had grown into. It was only two years since he started out with half-a-dozen hens scratching about in full view of the paying customers in the little wire-mesh run he'd built specially just outside the shop door. Then, as sales of eggs picked up, he reduced the flock to two, four having been culled to satisfy initial inquiries for oven-ready, free-range chickens. It wasn't long before the news spread throughout the nearby commuting community, and demand for his farmyard-fresh eggs and table chickens really took off. The surviving duo of hens was duly cashed in, and their run demolished.

This curious transposition of the accepted supply-and-demand formula had only been possible because all six of Jigger's exhibition hens had been well clapped-out and off-the-lay from the very first day they appeared in the hen run, anyway. All the eggs and all the oven-ready chickens (except the first six) were purchased wholesale by Jigger from a giant battery set-up down at the coast near North Crabswick, close to where he kept a few pigs in a disused WW2 RAF radar station. The one small snag was that the factory farm produced only white eggs, but by dipping them overnight in buckets of cold tea, Jigger quickly transformed them into the tastier brown variety for his discerning, premium-paying customers.

The continuing illusion of an unseen flock of hens ranging about, scraping and picking freely in the open air, was achieved by Jigger and young Davie, who was a dab hand at electronics, linking up a cassette player loaded with a C90 full of BBC cock-and-hen sound effects to the sensor of an old security light mounted above the stable door. Thus, whenever a customer's vehicle approached, the amplified poultry tape was switched on automatically and relayed through a loudspeaker craftily concealed behind the shop.

Jigger indulged himself in a smug smile. Old Tam would have been proud of him. His smirk was soon replaced, however, by a startled scowl when the BBC cockerel suddenly started to sound as if he was crowing under six feet of boiling water.

Tabetha caught her breath. "Coo!" she exclaimed, while clasping her hand to her breast. "Coo!" she reiterated, "Doesn't your cock ... er, rooster sound queer!"

"Cockadoodliosis," said Jigger. He spoke in cool tones as his right foot feverishly felt for the cassette player on the floor under the counter.

"*Ree-lee?*" The familiar bamboozlement was returning. "Cocka — cockadilly —"

"Cockadoodliosis, Mrs Spriggs!"

Jigger was winging it like crazy. If he couldn't sort that snarled cassette smartly, his lovely little scam would be rumbled by trembling Tabetha and duly exposed to all of his premium-paying clientele. Keep talking, that was the game . . .

"Yes, cockadoodliosis. It's a kind of poultry tonsillitis . . . ehm, but more to do with the gizzard, if you see what I'm saying."

"Gizzard? Ree-*lee?* Golly!"

"Strangulated giblets is the layman's term, I think."

"*Ree-ee*-lee? Giblets? Oo, I say!"

"Yes, that's your cockadoodliosis for you." Jigger's frantic foot finally found the cassette machine. "But it's usually only a temporary condition." He gave the offending apparatus a surreptitious boot, and was relieved to hear normal service being resumed over the Tannoy. "See what I mean?"

A look of transparent wonderment spread over Tabetha's face. Somewhere in there an idea was trying hard to form, Jigger suspected.

"That sound," she ventured timidly, "that funny crowing sound sounded a bit like a snarled up tape re —"

"That sound," Jigger dominatingly declared, while leaning over the counter and fixing the cowering Tabetha in a Connery-eyebrowed stare, "that funny crowing sound, sounded just like cockadoodliosis. Because that's exactly what it was, wasn't it, Mrs Spriggs?" He handed her the tray of eggs. Then, his hands lingering for a moment against hers, their eyes playing close-up peek-a-boo between the uniformly-tinted ranks of Grade Two single-yolkers, he huskily repeated, "Wasn't it, Mrs Spriggs?"

"Oh-h-h, yes," quaked Tabetha in a febrile whisper.

"Good! That'll be three pounds, please," said Jigger, abruptly breaking the spell. "As you say, Mrs Spriggs, it's always worth paying the extra for the free-range quality. Here, let me help you out to the car with that tray. You don't want to drop any eggs when you're paying as much as that for them, do you?"

Tabetha didn't reply. She was too busy struggling to pull her trembling self together. Besides, another idea was trying hard to form.

Jigger closed the car door behind her, then handed her a plump spring cabbage, the one Toby had kicked in his tantrum build-up.

"I hope you'll accept this little gift, Mrs Spriggs."

"Oh, no, I couldn't poss —"

"Please, it's only a small token of my appreciation to a valued customer." He gestured towards his conspicuously parked pickup truck, heaped with dung from which the old bath and doors had already been circumspectly removed. "Organically grown, these cabbages — like all our produce."

Jigger never missed a trick when it came to advertising. The small detail that the horse manure, after a brief period on display in the farmyard, was always flogged at a tidy price to a keen amateur mushroom grower at North Crabswick, without having fertilized a single cabbage or anything else on Jigger's land, was kept, as a matter of necessity, absolutely shtum.

The expression of transparent wonderment returned to Tabetha's face, passing Jigger the hint that her second idea of the morning had hatched, or was about to.

"I've just been thinking," she claimed, "and I was wondering how you always seem to know when I'm coming."

Jigger raised an inquisitive eyebrow, but said nothing.

"You see, it's only that, every time I drive into your farmyard, you always seem to appear suddenly from nowhere before I even beep the car horn."

He liked this woman a lot better when she wasn't allowing ideas to form, Jigger decided. Something had to be done about it. Leaning his elbow seductively on her open window, he passed his head through and stared once more into her cornered hare's eyes. With eyebrows working overtime, he turned up the Connery to regulo mark 9 and droned, "Mrs Spriggs, I swore to myself that I'd never tell you this, because . . . because . . ."

"Yes?" Tabetha whimpered.

"Because you're a married woman. But . . ."

"Yes? Yes?" she whispered.

"But . . . but I can't keep it a secret any longer, dammit!"

"Oo, *ree-ee-lee?*"

"I know when you're coming, Mrs Spriggs, because I sit there at the kitchen window all day, watching and waiting, looking and hoping."

"Coo!"

"And when I see your car coming down the road, I can't stop myself from rushing out, because . . ."

"Yes?" Tabetha's breath was coming in short pants now, like a procession of 1970s marathon runners, Jigger mused.

"Because, Mrs Spriggs — or may I call you Tabetha?" He didn't wait for the overwhelmed Tabetha to answer. "Because Mrs Tabetha Spriggs, when I cast my eyes upon you . . ." He paused, allowing his eyebrows to raise themselves into a ceremonial arch and his mouth to arrange itself into a full-blown, bottom-lip-only 007 pout. "When I cast my eyes upon you, Tabetha, I'm both shaken and stirred."

Cringe-makingly corny as Jigger's patter had been, Tabetha dissolved into coy flutterings of excitement. Crunching her 4×4 into first gear with a quivering hand, she sped off homeward in full tremble — no doubt, Jigger speculated, to the waiting pages of her favourite pirate book.

"You been teasing that poor Spriggs girl again?" Nessie called when she heard Jigger come chuckling back into the kitchen.

"Just protecting the trade secrets, and having a bit of harmless sport at the same time, that's all."

Nessie shot him a wry look. "Something tells me I'm better off not knowing the sordid details. Anyway," she went on, "the Duke was on the phone a moment ago. He wonders if you can pop over to Craigcuddy Castle and see him right away. Seems to be in a real blue funk, the poor old sod."

CHAPTER
THREE

Crisis at Craigcuddy

Jigger still missed old Tam, though ten years had passed since he walked into the sitting room on that Christmas evening and saw his grandfather sleeping peacefully by the fire, his hand still holding a whisky glass on the little table at the side of his favourite easy chair.

It had been a good day, a typical Christmas. The kids were still of an age to believe in the simple joys of the occasion, and to enjoy without question the warmth and security of their little family group. It would be a while yet before the distractions and attractions of adolescence would steal up on them unnoticed and carry off their precious innocence for ever.

"Time for Nessie and me to take wee Maggie and Davie home to bed," Jigger had said to his grandfather. "They've had a great day. We all have. Here, I'll put another log on the fire for you before we go. We don't want your whisky catching cold, eh?" he laughed.

He had stood for a moment, looking down at the old man. He was a picture of peace and contentment, the corners of his mouth turned up in that mischievous little smile of his, the laugh lines at his eyes testimony to the easy nature and pawky humour that had seen him safely through an often hard, but always contented life. Jigger had forever regarded old Tam as someone who would always be there, someone whose permanent presence could be taken for granted as surely as the coming of each new day. He had never even thought of life without his grandfather. Perhaps, as many do when it involves a loved one who had been as close to old Tam as Jigger, he simply couldn't bring himself to think of such an eventuality, no matter how inevitable.

But, on giving the old man's head a goodnight pat on that Christmas night, the marble-like cold that his hand encountered had chilled Jigger's very soul.

What immediately followed now seemed like a distant, hazy dream. A bad dream, of Granny devastated and shattered, but bravely trying to hide her crushing grief from the confused, but suddenly less innocent, children, of Nessie, somehow managing to control her own distraught feelings enough to help do all the things that have to be done at such a tragic time.

It had been a dream from which Jigger only fully awakened some hours later, when he found himself sitting alone on a tree stump at the edge of a little wooded knoll. It overlooked the village on one side, and the neat, hedge-enclosed fields of Acredales of Cuddyford on the other. It was a place where, since Jigger's earliest recollections of childhood, old Tam had taken him to look out over the ripening crops of golden barley on warm August evenings, to check on young calves turned out for their first, tail-high romps on the fresh April swards, and to show him how to make whistles from little green twigs cut from the big ash tree whose spreading branches overhung that very stump on which he was now sitting.

This spot evoked so many memories. Memories of winter days spent sledging on the snowy slopes with his school pals. Memories of still autumn evenings, strolling hand in teenage hand with Nessie, and whiling away timeless moments gazing down at the wood smoke drifting up from the chimneys that crowned the pantiled village roofs. Memories of Easter Sunday mornings when Maggie and Davie were small, and Nessie and Jigger would help them roll their hard-boiled eggs all the way back down the hill to the farmhouse, where Granny and old Tam would be waiting for them in a kitchen filled with the spicy smell of hot cross buns fresh from the oven of the old range. All those memories had come drifting through, easing Jigger's stunned senses back into bitter-sweet reality.

He had no idea of how long he'd been sitting there, nor even that he had company, until the cold nuzzle of a dog's nose against his hand made him turn his head to see the gaunt figure standing by his side. In the dim moonlight, he had only just been able to make out that it was old Horace, the Duke of Gormlie himself.

"I — I hope I didn't startle you, m'boy," the Duke had said awkwardly, "but, you see, it was such a fine night, and I decided to stroll with the labs through the woods from the castle to wish your, ah-ehm, your grandparents the compliments of the season as usual, and —"

Jigger had tried to speak, but the words stuck in his throat as he made to get to his feet.

The old Duke had laid a hand on his shoulder. "Please don't get up. If I may, I'd like to sit with you a while. They, uhm, told me at the farmhouse that I might find you here, and so I . . ." He caught his breath, then coughed such a cough as befits a gentleman of breeding when faced with the task of fighting back a sob. "Look here, m'boy, I — well, I'm most dreadfully sorry. If only there was somethin' I could say, somethin' I could do . . ."

Jigger had shaken his head silently.

Countless minutes had then passed, during which even the usually boisterous labs had sat motionless. The only sounds to penetrate the frosty hush of the night air were an occasional little sniff from Jigger and a feigned clearing of the throat by the Duke. Both men were trying, each in his own way, to mask their emotions, the one hoping that the other wouldn't notice the tears rolling down his cheeks and falling silently onto the carpet of dead leaves at their feet.

"It was all so very sad," the Duke had said at length, talking in a hoarse whisper now, almost as if he were speaking to himself, unaware of anyone else's presence. "At the farmhouse there. All so very sad. It took me back . . . all those years to that night when young Nell . . . beautiful young Nell —" He stopped short, seeming suddenly to remember where he was and who was with him. "Ah-uhm, my God, I'm dreadfully sorry, m'boy," he flustered. "I — I didn't think . . . Er, that's to say, I forgot for a moment that —"

"Don't worry," Jigger had said, the overpowering feeling of loss that had been smothering him lifting

41

strangely as he attempted to placate the patently upset Duke. "You see, I never knew my mother, so I've never grieved for her. It's only now, tonight, that I'm learning what agony it is to lose someone that you . . ." He swallowed hard to quell the rising tears.

"Thank you, Thomas." The Duke's hand had returned then to Jigger's shoulder. "You're a credit to your mother's memory, the dear girl. Good night, m'boy. And — and if there's anything . . ."

No more had been said. The two men had shaken hands and had gone their separate ways, each knowing that words were not required to seal the bond that had been created between them on that sad Christmas night.

It all returned so vividly to Jigger when he looked up to the little hillock while walking this fine spring morning along the old cart track that led from the farm through the woods to Craigcuddy Castle. He still thought fondly of old Tam every time he passed that place, and of that meeting with the Duke those ten Christmases ago.

That had been the first time old Duke Horace had called him by his real name, Thomas. In fact, the Duke was the only person he could ever remember calling him that, except his teacher at Cuddyford Infant School, of course. But even she had soon opted for the less formal "Tommy", the name he answered to at home. It had also been the first time, and the last, that the Duke had talked of Jigger's mother. Beautiful young Nell, the dear girl, he had called her. Those few words, and the touching way the Duke uttered them, had haunted Jigger ever since. Only a few words, but words which posed so many questions — questions which Jigger suspected might never be answered in full.

But the passing of the years and his involvement in the raising of his own little family had gradually diminished any preoccupation he may have developed then regarding his veiled parentage. Whoever his real father might have been, old Tam had been the one to mould him, the one to teach him everything he needed to know about life. Above all else, he'd taught him how to make the most of every minute of every day by trying to look on the bright side, no matter how impossible that might seem at times. It was certainly a simple philosophy that Jigger tried his best to follow. "You've cracked the secret of a happy life," old Tam used to say, "when you can make Monday mornings seem like Sunday mornings," and although Jigger wasn't sure that he'd achieved that goal just yet, he was having a darned good time trying.

Even the nickname "Jigger" had come about as the indirect result of his grandfather's early influence. For Tam McCloud happened to have been more than just another Horseburghshire small farmer. He was also an accomplished fiddler, well known throughout the county, and for many years in great demand to play at barn dances and ceilidhs and weddings and wakes. And it became old Tam's determined intent that young Jigger should learn to play the fiddle just like him. So, on the wee fellow's fourth birthday, he set about teaching him on the same little half-size instrument on which he himself had learned to play when a lad. Every trick, quirk and nuance of Tam's personal fiddling prowess was revealed to and instilled upon young Tommy (as he was still known), and he was soon playing simple melodies in his grandfather's unique style. It was a technique that involved the idiosyncrasy of holding the forefinger of his left hand rigidly erect, sticking up like a pointer to paradise, while the other three digits danced and glided conventionally over the fingerboard.

The stiff forefinger foible had been forced upon Tam following a minor misfortune soon after starting work as a novice horseman on Craigcuddy estate. A particularly frisky Clydesdale mare had taken it into her head to rear up just as thirteen year-old Tam was yoking her to a cart one morning, trapping his hand between the harness and a cart shaft, and snapping his finger like a twig. Mrs McCurdy, the Craigcuddy Castle cook (and general estate first-aid factotum) promptly applied a splint, improvised from a broken ladle handle, and a swathe of binding torn from the hem of her ample apron. Without further ado, she despatched young Tam back to work with the secure pledge: "It'll be as good as new when you peel yon wee bandage off in a month's time."

She spoke the truth — if a good, new miniature flagpole was what she had in mind!

And so, almost half a century later, Tommy McCloud, now five years old, made his first public appearance as a guest artist with his grandfather's band, the Cuddyford Cornkisters, at a Saturday night dance in the Cuddyford village hall. And what a sensation he was. He stood there in front of the band, all two feet, eleven and three-quarter inches of him, apple-shiny cheeks dimpled into a delighted grin, scaled-down kilt swinging to the beat, his bowing elbow sawing away furiously, and his left forefinger flying back and forth like a perpendicular pin on a weaver's shuttle as he belted out a set of lively hornpipes.

The crowd were spellbound, abandoning all thoughts of dancing to stand clapping time in front of the stage. Even dedicated dance-night drinkers were compelled to exit their make-shift bar room in the gents' toilets to gawp, half bottles of whisky in hand, at this pint-sized fiddling phenomenon.

A new star had exploded into their midst. The entire audience knew it, but more significantly, wee Tommy knew it as well. He was on a high. Suddenly, with a buttock-airing flick of his kilt, he spun through 180 degrees and, still fiddling, launched his feet into a wild, sporran-swinging jig, the likes of which no one in the hall had ever seen.

"Jigger" McCloud had arrived!

Such uninhibited dance routines became a hallmark of Jigger's fiddle-playing performances in the years to come. And, as childhood blossomed into puberty, and puberty flowered into manhood, he became ever more aware of the favourable effect that his kilt-clad gyrations were having on the female members of his audiences. He exploited every tartan-pleated bum-waggle to the full.

Jigger formed his own band, while still at school, playing the traditional Scottish dance music he'd learned from his grandfather. As the years passed, however, the band's repertoire broadened to include the unique fusion of "Celtic Rock" and jazz that eventually became its speciality. Old Tam, a fan (though never a master) of the swinging fiddle style, had introduced his young grandson to the records of the master, Stephane Grappelli, and Jigger took to jazz as if he'd been born to it. He was a natural, and it was this ability to "swing it" that was ultimately to make Jigger and his boys the darlings of the "reeling" society set at posh tartan shindigs from Balmoral to Windsor. In fact, its popularity was such that the Jigger McCloud Band could have turned professional many times over. But their canny leader had always resisted the lucrative temptation. He knew how to have his cake *and* eat it too.

It was not, after all, the prospect of trekking incessantly up and down the country and drinking coffee bleary-eyed at motorway service stations in the middle of the night that had attracted him to having a band in the first place. It was the music. So, if he could enjoy himself playing with his band on selected occasions, while still keeping his feet firmly on the Cuddyford ground that he loved so much, then that would do him nicely. And it did. His sidemen, too, preferred it that way — "doing their own thing" around the city scene until receiving the periodic mustering call from Jigger. That way, the band kept its music jumping fresh, just the way its fans liked it.

Apart from his son Davie, who had developed into a real star turn of a drummer and had played with the band since turning thirteen, the only other of Jigger's musicians who lived locally was his shiny-domed, long-haired enigma of a bass player, Bertola Harvey. Bertola lived in a disused forester's hut deep within the woods of Craigcuddy Estate, a pad that Jigger had procured for him after Bertola's long-suffering wife had finally kicked him out of their tiny basement flat in Edinburgh's old Town. She'd felt compelled to give herself some well-earned peace and quiet after enduring years of his falling-about, door-banging, bottle-clinking, post-gig home-comings in the wee-small hours. Her other, perhaps more crucial, reason for evicting Bertola had been to provide sleeping space for some of their five kids in the box room that he, being a professional musician, had always reserved as an exclusive resting place for his double bass.

Initially, city boy Bertola saw the woodland hut as no more than a place for a two-night doss until he could find another city-centre gaff. Yet what he considered to be the "arsehole of the world" seclusion of Craigcuddy Estate soon morphed, in his eyes, into a veritable Garden of Eden. For, while stumbling through the woods on his way home from the Cuddy's Rest pub in the village one moonlit night, he chanced upon (or, more correctly, fell flat on his face into) a ring of magic mushrooms in a little glade not twenty paces from his shack. A secret source of fun fungus right there in his own back yard — and all free!

"Craigcuddy?" he called to the moon. "Man, this is what I really call *home!*"

An open-ended lease of the hut was then urgently agreed with the Duke, in exchange for Bertola doing a few odd jobs around the estate when needed.

Naturally, Bertola wasted no time in putting the quality of his fortuitous magic mushroom find to the test. "ACE!" was his yelled verdict on lift-off. But when he eventually came back down to Earth from his inaugural fungus-fuelled space trip, he discovered to his horror that, while in orbit, he had converted his beloved bull fiddle into a cocktail cabinet.

What the fuck, the distraught Bertola asked himself, was he gonna do for gigs now?

But Fate, having dealt him such a sneaky blow, then showed an appreciably less sadistic face. It happened to be in the guise of the old Duke's son and heir, Lord Ludovic Gormlie-Crighton II, now approaching his thirtieth summer at as leisurely a pace as was humanly possible, and blissfully ignorant of his local standing as the very epitome of the popular Gormless-Cretin distortion of his illustrious family name.

Young Ludo, as luck would have it, had owned a rather splendid bass guitar since school days, when he and a few other tone-deaf chaps had formed a rock band. Fortunately for the world of pop, the combo never progressed beyond a few expensively-equipped, promisingly-deafening, but predictably-barren rehearsals in the bike shed. Unlike the rest of his equally talentless, though more pragmatic chums, however, Ludo continued to harbour musical ambitions. These aspirations lay dormant until he chanced to win a portable Yamaha electric keyboard in a side bet on a pint-drinking competition in the Cuddy's Rest public bar one afternoon. This wager came good, coincidentally, on the very day that Bertola Harvey emerged from his disastrous boletus blackout. So, as word was about the pub that Bertola, in addition to being a master bass-player, was no slouch at the old ivory-tickling either, Lord Ludovic had little trouble in coaxing him to provide a few Yamaha-tickling lessons as a straight swap for one hardly-used bass guitar.

Bertola was back in business.

Ludo, for his part, stuck keenly to his keyboard studies until he had finally mastered a one-fingered rendition of *The Saints*, complete with bossa nova auto-rhythm accompaniment. This bizarre party piece was then summarily inflicted on anyone who had the misfortune to stray within earshot of his dreaded Yamaha.

Music was also on Jigger's mind as he stepped from the woods onto the sunlit gravel behind Craigcuddy Castle this fine spring morning.

"That'll be what the old Duke's getting his Harris Tweed plus fours in a fankle about," he told himself. "Yeah, he'll be wondering if I've got the band lined up and all the rest of the preparations in hand for his up-coming Hunt Ball." That'd be no sweat, Jigger figured. As ever, he'd soon get the old boy's blood pressure back down to normal.

"Ah-uhm, hello there, m'boy! Here you are at 1 — last!" spluttered old Horace, the 12th Duke of Gormlie, eagerly hailing Jigger from his castellated ramparts. "I was lookin' for you in the other direction — expectin' to see your truck comin' up the drive through the rhodo-, rhodo-, rhodo-"

"'Dendrons?" prompted Jigger, giving old Horace's stuck stylus a gentle shove, as was invariably necessary in moments of particular stress or excitement nowadays. The Duke's mental agility hadn't increased in tandem with his increasingly paranoid eccentricities over the years. "No, no," Jigger explained, "the pickup's otherwise occupied this morning, Duke. Tied up back there at the farmyard in a little PR exercise, in fact."

"P-uhm, P-uhm . . .?"

"R," said Jigger, with a further nudge of the needle. "Horse shit, to be exact."

"Ah, splendid! Stalwart stuff!" declared the Duke, suddenly sporting the confident air of a man well-versed in the subject. He descended the stone steps from his buttressed terrace. "Look here, Thomas, old boy," he blustered, pickled-onion eyes chameleoning in a wild way that told Jigger he was dealing with a well-distressed Duke here, "there are one or two, er, *problems* that I'm needin' to discuss with you . . . in confidence."

Ominously humming *The Dead March from Saul*, he shepherded Jigger by the elbow towards the hush-hush asylum of a nearby rhododendron clump.

There was more to this particular Gormlie-Crighton flap than mere Hunt Ball trivialities, Jigger guessed,

50

loping in step with the Duke rhododendron-wards. Surely there couldn't be any major panic in connection with the little Craigcuddy Home Farm? It was the only farm, of the seven that originally comprised the bulk of the estate, still in the Duke's ownership. Over the years, the others had been sold off sequentially to their sitting tenants (including, apparently, old Tam) in order to temporarily plug some new hole or other that had appeared in the increasingly porous Craigcuddy coffers. No, Jigger figured, it couldn't be anything to do with the Home Farm that was troubling the Duke. He was pretty sure about that. After all, he looked after the running of it himself, the Duke being totally clueless about the practicalities of farming and all the form-filling complexities linked to EU agricultural subsidies and the like. Indeed, it had been a long time since the Duke could afford to employ a bona fide estate factor, so such bothersome matters were now left in the capable and trusted hands of Thomas "Jigger" McCloud. Jigger saw to it that, while profits were carefully and creatively manipulated to appear minimal to his employer, losses *were* diligently kept at bay. Tidy.

So, what was up with the Duke this morning?

"What's the problem?" asked Jigger after the Duke had chosen a suitably secure rhododendron bush to converse behind.

"Prob*lems* plural, m'boy," the Duke confided, a look of deep anguish rippling his noble brow under the for'ard peak of his Harris Tweed deerstalker. "I fear, in fact, that we may be goin' to the wall. Mmm, problems, problems . . ."

The Yamaha-toned strains of *The Saints* in bossa nova time blared suddenly forth from a north-facing turret window in the castle. This indicated that young Lord Ludovic was now up, if not exactly about. It further suggested that, in all likelihood, an unsuspecting upstairs maid had swept, dusted and polished her busy way to within listening distance of Ludo's lofty lair.

"Prob*lems* plural," the Duke repeated, alluding now to the tuneless turret, "and *that* is only one of 'em!"

"Jeez! I see what you're saying," grimaced Jigger. "Must be bloody awful having to listen to that racket all the time. Enough to drive anyone nuts. But worry no more!" He gave the Duke an optimistic wink. "Tell you what — I'll ask Bertola to teach him another brace o' tunes. Yeah, at least that'll break the monotony, eh?"

"You miss the point, old boy," cautioned the Duke, also grimacing. "It's not the music. It's *him*!"

Young Ludovic, old Horace explained for openers, had become a layabout luxury that the through-at-the-knees estate could no longer afford. Astonishing as it might seem, for the first time in the history of the family, a Gormlie-Crighton heir would have to *earn* a living. Something easier said than done, the Duke was at pains to point out. For, at thirty years of age, young Ludo was, was he not, qualified for nothing but lying about, running up tick at the Cuddy's Rest, running up more tick at the bookie's, getting arrested for drink-driving, playing *The Saints* on his organ, getting château'd of an afternoon on what little remained of the claret stocks in the Craigcuddy Castle wine cellars, more lying about, and generally keeping himself permanently in a state of availability for possible commissions as a freelance paracetamol tester.

Jigger, who had been contemplating his cuticles during the Duke's discourse, nodded dolefully and was obliged to concur that finding a remunerative role in the real world for the young Lord could make the looking for needles in haystacks seem, by comparison, a piece of cake. Here was a fellow, after all, whose most notable achievement in life to date had been one of singularly negative description — an act of ungovernable profanity which had led to his formal education being abruptly ended at the tender age of eight. Jigger recalled the legendary details well . . .

One afternoon, in the small public school located in the old Dower House of Craigcuddy Estate, (the boy Ludovic's acceptance as a boarder having been a precondition of the Duke's lease of the property to the governors), the science master, as was his wont, had popped out of his classroom for a fly smoke in the staff latrine. In his brief absence, young Gormlie-Crighton blew up the entire colony of frogs that had been raised in the lab from frogspawn collected in the nearby Cuddy Burn for the furtherance of the pupils' studies. But the peerless perversity of the deed lay not in the mere fact that he blew up three dozen living Kermits in broad daylight, but more in the manner in which the blowing-up was executed.

Young Ludo, you see, didn't aim for the desired amusing result by employing the explosive properties of

TNT or dynamite, the obvious reason for this being that such a foolhardy experiment might well have led to his classmates (or, more importantly, himself) being injured or even snuffed-out completely. No, he blew the little creatures up by stuffing plastic tubes up their bums and inflating them with helium. The result was a thirty-six-strong flight of bouncing, bobbing, four-legged, pop-eyed, lighter-than-air, green balloons. And the sought-for acclaim of his fellow half-wits wasn't the only consequence of Ludo's scientific achievement. The lab, thanks to the voice-distorting effect of the spilled gas, was soon ringing to a cacophony of high-pitched giggles of the type you'd expect to hear at a gathering of the Jimmy Krankie Fan Club.

On returning from his clandestine puff, the horrified science master instantly confiscated the globular amphibians and dribbled, headed and punted them like verdant footballs into the adjacent apparatus store. The self-satisfied culprit was then frogmarched to the beak's office, where he was summarily instructed to hop it — permanently!

Later that same evening, the sound of muffled voices engaged in serious and sometimes heated negotiation was heard emanating from the science lab by a passing fifth-former. One of the voices he instantly recognised as that of the science master. The other, he suspected, belonged to a local youth by the name of Jigger McCloud, a crafty young wheeler-dealer, who was the senior boys' main supplier of alcoholic beverages, cigarettes, condoms, porn magazines and any other items of essential-but-forbidden kit that they cared to order.

The science lab bargainings concluded with a series of minor explosions, followed by what sounded to the fifth-former like two animated chipmunks bidding each other a back-slapping farewell.

Later still that same evening, the dinner menu in the Cuddyford Arms Hotel boasted an additional special, "*Les Cuisses de Grenouilles Provençale*", boldly sub-titled for the benefit of those not versed in Gallic menu-speak, "FRIED FROG LEGS WITH GARLIC". Jigger, meanwhile, was making his way jauntily homeward from the hotel with a noticeable bulge in his hip pocket, while the science master sat in his lonely room at the school, dreamily admiring a gleaming new wrist watch. A genuine Rolex Oyster, of course. Or so Jigger had said!

And so it appeared that, at the end of this grotesque little episode, young Lord Ludovic was (if we exclude the frogs) the only loser — an early example of the inherited art of which he was to become a dedicated patron.

Back behind the rhododendron bush, Jigger was soon to concede that old Horace did not have his problems to seek.

The Duke silently produced two letters from the breast pocket of his Harris Tweed shooting jacket. Letter number one, emblazoned with the distinctive triple-balls logo of the Royal Scottish Commerce Bank, was passed to Jigger with furtive glances through, above, around and beneath the bush. "Can't be too careful, m'boy," was the Duke's whispered assertion.

It took Jigger but a few seconds to scan and assimilate the letter's euphemistically-cushioned contents. The bank, in essence, were cheesed off with forking out ever-increasing amounts of loot to the Gormlie-Crightons without receiving in return one solitary penny of interest for more years than it was commercially prudent to remember. Bluntly, the time had come for the Duke to cough up or sell up. A substantial reduction in his overdraft would have to be effected. And soon!

"Change banks," said Jigger with a shrug.

"Uhm-ah . . . can't actually do that, old boy."

"Why not? Everyone else does."

The Duke double checked that the rhododendron bush was neither wired for sound, nor harbouring any transparent satellite dishes, then uttered a disclosure in tones so hushed that Jigger was obliged to say:

"Come again?"

The Duke put his lips to Jigger's ear and whispered, "Because, as I was sayin', old boy, I'm the Chairman of the Board of Governors of the jolly old Royal Scottish Commerce Bank m'self."

Jigger pulled a facial shrug and handed the letter back to the Duke. "So where's the problem, then? Use your chairman's clout to see off this hyena that's nipping at your heels. Arrange to have his arse kicked, then see to it that he spends the rest of his career in the bank's branch in the Falklands. He won't bother you from there, and it'll be a lesson to his mates to keep off your back an' all."

Jigger noted a nostalgic glaze clouding the Duke's eyes. "You all right?" he asked.

The Duke cleared his throat, gulped, swallowed, coughed, spluttered and spoke simultaneously in the way that only hereditary peers can do, saying, "Ahum, you — you sounded devilishly like one's own father just then. So firm, decisive. Hmm, quite uncanny, really." He rubbed his eyes, then proceeded to elucidate the full nature of his banking problem.

The hyena in question, Jigger would perceive if he cared to check the identity of the offending letter's signatory, was none other than the bank's Managing Director and Chief Treasurer, the autographer of the fivers himself, the top hyena to whom all other hyenas, up to and including the Chairman of the Board of Governors, were obliged to bow and scrape. The debt-laden Gormlie-Crighton buck, which had been bobbing about successfully soliciting favours of leniency from lesser bank hyenas for generations, had finally run out of privileged wind and had come to a cringing stop at the feet of the hungry leader of the pack. "Under such circumstances," the Duke went on, "and with due regard to one's social position, it would be totally inappropriate to redistribute, as it were, one's liabilities elsewhere." Besides, he added with commendable frankness, he had already tried all the other banks and, without exception, they had told him to carefully select the tallest tree on the Craigcuddy estate and go climb it forthwith. Negative collateral, they had all advised, was the only commodity that he had an abundance of. He was, in plain language, skint!

Well, well, the high-flying Gormlie-Crightons were at last losing their grip on the trapeze, Jigger mused. And as the safety net (a.k.a. their tenanted farms) had been sold years ago, the floor of the Craigcuddy circus ring seemed about to be splattered with a family of aristocratic crash-landers.

"The dynasty is d — doomed!" the Duke concluded, his pseudo-noble bearing slumping into a natural stoop of defeat.

Jigger, deep in thought, chewed his bottom lip while he contemplated his cuticles yet again. This was a tricky one and no mistake. OK, so the surviving rump of Craigcuddy Estate was all that remained of the once-immense spread of Gormlie-Crighton landhold-ings. Yet, it was common knowledge around Cuddyford that the recent auctioning of the castle's most valuable contents — almost totally comprised of rare artefacts and treasured effects "gleaned" by Duke Horace's great-grandfather, Robert the Bruce Gormlie-Crighton, during his years of imperial service in India — had realised well over two million pounds under the Sotheby hammer. It didn't take particularly shrewd reading between the lines, therefore, to deduce that those proceeds had flown directly into the vaults of that long-abused and patient creditor, the Royal Scottish Commerce Bank.

So, what to do? Would selling Cuddyford Home Farm, say, raise enough to keep the bank placid, if not totally happy, for a while? Jigger had no way of telling, and what's more, he would only suggest such a course of action to the Duke as an absolute last resort. Not that he was paid anything for farming the place — directly, at any rate. But there were obvious financial advantages to be gained for him from the increased efficiency of running the two relatively small units of the Home Farm and Acredales as one. And there were other perks, too, like the Land Set Aside hand-outs and the Cereal Acreage Subsidies and other multifarious pieces of EU money-for-nothing agricultural schemes that were better able to be "massaged" to his own advantage when the two holdings were farmed as a single unit.

Naturally, there was no question of his trying to diddle the Duke. Left to his own devices, old Horace would only have run the Home Farm into terminal ruin years ago. So, as long as Jigger was satisfied that he was keeping the land in good heart and maintaining a modest black figure on the Home Farm's annual balance sheet, he felt quite entitled to benefit, in whatever way possible, from his efforts. After all, it couldn't be denied that, in so doing, he was still protecting the best long-term interests of one of the Duke's few remaining assets.

"Er, I have, of course, thought of f — flogging the Home Farm," the Duke muttered, stinging Jigger's deeply-ruminating brain into a state of red alert. Then, to Jigger's great relief, the Duke solemnly added, "But, m'boy, it appears not to be a viable option." He then handed Jigger letter number two.

This turned out to be a brief, hand-printed note under a New York general delivery address. It was signed (in joined-up writing — just) by one Archibald Gormlie-Crighton, who stated in simple but unambiguous terms that he would be "visiting Craigcuddy Castle a.s.a.p. to claim my back-pay."

Jigger scratched his head. "OK," he said, "I get the layabout Ludovic and browbeating bank bits. In fact, I've already got a joint solution cooking for them. But this second letter . . . I mean, who *is* this bloke? Yeah, and what's all this back-pay business?"

The 12th Duke's expression changed from one of helplessness, through embarrassment, to indecision, and back again before he finally mumbled, "Uhm, perhaps I shouldn't really be botherin' you with this one, old chap."

But Jigger was having none of that. It was time to give old Horace a good shake. "Suit yourself," he stated bluntly, "but if this Archibald guy is going to make matters worse for you at the bank, it could blow the ploy I've got brewing for putting paid to your existing financial hassles." He looked at the Duke's bowed head in the way that a father would regard a little boy who was being goaded into admitting that it was he who released a noisy fart under the minister's chair while the padre was taking genteel afternoon tea with the family. "I think you'd better tell me all about it, eh?"

An arrow of reason penetrated the Duke's tortured mind, compelling him to mutely agree that, yes, of course Jigger *was* right. The three problems *were* interconnected. Their denominators *were* common.

There was nothing else for it, then; he would have to spill some previously un-spillable beans about Archibald.

It was a rather complex and extremely delicate subject, he hesitantly began, edging the first reluctant bean off the plate. And it was mandatory, he emphasised, that Jigger would be the very model of discretion in regard to all hitherto undisclosed details relating, as it were, thereto. The precincts of the rhododendron bush were surveyed once more for eavesdroppers, and when he was satisfied that none were about, the Duke commenced his revelations, albeit with a perceptible note of misgiving.

Archibald, it transpired, was a first cousin of Duke Horace, and about the same age. He was one of the Gormlie-and-Crighton Gormlie-Crightons. This meant, the Duke explained, that he was a member of the branch of the tribe that had remained resident at the estate adjacent to the twin towns of that ilk, far away in the industrial west of the country, when the leading shoot of the family tree turned eastward to Craigcuddy a century-and-a-half previously.

Jigger already knew all about this "exodus to Craigcuddy" stuff. Everyone around Cuddyford knew how the Dukes of Gormlie had wallowed historically in the lower divisions of the nobility, happily chasing deer and damsels through the green and pleasant lands surrounding their estate hamlets of Gormlie and Crighton, until it was discovered that those same lands were sitting on top of one of the richest coalfields in the country. Soon, the green and pleasant countryside became a blackened moonscape of pits and slag heaps.

Sleepy little Gormlie and Crighton had become the local engine rooms of the Industrial Revolution — sulphur-choked, soot-smothered sprawls of urban squalor. Ironically, they were separated in this desolation by their only remaining link with the past, the same little river in whose crystal-clear waters the village children had once swum. On its fragrant banks, the village women had once washed their clothes, and in its cool pools and sunny shallows gliding trout had once abounded. But now the river gurgled forlornly by, unloved and un-noticed, rank brown and foaming yellow, on its sterile way to the sea.

But so what? The Gormlie-Crightons were suddenly rich. Filthy rich! They were coal barons, steel moguls, landlords of all the black and unpleasant land they now surveyed. Royalties, rents and financial favours beyond their wildest dreams poured continuously into their gaping coffers by the train load. And their standing at court grew apace with their accumulating wealth. Being down-at-heel dukes was no longer their lot. At last, they were right up there with the bluest of the blue bloods. The influx of so much green stuff engendered by the subterranean black stuff had seen to that.

But as the systematic rape and pillage of the lands around Gormlie and Crighton progressed, there came a time when only the walled grounds of the Gormlie-Crighton mansion remained verdant and untouched by the grim, insatiable cancer of industrial spread. No fit place that for the bluest of blue bloods.

On returning from his rebel-bashing stint in India, therefore, the doughty Duke Robert the Bruce

Gormlie-Crighton took one look at the old ancestral home and did a quick up-sticks. He removed his entire household, replete with Indian "gleanings", fifty miles eastward to the suitably green and pleasant lands of Craigcuddy Castle — bought, cash down, with the blood of colliers, the sweat of foundrymen and the tears of maharajahs.

A secondary branch of the family was installed in the old mansion as a sort of rent-collecting rear-guard for the absentee Duke. It was to this Gormlie-Crighton offshoot that the letter-writing Archibald — or cousin Archie, as Duke Horace knew him — belonged.

And the back pay to which his letter referred? Well, that alluded to a sort of compensation allowance, the Duke thought. It had been payable monthly from Craigcuddy funds following the post-war nationalisation of the coal mines and steel works, from which cousin Archie's family had received, until then, a small but jolly useful percentage of the take. With no more rent-and-royalty-counting to detain him, Archie had eventually buzzed off to the States. There, he'd spent the next forty years, as far as the Duke knew, happily gambling away his monthly Craigcuddy allowance in Las Vegas, Atlantic City or anywhere else where a poker game or slot machine could be located.

Archie had never earned an honest penny in his life, and now that those spoilsports at the Royal Scottish Commerce Bank had frozen all outgoings from the Craigcuddy account, he was forced at last to interpret, in his own peculiar manner, the meaning of that oft-heard but never personally-used phrase, "cash-flow

63

problem". And it didn't take him long. The source of the flow had dried up, he had no cash, so this was a problem. Consequently, he was winging back across the pond in urgent haste to unbung the good old Craigcuddy pipe — by fair means or, the Duke feared, foul.

As before, Jigger couldn't see what the Duke's problem was. "But if the well's dry," he reasoned, "the Archie guy's on a fool's errand. I mean, you can't get blood from a stone or take the breeks off a Heilan'man, can you?"

The Duke boldly side-stepped that barrage of metaphors with a quick: "Ah, but it's not as simple as that, m'boy."

"You mean he has a binding contract or something?"

"Well, uhm, there is a *document* of sorts . . . yes."

Jigger's nostrils picked up the unmistakable aroma of dukely bullshit. Old Horace was not coming totally clean about cousin Archie, of that he was sure. He came straight to the point. "So, how does this Archie wrangle stack with the bank hassle?"

The Duke had no hesitation in admitting (although Jigger was certain that his admission would have been accompanied by a quiver of the chin — if he'd had one) that the two problems were liable to add up to the compulsory selling of the Craigcuddy estate — Home Farm, Dower House, Castle and all. He could see no other way. Cousin Archie, he suspected, would insist upon it, in fact.

"But if he's only a month or two light on his allowance, surely he can be stalled for long enough to let us have a stab at solving problems one and two, which, in turn, would solve problem three, namely the continued payment of his allowance."

The old Duke shook his head distractedly and crushed a symbolic rhododendron leaf between his fingers. "Hmm," he droned, "I fear the dynasty is d — doomed."

A feeling of "serves you bloody right, too" rose up in Jigger. He was sorely tempted to ask the Duke just what the hell he expected him to do about all this, anyway. But he couldn't. He hadn't the heart. All he could do was stare in silence at the sad figure standing before him. Although he was certain that he and the Duke had absolutely nothing in common, he couldn't help but be touched again by the eerie sense of bonding that he'd first experienced on that tearful night of old Tam's death.

"Look, with the best will in the world," he said softly, "the only advice I can give you is to talk all this cousin Archie business over with your lawyers. It's a family matter, and I'm not really —"

"Already have," muttered the Duke, "and Messrs Leary, Byblow and Wyllie WS advised me to accept the offer."

Jigger stood stunned. "The . . . offer?"

The Duke drew himself into a stiffly-erect, aristocratic posture, then blurted out machine-gun-fashion that, yes, he'd had an offer to buy the estate that very morning from Babu Ng, the mysterious Asian millionaire, newly-resident in the old Cuddyford manse, and Ng had plans to turn Craigcuddy into a theme park, and the Home Farm into a golf course, and the castle into a luxury hotel, and he (the Duke) would be permitted to occupy one of the turrets and would be a tourist attraction and could continue to shoot pheasants and . . ." He drew in a shuddering breath and braced himself to continue the outpouring.

Jigger held up his hands to stem the threatened flow. "OK, OK, Duke," he said, "I get the picture. I've also got a plan, so just put the brakes on everything for as long as you can, right?"

Duke Horace looked at him, the expression on his face a picture of puzzlement.

Jigger turned to leave. "And don't panic," he called over his shoulder as he strode off. "I'll be back in a day or two to sort things out. Oh, and another thing," he added as an afterthought, "tell young Ludo to look out a double-breasted suit. A dark grey one!"

CHAPTER
FOUR

Altercations at Acredales

"Those old doors looks OK stripped," said Nessie. She was watching Jigger loading them onto his truck in the yard. "But the old bath . . . well, even with the new paint job, I don't know why anyone would want to clutter up their bathroom with a great, ugly lump of scrap like that."

"Listen, some people would use a rusty old horse trough for a bath, if rusty old horse troughs happened to be the current thing. Anyway, as long as this Babu Ng character is interested in buying *this* ugly lump of scrap for a tidy price, I'm not fussy if he decides to stand it by his fireside in the lounge and use it as a coal bunker."

"Mmm, you *might* be lucky . . ."

"Whatever. Nothing ventured, and all that. So I'm gonna nip over and try to flog him this stuff right now. I mean, if nothing else, it'll be a good excuse to pump him about his plans for buying Craigcuddy Estate from the Duke."

"Keep an eye open for Bert, then. I saw him hobbling off over the field towards the old manse a few minutes ago. And if he wanders near the main road . . .

Well, you know what I mean. He's half deaf now and —"

"Yeah, I'll watch out for him. We know what he's likely to be up to anyway," Jigger laughed. He reminded Nessie that it *was* spring, after all. "And don't worry about Bert. He's far too suave an operator to be a-wooin' and a-courtin anywhere within sight of the main road."

"Mm-hmm, a-wooin' and a-courtin'," Granny echoed as she emerged from the kitchen mumbling rheumatically. "Should've had the nuts off that horny mongrel years ago. Only one consolation," she grumped, "at his age, he'll screw himself to death one of these days. And it'll be good riddance, too — the smelly wee bugger."

Nessie suppressed a snigger, then told Granny that Jigger was about to go and introduce himself to the eastern millionaire who'd moved into the old manse.

"Yeah, maybe do a bit of business an' all," Jigger said as he climbed into his truck.

"Mm-hmm, business," Granny muttered. "Just watch out that he doesn't give *you* the business, that's all!" She shook her head, a determined look on her face. "Never trust foreigners, that's my motto — especially Saracens and infidels."

"Gerraway!" Jigger scoffed. "Easy to see you've never even met a foreigner. You and your Saracens and infidels nonsense," he chuckled. "I mean, for all you know, Babu Ng could be Indian, Pakistani, Chinese, Japanese, Jewish, Arab or a mixture of the lot."

"Hmm, mixture." Granny inclined her head with a wry, there-you-have-it smile. "A mongrel, just like that foul-breathed rake of a dog of yours." She stabbed a finger in Jigger's direction. "And for your information, my lad, I've met *plenty* of foreigners!"

"Oh yes?"

"Oh *yes!*" Granny was getting on her high horse. "What do you think all those Poles billeted around here during the war were if they weren't foreigners? And nobody trusted them — *if* they had any sense. Even your sex maniac dog would've been out-shafted by that lot."

Jigger laughed out loud. Granny's outrageously jingoistic pronouncement reminded him of some of the more bizarre wartime stories old Tam had told him. One of the favourites was about how Polish officers, newly arrived in this rural area at a time when most of the young local men were away on military service, would ask the wags in the Cuddy's Rest public bar for a crash course in English chat-up lines. This would be the norm before the regular Saturday hops in the village hall. Not that the local blokes had anything serious against these Slavonic visitors, of course. No, it was just that the Poles' gold-toothed smiles, flared trousers, snazzy kipper ties and somewhat flash demeanour set them slightly apart from the more down-to-earth native swains. Besides, the smooth-talking bastards were after the local talent, and as there was a war on, the wags considered that all would be fair in the thwarting of the amorous intentions of these over-charming ladies' men.

So, after much tireless tutoring over pints in the pub, each expectant exile would enter the hall and approach his chosen lovely, confidently inviting her to join him on the dance floor with a snappy click of the heels, a polite bow, and an exotically-accented, "Howzaboutafuck, dahlink?" He would then become the surprised recipient of a gold-tooth-loosening uppercut, or would find himself (in an even more surprised condition) whisked outside and pinned against the back wall of the hall while his proposed dancing partner tore the flared trousers off him. It was the luck of the wartime draw.

But not all of the displaced Poles had been like that. There was, for instance, the distinctly down-to-earth and notably un-smooth-talking Johnny Ardonski. He, though given the crudely-suggestive alias of Ivan Ardon by the Cuddy's Rest regulars, was known by Jigger to be nothing but a hard-working country fellow, torn long ago from his peasant roots by a war that he'd wanted no part of. Neither had it been of his choosing to be deposited far from his family and loved ones in a land where he would always be regarded as an outsider. For all that, this was the land that, ultimately, he had been obliged to choose as his adopted home. Unable, like many of his countrymen, to return to his motherland at the end of the war, Johnny had worked as a casual labourer for old Tam and other local farmers ever since, and had become by now just another of the Cuddyford characters. But still a "foreigner". And the detail that he was not actually Polish, but Ukrainian, made no difference to the xenophobes of the area. He was a bloody Polski like the rest of them!

Notwithstanding such local prejudice, Johnny Ardonski was, in Jigger's eyes, the salt of the earth. He was a trusty hand, a cheery companion and a willing teacher of useful old country skills that the pursuit of "progress" in this country had all but consigned to the dustbin of history. Jigger reminded Granny of this, and told her (in the nicest possible way) not to be such a chauvinistic old bumpkin.

Granny's glower of indignation said it all, but she added a verbal footnote, just in case Jigger wasn't getting the visual message. "Oh aye! Chauffeuristic, is it?" she snapped. "Right, I'll remember that, Mr Jigger Smartarse McCloud. And we'll see who the bumpkin is when ye've been ripped off by this Abdul Balloon, or whatever his name is!"

Jigger drove off smiling, content in the knowledge that he'd got Granny nicely wound-up for the day. She thrived on it, he reckoned. It was good for her circulation.

There was something about the old manse that always gave Jigger the creeps. Its grim, spiky-gabled silhouette reminded him of those doomy piles you saw in black-and-white horror films on late-night telly sometimes. It had been built nearly two hundred years ago to house the church's cheerless ministers, and to strike awe into the simple hearts of their cottage-dwelling parishioners. All those menacing yew trees lining the driveway like sentinels of death, and the petrified forest of chimneys rising in skeletal clusters from the sombre, grey-slated roofs. Pure Edgar Allan Poe. Jigger shivered at the very thought.

When he rang the bell, he half-expected the door to be opened, creaking and groaning, by a leering Vincent Price, a cawing raven flapping on his hump-backed shoulders. But the door-opener now standing in front of him was no spooky character out of the Hammer House of Horrors. Hair-raising, yes. But spooky, no.

"Yes?" she cooed, her come-hither voice emerging as a sensual whisper from voluptuously red lips, her long eyelashes batting dreamily over huge brown eyes that wandered approvingly over every inch of Jigger for as long as it takes to mentally disrobe a strange man standing fully-clothed on your doorstep in the middle of a working day. And that was certainly longer than it took Jigger to mutually unwrap her in his mind. As far as he could see (and that was far enough), she was clad only in a negligée of sheerest black gossamer. It was worn titillatingly off-the-shoulder, and deliberately draped to reveal, Jigger calculated, more leg than a row of Easter lambs in a butcher's window. Tidy!

"Christ," he thought, "if they could only take a gander at what's darkening their hallowed doorway now, those bible-thumping old ministers would turn in their miserable graves!"

"Yes?" the doorway-darkener repeated, satisfied that she liked what her mind's eye had seen. "Anything I can do for you?"

"Wow!" said Jigger. "Or, ehm, what I meant to say was . . . well! That is, I was hoping to meet the new owner, Babu Ng. But . . ."

"But?"

Jigger tried to regain control of his eyes, which were still working overtime for his mind, which, in turn, was frenziedly writing a Mickey Spillane novel. "Rampant Sex Romps with a Quenchless Nympho" (Explicitly Illustrated), it was called.

"But I'll settle for a rampant sex romp instead," his mouth said of its own volition, with but a little prompting from his mind.

"Well, you don't believe in beating about the bush, do you?" the voluptuous vision said. "But don't you think it would be more *comme il faut* for you to introduce yourself first?"

This siren was so cool that Jigger could feel the tempering effect of her breath on his fevered brow from six feet. "Just a slip of the tongue, if you'll pardon the shocking pun," he lisped in Connery tones, trying to produce a verbal equivalent of the X-ray vision of his naked body that he sensed she had already conjured up. "Forgive me, but I wasn't expecting anyone as — as *attractive* as you to materialise at these staid portals." He extended his hand. "I'm Jigger McCloud, your neighbour from the farm along the road there."

"Oo-ooh, a farmer! Well, well! How earthy!" She offered Jigger her own diamond-festooned hand, shifting her weight on her stiletto heels so that her pelvis moved with a tantalising suggestion of bump-and-grind. This blatantly seductive motion parted the flimsy material of her robe more than enough to confirm Jigger's hunch that she had a pair of shanks that would have made even one of those Easter lambs in the butcher's window look sexually irresistible. "I'm Sabrina," she breathed. "Sabrina Ng — or Mrs Babu Ng, to put you fully in the picture . . . Jigger."

Her studied pause before saying his name, and the almost obscene way she looked at him when she said it, was intended to convey a certain message to him, Jigger suspected. It was a raw, animal communication that would require summoning all his powers of self-restraint to resist. He was a happily married man, for heaven's sake!

But not his mind. It was still defiantly single, and was now typing away like crazy at a chapter of its very own Mickey Spillane book . . .

"Chapter two. The chapter where the drag-ass gumshoe McCloud gets hauled by his zoobrick into that pink-draped bedroom in a Manhattan apartment by this broad with the ring-a-ding garbonzas . . .

Holy crap, McCloud knew that this was the babe that stiffed the John Doe they found floatin' ass-over-teacups with his zeppelin missin' in the East River last night. He knew it, she knew it, the Feds knew it, even the shit-for-brains beat cops on the precinct knew it. But what the hell? This dame was a looker — Jesus H Christ she was! And if she had her ass on fire tonight, she wasn't gonna get no complaints from him.

McCloud stood by the Pacific-size water bed, pulling casually on his Marlboro as she chasséd momentarily into the bathroom. She reappeared in her back-lit birthday suit, standing in the orgasmic rhythm of the red light pulsating into the bedroom from the Coke sign across the street. She was standing in the same pose that had burned up the centrefold of "Playboy" just a month back.

Then she started to slink towards him, like a prowling she-panther on heat — hissing, claws bared, breathing fire. This dish was hotter than a Tex-Mex enchilada stuffed with jalapeño peppers.

Slowly, McCloud pushed his hat back and loosened his necktie. She stopped in front of him — close enough for him to see, to almost feel, the gravity-defying fullness of her cantaloupes. Close enough for him to breathe deep on the thousand-dollar-an-hour aroma of her perfume. McCloud gulped as she said in a voice that would have started a melt-down in a brass monkey factory . . ."

"Well, you'd better come on in, Jigger. I'm not exactly dressed for an April alfresco conversation in Cuddyford, am I?"

Jigger thumped the side of his head with his fist. Jeez, his mind was giving itself treats that even he didn't trust it to have!

"So you wanna see my husband?" purred Sabrina. She motioned him to follow her inside, in the way she might beckon a lapdog back from a peeing excursion to a yew tree.

Jigger was trying to place her accent. Difficult. He'd thought at first that it was straight south-of-the river London with the usual up-west overtones. But no, there was more to it than that. There was a touch of French there, too. Or was it Italian? And that trace of mid-Atlantic in the way she said "wanna". This lady had been around. In fact, it was surprising that she'd been allowed to settle in Cuddyford without an X-certificate stamped on her forehead. Even now, Jigger could visualise the mayhem that would be caused the first time she strutted her sultry stuff along the village High Street.

"That's right," he said, redirecting his attentions to the mission in hand. "I heard from the builders who were renovating your house that there were still a few missing period fitments to be replaced."

Sabrina showed zero interest in that. She held the drawing room door open for Jigger, taking up enough space in the threshold for him to be forced to brush against her as he passed through.

Their eyes met in an almost nose-touching close-up at that instant of physical contact. Einstein, had he been a fly on the wall just then, could have saved himself the long years he spent developing the theory that eventually led to the development of the A-bomb.

Jigger pulled himself clear of the magnetic attraction that was threatening to make him forget that he had a devoted wife and granny preparing toad-in-the-hole for his lunch not half a mile away. "Yeah, that's right," he croaked, "and just by chance, I managed to come by some tidy old doors and a bath that should fit the bill here nicely. All genuine period stuff, mind you. Yeah, and only five hundred quid, the lot." He cleared his throat. "I, ehm, I thought I'd pass them on to you at cost — as a neighbourly welcome gesture, if you see what I'm saying."

Sabrina shut the door behind them and stood with her back against it, smouldering.

That door, Jigger told himself, was the only door she was interested in right now. And a bath? Well, that could wait until after they ... He stopped his overheated imagination in its tracks, suddenly aware that he wasn't standing in the suicidally-depressing front room of the old manse, but on the Hollywood set of a Matt Helm movie. And this had nothing to do with the Mickey Spillane book his mind had been writing. This was for real!

Everything was gold and white. There were acres of white carpet, with a pile so deep it must have taken half the sheep in New South Wales several years to grow enough wool to make. There were golden chandeliers that wouldn't have looked out of place in Tutankhamun's tomb. There were vast couches of white leather that sprawled over the floor and filled the corners of the room in billows of overstuffed opulence. A scattering of polar bear rugs had snarling mouths so full of golden teeth that any self-respecting Polish officer would have wept with envy at the sight of them. Against one wall, there was a gold-topped bar with a front of padded white satin and stools to match. And through a newly-created archway supported on white marble columns, was another similarly appointed room. This one had a Busby Berkeley grand piano of gleaming white nestling in a vast alabaster scallop shell. Beside it, gold-ballustraded steps led down to a palm-fringed swimming pool within a conservatory so spacious that it could have been a direct descendant of the Crystal Palace, circa 1851. If Dean Martin had staggered in, champagne glass to the fore, accompanied by a bevy of bikini-clad starlets, Jigger wouldn't have been surprised.

"My husband is a very rich man," Sabrina cooed, draping herself along a silk-upholstered chaise longue.

"Shite," Jigger muttered under his breath. "Why did I open my big mouth about five hundred quid? I could've copped a grand for the doors and bath from this Babu Ng guy. He must be Adnan Khashoggi with a numby plum!"

"He's also a rather old man," Sabrina revealed. "At sixty, he's more than twice my age. So, just leave your, uh, period fitments in the garage." She raised her shoulders, then added throw-away style, "If I say so, Babu will buy them. He gives me everything I want." She paused. "Well, *almost* everything. As I say, he *is* a rather old guy."

"Yeah, well, that's very handy." Jigger's mouth was switching onto auto-pilot again. "I mean," he swiftly corrected, "I can't, you know, wait to meet him, if you see what I'm saying."

"Well then, I'm afraid you're out of luck . . . or maybe *in* it."

Jigger swallowed hard. "Come again?"

"He's gone overseas somewhere — on business, as ever." Sabrina then gave Jigger a come-on look that was about as subtle as a clip from a Madonna video. "And I'm not used to being left alone in Hicksville dumps like this. I'm a fun person," she pouted, "and I need fun *now!*" She lowered her voice to a breathy whisper. "See what I'm saying . . . Jigger?"

Hell, this woman was no Tabetha Spriggs! In fact, Jigger decided, if he wasn't on his mettle, Sabrina Ng was more than capable of making a right sprig out of *him*.

"I wanna throw a party like they've never seen around here," she went on, talking determinedly now. "I wanna get to know everybody, and I wanna get you to help me make out a guest list of *all* the fun people here in Hicksville. OK, honey?"

Jigger was trying to think of a suitably sharp riposte to Sabrina's Hicksville slight, but his eyes were too intent on surveying her contours curving dangerously along the couch for him to be able to come up with anything other than a mental image of that "Playboy" centrefold in his mind's ongoing Mickey Spillane narrative. He was only just rescued from his mouth coming out with, "Great pair a' garbonzas ya got there, babe," by the door opening. It wasn't, as he thought it might have been, Dean Martin in Matt Helm mode, but a diminutive Filipina maid with a micro-mini Yorkshire terrier tucked under her arm.

Curtsying continuously, the maid whimpered something apologetic-sounding while depositing the little dog on the carpet.

Sabrina dismissed her with a backwards wave of a diamond-dripping hand.

The dog matched the Hollywood movie set perfectly, dressed as it was in a white fur coat and a zircon-encrusted collar. It even had a white satin bow tied on top of its head. But the image was flawed. The pooch looked surprisingly bedraggled for such an obviously-pampered pet. Its fur coat was crumpled up round its shoulders, the silky hair that nature had provided was matted and soggy, and the white satin bow was half undone and dangling over one eye. The pathetic little mutt just stood there trembling, staring at Sabrina with a look that seemed to say: "Forgive me, mother, for I know not what I have done."

"Aw, my poor little Fifi," Sabrina crooned, peeling herself off the couch. "Did little snookums fall in a dirty old Hicksville ditch, huh?" She bent to pick the dog up. "Aw, come here, baby, and let Momma kiss her little Fifi all better."

Jigger glanced out of the window, and there, as he instinctively knew he would be, was Bert. He was shuffling homeward in an advanced state of knackeredness, his tongue flopping out of the corner of his mouth, his breathing rate up around the cardiac-arrest-imminent zone. Jigger was quick to note that Bert also had that wicked glint in his eye, and that well-pleased grin on his face that invariably indicated that he'd just nailed another incomer.

No need to dream up a sharp riposte to Sabrina's condescending quips about Cuddyford now, Jigger figured. His smelly, old, four-legged friend had already delivered the ultimate one.

"Welcome," as Bert might have said, if he'd had the words, "to Hicksville, baby!"

★　★　★

Nessie was dishing up the toad-in-the-hole. "So, Jigger, did you get a good deal from Babu Ng for the stuff?" she asked, apparently without much real interest.

Jigger adopted an equally indifferent air. "He wasn't there, but I spoke to his wife. Yeah," he shrugged, "we'll get a good deal. No problem."

Granny was already shaking her head, an ominously sceptical scowl on her face. "You haven't got the money yet, then?"

"No . . . no, but as good as." Jigger was about to quickly change the subject, but Granny got in there first.

"Good-looking woman, his wife?" she asked.

"Mm-hmm, quite tidy . . . if you like that sort o' thing."

Nessie flashed Granny a conspiratorial wink. "And, ehm, what sort of *thing* would that be, Jigger? A bit exotic, is she?"

Jigger could feel Granny's stare of suspicion searing the side of his face. He instinctively knew that she was indulging in her usual habit of putting two and two together and arriving at twenty-two.

"Nah, she's nothing out of the ordinary," he lied. "Tidy enough, if you see what I'm saying, but nothing special."

"Foreigner?" Granny asked bluntly.

Jigger casually tucked his napkin into his collar. "Don't think so," he shrugged. "But, eh, more to the point, has Bert come back yet?"

"And where are the old doors and bath?" enquired Nessie, glancing out of the window on her way over from the range. "I don't see them on the truck."

"Yeah, I just left them in the garage at the manse. No problem. I'll talk to Ng when —"

"Ye've *left* them at the manse, and ye haven't even got the money yet?" said Granny, her voice rising.

"Correct, but as I say —"

There was a flash of stainless steel as Granny severed a toad-in-the-hole sausage. "Ye're worse than that stinky dog of yours," she snapped. "At least he's only randy, but you're randy *and* stupid!"

"Bert's back, then, is he?" yawned Jigger, making a forlorn attempt at nonchalance, while silently hoping that Nessie would leave sausage dishes off the menu for a while.

"He came back just before you did," Nessie said with a knowing smirk, "but he was so bushed, he didn't even make it into the house." She gestured towards the window. "He's lying in the shade by the barn door — out for the count."

"Mm-hmm, barn door," mumbled Granny. "The horny little bugger would even mount that . . . *if* he could get his leg over!"

"You look a bit bushed yourself, Jigger," Nessie commented matter-of-factly. "Was it a struggle to get the load off by yourself, or did Mrs Ng give you a hand?"

Granny joined Nessie in a smutty little giggle.

Jigger was noticeably ruffled. "Never mind," he said, "you'll all get a chance to meet Sabrina soon enough."

"*Oo-oo-oo*, Sabrina, is it?" countered Nessie. "On first name terms already, are we? Mmm, *very* neighbourly!"

Jigger pulled a smug smile. "Neighbourly enough to throw a party for the locals, anyway. Yeah, in fact, I helped her make up the guest list myself. Oh yes, there could be a barrel and a half o' fun at that do — with any luck."

"Ye won't get me there," Granny grouched. "Don't like parties — especially foreign ones."

Just then, young Maggie breezed into the kitchen in a surge of grey serge. "Did someone say something about a party?" she called out.

"Yes," Nessie replied, "your father's hobnobbing with the millionaire at the old manse now. Or with the millionaire's *wife*, to be exact."

"Really?" Maggie cast Jigger a chastening look. "Philandering at your age! Well, there's no fool like an old fool. Or, in the immortal words of Edward Young, 'A fool at forty is a fool indeed'."

"A bit of respect, if you don't mind, young lady!" Jigger retorted. "And what's more," he added, perhaps just a tad too defensively, "forty isn't old!"

"What are you doing home at lunchtime, anyway?" Nessie asked Maggie. "Has the head librarian given you a half-day or something?"

"No, no, I'm on a working lunch today. Yes, I've been delivering a box of books to Craigcuddy Castle, as it happens."

"Delivering *books* to Craigcuddy Castle?" Granny checked with an incredulous frown. "Back numbers of *The Beano Annual*, are they?"

Maggie gave a snooty toss of her head. "Actually, it's an anthology of various historical works, ranging in chronological context from the mid-seventeenth century to the present, and by such diverse and eulogized chroniclers as —"

"OK, OK!" Jigger interrupted "Spare us the verbal diarrhoea — we're having lunch. And, anyway, Granny has a point. Who in blazes at Craigcuddy Castle is going to attempt to read serious stuff like that? Old Duke Horace got house guests, has he?"

"The books are for Lord Ludovic, if you must know."

"For young *Ludo?*" Jigger queried, his eyebrows raised to the well-I'll-be-buggered position. "I take it they're listening books you're talking about, then. You know, tape recordings of some actor or other doing the difficult bit."

"Well . . . not exactly," Maggie answered, her demeanour noticeably less bullish all of a sudden. "But I *do* take your point. You see, Lord Ludovic called by the library this morning and asked if we had any material that might assist him in researching a book that he's writing about the history of the Gormlie-Crighton family."

"I don't believe it!" Jigger gasped.

"Neither do I!" Granny and Nessie concurred in unison.

"And neither did I!" Maggie revealed, a note of confidentiality creeping into her hitherto cagey tone. "You see, he, uhm —"

"Can't read," all four chanted at once.

"And what's more," Maggie continued, her creeping confidentiality breaking into a jaunty jog, "he —"

"Can't write either," the four of them chorused.

"So, what's the score?" urged Jigger, keen to hear what the son and heir of the destitute Duke of Gormlie was up to.

Maggie joined her elders at the table. "The score, father, is that I dug out all the books that might be relevant and delivered them to the castle, where Lord Ludovic played me *The Saints* on his keyboard, then suggested that perhaps I might care to act as his 'literary consultant', as he put it."

"You mean, be his ghost writer," Nessie said bluntly.

Maggie nodded her head. "Mmm, for a fifty per cent share of the royalties."

Silence.

"Something wrong?" Maggie asked. "You've all gone a bit pale."

It was Jigger who eventually spoke up. "And when," he asked, "would these, ehm, *ghost-writing* sessions take place?"

Maggie adopted a pointedly offhand manner. "Oh, at nights, at weekends. You know — whenever I have the time."

"And *where*?" Nessie and Granny anxiously enquired.

"At the castle, of course," Maggie replied, clearly not sharing their concern. "In Lord Ludovic's turret, I suppose." Then, as if to emphasise her air of insouciance, she casually began to peel a banana.

Bananas! I don't like the symbology, thought Jigger, mentally aping his daughter's literary lingo. Hell, this was the nightmare scenario that every father of a pretty daughter dreaded. And he should know. After all, he'd faced many such frantic fathers himself in his time!

"Don't go thinking that I'm about to get sexually associated with Lord Ludovic, if that's what's bothering you," said Maggie between banana bites. She spoke with a candour that had her mother blinking, her father frowning, and her great-grandmother advising:

"Mm-hmm, and that's *just* what happens to young girls who go to work at that place. They get sexually associated . . . *and* sprogged!"

"Get modern, Granny!" Maggie scoffed. "We young women of today don't allow ourselves to get plucked like daisies by the so-called lairds. Not unless we happen to fancy the particular laird, that is. And *I* don't fancy Lord Ludovic." She haughtily flicked a stray lock of hair from her face. "He's skint!"

"It's not you fancying Lord Ludovic that bothers me," Nessie said.

"No, it's that lecherous lout Ludo fancying *you* that's putting the wind up us," Jigger went on. "He's just not to be trusted with women, believe me!"

"Aha, father," said Maggie, tapping the side of her nose, "every man's censure is first moulded in his own nature, as the old saying goes."

"Come again?"

"She means it takes one to know one," Nessie explained, then turned to Maggie. "But all we're saying, dear, is be careful. Know what I mean?"

"Mm-hmm, careful," Granny muttered. "Take the pill, in other words. Hmff! From what I hear, they're no bloody use, anyway. They keep fallin' out!"

The kitchen fairly rang with laughter — from three of the assembled four, at any rate.

"If you only knew," Maggie announced after the hilarity and Granny's cursing counter-attack had subsided, "you're all getting yourselves in a tizzy for nothing."

"You mean you elbowed Ludo's offer?" Jigger asked with an air of impending deliverance, almost as if it were already two months down the line and Maggie was about to announce a negative pregnancy-test result.

"Of course I did. I'm not *that* dumb, father."

"A wise decision, Maggie," Nessie said while sagely stuffing an onion ring into her mouth. "You were quite right not to trust him."

Maggie stood up to leave. "Trust is dead," she proclaimed. "Ill payment killed it, as the old proverb goes."

"Eh?" enquired her trio of elders.

"Did you honestly think I would agree to do a hundred per cent of the graft for fifty per cent of the rake-off? You must be joking! *And* I told Lord Ludovic as much. Up yours, Ludo, I said. You can take your Gormlie-Crighton history and stick it right up your family tree trunk — sideways!"

There was a swirl of grey serge, and Maggie was gone.

Jigger, Nessie and Granny smiled at each other in smug satisfaction. The kitchen now fairly reeked with delight. It had been heart-warming and touching to hear that Maggie could still talk like a little guttersnipe when the occasion warranted it. They were proud of her.

Granny swatted the air. "Ach, the book idea would never have got off the ground in any case."

"How's that?" asked Jigger, genuinely curious.

"Because, one look at all the skeletons in the Gormlie-Crighton cupboard, and young Ludo would've shit a brick, that's why."

"You mean . . ."

"I mean that the dark secrets of Craigcuddy Castle would be the ruin of that lot, if they were ever brought to light. Mark my words," Granny continued, warming to her theme, "over the years, the Gormlie-Crightons would've needed to employ a whole team of full-time shepherds if they'd wanted to guard all the black sheep in *that* family!"

"Gerraway?" said Jigger. He then contemplated his cuticles, while thinking of a tactful way of asking Granny if she knew anything about this Archibald Gormlie-Crighton character. Such a way didn't come easily to mind, so he eventually blurted out, "So, do you know anything about this mysterious Archibald Gormlie-Crighton that old Duke Horace has mentioned to me?"

"ARCHIBALD?" Granny's ears pricked up and her jaw dropped — as did her cutlery.

"Yeah. Cousin Archie, old Horace calls him."

"Oh, so it's *cousin* Archie now, is it?"

"You mean . . . he's *not* the Duke's cousin?"

An evasive look appeared in Granny's eyes.

Jigger was persistent. "You're saying that this Archie is *not* old Horace's cousin, right?"

"I'm saying nothing. If the Duke says he's a cousin, then he's a cousin." Granny thought for a moment, then added through clenched teeth, "But I'll tell you this — it's forty years or more since that Archibald man was seen around these parts, and he's best forgotten!"

Jigger could see that this was a thorny subject for Granny, and while he didn't want to upset the old woman by dredging up matters best left alone, he was fired, nevertheless, by a curiosity he found difficult to contain.

"Archibald Gormlie-Crighton is, ehm . . . coming back to Craigcuddy Castle," he said hesitantly, intending to put a metaphorical toe in the water, but realising too late that he'd plunged both feet right in it.

"COMING BACK?" Granny hollered, her face livid, her sausage-slicing knife brandished aloft. "Well, just you keep your distance from him, Thomas McCloud. He'll bring nothing but trouble to Cuddyford. TROUBLE! DO YOU HEAR?"

CHAPTER
FIVE

The End of A Perfect Day

The midday Saturday sight of the old, ride-on lawn mower parked outside the Cuddy's Rest public bar was a sure sign that winter was truly dead and gone. The grass-clipping season was here again, and for Bertola Harvey, the intrepid pilot of that ancient Atco machine, this signified nothing but good news.

It meant more little gardening jobs for him at Craigcuddy Castle — always good for a few extra beer vouchers. And even better news, it meant the heralding of the magic mushroom season — always good for a few extra trips to outer space. But the best news of all, perhaps, was that he could drive the mile-and-a-half from his shack to the pub on the old mower without attracting the unwanted attentions of Sergeant Brown, as had happened when he risked using this unorthodox mode of transport early one snowy and particularly sherry-sodden New Year's morning. He would never forget that he'd got away with it on that occasion only because the eagle-eyed policeman was as drunk as a brewery night-watchman himself.

"Stop in the name of the bloody law!" the bobby had bellowed, suddenly rising up before Bertola, who was busy manoeuvring the mower meanderingly homeward after an all-night Hogmanay carousal with the Cuddy's Rest wags.

"This is it — thirty days or three hundred quid, plus two years in the foot soldiers," Bertola thought, straining to bring his slithering steed to a put-putting stop in front of the sergeant. "How the fuck am I gonna get to the pub now?"

"A day return to Edinburgh, conductor," the sergeant slurred as he attempted to get aboard the mower. "And direct me, please, to the buffet car."

Making an on-the-spot New Year's resolution to subscribe to a life membership of the St Christopher Fan Club, Bertola raised a boot and placed it firmly on Sergeant Brown's broad chest. He then propelled the lurching lawman backwards into the ditch, from which — according to a fresh-but-weaving line of outsize Doc Marten prints in the snow — he had only just arisen. From that day forth, Bertola only travelled totally at ease on the old Atco in the mowing season, and today was the start of such peace of mind for another year.

"What do you think, then?" asked the Cuddy's Rest proprietor, the rotund and kilted Hamish Glenkinchie, his strawberry nose glowing like a welcome beacon to passing alcoholics in the late-April sunshine. He was looking up at the new sign swinging gently above the entrance to his inn.

Concentrating, Bertola scratched his shiny dome.

The new sign comprised a painting that manifested the inn's name in what might best be described as crudely-descriptive fashion. The idea for the featured scene had come from host Hamish himself, a man whose creative thinking was matched only, on this evidence, by his sense of good taste. For the sign depicted the upper torso of an immodestly buxom barmaid lying in bed beside the grinning head and crossed forelegs of a smug-looking horse (or "cuddy", in the local vernacular) with a newly-lit cigarette in his mouth.

"Well, man," Bertola drawled, after gaping upwards for the best part of five seconds, "I don't dig it. It's like somethin' outa the fuckin' *Godfather*. Yeah, daddy — too much. Even the chick's a dead ringer for Marlon Brando!"

The casual visitor to the Cuddy's Rest would walk into a bar, still "authentically humble", but these days frequented mainly by a scattering of ostensibly upwardly-mobile young men, dressed in deliberately-casual country clobber. This would typically consist of corduroy trousers (with or without green wellies), chunky Aran sweaters and boldly-checked Marks & Spencers shirts (with or without cravats). Some would invariably have unopened copies of the *Financial Times* wedged conspicuously under their deodorised armpits, as they stood in little unsociable huddles, talking loudly in unfamiliar accents to similarly-attired, silver-haired chaps, recently "retired to the country".

The few remaining local worthies would usually be found sitting in an equally unsociable corner playing dominoes, subconsciously trying not to feel out of place in their own playpen. They'd be taking frequent sidelong glances at the one-hand-behind-the-back stances of the new "regulars" and marvelling at how skilfully they could make their individually-purchased half pints of beer last for hours on end. Instead of ringing with the bawdy jokes and raucous laughter of old, the air of the bar would now be filled with intense discussions about mortgages, the merits of this never-to-go-off-road 4×4 off-roader compared to that, the tiresome peak-hour traffic jams on the way into and out of the city, how dashed difficult it was for little Elton and Kylie to understand what on *earth* those local kids were talking about at the village school, how annoyingly hard it could be to grow decent dahlias at this latitude, and countless other topics that were totally alien to this once-cosy community of happily-unpretentious country folk.

Meanwhile, if the corduroy and cravat crew were to cock an ear in the worthies' direction, they might well overhear quiet conversations, regularly punctuated with dram-downing interludes, on subjects such as how the trout were rising in the Cuddy Burn, what date the swallows arrived at so-and-so's barn this year, how the lambing had gone on the hill places this spring, how this one's field of winter wheat was looking better than that one's, and why and how the drink prices in the Cuddy's Rest were always that bit cheaper than over the road in the posher, scampi-in-a-basket setting of the Cuddyford Arms Hotel lounge bar. And this latter fact, it went without saying, was precisely why those borrowed-to-their-eyeballs, who's-kidding-who buggers in the green wellies were in here instead of over there, where everyone knew they'd much rather be, anyway.

At the bar, Johnny Ardonski — just returned from feeding Jigger's pigs, and already fixed up with his first Carlsberg Special and double vodka of the day — was telling some long-winded joke or other (which he purported to understand) to a visibly bored Bertola. Johnny's forced bellow of laughter on delivery of the punchline was greeted with predictable indifference by his one-man audience, staring stone-faced into his sherry schooner.

"Hey, you been workin' with pig shit, man," Bertola droned, stroking his emergent Frank Zappa moustache, "or did somebody in the old country send you a bottle of Ukrainian after-shave for Christmas?"

"Ha! Bertola, you fuckink baster," Johnny guffawed, "you alvays takink piss avay from Johnny like dat! But I likink you all da same." He gave Bertola a playful punch on the chest with a fist that was only marginally smaller than his Nikita Khruschev-like head. "And I likink you because you callink me Ukrainian baster — not Polski one like all dem odder peoples doink!" By way of confirming his affection, Johnny slapped Bertola on the back so heartily that he choked on his sherry.

Fortunately, Bertola was spared further painful proof of Johnny's fondness for him by the bar door flying noisily open. A lanky, elderly gentleman with chameleonic eyes and a snappy suit swept in, followed by a little man struggling with a massive suitcase.

"Barkeep!" the gentleman thundered at Hamish. "Kindly mix me a New Yorker!" Then, fixing Bertola in an asymmetrical stare, he further thundered, "And you, bellhop, be so good as to take my luggage from the cabbie!"

"Hey, cool it, Clyde! I'm no goddam bellhop! I'm a fuckin' bass player, so go hump your own bag!"

Hamish, ever the peace-mongering innkeeper, poured oil on potentially troubled waters by stepping swiftly from behind the bar and fawning, "Hamish Glenkinchie at your service, sir. Please, allow me to take your suitcase. It's the, ehm, porter's day off. My most humble apologies."

"Much obliged, Glenkinchie. Smith's the name. And now that New Yorker, if you will."

Hamish's confusion was conspicuous. "Right away, Mr Smith. A New Yorker. Yes, now, that's Scotch and . . . no, Bourbon . . . we have some Jack Daniels right here behind the, er, Advocaat —"

"A New Yorker, for your information, Glenkinchie," stated Mr Smith, striding behind the bar and selecting the appropriate bottles, "is a simple but peerless cocktail of gin, vermouth, sherry and Cointreau — over the rocks, naturally."

"Naturally," Hamish bluffed, while rummaging ambitiously in the water at the bottom of the ice bucket.

Bertola liked the sound of this New Yorker stuff. He was taking a sudden shine to this old dude, and his admiration increased further when the venerable visitor addressed him with a straightforward, "And you, good buddy, will be sociable enough to join me, what? Name your poison!"

"What you're havin' looks poisonous enough for me, daddy."

"Swell! I like your style, young chap."

"Please to introjoosink myself, Mr Schmidt," said a suddenly interested Slav pigman as he shuffled forward to claim his place at this new well of possible plenty. "Johnny Ardonski at your services."

Mr Smith acknowledged Johnny's servile bow with a magnanimous: "Another New Yorker, I take it?"

"Ah, no, Ukrainian, sir. I comink from little willage odder side Kiev they callink Che —"

"Relax, man," Bertola cut in. "Just take the guy's booze and hold the geography lesson!"

Suddenly, bonhomie was booming. Even the undeclared culture wars with the incomers were temporarily forgotten by the four domino-playing worthies currently present, as they, too, responded eagerly to stranger Smith's philanthropic invitation to, "Be my guests". The corduroy and cravat crew, the worthies concurred, were welcome to their penny-pinching half pints. Happy days — or, with any luck, a happy hour or two at least — were here again for the Cuddy's Rest natives.

And soon, the four worthies were six, then eight, ten, twelve and more. The Cuddyford bush telegraph had become swiftly lubricated by the steady flow of Mr Smith's freebie New Yorkers, and was transmitting a treat. Why, local wags who hadn't been seen inside the Cuddy's Rest since the arrival of the first incomer (a milestone coincidental, as it happens, with the opening of the Horseburgh branch of Tesco, where the off-licence booze prices were irresistibly reasonable) turned up to meet this munificent Messiah, their faces aglow with anticipation.

Before one happy hour had passed, the altruistic Mr Smith joined his devoted throng of dipsodisciples on the fun side of the bar, having reinstated host Hamish at his drink-dispensing post with clear instructions to, "Keep 'em coming, Glenkinchie. And get that sickly look off your face. I told you, goddammit — I'll pick up the tab . . . when I check out!"

"Pops, settle an argument I'm having with myself, OK?" Bertola asked, laying his hand on Mr Smith's mohair-suited shoulder and exhaling the spent gasses of a Roman-candle-proportioned joint into his face. "That accent of yours, man. All that Sloane, Hooray Henry English — no offence, daddy — with bits of Yankee Doodle Dandy in there. Hey, you related to Koo Stark or somethin'?"

"Never heard of the chap, old buddy. Gambling man, is he?"

At that, Mr Smith, still prudently nursing his first New Yorker while all about him were wallowing in a veritable Hudson River of the stuff, produced a sealed deck of playing cards, with the jovial call: "Anyone for poker?"

Before a second hour had passed, the untold happiness of the first had nosedived into gobsmacked gloom for all the beneficiaries of Mr Smith's benevolence, successively parted as they were from their modest wads amid an endless New Yorker-blurred flurry of the benefactor's straight flushes, full houses and five aces. The worthies were rooked to a man; to a man, that is, with two notable exceptions. One, Johnny Ardonski, had passed the poker period slouched in a solitary haze at the bar, gamely trying to fathom out the punch line of a joke someone had told him. The other, Bertola Harvey, being a jazzman and *au fait*, therefore, with such hustler's scams, had repaired upon commencement of Mr Smith's sting sequence to the out-of-tune piano in the green-welly quarter of the bar. There, he had elected to entertain the delighted customers to endless medleys of feel-at-home pub songs — for a reward, it has to be said, of endless medleys of those "supposedly" long-lasting half pints. Culture wars, like suitcases, were just not Bertola's bag.

"I say, Bertola, old buddy, old chap," murmured a contented Mr Smith as he flicked through his bulging billfold with a practised thumb, "care to hail me a cab? I have some business to attend to at Craigcuddy Castle."

Bertola closed the lid on a Chas and Dave selection. "A cab?" he said. "No way, man. The only cab's the one that brought you here, and that's based down at Horseburgh, five miles away. Costs too much loot, pops." He copped an eyeful of Mr Smith's misbegotten stash of crinkle, then added, "But stay cool, daddy-o. I'll fix some wheels for you. No pressure."

And so it transpired that Jigger, when returning home later that evening from a "business meeting" at the old coal-mining town of Cowdenbings along the coast, stopped at the crossroads outside Cuddyford village and was confronted with the somewhat odd spectre of an ancient Atco lawn mower put-putting by in the direction of the castle. A huge suitcase was sticking out of the grass box at the front, and a lanky, elderly gentleman was riding shotgun for the three-sheets-to-the-wind Bertola, who shouted over his shoulder to his passenger as the machine rattled past, "Hey, anybody ever tell you you're a dead ringer for Jack Elam, pops?"

To which the lanky, elderly gentleman replied, "Anybody ever tell you you're a dead ringer for the bandleader in the Muppet Show, old buddy, old chap?" He patted Bertola on the back. "And please be so good as to drop the 'pops' moniker, OK. Just call me Archie, dig?"

CHAPTER
SIX

A Lifeline for Ludo

Word, as word invariably does in rural parts, rapidly got about Cuddyford and district that the Duke was in shtuck and about to sell up, Jigger having shrewdly enlisted the tattling talents of Nessie and Granny to drop a fertile word or two in the eager ears of the *crème de la crème* of the local chinwags. Sooner than it takes to buy a loaf of bread, or borrow a cup of sugar, the wildfire was kindled and spreading at a satisfactory rate, fanned by a favourable wind blasting forth from some of the biggest mouths in the area.

By now, Jigger had laid the mental foundations of a scheme for stymying the plans that Babu Ng allegedly had for commercially developing Craigcuddy Estate. Such plans, if implemented, would ruin for ever the familiar working surroundings and way of life that Jigger and his family had cherished for so long at Acredales of Cuddyford. Even more crucially, though, they would effectively put paid to those vital financial perks that resulted from his "managing" Craigcuddy Home Farm and performing his various other "estate-factoring" duties for the Duke. But Jigger needed time to develop his scheme and make it work.

He had a large and complicated jigsaw puzzle to put together, and, as yet, he was only in possession of a few ill-defined pieces. Stalling tactics were urgently required, so stirring up a hornets' nest of local hysteria on the subject seemed like the most effective way of slamming the brakes on.

Details of the mysterious millionaire's designs on the estate grew more fantastic and far-fetched at every step of their whispered way throughout the locality. In the short space of time that it took to achieve blanket gossip coverage, the tiny seed of the vaguely-mooted theme park, which Nessie and Granny had carefully sown, had beanstalked into something to rival Euro Disney, no less.

"It's an absolute outrage!" seethed Commander Plimsoll-Pompey, MBE, RN (Retired) through his immaculately-trimmed white whiskers upon receipt of the news from the matronly waitress in the lounge of the Cuddyford Arms Hotel. "I didn't drop anchor in a sleepy little backwater like this just to have everything ruined by some damned, money-grabbing rag-head!"

"Certainly not!" concurred the like-minded Mrs Plimsoll-Pompey, her rigidly-sprayed coiffure quivering in indignation like a blue-rinsed Brillo Pad. "Something ought to be done about it, Horatio!"

"And something jolly well *will* be done about it, my dear. I didn't put myself forward for election to the chair of the Cuddyford Community Association to sit back and allow some plundering foreign opportunist to buy his way into the area and change everything to suit his own selfish ends. And, I'll wager, he's only here because property just happens to be cheaper than around London, Paris, Milan, or — or —"

"Or Poole, Horatio?"

"Absolutely, my dear! I didn't sell up the jolly old shore base at Canford Cliffs and tack five hundred miles to a bungalow in the frozen north just to put up with that sort of thing!"

"Certainly not!"

"An extraordinary general meeting of the Cuddyford Community Association will be convened at the absolute earliest!"

"Here, here, Commander! You show 'em!" called out-to-grass, senior civil servant, Jonathan Littleton-Nimby. He lowered his *Daily Telegraph* from the Redhill-to-Victoria rush-hour position and thumped the arm of his chair in hearty enjoinment. "If I'd wanted to see out my days in a funfair, I'd have settled for somewhere nearer civilization, like Margate. You can rely upon my unwavering support, Commander!"

"Good man, Littleton-Nimby. Glad to have you aboard, sir!"

"I shall telephone the members of the bridge club immediately and *insist* that they attend your EGM," trumpeted Mrs Littleton-Nimby, laying down her conspicuous copy of *Country Life* and dusting the rock cake crumbs off her impeccable Barbour jacket. "Seven-thirty in the village hall as usual, I take it?"

"Absolutely, madam!" confirmed the Commander.

Very soon the lounge was filled with cries of "Hear, hear!" and pledges of solidarity for the Commander's cause as the waitress' word was spread to the farthest

102

chintz-covered corner. People who had passed each other in the street every day since moving to Cuddyford, but had never mustered up sufficient sociability to actually speak, suddenly found themselves emerging from the protective cover of their broadsheets and joining together in genial communion.

"Indeed, Commander, it's at times like this, when the foreign heel is hovering over us," spoke up Littleton-Nimby, chin down, shoulders back, chest out, "that we British get together and show 'em who's *really* boss!"

"It's the spirit of the blitz!" an excited voice proclaimed amid the rattling of coffee cups.

"Yes! Land of hope and glory!" said another, almost singing.

"There'll always be an England!" yet another emotional voice reminded the glad-hearted assembly of true Brits.

"And a Scotland, too, if the Commander has anything to do with it," shouted the ingratiating Littleton-Nimby. "Three cheers for Commander Plimsoll-Pompey! HIP, HIP . . ."

"HOOR-AY-AY-AY!"

Over the road in the public bar of the Cuddy's Rest, meanwhile . . .

Hamish Glenkinchie was polishing a glass while peering out of the window. "What the hell's that racket coming from the hotel?" he mumbled. "Sounds like they're having some kind of a celebration over there."

"Maybe one o' them toffee-nosed incomers has kicked the bucket," said wag number one, of the solitary three seated at the dominoes table.

"Nah, no such luck," muttered wag number two.

"Aye, it's more likely to be a welcome party for another batch o' the buggers," suggested wag number three. He removed his pipe from his mouth and directed a symbolic spit into the fireplace.

They could afford to talk like this, because, being a working day, all of the corduroy-and-cravat "regulars" were away commuting.

"And there's gonny be a damned sight more o' them once that camel-shagger at the manse turns Craigcuddy Estate into this theme park thing."

"Bloody disgrace!"

"That's right. Should never be allowed!"

"Correct! Where's yer plannin' regulations now, eh?"

"Aye, and yer so-called conservation areas!"

"And green belts!"

"Aye, right enough."

"Aye, right a-bloody-nuff, right enough! And what can the man in the street do about it?"

"BUGGER ALL!" was the chorused conclusion.

There followed a short intermission for the gathering of thoughts and the sipping of nips of whisky.

When, after some minutes of silence, it was beginning to appear that the thought-gathering harvest had failed, Hamish Glenkinchie — ever the professional publican — posed the stimulating question, "Do any of you lot know what a theme park is, anyway?"

More silence.

"Come on," Hamish goaded, "how can you condemn something if you don't even know what it is, for Christ's sake?"

The goading worked . . . sort of.

"It doesnae matter what it is, we dinny want it here!"

"Dead right! We've managed fine up to now without bloody theme parks!"

"Aye — bloody disgrace!"

"It's the Government I blame, of course."

"Ye never spoke a truer word, pal. Bloody corruption and sleaze!"

"That's it in a nutshell. Money talks, as bloody usual."

"Maybe so, but all it ever says to me is goodbye!"

Wry chortles.

"Bloody foreigners!"

"Aye, politicians' palms are being well greased. Ye can bet yer last nip on that!"

"Just like that dodgy buy-yersel'-a-lordship business. Yes, and yer Arms-for-Iraq Scandal a while back."

"It was Iran."

"Same bloody difference."

"And how about the gormless cretin, then?"

"Ye mean ye even think the Prime Minister's in on this an' all?"

"Nothin' would surprise me, son, but I'm talkin' about the bloody Gormlie-Crighton gormless cretin — old Duke Horace up there at the castle."

"Just what I was thinkin'. This theme park thing'll be worth millions to that old bastard."

"Right! And what'll us common folk o' Cuddyford get out o' it?"

"BUGGER ALL!" the wags concluded in harmony. "THREE MORE NIPS, HAMISH!"

The cavernous Great Hall of Craigcuddy Castle was the venue chosen by old Duke Horace for the vital meeting with Jigger, which he hoped against hope might produce a plan for the salvation of the estate.

The once-magnificent hall was now but a desolate barn of a room, all the fine paintings, tapestries, Jacobean furniture, suits of armour and other historic trappings sold off by Sotheby's at the debt-reducing auction that had been the talk of the county at the time. All that now remained of the Great Hall's former glory was the high, vaulted ceiling, from which weighty wrought-metal chandeliers the size of cartwheels used to hang on stout chains, but where now only naked light bulbs dangled on lonely lengths of flex. On the dark wooden panelling of the walls, faded rectangular patches showed where portraits of successive Dukes of Gormlie and their immediate families had once hung, but where now tarnished brass picture lights illuminated nothing more lordly than dust and cobwebs. And the vast stone fireplace, in which whole bullocks were once roasted on the spit, now accommodated nothing more meaty than a solitary mouse, sniffing forlornly at a little fall of soot, in hope, perhaps, of locating a grain of corn dropped from above by a chimney-squatting crow. Even the mighty banqueting table and its ranks of stout chairs had gone. In their place — but only for today's assembly — was a rickety, folding card table and three canvas director's chairs so dilapidated that they might well have seen service on the set of an early Boris Karloff movie.

It was, indeed, Frankenstein's monster that Jigger's fertile imagination was calling to mind as he sat alone in the middle of the Great Hall awaiting the entry of the Duke. And his imagination had it about right. When a shadowy figure appeared through a concealed door in the oak panelling at the far corner of the hall and came shuffling stoop-shouldered and panting towards him, Jigger could have sworn, in the dim light, that there was a bulky bolt piercing the creature's neck.

The creature was, of course, nothing more monstrous than the Twelfth Duke himself, and the bolt nothing more sinister than a pair of ear protectors that he'd been wearing while popping off a few practice blasts at some clay pigeons on the east lawn.

"That was a secret passage you came out of, was it?" Jigger asked once the usual pleasantries had been exchanged.

The Duke nodded his confirmation. "Can't be too careful, m'boy. In Craigcuddy Castle, walls *do* have ears, y'know."

"So, where does the passage lead from — and to?"

"Er, nowhere but everywhere . . . if you do it right."

The Duke was giving nothing away, and Jigger didn't press him, although greatly intrigued. He was attracted to the notion of a maze of hidden passages riddling the wings and turrets of the old castle, and connecting it by underground tunnels, maybe, to stone-slabbed,

107

rhododendron-camouflaged exits and entrances in remote corners of the grounds . . . and perhaps, even beyond. But, for the moment, there were other, less romantic matters to be dealt with, and the Duke didn't delay in broaching the subject.

The bank, he intoned discreetly, had been guardedly pleased to hear that a way of reducing the Craigcuddy overdraft to an acceptable level might be forthcoming. However, unless details of such were provided soon and met with the bank's approval, formal procedures would have to be set in motion to ensure that the Duke's debt to the bank was recovered. This would be achieved by the sale of some or, if necessary, all of the Gormlie-Crighton assets. Expedition, the Duke stressed, was of the essence, if acceptance of Babu Ng's offer to buy the estate was not to become mandatory.

He fixed Jigger in an apprehensive stare. "You did say that you had a scheme in mind to, er, both alleviate the bank's threat and solve the pecuniary problems of young Ludovic, did you not?"

"Yes, and now that you mention young Ludovic — where is he? He was supposed to be in on this too, you know."

He would, indeed, be joining them presently, Jigger was informed, but it was better to clarify a few points in his absence first. For instance, just what did Jigger have in mind for Lord Ludovic on the remuneration-for-work front? His qualifications, as Jigger would be aware, were somewhat on the doodling side of sketchy, so career choices did appear to be on the Hobson's side of limited. Had Jigger miraculously found an opening for a *Saints*-playing frog-inflater in a travelling freak show, perchance?

Jigger gave the Duke silent credit for his last remark, which, for such a humourless old fogey, was on the knee-slapping side of whimsical. But no, he confessed, such openings were well nigh non-existent these days — even for someone so eminently equipped as young Lord Ludo.

"Hmm, as I feared," the Duke droned dolefully, leaping like a lordly lemming over the precipice of lost hope, "good fortune has failed us in our hour of need. You have been unable to locate a likely livelihood for Ludovic. An earner for my heir is, as it were, a non-runner." He heaved a shuddering sigh. "Sod's Law — or is it Murphy's? — prevails, and I am now resignin' myself to blowin' my bleedin' brains out."

He'd have to be a damned fine shot to manage that, Jigger silently mused.

Just then, the massive double doors at the end of the Great Hall boomed open, and in strode Lord Ludovic II himself. As he stomped over the stone floor, his footsteps reverberating around the bare walls and off the high ceiling arches, he was the very antithesis of his furtive father.

"Hi there, Jigger!" he bawled. "Hey, it just chimed eleven hundred hours on the old ancestral grandfather clock out there — or it would have done, if the good old ancestral timepiece hadn't been flogged off with the rest of the jolly old ancestral goodies. Arf, arf! Yah, but worry not — eleven o' clock it is, which in plain

109

parlance means that it's . . . OPENING TIME, RIGHT?"

He produced a hip flask and thrust it at Jigger with a boorish guffaw. "Have a belt of that, mate! Go on, enjoy yourself! Get some laughing liquor down you!"

"A bit early for me, Ludo, thanks all the same," said Jigger, taking a sideways glance at the old Duke, whose previous expression of self-pity was now replaced by one of deep despair.

Why was it, the hangdog Duke wanted to know, that his clear instructions to keep this meeting and its location absolutely covert had been totally ignored by his son? Did he not realise that discretion was of the utmost importance in this embarrassing and potentially ruinous matter? A rather less conspicuous entrance would have been more appropriate — surely!

"No point, pater. I mean, as dim and doddery as old Elephant Bollocks is, even he must have twigged that you didn't instruct him to direct Jigger to a table and three chairs marooned in the middle of an indoor rugger pitch unless some kind of q.t. convention was on the cards, right?" With a silly grin, he offered the hip flask to the Duke and enquired, "Fancy a snort yourself, your Grace? Arf, arf, arf, arf!"

Jigger contemplated his cuticles in a mixture of abashment and amazement.

"His name is Baldock — Mr Ellington Baldock!" the Duke barked, pointedly taking a defensive stance on behalf of his old retainer. "And a dashed fine butler he is, too!"

"Hah! Ellington Baldock! Arf, arf! Yah, I had totally forgotten that that was the old fart's real name. I mean, be fair, pater — anyone with a ridiculous handle like that is bound to inspire one to come up with the obviously-brilliant jibe, right?"

"Like gormless cretin, maybe?" Jigger muttered sardonically, still cuticle-contemplating.

Lord Ludovic gave a patronising, pig-like grunt. "I think you've rather missed the point, Jigger, old mate," he said. "The jolly old jibe has to relate to a proper name. Something like, er — uhm — ah —"

"Gormlie-Crighton?" Jigger's lips enunciated before his brain could button them.

"Dammitall, chaps, we are not here to play word games," the Duke spluttered, much to Jigger's relief. "We are here to discuss the savin' of the dukedom from disaster, financial and otherwise!"

"Ah, the last of the family bathwater about to gurgle down the old hereditary plug'ole, pater, yah? Damned pity. Still, never say die — say 'cheers!', right?" Grinning vacantly, Ludo raised his hip flask and took a slug.

"What the hell am I getting myself into?" Jigger asked himself. Looking at the truly gormless antics of Ludo and the pitiful floundering of his father, he wondered whether it was worth the bother of trying to bail out this pair of nincompoops. The answer to that would have been emphatically negative, had it not been that Jigger's own family fortunes were inexorably tied to the maintenance of the status quo at Craigcuddy Castle. He took the bit between his teeth . . .

"Is that the grey suit I suggested, Ludo?"

"Ah, absolutely right, Jigger mate. Yah — got it from the Oxfam Shop in Horseburgh. Damned smooth set of threads. And only fifteen quid, would you believe?"

"I sincerely hope you didn't pay by cheque!" the Duke exclaimed, panic suddenly ousting irritation from his fluctuating countenance.

"No fear! Got it on tick, mate. Oh yes, too many of the old Dunlopillo billets-doux have been bouncing back to one already of late. Damned annoying. Can't you fire a rocket up the arsehole of one of those chappies at the bank, pater? I mean, what the blazes are banks for if they can't come good with the old moolah when a chap needs it? Bit of a liberty, Jigger, what?"

"That," the Duke interceded, "is precisely the reason for this meetin', Ludovic m'boy." Then, turning swiftly to Jigger, he added, "The floor is yours, Thomas."

Jigger took time to have a closer look at the besuited Ludo. Until now, he had never seen him dressed in anything other than scruffy moleskin trousers, a pair of down-at-heel Hush Puppies — their beige suede uppers permanently decorated with fag ash and drink stains — and an antediluvian, hand-me-down hacking jacket of ginger tweed criss-crossed with custard-yellow checks and embellished with worn-through leather elbow patches. So, even if this Oxfam suit was a couple of sizes too big for him, it was grey, it was double-breasted and it did go a long way towards transforming Ludo's image into the one Jigger had envisaged for him. Yes, he decided, a decent haircut, a general clean-up and Lord Ludovic would be just the ticket!

"Tidy suit, Ludo," he said, fingering the lapels.

"Yah, I rather thought so myself, actually. The old memsahib in the Oxfam Shop said it belonged to old what'sisname, the local MP who croaked recently. Nothing but the best. And take sights at the shirt — his too — damned stylish — pink shirt, white collar — three pounds fifty. Fa-a-a-abulous! All top Savile Row kit, mate."

The old Duke's eyeballs rolled. "Savile Row?" he gasped. "B — but old what'sisname the MP was one of those *Labour* fellows, for God's sake!"

Ludo ignored his father, as usual. "And how about this?" he grinned at Jigger.

"The old school tie, if I'm not mistaken?" Jigger ventured.

"Ra-ther, mate! Yup, nipped into the old dower house on the way back from the boozer yesterday and did a deal with one of the sixth formers. Swapped him a hardcore porn video for it. Damned smart bit of trade, what?" He made a dismissive gesture with his hip flask. "I'd seen the video before, you see. Not my particular groove, if you get my drift." Then, leaning towards Jigger, Ludo appended in a confidential whisper, "I mean, there's this donkey, right, with an absolutely e-*nor*-mous schlong, and —"

"Er, I think the floor, as I said, is yours, Thomas," the Duke butted in, clearly discomfited by mention of a donkey. After all, he'd been an officer in the cavalry (a gentleman's institution, cynically referred to by those proles in the infantry as "donkey-wallopers"), so four-legged creatures of the asinine variety — no matter how cinematically versatile — were regarded by him as strictly *personae non gratae*.

"OK, let's recap," Jigger said in an effort to take hold of the situation. "The position, as I understand it, is that Craigcuddy Estate is stony-broke, and unless we can organise a quick turn for the better, the bank is going to pull the carpet from under your feet, correct?"

"Fat chance," quipped Ludo. "No carpets left! Those damned Sotheby's chappies saw to that, right? Arf, arf, arf."

"Ah-*hum*!" coughed the Duke, paying no heed to his son's crude attempt at repartee, but beckoning instead to Baldock the butler, who had materialised silently and was hovering a few discreet steps away with a cordless telephone on a silver tray.

"The manager of the Horseburgh branch of the Royal Scottish Commerce Bank is on the line, your Grace," he monotoned. "There is, I am informed, a matter of great urgency upon which he wishes to confer."

Baldock bowed stiffly, handed the phone to the Duke, then retreated a few paces backwards and stood to solemn attention, staring ahead at some inconsequential point high on the opposite wall, the silver tray held horizontally at his chest.

The Duke concluded a brief and distinctly one-sided telephone conversation with an uncharacteristically gruff, "Very well!"

Silence then prevailed, until Baldock had made his sombre exit, slow-marching with his tray across the hall.

"I think I should advise you, Thomas," the Duke eventually announced, pale-gilled and quaking, "that this Babu Ng fellow has now placed on deposit at the bank — as a token of the seriousness of his intentions, as it were — more than sufficient funds to buy us clean out." He heaved another of his shuddering sighs, then quavered, "The sh — shit has now hit the b — bally f — fan."

Jigger stroked his chin. Ng was really putting the pressure on now, and that was for sure. The old Duke was correct. Things were beginning to look pretty bleak, right enough. Or *were* they . . .?

"Wait a minute, Duke," he said, heartened by a sudden flash of inspiration. "Maybe Ng has done you a favour. See what I'm saying?"

"No," the Duke replied without hesitation.

Ludo took another slug from his hip flask and lit a fag. "All well beyond me, mate," he said. He glanced at his wrist watch. "I say, is this going to take much longer? I mean, I really must get to the bookie's before —"

"What I'm saying," Jigger cut in, "is that as long as that money of Ng's is in the bank, the more time we've got to sort something out. Ng's hooked, so we just have to play him along for as long as possible, get it?"

"And, uhm, how do we do that, m'boy?"

"Just leave that to me, Duke. I've got a tidy idea brewing here," Jigger lied. The truth was that he hadn't a clue what the hell to do about this latest hitch. The main thing, however, was to stay cool and busk like the clappers. "The first priority," he pronounced, "is to launch Ludo into his new job."

The Duke nodded in hopeful confusion.

Ludo dropped his hip flask. "*Job*, mate?" he wheezed. "In the words of the great McEnroe, you can-*not* be fuck-ing *SER*-I-OUS!"

Jigger glared at the Duke in exasperation. "You haven't clued him up on *any* of this, have you?"

"Uhm, well, no — I, er . . ."

Leaving the Duke to his stumbling search for excuses, Jigger turned to Ludo.

"Look, the simple fact is that your old man's skint, the bank has already lobbed him more money than the Craigcuddy Estate is worth, and there'll be no more mazuma forthcoming from *them* until they can be persuaded that they're gonna get a fair whack of *their* mazuma back from you! The bank and your lawyers have already advised selling out to Babu Ng, and if that happens, you'll be left with zilch. Get the picture *now*, Ludo?"

"But why, mate? The jolly old Gormlie-Crighton name must still be good for a bit of tick from the bank. I mean, steady on — what's good for the Cuddy's Rest must be good for *them*, right?"

"And how much more tick do you think you'll get at the Cuddy's Rest, or anywhere else, if your cheques keep bouncing?" Jigger's patience was rapidly being stretched to the limit. "No, Ludo," he went on, "the only way out is to persuade the bank to do what they're in business for, and that's to lend *you* money and cop *their* pound of flesh in return. But that's only gonna

116

happen if you can make the deal look safe for them, savvy?"

"Well, it's dashed unfair, mate," whined Lord Ludovic, pouting sulkily. "And what about those bastards, Leary, Byblow and Wyllie, right? I mean, they've had loads of lolly from this family for generations. You know, sorting out minor probs with silly, up-the-duff kitchen maids and such. So, why are they sinking the boot in now? Dashed unfair, that's what!"

"They're lawyers, Ludo. They're making bugger all from your family these days, but they can smell big money in the sale of Craigcuddy Estate, and they'd like to get their mitts on some of it. Simple as that."

Lord Ludovic looked as though he were about to burst into tears. "Dashed unfair, mate," he mumbled. "That's all I can say."

The Duke nodded in grim-faced accord. "Hmm, dashed unfair."

"Fair or unfair, it's a fact," Jigger bristled. "So, Ludo needs an earner, and if he can find a career that'll give you access to ways of keeping the estate in family hands, so much the better, agreed?"

The Duke and his heir nodded their heads, vaguely.

"Right," said Jigger, "so there's only one possible job for him, isn't there?"

The Duke and his heir shook their heads, categorically.

Jigger took a deep breath. "OK, let's be perfectly blunt," he sighed, drumming his fingers on the table. "Ludo wasn't exactly up there among the high rollers at school, was he? In fact, it's been said that the most he knows about the three Rs is how to spell them. He's never done a day's work in his life, and on top of that, he's a well-known gambler, womaniser and bevvy merchant. So, when we put all of that together, there *is* only one career open to him, isn't there?" In the absence of any visible sign of apprehension, Jigger declared, "Yes, Ludovic Gormlie-Crighton, *you* are going to be Horseburghshire's next Member of Parliament!"

The silence in the Great Hall was palpable.

"Member of *Parliament?*" the Duke and Ludo eventually gasped.

"The very same," Jigger affirmed. "So, the origins of that suit couldn't have been better suited to the task, Ludo — if you'll pardon the pun. Of course," he shrugged, "you'll have to be adopted as a candidate for the by-election first, but I've put out a few feelers, and I don't think we'll have much of a problem."

So stunned was the Duke that he could only stand up shakily, raise his right forefinger as if about to make a point, machine gun out a magazine of staccato "ahs", then sit down again. This he did three times, before Lord Ludovic broke the hypnotic spell by proclaiming with a noticeable note of relief, "Uhm, 'fraid not, Jigger, old mate. One has been somewhat blackballed by the local party, you see. Several years ago it was — during one of Maggie Thatcher's state visits to the Horseburghshire Conservative Club. Mistook her for a barmaid — asked her to fetch me a triple Drambuie —

gave her a fiver and a pat on the arse and told her to keep the change."

"And they booted you out for *that*?"

"No way, mate! No, it was a bit later, right? Got slightly shit-faced — did a wobbly on the way to the pisshouse — stumbled into Maggie's old man — knocked the large G&T out of his hand — club president went absolutely ape-shit nuclear — immediately barred me *sine die*. Yah, the permanent bum's rush."

"Hmm," hummed the Duke, dark storm clouds of despair gathering once more above his lowered head. "I f — fear, then, that we are s — sunk."

"Spot on, pater," said Ludo, a wild grin lighting his face. "As you your good self might say, we are now totally f — fucked. Arf, arf, arf!" He gave Jigger a slap on the shoulder and declared in celebratory fashion, "Nice try, mate, but the jolly old working life is not for me after all. Ho-hum, such is life. Righty-ho! Must be off to the bookie's."

Jigger laid a reining hand on his shoulder. "Hold your horses," he said before Ludo could rise from his chair. "Putting you forward as the Tory candidate was never the idea, anyway."

"You're not *seriously* suggesting that he should become Screaming Lord Ludovic of the Monster Raving Loony Party are you, m'boy?" the Duke enquired in a way that was too genuine to be jocular.

"No. Tidy thought, though, but not too practical, Duke."

"Er, 'fraid you've rather lost me, mate," Ludo finally admitted while preparing to decamp again. "Yep, way beyond me, all of this. Now, if you'll excuse me —"

"Not so fast, Ludo," Jigger growled. "I've gone to a lot of trouble for you, and if you don't sit on your backside and listen to what I've got to say, you can go and disappear down your family plug'ole with your hereditary bathwater. If *you* don't care, why the hell should I? OK, *mate*?"

The Duke turned puce, stung from his mood of despondency by Jigger's unexpected outburst, and feeling instinctively outraged on his heir's behalf by this verbal affront from someone who was, when all was said and done, a subordinate. He braced himself to register his objection in the most dignified but clearly-defined terms. He stood up, knocking over his chair in the process, took a deep breath, pointed a trembling finger at Jigger and declared: "I — er — er — uhm —"

"And the same goes for you, Duke," Jigger snapped. "*You* asked me for help, but if you can't get Ludo to take this seriously, you may as well go and accept Babu Ng's offer, *and* get ready to go on display in your turret. Is *that* what you want?"

Jigger's words reverberated around the hall and hung like the sword of Damocles in the strained hush that followed.

"Well?" Jigger enquired quietly after a suitable period for reflection had elapsed.

"I believe that the floor is still yours, m'boy," the Duke muttered, while fumbling with his collapsed director's chair in a forlorn attempt to regain some of his lost composure.

Ludovic lit another fag, nervously this time. "Yah . . . yah, I'm all ears, mate," he truckled.

"OK, it's like this," Jigger stated, bringing the proceedings firmly back to order. "I went along to see the local Party bosses at Cowdenbings yesterday, and although they thought I'd gone doolally at first, they soon warmed to the idea of Ludo being their candidate . . . once, that is, I'd put them wise to the potential benefits — for them." He flashed Lord Ludovic a wink. "Yeah, just a few minor formalities to sort out, and you're their boy, Ludo."

"Cowdenbings?" queried the Duke, frowning.

Jigger sighed again. "Right, let me spell it out for you." He spread an upturned hand and, pointing to each finger in turn, patiently explained, "One — well over half of the constituency's population lives in that same Cowdenbings area. Two — everybody there votes the same. Three — that means that the candidate chosen by the Party bosses in Cowdenbings is bound to win. And four — that means that you, Ludo, are going to be the next Horseburghshire MP, *if* you play your cards right. Get it now?"

Ludo scratched his head. "Party bosses in Cowdenbings?" he muttered.

"That's right," Jigger nodded. "Cowdenbings, where all the big political decisions for this county are made."

"But surely all such decisions are made in the County Buildings in Horseburgh," the Duke objected, his stiff upper lip twitching in bafflement.

Jigger shook his head despairingly. "No, no, no, Duke. They're made in the back room of the Miners' Welfare Club in Cowdenbings, believe me."

"They *are?*"

"Yeah, 'cos it's there that all the local Party godfathers do their drinking. With me now?"

"Ehm, no, actually," the Duke and his son admitted, their looks of vagueness striking a remarkable hereditary likeness in Jigger's view.

"Hell's bells," he barked, his tethered patience finally running out of rope, "I'm talking about the bloody *Labour* Party!"

The Gormlie-Crighton duo looked as if they'd just been diagnosed as having contracted bubonic plague. "THE LABOUR PARTY?" they yelled

"B — but you can't be *seriously* suggesting that Ludovic should stand as a *Labour* candidate," the Duke spluttered. "Why, they're bally socialists, and Ludovic is an a — a — a —"

"Aristocrat?" Jigger prompted.

"A — a — absolutely!"

"He won't be the first," Jigger shrugged.

"Yah, but then there *is* that drink-driving rap of mine," Ludo objected hopefully. "They wouldn't really want to take on a chap with a reputation as a piss artist, right?"

"Gerraway!" Jigger scoffed. "They'll love all that bit. It'll be like the second coming of Lord Brown."

"But Ludovic would never be accepted as a true *socialist*," the Duke persisted. "After all, he's not even c — c — c —"

"Common?" Jigger anticipated. "Oh, I think he'll pass. Just keep wearing those manky, old beige Hush Puppies with your dark grey suit, Ludo. That'll give you the authentic common touch all right."

"Oh, yah, right — magic," nodded Ludo, totally clueless. "But just one other point, mate," he continued, a look of genuine angst in his eyes. "Speeches, you know — I mean, how does one know what to say if one can't quite, er —?"

"Write 'em?" Jigger prompted. "Ah," he smiled, "that'll be the least of your worries. The Cowdenbings boys have got some hairy university lecturer bloke who does all that for them. And stop worrying." He gave Ludo an encouraging pat on his hunched shoulders. "The Labour Party are just the same as the Tories these days. They've only got different heroes, that's all. Take it from me, all you need to do is learn a few hallowed names and you're in. And once you get to Westminster, you just keep blaming the other lot for everything, while *you* concentrate on looking out for number one, fixing up a few well-paid consultancies for yourself, and generally lining your own pockets like the other creeps." Jigger folded his arms and flashed Lord Ludovic another wink. "Yeah, should be a cinch for you, Ludo."

Ludo beamed with pride. "Wow, thanks," he chuckled. "Line the old pockets, eh?" Jigger had hit the button at last, and it showed in the sudden sparkle glinting in Ludo's eyes. "Sounds fucking magic to me, mate!"

"Oh, another thing," Jigger added, "when you meet the selection committee at Cowdenbings Miners' Club, be sure to put on that fake local accent that you use when you're in the Cuddy's Rest public bar. That'll go down well — the lord-turned-man-of-the-people angle, you know."

"OK, can do . . . the noo! Arf, arf!" A look of doubt then returned to Ludo's face. "And this university chappie *will* keep one genned up on the old speechifying thing, right?"

"Yeah, yeah, just listen to him and he'll put all the right words into your mouth, until such time as you've learned the ropes and can spout all the glib Party clichés without even thinking. And anyway, if a TV interviewer ever asks you a question that you don't know the answer to — and that'll be most of 'em — just tell him that he's missed the point, then give him an answer that has nothing to do with the question at all. That's politics. Piece o' cake!"

"TV, eh? Sounds absolutely fabuloso, mate! Hey, one could become a political media star, just like —"

"I've been thinkin'," the Duke interrupted, his expression dark, "and I'm not at all happy. A Gormlie-Crighton standin' as a bally socialist? Why, I shall be the laughin' stock of the entire Lambsdale Hunt!"

"Sitting in a turret with a string of black-tipped, peroxide weasels draped round your shoulders for lines of Japanese tourists to snap might raise a few titters with the members of the Lambsdale Hunt as well," Jigger retorted dryly. He left the Duke to ponder that point, then went on to explain the finer details of the proposed deal with the Cowdenbings Politburo.

First of all, it would be a foregone conclusion that, in order to have his candidacy confirmed, Ludo would volunteer to "look after" the local Party Chairman, Mick Murphy, and his little soviet of fellow ex-miners. Many of them just happened to be descendents of those same men who first dug coal in the dark, claustrophobic seams beneath the then burgeoning towns of Gormlie and Crighton in the west of Scotland. But the improving lot of miners in modern times had afforded sharp lads, like Mick Murphy, the unprecedented opportunity of hanging up their miners' lamps for good, in favour of taking up more "socially-rewarding" careers in local politics. By the time the last of the pits around Cowdenbings had been closed — whether despite, or because of the efforts of selfless campaigners like Mick Murphy — he and his colleagues (the Murphia, as they became known) had gained control of the Horseburghshire Council. Once thus established, they soon attained the status of local folk heroes by providing dramatic face-lifts to the drab environments of their grateful constituents. To add to their political appeal, such highly expensive civic works were being performed despite the recipient communities being ranked among the most flagrant non-payers of local taxes in the whole county.

The arrival of someone like Lord Ludovic into his merry band, therefore, would bring a new and valuable dimension to Mick Murphy's particular variant of latter-day Robin Hoodery. In addition to that, Ludo possessed just the woolly mentality required — the essential quality that would prove no match for the guile of his potential political masters in Cowdenbings. Yes, as Jigger intuitively knew, Ludo was ideally suited to being chosen as the Murphia's Man at Westminster.

Aha, but what was really in it for those coalminer chappies, the Duke wanted to know, sniffing the air for a socialist rat? There was no chance of someone like Murphy doing a Gormlie-Crighton any favours. There had to be a price to pay, and of that he was certain.

"True enough," Jigger conceded, "for it's back-scratching that makes the world go round. But Mick Murphy's a man of fairly simple pleasures. A bit like yourself, Duke. I mean, I've a hunch he'd be well chuffed, for example, if you were to let him and his pals do an occasional bit of hare-chasing with their greyhounds on the estate here."

After a bout of momentous mumbling, the Duke consented.

"And maybe let them do a bit of rabbit-snaring?" Jigger tendered.

Though demanding that it should go on record that his consent was being given only under the most grave duress, the Duke again complied.

Jigger resisted the temptation to tell him that it wouldn't have made any difference either way, since those same Cowdenbings families had been poaching hares and rabbits on Craigcuddy Estate for generations in any case.

"And then, of course," Jigger continued deadpan, "there's Mick Murphy's homing pigeons."

"*Homing* pigeons?" the Duke thundered, his eyes chameleoning in fit-imminent fashion. "Did you say homing pi — pi —"

"Pigeons? Yes. He says it was all very well having a loft in the backyard when he lived in a cottage in the old miners' row, but it'd look a bit down-market on the lawn of his new villa in Murphy Gardens."

"Did you say *Murphy* Gardens?" the Duke enquired in whispering incredulity.

"Yeah, the new executive development on that nice site on the shore. You know, the one that was reclaimed from the old slag heaps at Cowdenbings coal pits? Oh yeah, *very* exclusive. Mick was the chairman of the Planning Committee that rubber stamped the project, you see, so he says the developers thought it would be a nice touch to name the estate after him. Anyhow, he needs somewhere for his pigeons, and I took the liberty of suggesting that a corner inside the old walled kitchen gardens here might be just what he's looking for." Jigger paused, then concluded in mock-innocence, "I mean, the gardens aren't used for anything else these days, are they?"

The Duke was now so incensed that the purple-faced snort that followed Jigger's flip proposition launched a missile resembling a biological Rice Krispie from his flaring left nostril and fired it at something approaching the speed of sound directly at the neck of Ludo's hip flask, just as his Lordship was about to partake of a Westminster-here-I-come nip.

"Have a care!" he yelled, dropping the fouled flask to the floor. "I say, you've pranged one's gargler with a bogey! Hey, unclean! OK, that is just *too* utterly gross, right!"

Before Jigger could grab him, Ludo stormed off, screaming for Baldock to get his senile arse into the Great Hall to clean up one's hip flask and replenish it with a gill of some damned fine single malt. "And be pretty dashed quick about it, mate! Yah, and don't spill a solitary drop, right, or I'll have it docked off your miserable wages! OK, Elephant Bollocks?"

"That would indeed be an ingenious trick, Master Ludovic, if I may be so bold," Baldock was then heard to broadcast loudly from the security of his pantry, "AS ONE HAS NOT BEEN IN RECEIPT OF ANY WAGES, MISERABLE OR OTHERWISE, FOR A PERIOD OF SOME SIX MONTHS!"

CHAPTER
SEVEN

Cuddles and Haggles

The helicopter flew in low from the west, skimming the tops of the tall Scots pines in the windbreak beyond the old stackyard. It hovered above the Acredales farmhouse for a few moments, before slowly circling the steading at rooftop height, its rotors thudding the air in a deafening clatter and throwing stinging swirls of straw and grit into Granny's face. She stood with her back to the wall outside the kitchen door, peering up at the machine through half-closed eyes, one hand shielding her brow, the other raised in a defiant fist.

"Bugger off out of it!" she yelled, her voice all but drowned by the din. "Get yer damned birliewhirler the hell out o' here!"

Bert, who had been having a quiet kip at his favourite spot over by the barn door, blinked at the commotion and barked skywards with all the menace he could muster — which wasn't much. He didn't even bother to stand up. However, to his great satisfaction (and even greater surprise), the giant mechanical grasshopper veered off at the sound of his yapping and headed towards the village. Sweeping low over the houses in a deliberate slow arc, it finally descended in a billow of dust and dead leaves behind the oak wood that screened the little glebe field at the back of the manse.

Granny rubbed her eyes. "So, Ali Baba's back," she muttered. "Bloody foreigner!"

Bert went back to sleep.

Just then, Nessie came out of the kitchen, buckling her crash helmet under her chin. "Jigger's just been on his mobile," she said. "He wants Davie to clear a bunged-up pipe over at the Littleton-Nimby's bungalow. Mind if I borrow your moped?"

Granny grunted and shrugged her consent. "Jigger too busy bungin' up somebody else's pipe to do it himself, is he? Horny git!"

Nessie pretended not to hear. There had been a heavy shower of rain during the night, so she knew that Granny's joints would be giving her laldy. "I won't be long," she called back as she fired up the little two-stroke. "It should be easy enough to find Davie at this time on a Saturday morning."

"Hmm, another horny git," Granny grumped, then turned and shuffled back indoors. "There's a lot to be said for whippin' the goolies off them when they're young, like we do wi' the piglets."

Nessie found the little moped's lack of power a bit frustrating. It really did feel puny compared to the back-jolting poke of her own Honda 500 motocross machine. Still, she thought, there would have been no point in unleashing that beast for the short trundle down to Cuddyford. Actually, she hadn't taken the

Honda into the village since last Hogmanay, when Jigger had given her a right ticking off for popping a celebration wheelie the entire length of the High Street — and in full view of all the local churchy folk coming out of the watch night service, as well. "You're a lady," he'd scolded, "so try an' act like one. Wear trousers next time, for Christ's sake!"

Nessie pulled up at the old stone bridge that straddled the Cuddy Burn at the entrance to the village. She laid the moped against the parapet and looked over. The ancient willows bordering the stream were just coming into leaf, spreading their delicate green fronds out over the limpid water. Pendent clusters of catkins touched the surface here and there, and wove a wispy web through which a pair of swans were gliding gracefully, aloof and apparently oblivious to the goings-on only a few feet away on the far bank.

Just as his mother had expected, young Davie was down there, leaning cross-legged against a tree trunk, his hands thrust characteristically into his jeans pockets, his John Deere baseball cap tilted back-to-front on his head. He was surrounded by a small harem of half-a-dozen girls. They'd have been about thirteen years old, Nessie figured, their modesty freed from the weekday restrictions of school uniforms, and each novice vamp foxily jostling for position to display her recently-arrived "equipment" to the fullest advantage. Two or three of the girls were incomers' kids too, Nessie suspected, so that was nice. A good omen for future Cuddyford relationships.

Looking down at all of this, she reflected that it was a scene which must have been played out countless times in that same idyllic setting by successive generations of the village youth. Little would have changed over the centuries, save for the attire of the female protagonists, of course. And when she thought about it, Nessie couldn't help but feel that she would still have plumped for an old-fashioned, flouncy frock herself. Nicer, more feminine, and more practical, too, (when you got down to it) than those skimpy tee shirts and tight jeans the girls favoured today.

She allowed herself to wallow in romantic reverie for a while, the adolescent tenor of Davie's voice drifting softly upwards as he entertained his wide-eyed entourage with some simple country yarn or other. He was in his element. Nessie couldn't really make out much of what he was saying. Not that she was trying to eavesdrop, anyway, of course! But she did *just* manage to catch the words "nun" and "cucumber patch", before a cascade of squeals and giggles shattered the tinkling burnside tranquillity, followed by a concerted howl of:

"Oh, Bugsy McCloud — you're TERRIBLE!"

The swans sailed discriminatingly downstream.

"Yoo-hoo, Davie!" Nessie hollered. "It's mehee!"

"Hi, Mum!" Davie yelled back. "I thought I recognised the crash helmet. What's up?"

"Your Dad's busy cutting up those blown beech trees in Craigcuddy Wood, so he wants you to hitch the digger arm onto the back of the wee tractor and drive it round the twenty-acre field to the Littleton-Nimby's.

There's a choked drain to clear. Your Dad's had a prod at it already this morning. Type-A problem, he says, so he's told them not to put anything down it 'til you've finished the job. Should keep you busy 'til tea time, he reckons."

"OK. Message received and understood, Mum. I'm on my way."

"Listen, now that I'm here, I think I'll just nip into the village for a few messages, so when you pass the house, tell Granny I'll be a bit longer than I thought. All right?"

Davie gave her the thumbs up, his face wreathed in smiles. She had made his day. He liked a good Type-A drainage problem, you see — nice and simple, and a tidy earner into the bargain. Although it all sounded very technical to the uninitiated, all that the Type-A code meant was that his father had already managed to dislodge the blockage with his draining rods, but had told the unsuspecting customer that extensive excavations would have to be carried out to find and expose the drain, then to locate the offending obstruction. Jigger always said that there was no point in earning a measly fiver for a five-minute plunger job when there was a good hundred quid or more to be picked up by having fun with a hydraulic digger in somebody's garden for a few hours. Then, if you leapt in smartly with a keen quote, there was a fair chance that you might pick up the contract for the restorative landscaping work an' all. If those townies hadn't twigged that they couldn't stuff as much trash down a four-inch pipe to a septic tank as they used to flush into

an eight-foot urban sewer, then that was their loss —
and Jigger's gain!

Granny tended to get a bit fed up when she was left
hanging about the house on her own these days. The
arrival of spring should have signalled brighter, busier
times, she knew, but that didn't seem to happen any
more. Now that young Maggie and Davie were bigger,
they didn't really want her company. And they were
never in, anyway, except to stuff their faces at
mealtimes. With the coming of the better weather, even
that dog of Jigger's was seldom underfoot enough to get
a good kick at — too busy away on the rake, or lying
about recovering outside in the yard. Also, she was
browned off with that silly karaoke machine Jigger had
given her for her birthday. It wasn't much fun singing
to yourself. And besides, although Bing Crosby was her
favourite, Jigger had only managed to get her one of his
songs, and you felt a bit daft belting out *I'm Dreaming
of a White Christmas* in the middle of bloody April.

Granny sighed and sat down stiffly in front of the old
range. Aye, it had all been so different when she and
her Tam were young. Acredales of Cuddyford had been
a thriving little dairy farm then, and there had never
been enough hours in the day. Yet they always seemed
to manage. They'd be up at five every day and out into
that cold byre in all weathers for the morning milking.
Then she would bucket feed all the young calves, fill
the bullocks' hecks with hay, gather the eggs and feed
the hens. And she would still have kindled the range,
got the bairns up and washed and dressed and the

breakfast on the table by the time Tam got back from his fresh-milk deliveries round the village.

Twenty-odd Ayrshire cows they milked by hand in those days — just the two of them, twice a day. She shook her head and smiled wistfully. Twenty-odd! My God, nobody would even dream of trying to make a living like that any more. It had to be a couple of hundred cows now, all milked and fed by machine in fancy parlours glittering with stainless steel and hanging with plastic pipes and weird clusters of suckers for clamping onto the teats and everything. Aye, and all looked after by one man, too. Ah well, it was maybe OK for the younger generation, but to Granny it seemed like just another dreary factory job, with production targets to meet and all sorts of silly regulations to abide by. And to make matters worse, most of the rules were dictated by those foreign buggers in Brussels, if you please! Nah, nah, it would never have suited Tam and her.

Granny had long since decided that, nowadays, farming was all too much about increased mechanisation and so-called efficiency, business plans and cash-flow projections for the bank, form-filling for the Ministry, form-filling for the EU, and a hundred other kinds of bureaucratic bletheration. What a scunner! And what was it all for? Just so you could have the pleasure of borrowing more and more money from the bank to fork out to multinational machinery manufacturers and chemical giants to help you grow more and more stuff on any given bit of land. And what was the point? All that was intended to do was to push up your income for the government to tax, so that they could employ thousands of pen-pushers to work out how much to give you back in subsidies for not growing anything at all. Yes, Tam and her had seen the best days of farming, right enough.

Still an' all, it wasn't that she blamed Jigger for getting out of dairying . . . although it had broken her heart to see the cows going at the time. Acredales without cows to milk? It just didn't seem right. But, as usual, it was the politicians to blame. No sooner had they doled out millions to help small dairy farmers like them to expand than they were throwing away even more millions to encourage them to stop producing milk altogether. Here's a nice lump sum for you, they said. Oh, and by the way — remember that milk production quota we slapped on you not so long ago? Well, we don't mind now if you sell it off to the highest bidder. An attractive enough idea then, Granny had to admit, but it was really only a back-door way of helping the big farmers grow even bigger by buying out the wee men. The quit-milking hand-outs soon evaporated, anyway.

And the country folk. That was another thing! Whatever happened to all the families that used to live and work on the farms? Not so long ago, there were just about as many of them as there were bloody bureaucrats now! And where were all the villagers who used to come out and help at the turnip slinging, and at haymaking, and at harvest time? And there used to be all those kids from Horseburgh, who would get special exemption from school every October to work at the tattie howkin'.

Oh aye, those were hard enough days in many ways, and nobody ever had much to show for their labours, truth to tell. But folks still found a minute or two to stand and have a good blether and a laugh . . . or a moan. And hardly a day went by without a neighbour dropping by to lend a hand at this, or ask for a bit of help with that. Dammit, there was *life* in the countryside then. Bairns being born in the cottages, spending their childhood and growing up within the same four walls, working on the land that reared them, marrying their sweethearts from along the road, and starting the whole simple cycle all over again. Until the day finally came when they had to leave their birthplace, at last, and return to the land — for ever.

Those folk, wholesome and natural, had been the *real* life of the country places. And, for Granny, all the coloured wellies, waxed coats, horsey headsquares, hee-haw accents, and all the Range-Rover-mounted, nose-in-the-air snobs on earth could never hold a candle to them.

Granny sat staring into the fire for a while, deep in thought. She'd never really been one to dwell on the past. But today . . . well, maybe it was the rheumatism acting up, or maybe it was because everyone had gone out and left her. Hell, she couldn't even scoot down to the village for a gossip and a nip or two in the pub with Camshaft McClung's granny, because Nessie had nicked her moped and wasn't even coming straight back now like she promised! Whatever the reason was for her thinking back a wee bit melancholy-like today, she couldn't help it. She longed for those bygone days in a way she'd never done before. Those days when she could heave a sheaf of oats off her pitchfork to the top of a stack without thinking about cricking her back. Those days when she would sit up all night in the byre with Tam, waiting for a heifer to calf for the first time, and never even feel tired. Those days when Jigger was wee and . . . or was it when his mother Nell was wee? Dear God, she was getting old, that was all. Old and soft in the head. She wiped a drip from her nose with the back of her hand and chuckled sadly to herself. What would Tam have said if he could have seen her now? She could almost feel his hand on her shoulder, almost hear his kindly, coaxing laugh as he murmured:

"Come on, lassie. Give yersel' a shake. Ye'll be a long time dead soon enough, mind."

She clasped a hand to her lips, slowly moving the other to her shoulder, where Tam's hand had just lain. It *had* been there. She'd felt it. But now, somehow, there was only her woolly shawl beneath her trembling fingers.

"Oh, Tam," she whispered. "Tam, Tam . . ."

"Talking to yourself, Gran? That's a sure sign, they say."

Granny hadn't heard young Maggie coming into the kitchen. Startled, she looked up, then turned her head away, trying to hide her tear-filled eyes from her great granddaughter's inquisitive gaze. "No, no, no," she flustered. "Just — just hummin' a wee song I used to know."

Maggie said nothing, but quietly pulled up a chair and sat down beside Granny. Putting an arm round her stooped shoulders, she drew the old woman gently to her and rested her cheek on the silver-thatched head, which now, for the first time, seemed so frail and vulnerable.

Granny took Maggie's hand and held it tightly in her lap. "A right turn up for the books, this," she sniffed after a while.

"Mmm?"

"*You* takin' *me* under your wing."

"So, what's wrong with that?" Maggie asked, in a way that Granny thought was uncharacteristically sympathetic.

"Well, it only seems like yesterday I was always havin' to do this for you, that's all. Every time you lost your dolly, or something."

"Well then, as the saying goes, one good turn deserves another, doesn't it?"

Granny blew her nose. "You and your sayings."

Maggie stroked the back of Granny's work-worn hand. "And I suppose you're never too old to miss your dolly . . . or something. Are you, Gran?"

Granny caught her breath, and a little tremor ran through her body. She remained silent for a time, save for a few gulping sobs, which she did her best to cloak in little high-pitched coughs.

"I think I've got a cold comin' on," she whimpered at length, dabbing her eyes with her hankie.

Maggie patted Granny's shoulder. "Yes, there's a lot of it about just now. Nearly everyone who came into the library this morning was complaining about how —"

She stopped short, sensing that Granny wanted to tell her something.

"It was April the fifteenth at . . ." She sniffed. Though a little of the sadness had gone out of Granny's voice, she still spoke her words very softly and with an unmistakable note of longing. "At a quarter to twelve . . ." sniff, ". . . in the morning."

Maggie was close to tears herself now. "Your — your wedding day."

"How did *you* know? I never told anybody."

"I just kind of guessed, Gran, and . . ."

Maggie's words faded away, and the tears began to well up as Granny's grip on her hand tightened. The recess of the old range was soon resounding to the sniffles and gulps of their combined blubbing.

"Sixty years today," Granny twittered in a Stan Laurel treble.

"Your diamond wedding," Maggie wailed, the flood gates open now, the water-works in full flow.

"Aye, and I still love him just as much today. Oh, Tam . . ."

"Oh, Granny . . ."

"Oh, Maggie . . ."

"OH, DEARY, DEARY ME . . ."

They hugged each other and bawled like a pair of abandoned babies. There hadn't been such uncontrolled blubbering and free-for-all back-patting in the kitchen since the harvest day many years ago when Granny was

140

preparing a huge pot of onion soup for the farm-hands and choked on a Berwick Cockle.

"So, all that hard-bitten thing of yours," Granny wept into Maggie's face, "— just a smoke screen, is it? Just an act?"

"Uh-huh," Maggie bleated. "And guess who I learned it from."

"So, you're still Granny's wee pet lamb after all, then?"

"Mmm-hmm. And you're still wee Maggie's favourite granny."

They howled in tearful unison, until Granny suddenly jerked her head away from Maggie's shoulder, fixed her in a watery stare and said:

"Wait a minute. I'm yer *only* bloody granny!"

An involuntary giggle crept in between Maggie's choking sobs as she nodded a shower of tears over Granny's shawl. "Right enough. So you are, too."

"Oh, Maggie, Maggie," Granny half laughed, half cried, "just tell me that ye'll never *ever* get married, except for all the right reasons. Promise me."

"I promise, Gran," Maggie sniggered, a dainty bubble popping at her nostril and melting into the stream of tears dripping from the end of her nose. "I promise, I'll only ever marry — for money."

Granny slapped her hands on her knees and let out a full-blooded cackle. "Ah, pet, there's nothin' better for a body than a right good laugh, eh?"

"No, not unless it's a right good greet," Maggie warbled, drying her eyes.

"And we won't tell anybody about this wee confab, will we?"

"Well, I won't, if you won't."

"That's a good lass," said Granny, blowing her nose again. "It'll be our wee secret."

Maggie smiled, inclined her head enquiringly and said, "You sure you're OK now, Gran?"

"Never better."

"You won't be humming that wee song of yours again if I go away, then?"

"No, no. I'll be fine now, never fear. I was just bein' a daft, old, sentimental besom."

"OK, I'd better go and get changed. I'm supposed to be going to a post-impressionist exhibition in Edinburgh with Roger this afternoon."

"Roger?"

"Yeah, Roger Pratt. He's the new young lawyer with the County Council in Horseburgh. Boring sod, but he's tipped for the Chief Executive's job some day." Maggie rubbed her forefinger and thumb together under Granny's nose. "All the right reasons, right?"

"I'll never understand you young folk," Granny laughed. She thought for a moment, then added, "I wonder whatever happened to Camshaft McClung's brother Doddie. He was what I would call a *champion* post-impressionist."

Maggie raised an incredulous eyebrow. "Old Camshaft's brother a post-impressionist?"

"That's right," said Granny, her face expressionless. "Never knew anybody that could make an impression on a post with a one-stone mallet like Doddie could.

Puttin' up two hundred yards o' five plain-wire, one barbed-wire fence in a day was nothin' to him. Single handed at that!"

The arrival of a car in the yard, triggering the amplified hen cassette, spared Maggie the tricky decision of whether or not to laugh.

Granny grimaced as she looked out of the window. "The mysterious Abdul Abulbul Amir himsel', if I'm not mistaken," she growled. "The very bugger I wanted to see!" She grabbed her twelve-bore shotgun from behind the door, and was out of the kitchen like a floral-overalled greyhound out of a trap. "OK, Abdul," she piped. "Make ma day!"

Had she been an aficionado of classic sports cars, Granny would have recognised the mean, black machine parked outside the farm shop as upwards of £300,000-worth of Porsche Carrera GT. But, instead, she barked a derisory, "Leave yer silly, wee Volkswagen Beetle there if ye want, laddie, but if Jigger comes back and runs over it with his tractor, on your head be it. Don't say I didnae warn ye!"

"Ah, little-old woman," boomed the suave, swarthy figure strolling over the yard towards her, "kindly inform your master that I, Babu Ng, wish to discuss a small matter of business with him."

Granny adjusted the specs on her nose and fixed her exotic visitor in a well-focused glare. "Hold it right there, pal," she said, standing squarely in front of him and wagging an intrepid finger. "For a start, I am *not* a little-old woman. I'm a little-old *lady*. And for yer information, sonny-boy, no man is *my* master!"

Forcing a condescending, who-are-you-kidding smile, Babu Ng replied, "Quite, but I would be obliged if you would now tell your —"

Granny cut him off in mid-patronise with a sharp: "And for yer further information, ma lad, ye're speakin' to the owner o' this spread. So, if ye don't show a bit o' instant respect, I'll run ye off ma bloody land wi' the arse o' yer fancy pants air-conditioned by two cartridge-loads o' lead pellets!"

The throaty roar of a diesel engine heralded Jigger's return. His big green John Deere tractor pulled into the yard, hauling a metal-sided trailer piled high with beech logs. Carefully navigating his way round the cavalierly-stationed black Porsche, which he eyed from his lofty seat with undisguised admiration (if not a little envy), he parked his rig in the most favourable PR position, and alighted from his cab, whistling, as was his wont, a jaunty jig. "Aye, aye, Annie Oakley," he shouted over to Granny. "Crow pie for dinner today, is it?"

"Hmm, shoot the crow. And that's what this impudent gink'll be doin' right away, if he knows what's good for him." She showed Babu Ng the business end of her twelve-bore. "On yer bike, china!"

Quailing, Ng raised his hands.

Omar Sharif, Jigger mused, weighing up Granny's victim and flipping through his mental Hollywood file. Yeah, that was it — Doctor Zhivago, but eyes a bit more oriental, more . . . inscrutable, like. Hmm, he'd take a bit of watching, this one.

"Mornin'! I'm Jigger McCloud," he called out to his visitor. Then, sauntering across the yard whistling the

144

fist few bars of *Lara's Theme*, he extended a hand in greeting. "And if I guess right, you'll be Babu Ng. Welcome to Acredales of Cuddyford. Granny and yourself have already had the pleasure, I see."

Transfixed by the twin barrels of Granny's unwavering twelve-bore, Babu Ng shakily lowered one clammy hand to meet Jigger's. He held on for dear life while he carefully positioned himself safely out of Granny's line of fire by using Jigger as a human shield.

"Ah, yes, yes," he quaked, "the old granny-woman, she —"

"Hey, hey, boy," Granny cut in, "less o' the old granny-woman stuff, eh!" She shuffled sideways to get a better bead on the whites of her target's eyes. "Mrs McCloud's the name, right?"

Ng flinched and nodded his head.

"But that's only to folks I like!"

Ng did a double flinch as she cocked both hammers.

"So you can call me 'madam'!"

"Come on now, Granny. That's no way to welcome a new neighbour to our door," Jigger said in tones both conciliatory and materialistic. "I mean, you're not exactly bathing our humble farmyard in the spirit of goodwill and —"

"Stuff goodwill! Ali Baba here knackered any chance o' that when he buzzed this place with his bloody birliewhirler this mornin' — frightenin' the daylights out of a frail, old lady an' everything!"

Babu Ng's black eyes darted back and forth between terror and puzzlement. "What is this, this *birlie*whirler of which the ancient one speaks?"

Jigger advanced swiftly into the verbal combat zone before Granny had time to respond to Ng's presumably innocent, but potentially suicidal, reference to her venerable status. "She means your whirlybird," he explained. "She's talking about your helicopter — your chopper."

"Hmm, chopper," Granny muttered ominously. "And if I ever see it above this farm again . . ." She contorted her face into an intimidating scowl, thrusting her gun skywards as if preparing to fire a salute at a funeral, ". . . ye'll know what to expect." Without a blink of an eye, she discharged both barrels into the air, then blew the gunsmoke from the muzzle in a cool, laid-back style that Jigger reckoned he hadn't seen since Gary Cooper did it in that old *High Noon* movie.

Ambling back towards the kitchen door in the nearest thing to a slow swagger that her arthritic hips would allow, Granny paused dramatically, half turned towards the mesmerised Babu Ng, gestured upward with her firearm and drawled, "That's McCloud air up there, kid, and nobody — I mean *nobody* — sticks his chopper into that!"

Jigger could have sworn that he heard the strains of Frankie Laine's *Do Not Forsake Me, Oh My Darling* mingling with the amplified cackle of the hen-effects tape as Granny faded into the shadows of the back lobby.

If Babu Ng had been of paler complexion, Jigger would most likely have waited until the colour had returned to his cheeks before picking up the conversation. But as there was no such visible clue, he proceeded nonchalantly . . .

"Some case, that Granny o' mine, eh?"

His self-confidence appearing to make a miraculous recovery following the retiring of the killer pensioner, Ng growled through a macho sneer, "Where I come from, a woman would be given a public flogging for daring to utter such insolence to a man."

Jigger was tempted to remark that it would take a foolhardy flogger indeed to threaten Granny with his birch. However, in the interests of neighbourly good manners (coupled with a fair measure of sheer nosiness), he elected instead to inquire:

"And where *do* you come from — apart from the old manse, if you see what I'm saying?"

Babu Ng's heavy moustache moved deviously, his eyes narrowing into shifty slits as he surveyed Jigger's openly smiling face. "I am from many places, my friend," he murmured. "From many places."

"A real man o' the world, then," quipped Jigger, unfazed. "A bit like myself, I daresay."

He returned Ng's penetrating stare and quickly concluded that his Omar Sharif lookalike theory had been a right bummer. Never mind Doctor Zhivago, this guy was more like Genghis Khan. Yeah, a dead ringer for Jack Palance, if ever he'd seen one!

At that, Nessie rode hell-for-leather back into the yard. She screeched Granny's over-heated moped to a broadsiding halt outside the barn. "Hi!" she shouted as she sprinted towards the kitchen door. "Can't stop. Got delayed in the village. Must rush!"

Jigger waved his acknowledgement. Ng didn't even give her a second glance, presuming, Jigger guessed, that the helmeted female biker in the baggy jumper and old jeans was just another of the farm's resident tribe of loony Amazons.

The BBC cockerel crowed from the loudspeaker behind the farm shop, prompting Jigger to steer matters businessward. A Mongolian's money was as good as the next man's, after all.

"Well then, Mr Ng — or can I call you Babu? Come over to buy some eggs, have you? You'll never buy fresher. All free-range brown ones, hot from the hens' ar —"

Ng raised a hand. "The purchase of eggs, or any other woman's work, is not something with which I occupy my time." He cocked an ear at the Tannoyed poultry sounds. His moustache moved again — upwards, and at one side only this time. Simultaneously, his mouth distorted into a sly leer as he gestured towards his Porsche. "One of the advantages of driving an open-top car," he smirked, "is that you hear more clearly the things which go on around you."

"Bloody cosmic!" were the words that sprang immediately to Jigger's mind. But, persevering with his adopted policy of neighbourly good manners, he replied in preference:

"Yeah, I've noticed that myself — when I'm on my tractor without the cab, like."

Paying scant heed to Jigger's polite rejoinder, Ng continued:

"So, when I drove into your yard a short time ago, it struck me as odd that your domestic fowls only began to make a noise when I approached your farm shop here."

"That's hens for you. Never know when one of 'em's gonna burst into song — unless you see the egg coming, of course."

Jigger's wisecrack and the laugh of bravado that followed were met by a stony stare.

"It struck me as doubly odd, because I had seen no poultry when I hovered over this farmstead earlier today."

Curbing his instinctive desire to grab this prying git by the throat (there was still the doors-and-bath business to conclude, it had to be remembered), Jigger merely smiled sweetly and said, "Ah well, that's your true country hens for you, in't it? I mean, it wouldn't surprise me if not one of the little yokels had ever clapped eyes on a chopper before. Not as close up as that, anyhow. One peep at you coming roaring over those old pine trees, and you can bet they'd be off into their henhouse as fast as their little legs would carry them." Jigger countered Ng's sceptical stare with the hopeful addendum: "And listen, I don't mind telling you that you scared the shit out of me when you zoomed over my head up there at Craigcuddy Wood, and I pride myself on being a wee bit less flighty than a chicken."

Ng was clearly not convinced. He caressed his moustache with descending strokes of forefinger and thumb, his eyes coldly scanning the stable wall until they finally lighted on the sensor of the old security light.

"Aha-a-a," he baritoned, a disquieting note of discovery in his voice.

Jigger couldn't have been more gobsmacked if Ng had actually shouted "Eureka!" The crafty bastard had rumbled his caper!

Tapping the side of his nose, Ng slowly turned to face his quarry, his head nodding in the patient, sinister rhythm of a skulking vulture.

"Your little tricks may fool the easily-hoodwinked members of this hillbilly society, my friend, but I, Babu Ng, am wise to such childish scams." He wagged a cautionary finger at Jigger. "Do not be tempted to play your fraudulent games with me, for you will always be the loser. And this I promise you."

Jigger shrugged in feigned innocence. "Fraudulent? Me?"

Nessie's sudden re-emergence from the house couldn't have been more timely, her appearance diverting Ng's attention from a subject that, for Jigger, was becoming more sticky by the second. But the Nessie on whom Babu Ng's rapacious eyes were now feasting was not the scruffy apparition that had scurried through that same kitchen door only a few minutes earlier. She was dressed now in an emerald green suit, which, whilst eminently elegant and conspicuously chic, was of a cut that showed off her curvaceous figure to its still-youthful best. Throwing back her billows of auburn hair with an unintentionally sensual toss of her head, she trotted towards the barn on high heels which did all the right things for her trimly-sculpted legs. She blew Jigger a kiss and shouted across the yard, "Granny'll fix your lunch. I'm nipping into Edinburgh to Jenners' sale. The postmistress in the village told me they've got some great bargains in the dress department. I'll take the car. See you later!"

Jigger watched Babu Ng ogling her. His eyes were full of eastern promise all right, but Jigger wasn't too delighted by the look of what they had on offer. He'd have to tell Nessie to drop her wiggle down to first gear when this bandit was around.

A few moments later, the old Humber Supersnipe purred out of the barn with Nessie at the wheel. She looked, Jigger imagined, every bit the Hollywood superstar, cruising Sunset Boulevard in her stretch limo. As she swept past them, she threw Babu Ng a wide-eyed, self-assured glance over the top of her sunglasses — a look that Jigger was convinced would have out-Dynastied even Joan Collins at her stunningly haughtiest.

Ng stroked his moustache. "Magnificent!" he crooned. "Mmm, absolutely delectable!"

"Yeah, the old Supersnipe's a real beauty, right enough," said Jigger, quick to attempt what he considered to be an urgent diversion of topic. "She's been round the clock twice and still on the same gearbox. Do all the maintenance myself, mind. Used to belong to the Duke of Gormlie, you know. Got her off him for . . . well, for services rendered, you might say."

Babu Ng wasn't listening, his thoughts more attracted to the current occupant of the car than its service history.

"That's right — services rendered," Jigger persisted. "Yeah, I do a lot for the Duke, you see. Kind of become his right-hand man over the years. Never does anything without checking with me first, sort o' style."

"The Duke of Gormlie?" Ng said absent-mindedly, his gaze still set on the old Humber speeding away down the farm road.

"That's right. Discusses everything with me, old Horace. Which reminds me," Jigger went on, deciding that now was as good a time as any to take the bull by the horns, "what's all this he tells me about you wanting to buy Craigcuddy Estate off him? All this theme park stuff an' everything."

Babu Ng rounded on Jigger with the speed of a striking rattlesnake. "Whatever business I may have with the Duke of Gormlie," he hissed, "I discuss with him, or his legal representatives, *not* with one of his flunkies!"

Jigger felt his hackles rising. "*Flunky?*" he exploded. "Don't you bloody well flunky me! I'm telling you, the Duke discusses *everything* with me!"

Ng looked him up and down dismissively. "In all my meetings with his solicitors — Messrs Leary, Byblow and Wyllie, I believe they are called — I cannot recall your name ever having been mentioned. The same applies to my meetings with his bankers, and to my talks with the Duke himself." He raised his shoulders. "Need I say more, my friend?"

Jigger was dumbstruck. For the first time in his life, he had been well and truly put in his place, and it hurt. A limp, "Well, anyway, I know how I stand with the Duke," was all he could offer by way of riposte.

Ng delivered his *coup de grâce* with gloating delight. "And so, sir, do I."

There followed an awkward silence, broken in his own good time by Babu Ng himself, capriciously altering his hitherto hostile demeanour to one of gushing affability.

He nodded towards the tractor and trailer, and smiled. "Ah, I see you also trade in firewood. How much for a load like that?"

"Two pound a bag. Yeah, most of my clients prefer their logs bagged. Tidier, easier to lug about." Then, with a cynical wink, he added, "Women's work, like?"

Ng treated Jigger's little gibe with the contempt he clearly felt it deserved. "I said, how much for a *load* like that?"

Jigger shifted his feet uneasily and did a bit of cuticle contemplating. This Ng bugger was a fly one, and no mistake. Flyer than a bag o' bloody monkeys. Keep the heid an' play him along, that was the game. "Let's see now — for a load like that, and it is a big one, we'd be talking about a hundred and fifty quid or so . . . delivered, like."

Babu Ng laughed mockingly. "Where I come from, my friend, even the poorest street urchin has the skill to quickly estimate the number of people in a crowded market place, the number of goats in a trader's herd, the number of pearls spread on a merchant's tray."

"Oh yeah — Kim's Game. I remember that movie. *Sabu the Elephant Boy*, wasn't it?"

"It is a skill which, once mastered, one never forgets," Ng replied.

"Mmm, I daresay . . ."

"And I say to you, sir, that buying your firewood in bags would cost me double the bulk price!"

Jigger cleared a frog from his throat. "Ehm, no, I wouldn't say that exactly. But, mind you, I do have to cover the time it takes to bag them and everything. And as I say, the bagged ones are handier for —"

Ng raised a checking hand. "It is only the foolish labourer who continues to dig when he finds himself in a deep hole, is it not? And please do not insult me with your clumsy attempts at petty swindling." He tapped his nose again. "I use this for sniffing out rackets, not for paying through. So kindly deliver to me a load of firewood like that one. The price of one hundred and ten pounds — and not one penny more — will be paid upon delivery."

With a resigned sigh, Jigger grabbed Babu Ng's hand and pumped it cordially. "OK, it's a deal. A hundred and ten quid it is. You drive a hard bargain, Babu," he shrugged. "But no hard feelings. Yeah, business is business, eh?"

Ng allowed himself a self-satisfied smirk.

Jigger allowed himself one too, secure in the knowledge that he'd never charged anyone more than eighty-five quid for a trailerful of logs before — not even Nigel Spriggs, and he was a right gullible eejit!

"And now that we have got down to business," Babu Ng said with an air of new-found assurance, "I wish to talk to you on the subject of the items which you deposited in my garage."

Jigger let out what he hoped was a suitably hillbilly-sounding chuckle. "Oh yeah, the antique doors and the period bath. Nearly forgot about them."

Shaking his head in the derisive manner of a master butcher at a fat stock auction, Ng continued, half laughing, "My wife informs me that you are asking five hundred pounds for those items, no?"

Anticipating another kasbah-style haggling shot, Jigger replied, "Tell you what, make it the round four hundred. No point in wasting time bickering over a few quid. Call it a token of goodwill to a new neighbour, if you like. Right?"

"Wrong! I would not even offer four pennies for such pieces of . . . well, shall I say that one could find similar items on a rubbish tip any day?"

"Four pence! Rubbish tip!" Jigger blustered, miffed. "OK then, if that's how it is, I'll go over in my pick-up and take the bloody stuff back right now. Don't worry, I know plenty people who'll give me —"

"Hold on, my friend, hold on." Ng laid a hand on Jigger's shoulder, but the skulking vulture look returned to his eyes as he continued, "Although I said that I would not give four pennies for those items, that did not mean that I might not be willing to pay you a thousand . . . pounds."

Good God almighty, McCloud, Jigger thought to himself, your fortunes are going up and down here

155

quicker than, as Granny would put it, a hoor's drawers on a busy Saturday night. "A thousand *pounds*?" he gasped.

The vulture's head nodded its confirmation. "A thousand pounds, my friend. For those items. *And*," he added with a cautionary raising of a finger, "for services to *be* rendered, you might say."

CHAPTER
EIGHT

Arithmetical Agonies

Hips swinging extravagantly, Nessie pranced across the bedroom floor, did a twirl at the door, and pranced back to where Jigger was sitting on the edge of the bed, his entire person a study in doomy preoccupation.

"Well, what do you think?" she said, doing another twirl.

"I think the bugger's up to something, that's what I think."

"Forget Babu Ng for a minute and look at my new dress. Come on, pay attention!"

"Oh, yeah . . . sorry. Yeah, lovely . . . very nice."

Nessie knew that Jigger was looking, but not seeing. "Reduced from two hundred and fifty pounds to a hundred and fifty," she breezed, posing in front of the wardrobe mirror.

"A hundred and fifty! A hundred and fifty bloody knicker?" Jigger almost choked.

"I thought that'd make you sit up. Now, seriously, what do you think?"

"I think that's the Littleton-Nimby drainage loot down the pipes! And I've still to give Davie his share for doing the work!"

"Never mind — I'm worth it. Now, how about the other one?"

"The *other* one?"

Nessie was a flurry of zippers and buttons, stepping out of one dress and wriggling into another. Under normal circumstances, Jigger would have been only too delighted to have been treated to an impromptu striptease show like this, but not tonight. Try as he might, he just couldn't get his mind focussed on Nessie's half-naked curvy bits bouncing and bobbing about in front of him. All he could see was Jack Palance's cobra eyes staring at him from a vulture's head. Trance-like, he reached out and took hold of the price tag hanging from frock number two.

He clapped a hand to his forehead. "A hundred and ten quid," he moaned. "Bugger it! There goes the log money up in smoke, and Ng hasn't even paid me for them yet!" Eyes downcast, he shook his head dejectedly. "When you come to the end of a perfect bloody day, right enough."

"Don't be such a miserable moaner. This little number's a Jacques Vert original, you know. How often does a girl get a chance to pick up a dress like this for peanuts like that?"

Jigger buried his face in his hands. "Thank God there's plenty more blown trees up in Craigcuddy Wood."

"That's more like it," Nessie chirped, standing sideways to the mirror and smoothing the exclusive Jacques Vert satin over her tummy. "Do what your grandfather always told you. Look on the bright side

158

. . . and get busy with your chainsaw again tomorrow morning."

Nessie's well-intentioned attempt at whimsy was wasted on Jigger. He reminded her in deeply foreboding tones that everything would change for the worse if Ng got his hands on the Estate. There would be no free logs to flog then, no Home Farm to glean an extra few grand from every year, no privacy, no peace and quiet. Nothing but thousands of punters swarming about, breaking fences and trampling the crops.

"Well, at least they won't be able to scare your non-existent hens off the lay, so that's something. In fact, all those extra punters should give your egg trade a boost."

There'd be no egg trade left to boost if Ng decided to blow the gaff, Jigger lamented. The slimy shite had him nicely by the short and curlies, and no mistake.

Nessie had never seen Jigger so down in the dumps, and she knew him well enough to suspect that it wasn't really the Craigcuddy Estate situation that was vexing him. That was no more serious than before. No, what was really getting to him, she guessed, was the very idea that Babu Ng had put one over on him. Jigger was more used to giving than taking in the one-upmanship game, and his silly male pride had been dented, that was all. On top of that, Ng's rubbishing of Jigger's close association with the Duke had hurt. And it showed, even if, as Nessie fancied, it had only been a bit of cheap divide-and-rule propaganda, a ploy of Ng's to sicken Jigger and get him out of his way. That's what she reckoned, anyway, and she told Jigger so.

"Mmm, could be. But I'll say this — it's made me think, and from now on, anything I do to snooker Ng's plans for Craigcuddy will be for the future benefit of the McClouds, not for old Horace Gormlie-Crighton and his numpty offspring."

Nessie smiled impishly. "So what's new? That's exactly what you'd have done in any case."

Jigger had to concede a wry smile in response to that one. He sat lost in thought for a while, with Nessie fluttering about, trying on the first dress again, then back to the second, and so on. She was probably right, Jigger admitted to himself at last. Ng was a sharp one all right, but he couldn't expect to get the better of him by moping about and sulking. He'd have to keep his wits about him, for sure, but he'd find a way of sorting out that damned mystery man — somehow.

"So, which one *do* you like best?" Nessie asked for the umpteenth time. She was doing slow pirouettes in front of the mirror. "The flared one, or the slinky one?"

"Yeah . . . very nice," Jigger mumbled, still miles away.

"You're absolutely useless, Jigger McCloud! You wouldn't even notice the difference if I was standing here dressed in an old tattie bag. Get with it, and cheer up, for heaven's sake! Just think of that lovely thousand pounds you're going to get from Ng for the scabby old bath and doors."

"Yeah, but what services am I gonna have to render to get it? That's what bothers me."

"He said he'd tell you more about it at their party, didn't he?"

160

"That's what he said."

"Well then, you won't have long to wait, because the party's tomorrow night. Which is precisely why I want to know which of these dresses you prefer. So speak up! Which one?"

Jigger made the supreme effort to concentrate on his wife's dilemma. "OK, OK," he sighed, "just try 'em both on in turn an' I'll give you my verdict."

Nessie's shriek of exasperation could well have been heard at the other side of Cuddyford Village. "I've had these bloody frocks on and off, and on again, half a dozen times already for your benefit, Bruce Oldfield, so you can forget it! I'll wear the dress that *I* want to wear to the party!"

It was now Jigger's turn to smile impishly. "So what's new?" he said. "That's exactly what you'd have done in any case."

A low-flying, high-heeled shoe narrowly missed his head.

"Just think yourself lucky that I didn't know about Ng's thousand pounds thing before I went to Jenners this morning, or I'd have come back *well* laden, I can tell you!"

"That's what worries me. I see in the paper that their sale's on for another three days yet."

Nessie rummaged furiously in a carrier bag that she'd left lying on the bed. "Don't get your breeks in a fankle, McScrooge. I won't blow your precious money. There's nobody more thrifty than me," she stormed, throwing Jigger a small paper packet. "And that's to prove it!"

"Hey, you've been thinking about me! Tidy! I like a wee surprise now an' then."

Beaming expectantly, he opened the packet and pulled out the contents — a three-pack of Marks and Sparks black socks. Emblazoned in bright red on the label was the deflating message:

"REDUCED . . . FROM £4 TO £2 !!!"

To cheer herself up, Granny had prepared, according to her very own recipe, the family's favourite treat for supper — poached salmon. As usual, the great fish had been poached down at the mouth of the Cuddy Burn, and handed over gratuitously to Sergeant Brown, the stalwart village policeman, who had an ongoing "understanding" with the poachers. The sergeant, in turn, had bartered the salmon, a splendid specimen of his regal caste, for a bottle of Jigger's renowned "Home Brew". A neat enough wee system, Granny admitted, though not quite so cost efficient, of course, as the days before the damned rheumatism put paid to her preferred practice of poaching the salmon for herself. No bloody polisman had ever got a slice of her action after she'd been standing up to the reinforced gusset of her bloomers in freezing water half the night!

Still, everything in the kitchen was lovely enough tonight, save for one thing — young Davie. To Granny, he seemed unusually subdued. Fair enough, he was still guzzling his salmon and all the trimmings as if a ten-year famine warning had just been announced on the news, so there was nothing wrong in the appetite department. But there *was* something up. Granny was certain of it.

"You alright, young McCloud?" she asked, squinting at him over the table between his personal array of tartar sauce, salad cream, tomato ketchup and HP Sauce bottles. "Ye're too quiet. It's suspicious. Haven't picked up one o' them sociable diseases, have ye?"

Davie shrugged and gobbled a new potato.

Despite her recently-acquired and impassioned aversion to the eating of the remains of dead animals, even Maggie made no attempt to hide the fact that she was more than a little partial to getting her choppers into a lump of deceased fish — particularly if it happened to be a nice lump of freshly-expired salmon.

"It's *social* diseases, for goodness' sake, Gran," she tutted between mouthfuls, plainly back in top, self-assured, clever-clogs form. "And there's no need for the aware individual to fall prey to such antediluvian maladies in these enlightened times, *if* all readily-available precautions are taken, needless to say."

"Never mind yer fancy lingo. Say what ye mean . . . CONDORS!"

"It's cond*oms*, Gran. Honestly!"

"That's what I said — condors. And a lassie your age shouldn't even know words like that. It's disgusting!"

Jigger and Nessie both rolled their eyes heavenwards.

Davie, meanwhile, was toying with another spud. "Nah, I've just been thinking," he muttered.

Maggie crooked her brother a mocking thumb. "Say no more, then. *That's* what's ailing him. He's strained himself."

For once, Davie didn't rise to the bait, but instead pulled a little wad of notes from his shirt pocket and laid it sombrely on the table. "This money you gave me for the drainage job, Dad. There's something not right about it."

Jigger took the notes and held each one up to the light in turn. "Look OK to me. But if you don't want 'em . . ."

"No, no, it's not that," said Davie, prudently snatching the money back. "No, it's just that the divvy-up seems a bit one-sided. And I'm on the wrong side."

All eyes were on Jigger.

"*Do* me a favour, Davie lad," he said, just a tad sheepishly. "You surely don't think I'd short change my own son — exploit my own flesh an' blood, sort o' style?"

"Yes!" said Granny with instant conviction. "Ye'd sell me into hoordom, if anybody was daft enough to part wi' a tenner."

"Don't overvalue yerself," Jigger mumbled out of the corner of his mouth.

"I mean, I was always happy to do these Type-A drainage jobs for a fifty-spot, Dad," Davie continued, his confidence buoyed up by the sudden ambient feeling of feminine support for his case, "but that was before I found out how much you were actually socking it to those incomers."

"Now, now, they'd never get a better price from anybody else for that kind o' work, and that's a fact,"

164

Jigger bluffed, while silently cursing the Littleton-Nimby's for spilling the financial beans to Davie.

"Except, maybe, from an honest plumber with a set of drainage rods and five minutes to spare," Nessie suggested, winking mischievously at Granny and the kids.

Jigger found himself having to do his best to appear uncowed by the growing atmosphere of hostility in the kitchen. "Oh yeah?" he retorted. "And when did you ever hear of an honest plumber?"

Letting that question pass unanswered, Davie said, "You see, I was kinda under the impression that you and I were on a fifty-fifty split for these drainage jobs, Dad."

"And so we are, son. So we are."

"But when old Littleton-Nimby started whining about having to lob you a hundred and fifty for today's caper, it got me thinking. Fifty to me and a ton to you . . . not exactly a down-the-middle split, is it?"

"Expenses, son. Expenses. One o' yer basic elements o' business, that. Deduct the exies before you divvy out the old profiteroles, like. Common sense, eh?"

Davie sensed that he had his old man on the run now, and the smirks of encouragement he was receiving from the three females of the family were all he needed to take up the chase.

"So, Dad, what exies are we talking about exactly? See, the way I figure it, a fifty-spot to me and a hundred-spot to you would leave you a spare fifty quid to play with. Big exies, eh?"

All four fellow McClouds were now staring along the table at Jigger, chins on hands, their eyes sparkling with anticipation.

"OK, Houdini," Granny challenged, "get out o' that!"

Jigger looked imploringly at Nessie. When all was said and done, she was the one who'd blown the Littleton-Nimby spondoolicks on herself, albeit indirectly, so surely it wasn't too much to expect some backup from her now. The look of barely-disguised glee that she was radiating left him in no doubt, however, that no such support would be forthcoming.

"Ehm, well, there's the cost o' the fuel for a start," he declared falteringly. "That's a day's diesel for the tractor, at say . . . that'd come to . . . let me see . . ."

"A tenner, top whack," said Davie, crisply.

"And — and depreciation. You've always got to count in the depreciation of the machinery, son. So that would be, ehm . . ."

"That wee tractor's ancient," Nessie cut in. "It's value was written off for tax purposes in the books years ago."

"OK, but it still cost money to buy it originally," Jigger protested, a note of desperation creeping into his voice. "Which means it's still got a hire value for the job, so to speak. And that's got to be worth another twenty knicker a day."

"Is that all?" Granny queried.

"No, you're right, Granny. Good thinking," Jigger said, grasping at the straw so humanely offered. "It would have to be nearer thirty, for sure."

"Fine! I'll have that, then, because the wee tractor belongs to me. Yer grandfather and me bought it twenty-five years ago, God rest his soul."

Squirming, Jigger dug into his trouser pocket and pulled out the Littleton-Nimby wad, from which he dealt Granny three tenners.

"That still leaves another ten pounds unaccounted for, Dad," said Davie, closing in for the kill. "Even allowing for the diesel."

"Administration charges, Davie. It takes time to fix these jobs up, you know. So, that's the ten quid, right?"

"Right!" said Nessie. "And *I'll* have that, because it was me that Mrs Littleton-Nimby got in touch with."

Jigger was visibly distraught, staring incredulously at the remains of the wad in his hand. "But that only leaves me with these five measly tenners for a whole day's drainage work."

"You didn't do the work," Nessie rounded. "Davie did, and that's why I'm donating the administration money to him."

"And that's why I'm donatin' the tractor-hire money to him, too," Granny added.

"But that means Davie's got ninety pounds to my fifty!"

"It seems merited recompense to my mind," Maggie opined. "To labour and not to receive just reward, to paraphrase St Ignatius Loyola, is a right bleedin' mug's game."

"Gee, thanks, sis!" Davie grinned in amazement. "That's one I owe you!"

"No," Maggie stated firmly, "that's *forty* you owe me." She grabbed the folding money that her mother and Granny had just donated to her brother. "The readies you bummed off me to take Hot Pants Lyback to the Horseburgh Young Farmers' Christmas disco, remember?"

"Get lost! I only bummed thirty!"

"Well, that'll teach you to pay back your debts on time, won't it, brother dear?"

"Aw jeez," Davie wailed, "that means I'm back down to the mingy fifty-spot again."

"Shake on it, partner," Jigger mumbled in reluctant agreement. "Now we're both on the wrong side of the divvy-up. But at least it *is* fifty-fifty, agreed?

Davie nodded glumly. "And to think I jacked in a hot date with one o' them wee birds under the old bridge this morning for this."

Jigger patted his shoulder. "Aye, when you come to the end of a perfect bloody day, right enough!"

CHAPTER
NINE

That's the Spirit!

Inside the Cuddy's rest, there was only one solitary customer — a living, breathing ad for Panadol Plus, sitting slumped at the bar.

Jigger looked at his watch. Just after eleven o'clock. "'Mornin', Bertola. I noticed your lawnmower outside. Bit early on a Sunday, even for you, in't it?"

Bertola took a wobbly-handed sip of his sherry and blinked at Jigger through bloodshot eyes. "It's not early, man — it's late. Only got dropped off at the shack from an all-night gig in Aberdeen half an hour ago. Thought I'd slip over here for a noon nightcap before I hit the sack. Anyway, what's happenin'?"

Jigger pulled up a stool and asked for a glass of water from Hamish Glenkinchie, who was grumpily clearing up the Saturday night flotsam and jetsam behind the bar. The smell of stale beer slops and fag ash, mingled with the acrid pong of Jeyes Fluid and bad aiming drifting through from the gents' toilet stung Jigger's nostrils.

"Breath o' spring in the air this mornin', Hamish," he remarked, with just a hint of irony.

"It'll be the crocuses," Hamish grunted. Po-faced, he jerked his head backwards in the general direction of the gantry, where stood a half-pint glass containing a handful of semi-decayed vegetation.

"Yeah," Bertola droned, "I remember it well, man. A great year for the crocuses, 1965."

Muttering incoherently, Hamish set off with a damp cloth and an empty Golden Wonder Crisps box on a grudging tour of his debris-strewn tables.

Bertola started to roll a reefer. "Got this dope from a Spanish sailor in Aberdeen last night. Supposed to be primo grass. Fancy a drag, daddy?"

Jigger declined with a wave of his hand. "Listen, Bertola," he said, lowering his voice to an urgent whisper, "that old bloke I saw you giving a lift to the other night . . ."

"Yeah?"

"Well, what do you know about him?"

Bertola lit his joint, coughed to the rheumy-eyed verge of puking, shrugged and wheezed, "New Yorkers. He drinks New Yorkers, plays poker and calls himself Archie. That's it. What else can I tell you, man?"

"For starters, where did you drop him off?"

"At the castle. Round the back." Bertola went all confidential, then added, "Told him to keep shtum to the Duke about me using his mower as a taxi, natch."

"So, what did this Archie guy want at the castle?"

Bertola drew deeply on his spliff, holding the smoke in his lungs until the veins stood out like subcutaneous earthworms on his shiny pate. "Inheritance, man," he coughed. "Said he had to sort out some inheritance stuff." He pulled a one-shouldered shrug. "Maybe he's in the insurance business." He raised the other shoulder. "Fucked if I know."

Jigger sat pensively silent for a moment or two. Inheritance, eh? That was a bit different from the back-pay Archie had mentioned in his letter to old Horace. Interesting. And why hadn't the Duke owned up about Archie's arrival during the meeting with Jigger and Ludo in the Great Hall the next morning?

"So, what else did he tell you? Anything come to mind?"

Bertola twirled a rat's tail of straggly hair between his fingers, a cannabis-induced feeling of indifferent amusement spreading magically through him. He laughed out loud. "Yeah, the old dude told me I looked like the Muppet bandleader. Cheeky old bastard."

"Mmm, maybe the bandleader bit *is* taking it too far, right enough. But what else did he say? Come on, Bertola — think hard!"

"Aw, gimme a break, daddy," Bertola groaned. "I can't remember." He started to massage his temples. "I mean, I was well stoned. Like gassed, all right?"

"Hey, Jigger!" Hamish called from the other side of the room. "Catch this pint mug and stick it on the bar for me, will you? Some untidy slob must've dumped it on the floor over here last night."

The heavy, dimpled glass arched slowly through the air and descended, just a couple of crucial feet off target, bang onto the back of Bertola's marijuana-inhaling head, then cannoned safely into Jigger's outstretched fingers. Hamish clapped his hands to his mouth, eyes staring in horror as he waited for Bertola to keel over — concussed at best, dead at worst.

Bertola sat poker-backed and paralysed on his high stool, gazing straight ahead, glassy eyes unseeing. After several heart-stopping moments, he blinked, shook his head and looked down at the reeking roll-up in his right hand, a grin of delighted amazement spreading over his haggard face.

"Wow, man!" he declared, fingering the reefer in awe-struck adoration. "Ace grass!"

Jigger nodded reassuringly to Hamish. Relax — Bertola was going to be OK.

"Come on, Bertola," Jigger persisted, "you must be able to think of *something* else this Archie guy said."

"Just asked how Robert Chan was doin'," Bertola replied with a new-found presence-of-mind, the blow from the errant tumbler evidently having acted as a memory jolter. "Yeah, I remember that, 'cos it's the same name as mine."

"Chan?"

"Nah, Robert, man." He threw Jigger a get-with-it look. "I mean, like Robert — Bert — Bertola. Can you dig?"

"So, who the hell's Robert Chan?"

"My lyrics exactly, pops. *Jackie* Chan, sure, but Robert, zippo!"

"So?"

"So, the old dude ran a few other weird names by me 'til he came up with Babu Ng. Yeah, daddy, I said — now you're talkin'. I've heard about him. He's the far-out cat at the old manse who's gonna like do a

Disneyland number at Craigcuddy. Disneyland? says the old dude, shakin' his head and laughin' like a drain. Hey, you're pulling my leg, old buddy, old chap, he says. Then he makes a well-whadda-ya-know? kinda face and tells me that nothin's what it seems on the surface."

"Nothing's what it seems on the surface? What'd he mean by that?"

"Search me, man, but that's what he said. Then he slipped me a fiver for the lift, and I split. Like end of story."

The words echoed in Jigger's mind during the short drive down to his piggery near North Crabswick.

"Nothing's what it seems on the surface . . ."

Just what Jigger had been suspecting himself. There had to be more to Ng's interest in buying Craigcuddy Castle than met the eye. There *had* to be. Why else would someone with as many trappings of wealth as that, want to spend fortunes making a theme park in a back-of-beyond place like Cuddyford? To make even more money? No way. It would take too long — if ever — to recoup the outlay. And what about Ng's other names, Robert Chan and so on? And just what was old Archie Gormlie-Crighton's connection with him? And now there was this inheritance business of Archie's as well . . .

"No, boy, nothing's what it seems on the surface, and that's a fact," Jigger affirmed, turning the pickup off the main road and into the narrow track that led down to the old radar station.

Bert barked his agreement, so Jigger thumb-flicked a chunk of Yorkie bar to him for being such a clever wee bugger.

"I'm tellin' you, Bert, the mystery deepens. And the deeper it gets, the more I'm flummoxed, if you see what I'm saying."

Bert elected not to bother responding to that particular verbal composition. He was too busy trying to crunch the Yorkie chunk into gulpable lumps without allowing them to become nerve-stingingly lodged in the cavities of any decayed teeth. No easy task for an old dog with a mouthful of rotting tombstones like his, but worth the effort, all the same.

Jigger gazed ahead in contemplative silence, while Bert twitched his head about and gnawed his Yorkie in smiling, ears-back bliss. Little rivulets of saliva dribbled through his spiky whiskers and plopped onto the floor like delicious, chocolate-hewed raindrops. But not to worry — he would lap them all up later.

From the main road which ran parallel to the coast at that point, the track followed a barely-perceptible decline between broad fields of sandy loam. The fine, friable soil was already pierced by the first leafy shoots of early potatoes, their ranks of perfectly-drawn drills stretching away towards the far headlands like an object lesson in perspective. Half a mile or so ahead, an undulating ribbon of dunes, sparsely clad in clumps of gorse and tufts of coarse grass, separated the fields from the shore. Those low ridges afforded the cultivated land some protection from the salty ravages of the northerlies which, in these parts, can howl down from the Arctic during the long months from capricious autumn, through to fickle spring.

Jigger's gaze wandered out over the wide waters of the Forrit Firth to the distant coastline of Drummy. The lower flanks of its hills were veiled under a hazy wash of mist that melted the delicate greys of the sea into the pale blue above. Up there, the silver speck of a high-flying jet drew its unwavering chalk mark over the vast expanse of sky.

Below, the softly-rounded summits of twin peaks known descriptively as the Paps o' Drummy thrust their mammary curves up through the shroud of mist. To Jigger, their legendary feminine form seemed more exaggerated than usual and appeared more sensual than ever, exposed, as it was today, in such wonderful, gossamer-draped isolation.

His thoughts turned to Sabrina Ng . . .

There was more to her than met the eye an' all, if he was any judge — and he judged himself to be not a bad one. With any luck, more — if not all — would be revealed at her party tonight.

The flat-roofed buildings of the old radar station were huddled together only a few hundred yards from the shore. They were totally enclosed now by a mature garland of spruce, larch and birch that had been planted, presumably, during the war to afford the place a measure of camouflage from both land and sea. Nowadays, only a few of the older locals even knew of the old station's existence, and as the track leading to it led nowhere else, only occasional cars containing nocturnal courting couples ever ventured near. And, no matter how furtive or desperate their motives, none but the most nasally-congested lovers dared approach within a down-wind furlong of the foul stench that emanated permanently from Jigger's piggery. The place was, in effect, akin to a stink-shielded Fort Knox.

Jigger parked his pick-up alongside Johnny Ardonski's rusty old Lada estate outside what had been, in RAF times, the main admin block. Bert sniffed the air appreciatively through the open passenger window. Nothing quite like a nice, sharp whiff of pig shit to savoury up the aftertaste of a lump of Yorkie bar. That would be Bert's opinion, Jigger reckoned.

"Ah, Yigger! Goot to seeink you. Wery nice mornink for da size o' da place, no?" Johnny was filing away happily at a piece of metal rod which he was holding with one knee on the edge of the doorstep. The nodding heads of a trio of floppy-eared pigs grunted a running commentary over the concrete parapet of their adjacent pen.

"Aye, aye, Johnny," Jigger smiled. He gestured towards Johnny's job-in-hand. "Got a problem?"

"Is vater. Doon da stairs in da cellar. Is leakink in under da old metal door dat never ever beink opened. I am tryink to makink key here. Like boils on da arseholes ve are needink floodink in da sti —"

Jigger clapped a hand over Johnny's mouth. "I've told you," he whispered, casting darting glances towards the encircling woods, "— never mention that word. You'll get us bloody well locked up, for Christ's sake!"

"Ah, bollocks, Yigger!" pooh-poohed Johnny, his pumpkin lantern of a face opening into a great half moon of a grin. "Da only peoples dat beink here is dem pigs, and dey don't givink a shit about no vords." He dismissively waved a banana-fingered hand. "So, don't gettink your knickers tvistink!" The grin waxed outwards and upwards, drawn by the subtle magnetism of Ardonski-style word association. "Da!" he beamed, "let's tvistink again like ve done last summer, eh!"

Johnny's troll-like guffaws reverberated off the walls and through the trees as he struggled to his feet and wriggled his podgy legs in a baggy-trousered take-off of Chubby Checker. The three onlooking pigs bobbed their heads from side to side in rhythmic approval of the singing swineherd's impromptu cabaret, while Bert yapped excitedly from his grandstand position in the truck cab.

Jigger got hold of Johnny by the scruff of the neck and hauled him unceremoniously inside the building. He screwed up his nose as it passed within a couple of inches of the beaming pumpkin. "I thought so," he gasped. "Bloody stotious! Bugger me, your breath smells like a brewery horse's fart! I thought I told you — no nippin' 'til I get here!"

As much as he was fond of old Johnny, and as much as he'd learned to put up with his bibulous ways over the years, Jigger felt justified in losing the rag with him on this occasion. One careless moment like that, and this little caper (or pig-farming diversification scheme, as he liked to refer to it in trendy EU Common Agricultural Policy jargon) could be down the tubes for ever, with Jigger in the slammer for a ten-stretch. That, on top of all his other current hassles, he did not need.

Holding Johnny firmly by the collar, he briskly marshalled him through the secret trapdoor and down metal steps into the reinforced concrete subterranean chamber that was the long-forgotten wartime radar ops room. In place of sprawling plotting tables displaying maps of the theatres of aerial warfare, the floor was now occupied by nothing more exciting than a conglomeration of metalwork that may have looked, to the untrained eye, like a Heath Robinson version of an early launderette. This was, nonetheless, the highly hush-hush stuff of the cellar to which Johnny had been about to so incautiously allude.

To Jigger, that cellar was the nerve-centre of a clandestine operation that had produced handsome profits for many years, not only in much-needed financial terms, but more importantly, perhaps, in the business of gaining and maintaining friends among people of influence. Johnny Ardonski, on the other hand, thought of it as no more than a "modernised" extension of the mundane task he'd performed throughout the latter war years for his masters, the Polish officers who were billeted for the duration of hostilities in the commandeered Dower House on Craigcuddy Estate. Of all the obscure peasant skills of his homeland of which Johnny was a renowned exponent, his ability to make vodka from potato skins was the one that had appealed most to the Poles, and they'd seen to it that his rare rustic talent was well encouraged and exploited. For his part, Johnny had been eminently more content making moonshine for the Polskis in Cuddyford than he would have been — as he had been known to say — gettink his chuckies frozen offski on da fuckink Russian Front. And who would have questioned the wisdom of his reasoning? Certainly not the Cuddyford Polskis.

Many years later, on overhearing Johnny relating a long-winded yarn about this particularly illicit military activity to a group of bored worthies in the Cuddy's Rest, tiny cogs in the young Jigger's brain began to turn and mesh commercially. It wasn't long, therefore, before the old Ukrainian alchemist was back in action, a basic DIY still (a la Dower House, circa 1945) having been set up in the basement of the remote radar-station-turned-piggery.

But the manufacture of rotgut, gold-tooth-dissolving vodka was not Jigger's objective. For one thing, unlike the war years, when military bases and their vital cookhouses abounded in the area, unlimited supplies of potato peelings were no longer freely available. Conversely, other more potentially-lucrative raw materials were. There was the purest of crystal-clear water in abundance right there in the cellar, courtesy of a bore hole that had been drilled by the RAF to ensure a reliable, independent supply, no matter what might befall conventional sources in times of enemy action. And nearby, there was assured access to some of the best malt in Scotland. Suddenly, Jigger McCloud was in the Scotch-Whisky-making business!

The setup was perfect — a bootleg distillery in a near-impregnable underground labyrinth that nobody knew existed any more, with foolproof cover provided by the token presence of the pigs, which, though few in number, could always be relied upon to out-stink the give-away aroma of exhausts from the still room. Even the transportation to the premises of a trailer-load of essential malted barley from time to time could quite plausibly be described to any inquisitive police patrolman as merely another batch of spent brewers' grains to supplement the diet of the pigs. Yes, to the outside world, all appeared quite conventional and totally beyond suspicion.

Like his free-range egg-and-chicken business, Jigger's little whisky-distilling wheeze had steadily developed from the most inauspicious and tentative of beginnings into an admirably slick operation. It was what he liked to think of as a naturally-renewable production cycle, not unlike his hay/horse-manure/mushroom-compost enterprise in some respects, not least of which was that the only movement of money just happened to be in the direction of his own pocket.

This was how it worked . . .

Every harvest, Jigger sold all the malting barley that he grew on the two farms (usually in the region of three hundred tons) to the world-famous Glenreekie Distillery, situated by the Cuddy Burn in the Lambsfoot Hills some five miles upstream from Cuddyford. A nod-and-a-wink arrangement with the distillery foreman allowed for one ten-ton load of barley per year (always from the Duke's Home Farm) to be omitted from the weighbridge paperwork, which recorded all grain entering the distillery. What the foreman did with the phantom load was anybody's guess, and Jigger wasn't bothered in the least about that. All he knew was that the ten tons was worth about £1,000 on the black market, and that grand was one of the little bits of payment in kind that he covertly extracted from the Duke, "for unremunerated factoring duties, like."

But the deal was, that, instead of actually paying Jigger cash for the purloined grain, the accommodating distillery foreman would provide him with his annual requirement of malted barley, after the raw grain had been subjected to the inimitable Glenreekie malting process. This was an unsurpassable and priceless constituent of Jigger's liquid gold, an essential ingredient which he couldn't even have attempted to replicate in his cottage-industry operation.

Once in possession of the malted barley, it was simply a case of being patient and relying on Johnny Ardonski's talents. And when the production procedure reached the stage of requiring a few oak barrels, or cases of empty bottles, the Glenreekie foreman came good again. This time, he provided the goods in exchange for a few radar station porkers, all butchered freezer-ready by the multi-skilled Johnny Ardonski in a neat mini-abattoir that he had improvised in the old Waffs' ablutions, right there beneath the piggery.

Looking at his compact and highly efficient distillation system now, Jigger felt that he had a right to be proud of how (with the backing of his own sophisticated, capitalist know-how) old Johnny had managed to continually improve and develop the equipment over the years. No more the primitive Eastern European moonshine-making odds and ends of the frugal war years for them. With strict adherence to the old business adage that you must speculate to accumulate, all access to modern technology made affordable by the fruits of his strictly COD sales policy had been keenly turned to account by Jigger. That said, he wasn't above admitting to himself that the proximity of a domestic equipment graveyard at the old North Crabswick Gasworks site just might have been the single most significant dynamic of his ongoing distillery-development programme.

The current state-of-the-art modus operandi involved simmering a brew of the essential ingredients in an old washing machine for a few days, the drum of the resuscitated Hotpoint Automatic having been set to spin at key intervals, thus obviating the labour-intensive requirement for manual stirring. The juvenile liquor was then regurgitated at the end of the Hotpoint's final spin cycle into a patched-up, copper, hot-water cylinder. The precious fluid was allowed to snooze cosily in there at a precisely pre-determined temperature, kept constant by the tank's enveloping electric blanket, whose exposed thermal wiring had long since prompted its expulsion from someone's comfy Slumberland King-size.

When master distiller Ardonski deemed it chemically crucial, an ex-caravan bottled-gas ring under the cylinder was ignited and the brew set aboiling. The resultant captive vapour was ducted through a copper coil immersed in a neighbouring terminally-chipped domestic bath, which was kept continuously full to overflowing by a hosepipe running water direct from the chilly depths of the borehole. The ensuing distillation was funnelled into an old glass carboy, fitted with a tap from which (for the purpose of scientific purity-evaluation) Johnny would lovingly draw samples of his new-born creation into a frying pan. A lighted match was then passed over the pan, and if the ignited spirit burned blue and bright, the virginal water of life was declared pure and perfect. An orange-coloured blaze, on the other hand, would indicate impurities unacceptable in such a deluxe whisky, though Johnny Ardonski's high-tech production methods ensured that no such wasteful hiccup ever occurred in Jigger's distillery. Well, not to such a degree of orangeness, at any rate, that the contaminated booze was beyond a bit of "doctoring" to elevate it to the required standard. This involved a complex technical process known only to Johnny himself, and entailing, as far as Jigger had been able to espy, a unique filtration system made up of such diverse components as pigs' intestines, sliced parboiled jacket potatoes, and crushed eggshells.

The purpose of today's on-site get-together had been to taste-test a specimen from a cask now nearing its momentous twelfth birthday. As Jigger had correctly discerned, however, his master distiller had yielded to impatience, had scaled the bugger-it barrier of his low resistance-to-temptation threshold, and had downed a tidy few drams of the examinee whisky well before the appointed meeting time.

"What's the verdict, then?" said Jigger in an almost detached way, his attention immediately divided between the barrel from which Johnny was already tapping another two sample glasses and the disquieting squelch of water underfoot.

Unrestrained pride was oozing from Johnny's glee-filled face — a feel-good feature that Jigger hadn't noticed in the old fellow since the one and only time he so magnanimously condescended to putting a five-pence piece in the Salvation Army swear box in the Cuddy's Rest. "Da werdick?" he replied. "Yigger, dis new wintage is fuckink braw!" Circumspectly holding onto his trouser belt with both hands, he pulled in his paunch, puffed out his chest and proclaimed majestically, "I am tellink you true, is da wery best bevvy I ever been makink in my whole baster life!" With an exaggerated flourish, he raised his glass and clinked it against Jigger's. "MY WERY BEST RESPECKS, EH!"

Expressionless, Jigger sniffed the amber contents of his glass with an extravagant lack of urgency.

"Hmmm," he droned flatly, "fairly tidy nose, I daresay . . ."

"Tidy? Is *wery* tidy!" Johnny objected, his piggy eyes wide and illuminated with expectant tension. Without attempting to hide his mounting frustration, he clinked Jigger's glass again and urged, "Now, cop yer whacks for a fuckink swallae!"

Strange, Jigger thought behind a wry smirk, to hear the broad Scots patter of Billy Connolly spoken so naturally in a thick Ukrainian accent. But it proved that here at least was one incomer who had truly graduated with honours from the Cuddyford school of integration.

"Hmm," Jigger hummed as he swilled a sip of whisky round his teeth with deliberate languor. "Mmm-hmm . . ."

Johnny was beside himself with sheer exasperation. "Vell?" he pressed. "Vot you bloody tinkink?"

Jigger further silently swilled, then finally swallowed the well-swilled swallae, frowning sourly.

"Vell? Vot's da bleedink score? Da cat been nickink your tongue or somesinks!"

Jigger relaxed his frown into a look of reflective reservation, savouring a further moment or two of Johnny's mouth-gaping agony before spreading his own lips into a laudatory grin.

"Ardonski," he beamed, "you were dead right, and I couldn't have put it better myself. Dis new wintage is fuckink braw!"

Relishing the prospect of all those lovely greenbacks to come, he gave Johnny a hearty slap on the back, sending the old fellow into another celebratory dancing spasm, but one in which Jigger was this time delighted to join . . .

"OH-H-H, LET'S TVISTINK AGAIN LIKE VE DONE LAST SUMMER!" they sang at the top of their voices — knees, elbows and hips grooving wildly, one foot rhythmically grinding an imaginary fag end into the floor in the style of the legendary Chubby himself. "YEAH, LET'S TVISTINK AGAIN LIKE VE DONE LAST YEAR!"

It was only the cold, soggy feeling of his wet trouser cuffs clinging to his ankles that eventually put the dampeners on Jigger's euphoria and drew his attention back to the problem of the flooded floor. There was still less than an inch of water covering the concrete, but if it got much deeper, Jigger predicted, the electrics of the distillation gear would be knackered. And if the water seeped into the adjoining underground rooms where his casks of maturing whisky were racked . . . Well, perish the thought. Jigger was a worried man.

"I'd better fill some sandbags and lay them along the bottom of that old metal door for the moment, Johnny," he muttered. "That'll buy us some time. But keep trying to unlock it. It likely only leads into an old ventilation shaft or something, but we've got to find out where that water's coming from before we have a disaster on our hands here."

Jigger did the necessary with the sandbags, then, explaining that he had another important meeting to attend, he left his mobile phone with Johnny — just in case — and set off for Cowdenbings with a large bottle of the new 12 year-old "Home Brew" stashed behind Bert's seat in the pick-up.

The extensive car park of the Miners' Welfare Club was already almost full when Jigger drove in; a reminder that, being the Sabbath, the faithful of Cowdenbings and surrounding district would already be gathering inside for the major bingo session of the week. Jigger had arrived deliberately early, having stressed to Lord Ludovic the importance of turning up in good time for a final pep talk before his crucial interview with the supreme soviet of the Horseburghshire Constituency Labour Party. However, a cursory cruise around the car park confirmed what Jigger instinctively knew would be the case — Ludo hadn't yet showed up. Jigger parked the pick-up by the entrance and glanced at his watch. Still quarter of an hour to go. Plenty of time. He settled back in his seat, casually planting his feet on the dashboard, where they caught the sunshine that was being filtered by the smoke of a thousand coal fires burning briskly in the hearths of the surrounding houses.

Strange, Jigger mused, how there was always that smell of hard-boiled eggs around Cowdenbings. Nothing to do with what folk had had for breakfast, of course. No, it was the sulphuric waft of coal smoke, nothing more. For, although only ex-miners occupied those trim ranks of little red brick cottages these days, their former contracts of employment with the National Coal Board pledged them free supplies of domestic fuel in perpetuity. And it mattered not that there was no real need to kindle a fire on a pleasant April day like today. The maxim seemed to be that, if you get the coal for nothing, you damn well use it with a vengeance!

"The sun's nice and warm shining in through the windscreen there, Bert," Jigger said. "Better try and get the old trouser legs dried out before I go public. Bad enough if the prospective parliamentary candidate looks like a close relative of Worzel Gummidge, without his agent looking like a drookit scarecrow an' all, huh?"

Bert had already curled up on his own sunny patch of seat, and one heavy eyelid was the only bit of his anatomy that he could mobilise in token acknowledgement of his master's words.

Jigger rested his head against the back of the cab, folded his arms and smacked his lips, delighting in the lingering malty tang of his latest whisky classic. He smiled a contented smile and closed his eyes, trying his best to ignore the hum of the piggery being coaxed from his damp trouser-leg bottoms by those sultry sunbeams.

"That old lush Ardonski," he chuckled to himself. "He'd drink the whole wee distillery dry, given half a chance."

But, for all that, Johnny was worth his weight in gold — literally. Without him, there would have been no wee distillery at all. And it wasn't as if he expected much for his sub-piggery jiggery-pokery, either. He was happy enough to pocket a modest share of the convertible proceeds, so to speak, and it suited Jigger just fine to protect the modesty of that share with all the devotion of a head eunuch in a paranoid sultan's harem. Not that he was trying to rip Johnny off, mind. Hell's bells, Johnny only went and blew his whisky takings on vodka in the Cuddy's Rest, anyway. It was some sort of perverse way, Jigger suspected, that Johnny's addled brain had dreamed up for returning a contribution from his corrupt capitalist gains to the motherland. Whatever, there wasn't *that* much profit in the bootleg booze business in any case, particularly when you remembered that the radar station "Single Malt" was being retailed at well under the price of an ordinary blended Scotch.

Jigger shook his head meditatively. Of course, you had to own up that there was no alcohol duty to pay, and, fair enough, that tended to help the margins a wee bit. And who cared if Nessie was always saying that diddling the Customs and Excise was the height of dishonesty? Jigger certainly didn't see eye-to-eye with her on that score. And he had given the matter a lot of thought — once.

See, the way he saw it was that all those highfalutin EU-backed farm diversification schemes that were sprouting like mushrooms these days added up to millions of pounds of tax-payers' money being doled out to any old farmer who could convince some pen-pusher from the Ministry that this screwball caper, or that, was likely to be a goer. And most of them weren't. So, the tax-payers' hard-earned cash just went straight down the drain. Conversely, *his* scheme required neither government subsidy nor the expensive employment of countless civil servants to administer it. By Jigger's reckoning, therefore, his wee distillery was actually saving the tax-payer money. Why, if only more people would bother to think things through as precisely as he did, Income Tax in this country could be cut by half — or maybe even three-quarters!

He would need to have a word with Ludo about that once he was an MP. Could even make a tidy theme for his maiden speech, a revolutionary theory like that. Hmm, but then again, he thought after a while, why give away his good ideas, particularly when the

McCloud system of creative accountancy — or bent book-keeping, as Granny dubbed it (and she should know, since she invented it!) — ensured that he never paid Income Tax himself in the first place? Yeah, Ludo could dream up his own vote-winners . . .

The combined soporific effects of Bert's snoring and the pig-tainted warmth of the sunshine percolating through the cosy confines of the cab soon had Jigger nodding off himself. He drifted into a little B-feature daydream, starring himself as a macho mountaineer scaling the silky-smooth curves of the Paps o' Drummie. He eventually arrived breathless at the erotic pinkish-brown tip of one of the voluptuous twin summits to find Sabrina Ng, scantily clad in three strategically-placed banknotes. She was doing a sexy, slow-motion interpretation of the twist inside a giant whisky bottle that had Johnny Ardonski's grinning head as a stopper. Peering through the greenish haze of the bottle's glass, Jigger could just recognise the outline of a face on the bottom-most of the three banknotes. It was the face of Lord Ludovic, his gawky features contorting grotesquely as the note was pulled and stretched one way, then the other, by Sabrina's sensual gyrations. Talk about turning a dream into a nightmare! Why the hell did the image of that ugly mug have to materialise now of all times, and there of all places? Look! The face was even trying to speak to him. Jigger laboured to read the distorted, writhing lips. They seemed to be calling his name. Yes, he could hear them now — those unmistakable Hooray Henry tones echoing spookily from within the monster flask . . .

"Jigger . . . Jigger . . . I say, Jigger, old mate . . ."

Jigger's eyes tried to blink his drowsy senses back to semi-consciousness, while Ludo's face faded in and out of focus through the shimmering, transparent barrier. His Lordship had now sprouted arms, and hands, and one of the hands was tapping urgently on the glass.

"Jigger . . . Jigger . . . *Jigger*, WAKE UP, FOR CHRIST'S SAKE!"

Jigger rubbed his eyes and wound down the pickup's window. "Hi, Ludo," he yawned. "Where's Sabrina?"

"Where's *who?* Hey look, I'm dreadfully sorry, mate. Got slightly waylaid by Bertola at the Cuddy's Rest, OK. Just popped in for a swift eye-opener en route, in fact, then one turned into two, right, then two into, well, you know. And then, when I told Bertola what I was going to be up to today, he took me over to the old pub piano and taught me how to play another tune. Pretty dashed catchy, right. It's called —"

"Shite!" yelled Jigger, snapping fully awake. He glared at his watch. "You're late for the bloody interview! Ten minutes bloody late! What the hell were you thinking about? No, on second thoughts, don't even bother trying to answer that!"

Jigger grabbed the bottle of "Home Brew" and stuffed it inside his jacket.

"Right, let's get our arses into gear," he panted as he scrambled out of the pick-up. "And let's just hope you haven't blown your career in politics before it's even started."

"Yah, too true, mate," Ludo replied through a feckless grin. "Which reminds me — now that I'm going to be a politician, I shan't be needing these any more. No time for the old literary game now, I fancy. Well, not until it's bye-bye Westminster and hello memoirs time, right? Arf, arf, arf!"

He handed Jigger the box of books that Maggie had delivered to him at the castle a few days earlier.

"Jolly kind of your daughter to dig these out for me, Jigger. Uhm, didn't quite recognise her at first when I popped into the library, though. Used to be a real knock-'em-dead looker, as I remember. Gone a bit frumpy now, if I may say so." He stuck out his bottom lip and nodded sagely. "Too bad, mate. Yah, too piss-poor bad."

Jigger was only half-listening to Ludo's prattle, being too intent on propelling him without further ado towards his waiting fate. They had almost reached the top of the club's stone steps when Jigger grabbed him by the arm and drew him to one side.

"Now listen, Ludo, there's no time to go over everything again, and I can't go into the interview room with you, so I won't be there to cover for you if you make a balls-up. Understand?"

"OK, yah, got it on board. Oh, and I've been thinking — would this be the time to put the old bite on the politburo for a London pied-à-terre? You know — a modest little love nest around Mayfair or somewhere would be absolutely —"

"Screw the nut, Ludo!" Jigger hissed. He tapped the side of his head. "If that's the kind of stuff you come up with when you've been thinking — don't! Just remember the basics in there. The committee comes before everything, then it's the Party, then the people." He looked Ludo squarely in the eye. "We're talking hardcore socialism here, OK?"

"Yah?"

"Yeah, and don't forget to give them a bit of your local-accent act occasionally. The common touch, remember? And if you're really cornered, just name-drop a few red heroes like I told you before. Savvy?"

"Righty-ho! Red heroes it is," Ludo bumbled in his customary manner of studied vagueness. "Yah! Nice one, mate!"

Jigger stood back and took one final look at his unlikely protégé. God, he was an even bigger disaster area than ever. The grey suit had the appearance of having been slept in every night since leaving the Oxfam shop. Its wide lapels were now decorated with a multi-coloured array of organic ribbons, commemorating, presumably, some late-night battles with take-away pizzas, fish suppers, doner kebabs and, if Jigger was not mistaken, a few of the notorious Hamish Glenkinchie greasy pies and baked beans as well. All this and the fouled Hush Puppies, too? Hell, he made even the venerated Michael Foot look like a podium-placed contestant in a Beau Brummell competition. Perfect!

"OK, LUDO," he barked, "LET'S GO FOR IT!"

With Jigger leading the way, they marched boldly into the main public area of the club, striding between long rows of tables already laden with seemingly inexhaustible supplies of beers and spirits. They sailed through a smoke-hazed sea of seated punters, all gabbling away merrily with ballpoints and bingo cards at the ready.

"Heh, two thousand quid in the snowball today," one matronly lady clutching a pint was heard to remind her companion. "Benidorm, here we come, eh?"

Jigger squinted through the fug as he pressed onwards towards the rear of the hall. "So, there's two grand in the jackpot," he muttered to himself. That meant just one thing — the Selection Committee meeting would be short and sweet. No chance of Mick Murphy and his mates missing out on a go at the numbers with that kind of loot at stake. Ludo being late was a stroke of luck, too. That would make the selection session shorter still. Things were looking up. And so what if Ludo was attracting some fairly wonder-struck gawps from his unsuspecting future constituents? It could only be a sign that the lad had charisma. Tidy!

"'Afternoon, Mr Murphy, sir . . . gentlemen," Jigger called in businesslike fashion as he approached the raised executive alcove, where Mick and three other men were sitting in relaxed, if slightly pompous, poses. "Sorry we're a bit late."

Mick and his henchmen were dressed in immaculate and matching navy blue suits. They were sipping Red Stripe beer straight from the bottle, while surveying the club's swarming clientele like the occupants of the royal box at Wimbledon — if not the balcony of the Kremlin on May Day. Without taking his patent-shod feet off the table, Mick Murphy indicated with a languid movement of his hand that his two visitors should be seated.

"And," he said, "you can forget the sir and gentlemen stuff." He paused to take a sideways glance at Lord Ludovic. "There's no fuckin' sirs or gentlemen in this establishment — and that's official!"

"Aye, I daresay," said Jigger, trusting that his face didn't betray his private ponderings of: "Who the hell does this jumped-up little nyaff think he is?"

"Ludovic Gormlie-Crighton," boomed Ludo, his voice brimming with well-bred bonhomie and his right hand pumping the Murphy mitt with exaggerated heartiness. "Delighted to meet at last, Micky mate." He looked around, almost furtively. "I say — frightfully bad form — but Nature calls. Would, uhm — would you be so kind as to direct one to the jolly old karzi?" Then, recalling Jigger's advice on the benefits of employing the local vernacular, he added with a wink, "Or, rather, would you be so kind as to direct one to the shite hoose, ye ken? Arf, arf!"

Without saying a word, Mick motioned towards the nearest gents, but Jigger could tell from the incredulous frown that descended over his features that he was wondering if this guy was for real.

At that, one of his serge-suited sidekicks leaned across the table, cocked a bushy Celtic eyebrow and mumbled out of the corner of his mouth, "Here, Mick, is that guy for real?"

Mick gave a "search me" shrug and looked at Jigger for enlightenment.

"As real as they come, believe me," Jigger confidently declared. "What you have there, comrades, is thirteen stone of twenty-four carat Plasticine."

No sooner had he said it than Jigger remembered that he'd heard it on the telly that all that "comrades" stuff was reckoned to be way behind the times nowadays. It just wasn't reckoned to convey the right image for the new, forward-thinking Left. Dammit, Mick and his men would think he had been taking the piss!

Several moments of gravid silence ensued while the Murphia exchanged cryptic glances round the table. It was Mick himself who finally peered at Jigger through half-closed eyes and delivered the probing line:

"Are you tryin' to say, comrade, that he'd be like putty in our hands, like?"

Relief spread through Jigger like a gulp of cool burn water on a hot harvest day. "Yeah," he grinned, "and virgin putty at that. You'll be able to mould him into your very own six-million-dollar man, if you see what I'm saying." Jigger rubbed his forefinger and thumb together, and a communal grunt of approval resounded in the alcove. But only, Jigger noticed, after one Murphia member had taken the precaution of crossing himself at the mention of the word "virgin".

"And all the composites of the relevant motion relating to selective executive access to hitherto exclusive Gormlie-Crighton privileges have been duly agreed by you-know-who?" asked Mick Murphy in fluent conference-speak. His colleagues looked at each other in concerted puzzlement, before nodding their cogent assent.

"You-know-who agreed to the lot," Jigger confirmed with a reassuring smile. "Homing pigeons an' all."

Mick Murphy could only do his best to conceal an involuntary smirk of satisfaction by taking another slug of Red Stripe.

"And what are you gettin' out of all this, fiddler?" croaked one committee member, his physique suggesting a post-wall Humpty Dumpty, who himself had been put together again, by committee.

"Same as you, brother," Jigger countered, opting for the politically-fraternal appellation in preference to the more aesthetically-accurate "Quasimodo". "Same as you — that nice feeling all us public-spirited folk get when we've done the proletariat a wee favour at somebody else's expense. Oh, and the name's Jigger, by the way — or Mr McCloud, if you want to keep it formal."

Sensing that brother Dumpty was about to cop the hump, Jigger decided that the time had come to build a less contentious bridge — towards the common good, so to speak. He reached inside his jacket and produced the bottle of his liquid ambrosia. Four glasses were requested from, and promptly supplied by, the handily-placed Committee-Members-Only Bar, then Jigger sat back to allow the quartet of exalted incumbents to sip and savour their generously-administered drams.

Ludo, meanwhile, had emerged from the gents' toilet and was punctuating his unhurried way back to the executive alcove with short pauses at randomly-selected tables. The open-mouthed occupants were being subjected to a ritual of polite bows, handshakes all round and bursts of animated and, in all probability, meaningless rhetoric, culminating in raucous peals of his manic guffawing.

Jigger could hardly believe his eyes. Well, he'd be blown away by a fly's fart if the cocky young bugger wasn't electioneering already! Aye, and him not even confirmed as the bloody candidate yet! No doubt about it — the lad was well fixed for charisma, all right, and it was already common knowledge that he could produce enough natural bullshit to fill a jumbo muck-spreader at will. Yes sirree, all the essential rudiments for a career politician were there. With the right breaks, as they said in the best boxing movies, this kid could go all the way. Jigger was well pleased.

And Lord Ludovic's easy rapport with the plebs hadn't gone un-noticed by Mick Murphy either, although the only outward indications of his approbation were a hint of a pout and a lethargic lift of the eyebrows. However, in Jigger's opinion, those minor details of body language might just as well have related to the subtle potency of his peerless new "Home Brew".

It was to the latter, indeed, that Chairman Murphy now happened to refer.

"Nice drop o' poteen, to be sure," he murmured, drifting absentmindedly into his ancestral patois, while studying the honey-hewed contents of his glass. He cast Jigger an any-more-where-that-came-from? glance.

Jigger's return look was of the plenty-more-where-that-came-from variety.

No words were necessary. Business had been done.

198

Downing the dregs of his dram, Mick marshalled his three cohorts with the stirring words: "Better get this fuckin' Selection Committee show on the road, boys." He nodded towards the seated hordes of expectant bingo-players. "It'll soon be eyes-down-for-a-full-house time."

"But what about the rest o' the lads?" brother Dumpty objected. "There's no even half the committee here yet and —"

"Ach, forget it," Mick butted in. "It's ten-to-one they've all went to the dog races over at Wallybings gaff track. Fuck it — I'll cast their votes for them myself, as usual." Turning then to Jigger, he explained indulgently: "It's what's known in the politics trade as votin' by poxy, by the way."

Ludo was summarily retrieved from his gladhanding practice and shepherded, waving regally to his bemused public as he went, towards a door at the rear of the alcove. A sign on it stated, predictably enough, "Committee Room — Strictly Private". This, then, was the unofficial but veritable hub of Horseburghshire power politics. Jigger gave Ludo a wink of encouragement as he passed into the inner sanctum. His fate was now in the hands of God. Or, rather, his fate was now in the even more powerful hands (locally, at least!) of Mick Murphy. Those hands were more immediately occupied, however, in discreetly accepting from Jigger, and secreting in his copious briefcase, the unmarked one-litre bottle with its abundant residual contents of radar station nectar.

Left now to his own devices, Jigger sidled over to a quiet seat by a frosted glass service hatch that was conveniently positioned for dispensing drinks into the committee's holy of holies. He lifted a copy of the *Sunday Post* from the bar and made the outward appearance of being absorbed in the further adventures of "Oor Wullie" and "The Broons", while straining his ears hatchwards in a resolute attempt at picking up a clue or two as to how the selection process was proceeding within. All that could be heard, though, was the muffled drone of voices, and only two voices at that — those of Mick and Ludo, their indecipherable exchanges peppered with routine grunts from the chairman's three minions.

Jigger's curiosity was killing him.

The hall's public address system crackled into life, and a series of thunderous bangs and woofs shook the building as the MC blew into and tapped the mike:

"TESTING . . . POOH! . . . ONE, TWO . . . THUMP! . . . ONE, TWO . . . PHRRRP!"

BOOM!

Silence . . . goosed amplifier.

Taking advantage of the ensuing interlude of catcalls and general mayhem, Jigger gave the hatch door a surreptitious nudge with his elbow and craned his ear to the gap.

"Obviously, Ludovic son, it has been took for granted that you have did your homework on the history of our socialist movement, like."

"Oh, too true, Micky. Right on."

"So, you'll be familiar wi' the works o' Lenin and Marx an' that, then?"

"Absolutely, mate, absolutely! One has all John's records. And, uhm, although he was a bit before my time, I'm *right* into Groucho's movies. Yah, absolutely magic!"

Jigger's heart turned a summersault. So much for his pep talk on red heroes! But his worries were premature. Squinting one-eyed through the narrow opening, he could just about see half of Mick Murphy's face. Ludo's silly clanger had really rung the bell, but, contrary to Jigger's knee-jerk reaction, it had been in the most positive of ways. Mick's look of scheming fulfilment bore ample testament to that. Any nagging doubts he may have had were now dispelled. This guy *was* for real after all, and Mick couldn't wait to get his manipulative fingers on that prize lump of political putty.

"Your name Yigger, pal?" yelled the barman. "Phone call for ye," he said in response to Jigger's nod of affirmation.

The combined feeling of deliverance and elation that had only just enveloped him was compounded to one of near lottery-winning hysteria by Johnny Ardonski's telephone revelation of what lay behind that old steel door beneath the piggery. It was all Jigger could do to stop himself from shouting "House!" before the bingo had even started. OK, there were still a few pieces missing, but the jigsaw puzzle *was* beginning to take shape at last!

BOOM!

"TESTING, TESTING ... ONE, TWO ... THUMP! ... MARY HAD A LITTLE LAMB — THE MIDWIFE CRAPPED HERSEL'."

The MC, armed with restored amplification, proceeded to warn the gathered punters that the very best of order would now be required, and any noisy bugger not giving the upcoming "turns" a fair chance would be booted out — smuckin' fartly!

If Jigger needed any further excuse to leave Ludo to what now seemed to be his favourably-ordained fate, this was it — the commencement of the pre-bingo cabaret.

"Tell the boys in the committee room I'll catch them later," he called to the barman over the resident organist's blaring intro to *My Way*. "Got some urgent business to see to. Pig business!"

Jigger made a beeline for the car park, unaware of Ludovic emerging with a triumphant smile from the confines of the committee room, just as a middle-aged midget — who'd been hailed by the MC as "The Ten-year-old Glasgow Sinatra!" — squealed out the unwittingly-apt line ...

"BUT MORE, MUCH MORE THAN THAT, I DONE IT A-MY WAYYYY!"

CHAPTER
TEN

The Natives are Revolting

Maggie glanced over Jigger's shoulder. "That's one of the books I got out of the library for Ludo, isn't it?"

"Yeah. Thought I'd have a quick flick through before you take 'em back."

"Finally decided to jack in all his great plans for writing his family history, then, has he?"

Jigger didn't answer, rapt as he was in a reference to Craigcuddy Castle that he'd just stumbled upon. He rose from his seat beside the old range and moved over to the window, the better to read the faded print on the aged, yellowing pages.

"When was the last time anyone borrowed this book from the library, Maggie? — before you took it out for Ludo, I mean."

Maggie turned the book in her father's hands so that she could make out the title on the cover.

"Let me see — *Legends of Lowland Scottish Castles*." She shook her head. "I'm pretty certain it hasn't left the library in donkey's years." She opened the book and pointed to the flyleaf. "See, I even had to stick in a new borrowing-record sheet to take it out for Ludo. The original one probably fell out ages ago."

"So, there's no way Babu Ng would have seen this book since he came on the scene?"

"No way. He's never even been in the library, as far as I know." Maggie looked closely at the corner of the flyleaf. "What's that scrawled in pencil there? Somebody's initials, maybe? Mmm, looks a bit like 'AGC 1945'. Yes, and that's probably the last time this ancient tome left the library, judging by the amount of dust on it. Phew!" She fanned her face, then poked a finger into her father's ribs. "But, come on, Dad. Out with it! Why all the interest in this boring old book all of a sudden?"

"Oh, nothing really. Just something that maybe ties in with what Johnny Ardonski came across down at the piggery today, that's all."

Maggie gave him a disbelieving look. "The *piggery*? And just what does your World War Two radar station have in common with the history of Lowland Scottish castles, if you don't mind me asking?"

"Well now, that remains to be seen, Maggie, doesn't it?" Jigger closed the book and drummed a pensive tattoo with his fingers on the scuffed leather cover. "Mind if I hold onto this one for a while?"

"Be my guest," Maggie shrugged. "It'll probably be another sixty years before anyone else wants to borrow it again, anyway."

Just then, Nessie scurried into the kitchen with Granny in hot, shuffling pursuit. "Get a move on, Maggie!" Nessie urged. "We'll miss the start of the

204

Community Association EGM if we don't shift ourselves . . . *now!*"

This was the one and only time that Jigger had known even one member of the McCloud family to be interested in what the Cuddyford Community Association was up to. For one thing, it was totally dominated by incomers, and for another, there hadn't been a Community Association in the village at all before old Commander Plimsoll-Pompey blew into town and set the whole thing up with himself at the helm. Shades of the Mick Murphy school of democracy there, Jigger reflected with a smile — particularly as the bulldozing Commander had also managed to have *himself* voted in as chairman of the Horseburghshire Constituency Conservative Party, in direct opposition to Mick's ruling politburo. But all such political shenanigans apart, Granny and Nessie couldn't resist going along to this particular meeting. After all, it was their spreading the word of Babu Ng's alleged plans for Craigcuddy Estate that had sparked off the whole local furore in the first place.

For her part, Maggie had decided at the last moment to tag along "just for the fun of it", although her mood suddenly became far removed from one of amusement, after Jigger called out to her just as she was heading out the kitchen door:

"Hey, Maggie! I almost forgot. Ludo asked me to pass on a message to you."

"Oh yeah? How un*bear*ably exciting! Wants me to give him private lessons in public speaking now, I suppose."

"Nah, nothing quite so romantic as that. No, he just said it's too bad you turned out to be such a dowdy little frump."

For the first time in its brief history, the Cuddyford Community Association had succeeded in attracting a large and truly representative cross-section of the local population to one of its meetings. The village hall was packed to overflowing. Some of the natives were attending, like Maggie, just for the fun of it, others out of sheer nosiness. But few, if any, were there because they shared the pompous Commander Plimsoll-Pompey's notion that the general public's opinion would count for something at the end of the day. As one of the Cuddy's Rest wags had put it, the powers-that-be would generally pay as much heed to what Joe Bloggs had to say as they would to a flea's fart in a thunderstorm.

Undaunted by, or more likely totally uninterested in, these fainthearted, parish-pump bodings of inevitability, the Commander imperiously brought the meeting to order. He was flanked on the platform, as ever, by the redoubtable presence of his wife and the fawning Littleton-Nimbys. To add weight to this particularly auspicious occasion, however, he had also called on the services of the Lilliputian Dr Quentin Spon, an early-retired lecturer in urban ecology at Piddling-in-the-Marsh Polytechnic, or some other equally-obscure seat of further education. During his short residence in the village, Dr Spon had also become prospective Green Party candidate for the Cuddyford and

206

Lambsfoot ward of Horseburghshire Council, president of the recently-formed Horseburghshire Ramblers' Club, founder and spokesperson of the affiliated Horseburghshire Countryside Rights-of-Way Identification and Preservation Society, and author of the newly self-published book, *The Double-Crested Spotted Newt of Craigcuddy Castle Duck Pond — An Endangered Species.*

In a stirring introductory oration, the Commander took it upon himself to remind all members of the community that it was their abiding responsibility — nay duty — to steadfastly resist all threats to the ancient, sylvan sanctity of this precious corner of rural England, ehm, Britain (he never could fathom the difference) made by any pillaging, entrepreneurial blackguard who dared to defile these hallowed shores with his barbaric feet, and to cast his alien shadow of tawdry commercial development over these green and pleasant lands. The floor was then formally passed to the fidgeting, bespectacled Dr Spon.

"What about the extra jobs for us local folk, then?" came the strident call from the back of the hall, before the C-list boffin could utter a word.

"Aye, that's right!" shouted another native voice. "When ye're on the bloody dole, there's nothing very precious about this corner of rural *Scotland*." Then, stabbing a finger in the direction of Commander Plimsoll-Pompey, he caustically added, "Just try an' get yer navigation right, Cap'n Birdseye, eh!"

Muted sniggers and general mutterings of approval rippled through the body of the hall, accompanied by shocked tut-tuttings from the blue-rinse and Barbour-jacket brigade occupying the front two rows.

"Ordah! Ordah!" bellowed the Commander, puce-faced and fuming. There would be ample opportunity for questions in due course, he decreed, but he was now bound to insist upon complete silence for Dr Spon. "A measure of decorum, ladies and gentlemen, *please!*"

Holding aloft a copy of his new book, the diminutive Doctor sought to draw everyone's attention to the potential plight of wildlife in the area if the mooted theme park were to be built. No species would be more vulnerable, he stressed, than the subject of this book, signed copies of which, incidentally, would be on sale in the foyer at the termination of the meeting — £12.50 apiece.

"Stuff yer book and yer wildlife up yer bahookie!" yelled a balcony-seated village worthy. "We cannae eat damned newts! Work — *that's* what we need around here!"

"Well said, Jock! That's right, there used tae be fifty men workin' on Craigcuddy Estate when we were laddies, and how many work there now?"

"Just one, Wullie!"

"Aye — the Muppet!"

"Correct! One bloody Muppet, instead o' fifty men!"

"ORDAH!" boomed the Commander. "Silence for Dr Spon!"

"Away an' claw yer barnacles!" retorted balcony Jock, the newly-emerging voice of the people. "Where's the old Duke and this Baba bloke? *They're* the ones we want tae hear, no youse take-over chancers!"

The Duke of Gormlie, the bristling-whiskered Commander stated defiantly, and Mr Babu Ng, to whom he presumed the gentleman was *attempting* to refer, had been invited to join the members of the committee on the platform, but had, for reasons best known to themselves, declined.

"Stuff them an' all, then!" countered vox populi from aloft. "Stuff the lot o' yiz!"

Visibly shaking now, Dr Quentin Spon resumed his address, encouraged as he was by a carillon of hesitant applause from the front two rows. Resolutely adhering to his well-rehearsed theme, he went on to proclaim in a nervous yodel that it was his avowed intention, and that of his Party, to see to it that much greater access to estates like Craigcuddy should be afforded the public, though on an efficiently organised basis, of course. Indeed, it was a fundamental part of his policy that due consideration should at all times be paid to Nature, and to the integrity of the habitats of the non-human occupants of those lands, right down to, and including, the merest moth and, dare he say it, newt.

Jock's jeering chortle from the balcony was greeted with an irritated discharge of blue-rinsed shushing and tutting. "That vulgar person!"

And so it would be imperative, Dr Spon continued (with a nod of indebtedness to the front row matrons), for those wishing to partake of this new freedom of enjoyment of God's given countryside — if he might describe it thus — that such enjoyment be developed and safeguarded by the regular walking of this area's ancient rights of way by as many people as possible. It went without saying, he said, that this free-to-all activity would have to be policed — if that were not too strong a word — by a responsible body, such as the Horseburghshire Ramblers' Club, of which (cough) he himself was proud to be president. Membership of the Club, he announced, would be open to all those sympathetic to the cause, for a modest annual subscription of (cough) £30 — application forms available (in addition to the aforementioned copies of his new book) in the foyer.

"Away back tae Pishy Marsh where ye came from, an' take a runnin' jump at yersel' while ye're at it!" shouted Granny McCloud, standing up on her bench at the back of the hall and brandishing her fists. "Us Cuddyforders have been poachin' rabbits an' trouts an' pheasants all over Craigcuddy Estate for generations — for hundreds o' years before yer daft, hoity-toity Ramblers' Clubs and the like were even thought about by you creepin' townies!"

"ORDAH!" thundered the Commander, as the old-timers in the audience mumbled their appreciation of Granny's astute observation. "Through the chair, madam!" he bellowed at Granny. "How *dare* you take —"

"And you can shut yer hairy face, Popeye-Plimsole!" Granny cut in, inspired by the success of her own magniloquence. "I'm no finished yet. And anyhow, I've got as much right to speak here as you. Aye, who in the name o' the wee man gave *you* the right to hijack this village, anyway?"

A loud stomping of like-minded feet rumbled over the hall's wooden floor. That was all Granny needed. She was really buzzing now, and she aimed her next verbal rocket at Dr Spon . . .

"And don't you lecture *us* about *our* wildlife, Mr Spock. *Nobody* looks after wildlife better than us country folk." Then, thumping her chest with her fist, she trumpeted, "We *always* treat the wild beasties right — for it's *us* that has tae eat them!"

Howls of "Good for you, Mrs McCloud!" and "Just you tell them, Granny!" resounded round the hall.

Dr Spon, meanwhile, had come over all useless upon hearing Granny's last statement, and, as befitted the founding President of Horseburghshire Vegetarian and Vegan Alliance, slumped back down on his seat and concentrated hard on not throwing up.

"And as far as yer so-called ancient rights o' way are concerned," Granny exclaimed, "any o' yer fell-booted, knapsack-totin', free-to-all, fairweather, weekend . . ." (Granny paused there to draw breath and to think up a few more pawky adjectives) . . . "Soft-handed, city-slicker, binocular-peepin', born-again country people that trespass on *my* land will be pickin' lead shot out o' the arses o' their designer plus fours 'til the morn-come-never!"

A standing ovation followed, observed in shrinking silence by the platform quintet and their front-rows vanguard of the Cuddyford Community Association.

Granny's dander was well up now, and she was all set to have a right go at that puffed-up Popeye and his clique of high-and-mighty white settlers about how there were no wee houses left that the young folk of Cuddyford could afford any more, because they and their like had swarmed in and snapped them all up and shoved the prices through the roof with their fantoosh, big-city money. It was only a whispered caution from Nessie, however, that spared Granny the ignominy of putting her foot right in it. Nessie reminded her, from behind a cupped hand, that it had been Jigger, courtesy of his conversion of the old steading into a bijou residential development, who had benefited more than anyone to date from the exploitation of this unjust state of affairs.

So it was that the three McCloud ladies retired discreetly from the hall with the roars of acclamation from Granny's fans still ringing in their ears. She had made her point, though quite what good it had done was difficult to determine. It would certainly take more than a belligerent old woman to knock the wind out of the "Popeye's" sails for long. Still, at least he and his crew now knew that, in the eyes of some Cuddyforders at least, there was precious little difference between theme park customers trampling over their land and "Mr Spock's" ramblers and twitchers doing likewise.

It was, nevertheless, a noticeably more subdued Commander Plimsoll-Pompey who eventually succeeded in restoring order to the meeting, after most of the locals had drifted away in Granny's wake. For them, the fun was over for the evening, and it remained only for them to get on with their lives as usual. As vox-populi Jock remarked on descending from the balcony, they'd leave it to windbags like the Commander to waste time fartin' against thunder, if that was what turned the meddlesome old scunner on, like.

The vote on the Commander's motion to resist any unsavoury development of Craigcuddy Estate, whilst also putting pressure on the Duke to allow increased access to his lands by selected members of the community, was carried by a 100% majority. The few natives who remained seated behind the front two rows abstained — except, it was minuted by Mrs Littleton-Nimby, the giggling and slavering wee Eck "Napoleon" McClarty. However, by raising his hand in support of both the "Ayes" *and* the "Noes", his vote had been declared null and void, anyway.

CHAPTER
ELEVEN

If Music Be The Food
of. . . Love?

While the ladies were at the meeting in the village hall, Jigger had got himself all dandied up in his best kilt gear, complete with silver-mounted, sealskin sporran and silver-buttoned, black-velvet doublet, embellished at the throat and cuffs with cascading jabot and ruffles of white lace. He'd then put on his black dress brogues, with their long laces criss-crossed over white kilt hose and tied above the ankle in pendent, tasselled bows. To set it all off, just the right amount of the jewelled hilt of his skean dhu dirk had been left showing at the top of his right stocking.

He had also been tempted to wear — at a jaunty cant — his toorie-topped Balmoral bonnet with the gilded Clan McCloud crest, white cockade and pheasant's-tail-feather aigrette. But he finally thought better of it. Although he could never share Granny's opinion that it made him look like a pansified imitation of that heather-loupin' Alan Breck in *Kidnapped*, Jigger had to admit that the Balmoral was maybe just a *wee* bit over the top for this particular occasion, right enough.

214

That decided, he stood back and took one last look at himself in the mirror. Mmm-hmm, he concluded, he would do just fine. No, wait a minute. In all modesty, and although he said it himself, he would do better than fine. Aye, he looked the absolute bee's knees!

The arrangement was that, seeing as how he had helped make up the guest list for Sabrina Ng, Jigger thought it only right and proper that he should arrive at the party early doors — to help introduce the folk, sort o' style. He'd told Nessie, therefore, that she could "just follow on with Maggie and Davie a wee bit later." Normally, a suggestion of this provocative kind from Jigger would have prompted Nessie to tell him to go and get well and truly raffled, but for some reason, she'd appeared quite happy — almost keen, in fact — for him to "go solo for an hour or so tonight."

Granny didn't give a monkey's what they all did. No amount of cajoling from the rest of the family for her to go along and let her hair down for a change would shift her from her dourly declared policy. She didn't like parties, particularly foreign ones, so she was *not* going!

Guards of honour of specially-installed lanterns lit the pick-up's way along the old manse's gravelled sweep, the tall yew trees lining either side somehow looking less foreboding than normal in the warm, amber glow. And OK, it wasn't exactly a Beverley Hills mansion, Jigger conceded, but the stern façade of this former home of those dreich ministers o' the kirk certainly did have something of a near-glamorous look about it, illuminated as it now was in the flattering beams of

215

concealed banks of multi-coloured floodlights. In truth, if he forgot about the lack of a claymore in his hand and the absence of a plaid over his shoulder, Jigger felt a bit like Errol Flynn in *The Master of Ballantrae* as he swashbuckled up the manse's stone steps two at a time. Here! he thought, maybe that pheasant-plumed Balmoral wouldn't have been such a bad touch after all!

Despite those irrepressible Hollywood fancies of his, Jigger was totally unprepared for the sight of what awaited him at the open front door. It was a reincarnation of Stewart Granger, no less! He was resplendent in his sartorially-extravagant Scarlet Pimpernel gear of gold-buckled shoes, white silk knee-breeches and satin frock coat of palest blue worn over a thigh-length silver lamé tunic. He wore a powdered wig and face to match, complete with gold-star beauty spot stuck to the left of his upper lip.

"Welcome, monsieur," the lipstick-painted mouth articulated in stentorian RADA tones from beneath the bowing wig. A gloved hand was extended towards the startled Jigger.

"Monsieur's invitation card, *s'il vous plaît?*"

Jigger fumbled in his sporran, his eyes fixed unwaveringly on the Pimpernel, his back pressed even more unwaveringly against the door jamb. He had worn the kilt for enough years, man and boy, to know that you had to keep your tradesman's entrance well out of range of weirdoes like this.

The Pimpernel scrutinised Jigger's card, then, inclining his head towards the recoiling invitee, whispered amid much fluttering of false eyelashes, "Ahem, is there no *Madame* McCloud?"

"Well, no — not at the moment. *But*," Jigger hastened to add, "she *will* be coming along later, all right? Eh, and *with* my two kids an' all!"

"JIGGER McCLOUD, ESQUIRE!" the Pimpernel haughtily announced without further ado. He returned the card to Jigger, whom he then looked up and down with a pout of undisguised pique.

"Butch kiltie bitch!" were the words the foppish footman lisped under his breath as Jigger sidled cautiously past, then swaggered off, kilt swinging, across the entrance hall.

"Well, at least there's no need for me to bother about introducing anybody now," he muttered to himself, tugging suavely at his frilly cuffs while standing straight-backed in the drawing room doorway and surveying the sumptuous scene within, ". . . not with that big, nosey Jessie on the door!"

Having made sure that he himself was well ahead of time, Jigger was surprised to see that there were already three guests in the room — all men and all in a huddle over by the bar. They were, predictably, young Lord Ludovic, Bertola Harvey and Johnny Ardonski, each one a habitual early bird at any such freeloader-friendly function.

The strains of genteel elevator music rippled through the archway from what Jigger remembered as the Busby Berkeley room, where the tuxedo-clad purveyors of the insipid tinkling were presently located. A pianist was seated at the gleaming white grand piano inside the great alabaster scallop shell overlooking the swimming pool. He was accompanied by a double bass player and drummer. All three po-faced musicians looked, Jigger judged, as if they specialised in post-funeral gigs and had turned up at the wrong venue.

"Hell's bells!" he sighed, "Sabrina's dropped a right one if booking that powder-puff doorman and the Count Dracula Trio there is her idea of what's likely to add up to a hot time in Cuddyford." What a letdown she'd turned out to be — and him having had her sussed as a woman of superior intellect, would you believe!

Oddly enough, neither Sabrina nor Babu Ng were anywhere to be seen. A bit bad-mannered of the host and hostess, Jigger reckoned. Looking around, his eye was caught by an expansive wall painting above the fireplace. It depicted a freaky modern-art portrayal of a naked woman (whom he took to be Sabrina), doing what appeared to be something dodgy with a human-headed python. Funny, he pondered, that he hadn't noticed it when he was in here before. But, then again, maybe that was only because he hadn't been able to keep his bins off the real thing . . .

He was stirred from his wanton wool-gathering by a cordial holler of:

"Hi there, Jigger, my old mate!"

Ludo was striding towards him in a threadbare, blue-grey smoking jacket that gave the impression of having started life as part of the upholstery of some long-abandoned Victorian sofa. His Lordship was clearly out to make an impression.

"OK, Jigger," he gushed, "shake hands with Horseburghshire's future man at Westminster! Magic, right? Arf, arf, arf!"

"So, you've been adopted as the official candidate, then?"

"Uhm, near as dammit, mate — subject to a ballot of all party members in the constituency, naturally. Must follow strictest democratic principles, what?"

Well, well! The young laird was getting a grip of the essential jargon already, Jigger marvelled, stroking his chin and smiling proudly.

"Still," Ludo continued with an airy wave of his whisky glass, "as Micky Murphy says that no other candidate will be put against me, it all seems as cut and dried as a gelded camel's passion fruits on a Sahara sand dune, no?"

Jigger threw a congratulatory arm round Ludo's shoulder. "I couldn't have put it better myself," he beamed. "Bloody marvellous!" Yes sirree, he mused, those jigsaw pieces were coming together tidily. This called for a drink!

"What'll you have, Ludo? This one's on me!"

"Better than that, mate — all the drinks are on the house. So, I'll have a jolly old double Glenreekie, OK?"

"Make it a treble!" said Jigger, overcome by a spontaneous surge of generosity. "Yeah, and I'll have one, too!"

Although Johnny Ardonski had been well warned to keep absolutely quiet about the discovery at the piggery during the afternoon, Jigger, on approaching the bar, gave him a button-your-lip-or-else glare, just in case.

"Ah, Yigger!" the old fellow grinned, offering a welcoming hand. "Is amazink vot ve can findink under fuckink pigs, *da*?"

Bertola was peering down mistily into his sherry schooner. "Yeah," he drawled, "like fuckink pig shit, man."

An awkward silence followed, during which Jigger's intensified death-ray stare at Johnny had the bumbling pigman gulping at his vodka and fumbling with the unfastenable waistcoat buttons of his seldom-aired Sunday suit. The tension was soon relieved, however, by an unseen penny dropping on the meditative head of young Lord Ludovic.

"Oh, yah! I get it now, Bertola. Pig shit! Arf, arf! Nice one, mate! Jolly droll!"

Johnny's blabber-mouthed greeting having done no apparent harm after all, Jigger proceeded to propose a congratulatory toast to Ludo, who, bursting now with bonhomie and pent-up excitement, courteously acknowledged his friends' compliments before blurting out that there was even more good news to celebrate. As if it hadn't been enough of a windfall to be handed a House of Commons seat (with a jolly comfortable cushion of sixty grand a year, plus three times as much again in exies attached), the Cowdenbings Miners' Welfare Association had also bestowed upon him, as a mark of their appreciation for lending his lordly services to their humble cause, an honorary life membership of their Bingo Club. To back up that magnanimous gesture, he added, they'd even given him a free go at today's "eyes down". And what had been the upshot of all this good fortune? Why, even better fortune! He had won, would they Adam and Eve it? The jolly old Snowball, no less!

"Yah, two thousand smackers, OK, right there in one's paw in crispy new twenties!"

And what, Jigger enquired with not unjustified apprehension, had his Lordship done with the two big ones so providently gained?

That, Lord Ludovic proclaimed (a shade too loftily for Jigger's liking), had been where his hereditary instincts came in. "Noblesse oblige and all that stuff, right?"

"Don't tell me," Jigger groaned in despair. "You bought a round of drinks for everybody in the place. I might have bloody well known it!"

"Hey, uncanny, mate!" Ludo beamed, stepping a half pace backwards. "Right on!"

Bertola raised a half-opened eye. "You get my vote, daddy-o," he mumbled. "Yeah, I dig your political style, man. Cool platform."

"Platform! Absolutely spot on, Bertola," Ludo gasped. "Talk about telepathy, mate!"

The crowd in the hall, he went on, had actually pushed him, applauding and cheering, onto the platform following the announcement by the bingo caller of their prospective parliamentary candidate's big-hearted donation of "free bevvy fur the lotta yiz". Ludo had then felt inspired, under such emotive circumstances, to make an impromptu speech. "One had felt," he confided to his three friends, "rather as how Montgomery must have felt at the Alamo,

221

actually." He had made only a brief oration, of course, during which he'd once more slotted in — jolly skilfully, he thought — a couple of pithy references to those revered socialists, Lenin and Marx, or John and Groucho as he felt he could now more familiarly refer to them in public.

Amazingly, according to Ludo, the crowd had gone absolutely berserk, some even jumping on chairs and yelling his name, others so overcome with communal joy that they were laughing uncontrollably, some actually moved to the point of tears. It had been a very touching moment, and the second time that Lenin and Marx had done the business for him in one afternoon. "Nice one!" In fact, Ludo had been so touched himself, he was obliged to admit, that he had yielded eventually to the overwhelming mood of mass goodwill — of true socialist amity; indeed, had suppressed his natural tendency to modesty, and had seated himself behind the resident organist's Yamaha. He'd then invited the large gathering of his constituents-in-waiting to sing along to a jolly rousing rendition of the new tune Bertola had taught him in the Cuddy's Rest earlier in the day.

Jigger kneaded his temples with his middle finger and thumb. "Not *The Red Flag*?" he groaned, his eyes drawn to Bertola's laid-back, "what else, man?" shrug. "Not the bloody *Red Flag*, surely!"

"Wow! Telepathy it is again, mate," Ludo enthused. "You named that tune in one!"

And so it had transpired that, after a summary execution of *The Saints* as an encore, Lord Ludovic

Gormlie-Crighton II was, in his own words, escorted from the stage by Mick Murphy's three lieutenants and carried shoulder high through the hall amid fanatical chants of "LUDO! LUDO! LUDO!". They bore him, like some latter day Caesar, all the way out to the car park, where awaited his trusty old Land Rover with butler-cum-chauffeur Ellington Baldock, alias Elephant Bollocks, seated loyally at the wheel.

"Jigger, Bertola, Johnny, my old chums," Ludo concluded with an emotional break in his voice, "one feels it in one's water that one has met one's true calling." Laying a hand on Jigger's arm, he solemnly conceded, "You were absolutely right, mate. Forget the old pied-à-terre in Mayfair. Yah, Number Ten is just around the corner!"

Johnny raised his vodka glass. "My wery best respecks," he sniffed, his piggy eyes moist with befuddled sentiment. "You got my wote too, Ludowic, my wery goot friend."

Bertola leaned away from Ludo to get his focus fixed, then tapped him on the chest. "Become an organ donor, pops," he muttered. "Like, that's *my* advice for your future success in public life."

"Hey, good thinking!" Ludo enthused. "Oh yah, all that public-spirited stuff, right? Nice socialist touch there. Hmm, must get a donor's card pronto. Invite the press chaps along to cover the event." He gazed skyward, inspired. "I can see the headline now — 'Humanitarian new MP registers as organ donor'. Wow, excellent PR, Bertola mate." He took a generous swallow of Glenreekie single malt while he developed the thought.

"But just one thing, man," Bertola slurred dryly. "Do the world a double favour, huh? Yeah, hold onto your liver and donate your fuckin' Yamaha!"

"I take it, Ludo, that you entertained your two half-canned chums here to a few in the Cuddy's Rest on the way over here?" Jigger enquired. "*If* you had any of the bingo winnings left at all, that is."

Despite the whiff of cynicism in Jigger's query, Ludo showed not a trace of rancour. "Right you are there, Jigger," he confirmed. "One had a bit of, well, a bit of family business to clear up with Hamish Glenkinchie. So, as you so rightly surmised, one had old Elephant Bollocks drop one off at the pub en route. Wiped the old Cuddy's slate clean with the bingo boodle too, OK? Hmm, Mr Skint, therefore, will soon be the sole tenant of one's wallet once again." He hunched his shoulders, then added with a stoical sigh, "Hey-ho, *c'est la vie*."

At that moment, a door at the side of the bar opened, and out of the room, that Jigger remembered as the former ministers' study, emerged the dapper, white-jacketed Babu Ng, accompanied by none other than old Archibald Gormlie-Crighton himself. Jigger was flabbergasted. Archie hadn't been on the list of guests he'd drawn up for Sabrina, so it followed that these two mystery men were already acquainted — just as Archie's lawnmower-mounted conversation with Bertola had implied. Interesting.

"Always a pleasure doing business with you," Archie said, while stopping briefly in the doorway to shake

Ng's hand. "I guess we should have the whole deal concluded to our mutual benefit real soon, Robert. Yes, and then —"

"Quite so, quite so," Ng interjected, his tone revealing a note of disquiet as he glanced at Jigger and his companions standing only a few feet away. "And please do call me Babu, my friend. I tend to prefer that to the, er, *westernised* version these days."

If Archie realised that he had made a faux pas, he gave no indication of it. Rather, he turned purposefully towards the bar and expressed the genial greeting: "Aha! My two good buddies from the Cuddy's Rest, I do believe. Now then, let me see — it's Bertola, isn't it? And, yes, I recall the vodka glass — Johnny from the Ukraine, if I'm not mistaken."

Archie then diverted his attention to Jigger, and his manner instantly changed from glib affability to one of near shock. It was a sensation that Jigger shared. Although the two men had only now come face to face for the first time in their lives, there seemed a strange feeling of familiarity — that same, almost eerie sense of bonding that Jigger had experienced during that poignant encounter with the Duke on the night of old Tam's death.

"You — you must be —" Archie stammered, his customary flamboyance gone, his voice hushed, his expression that of a man who had just seen a ghost.

"Uhm, allow me," Ludo volunteered, his own demeanour unexpectedly uneasy and oddly restrained. "Jigger McCloud, this is my father's cousin, Archibald Gormlie-Crighton. Uncle Archie . . . Jigger."

The two men stood and stared at each other in silence, their right hands tightly clasped and unmoving. Although he knew it was irrational, Jigger couldn't dispel the overwhelming conviction that he knew this person well. There was something about him that was so familiar, something about his smile, something about the way he inclined his head inquisitively as he looked at you. A shiver ran down Jigger's spine. What he saw in old Archie was like a barely distinguishable image in a clouded, broken mirror. What he saw in Archie was something of . . . himself.

"Nell," Archie whispered almost inaudibly. "Nell . . . the dear, sweet girl."

Releasing Jigger's hand as if suddenly realising that he may have already revealed too much, he drew himself up to his full height and continued, though now in a deliberately firm voice: "You must forgive me, my boy, er, Tommy, but your mother — you reminded me so much of Nell. And it's been so long — forty years or more. Seeing you just then brought it all back. I — I'm so pleased to meet you after all this time."

Jigger found himself unable to answer. For the first time he could remember, a lump had risen in his throat at the mention of the mother he had never known. What was it about this stranger that could tug at his heartstrings in such a peculiar, unsettling way? And he had called him Tommy, too . . .

The silence was interrupted by Babu Ng. "I hope you will excuse me if I borrow Mr McCloud for a few minutes, gentlemen. We have a rather pressing matter of

226

business to discuss." He took Jigger by the elbow. "This way, Mr McCloud."

Once inside the study, Ng offered Jigger a seat by his desk. He then gently lifted a bottle of wine from a rack behind the door, uncorked it and, with infinite caution, poured the rich, ruby liquid into a crystal decanter.

"Do you know what this is, Mr McCloud?"

"Wine?" said Jigger with decided indifference, his thoughts still wrapped up in those moments with old Archie.

"Ah yes, but such a wine, my friend. Such a wine." Ng lovingly poured a measure into an enormous wine tulip.

A wee bit like a goldfish bowl on a stick, Jigger thought.

Ng then returned the decanter to the vertical, with a neat twist of the wrist, when the glass was precisely one-third full. "It goes without saying that we insult such a glorious wine by not allowing it sufficient time to breathe, but circumstances dictate that insult it we must." He passed the goblet to Jigger. "But please, Mr McCloud, do at least take a moment to savour the fabulous bouquet before tasting. Ah, it is *such* a wine."

Jigger took a quick sniff, then slurped up a manly mouthful, swilling the wine around his teeth in the way he had seen the experts doing on telly, before swallowing it down with a resounding smack of the lips.

"Yeah, tidy enough drop o' plonk," he said, then prepared to have a second swig. But, in acknowledgement of Babu Ng's startled expression, he paused with the glass at his lips and added, "Sorry — was I supposed to spit it out, like? I never noticed any bucket, so I —"

"Spit it out? Plonk! *Spit*? Spit out a wine such as *this*?" Ng was clearly distressed. "My friend, do you not appreciate that in your hand you are holding a glass of one of the world's greatest wines?" He thrust the empty bottle at Jigger and barked, "This is a Château Lafite-Rothschild 1961! Have you no idea what it is worth?"

"Not the foggiest, Babu. Nah, I prefer a nice pint o' lager, myself — maybe with a wee squirt o' lime juice in the summer, ye know. Nice an' refreshin', like. Still, to each his own, as they say." He clinked his glass against the empty bottle. "Cheers!"

His words, though tantamount to sacrilege to a dedicated wine buff, were like music to Babu Ng's ears.

"Then I had better not enlighten you as to the value of this wine, Mr McCloud," he said, his sly smile hidden from Jigger as he turned and walked over to a wall safe, from which he extracted a thick bundle of banknotes. "It may scare you off the business proposition which I was about to put to you."

Jigger eyed up the wad. "I'm braver than I look," he swiftly countered.

Ng sat down at his desk opposite Jigger and thumbed teasingly through the money. "The small matter of the bath and two doors, I believe. Five hundred pounds you asked?"

"But one thousand pounds you offered."

The skulking vulture look returned to Ng's eyes, his moustache twitching schemingly. "Quite so. And for services to *be* rendered, was it not?"

All ears, Jigger leaned back in his chair and folded his arms. "So, tell me more," he nodded.

"You will have gathered, my friend, that I, Babu Ng, am a connoisseur of the finer things in life — art, furniture, motor cars, women and, of course . . ." he gestured with a gold festooned hand towards the decanter which sat between them like a glittering chesspiece, ". . . the noble wines of France."

"A man after ma own heart," said Jigger, breezily taking another slurp of the Château Lafite. "Aye, I think I could get to like this stuff maself."

Ng sniffed disdainfully. "You will also have gathered that I have the wherewithal to indulge such expensive tastes." He poured Jigger another measure of wine. (Queen to King's Rook Five). "And that is why I can afford to offer you such a generous remuneration for the simple service which I wish you to perform for me."

With practised poise, he peeled ten one-hundred-pound notes from the bundle and laid them beside the decanter. (Knight to Queen's Bishop Four). At his Paris home, he disclosed, his cellar was stocked with the rarest of wines — priceless masterpieces of Gallic viniculture, which even he felt privileged to own. Yet, in the final analyses, even classic wines, like beautiful women, were only expensive bagatelles, desirable baubles to be flaunted to one's own advantage and then enjoyed while at the zenith of their perfection. He stroked his moustache salaciously for a moment. Thus, he had concluded, there was no benefit to be gained from leaving his prized collection of Bordeaux and Burgundies buried in Paris when he intended to spend most of his future time here in Cuddyford. He had decided, therefore, to transport a selection of his most cherished vintages to Scotland — though, in the interests of security, only a few at a time. The operation would be undertaken by using his ocean-going motor cruiser, commencing with two cases, perhaps, in the very near future.

Jigger felt like saying that maybe a better way to go about all this would be for Ng to fly the stuff over himself in his helicopter. But, realising that continuing to act the lager-loving lout was clearly the more profitable option, he noisily gulped down another draught of wine and bade his host continue.

In order to avoid the unwanted attentions of any "undesirables" who might be covetous of his cache (for coteries of such people did exist in the world of fine wines), the utmost secrecy would be applied to the timing of the shipment and, until the very last moment, to the location of its landing place. All that Ng could divulge at this time was that the mission would be carried out under cover of darkness somewhere along the local coast. Once the cases were safely on land, the essential mode of transport to Cuddyford would be a four-wheel-drive truck, such as Jigger's. A simple enough operation, of course. But, Ng wanted to know, was Jigger confident that he was capable of executing *his* part of it satisfactorily?

"You bet your cotton socks, I am," said Jigger without resort to undue deliberation. "Just tell me where and when, and I'll be there!"

"Excellent!" smiled Ng, his hand beating Jigger's to the £1,000. "But I only pay cash . . . on delivery!" (Checkmate!).

The invited guests were already beginning to arrive in numbers when Jigger returned to the reception room. Local traders were mingling with their customers from the surrounding farms, their wives already jawing with the wives of the Cuddy's Rest wags, many of whom were being seen in public with their spouses for the first time in living memory. Everyone, though, was goggling at the sheer extravagance of the reformations that had been carried out inside the old manse.

"Jeez! An indoor pond ye could dip all ma bloody sheep in at one go!" roared one tweedy old livestock farmer on espying the massive swimming pool.

"And inside a greenhouse big enough to grow all the tomatoes ye'd need to keep the folk around here goin' 'til the cows come home!" marvelled his ruddy-cheeked missus.

"My, my, ye'd hardly credit it, would ye!"

A clutch of bewigged clones of the front-door footman had materialised during Jigger's absence, and were waltzing around with silver trays, offering flutes of vintage champagne to the wonder-struck guests. They were also prompting an epidemic of obscene fairy jokes to escape the corners of the mouths of the worthies already assembled at the bar for their preferred consumption of "some *real* drink".

"No thanks, hen," one worthy said to a particularly precious Pimpernel. "Nah, I've tasted that froggy bubbly before. Just like vinegar wi' Andrew's Liver Salts in it — and wi' the same effect on ma bowels!"

Jigger stood outside the study door for a few moments, surveying the scene, tasting the atmosphere. He was experienced enough as a bandleader to sense when a crowd of punters was shaping up for a good time. He had a nose for *that*, even if he couldn't smell much of a difference between Chateau Left Feet 1961 and a wine-of-the-month Lambrusco from Asda. And his bandleader's nose told him that this party bore all the hallmarks of turning out to be a right bummer.

Count Dracula and his two undead sidemen were still grinding out an endless dirge of crematorium music from the Busby Berkeley twilight zone. The guests, meanwhile, were already separating out like butterfat on sour milk into little, chattering dollops of ethnic xenophobia — the natives here, the incomers there. Jigger shook his head gloomily. Why the blazes had he allowed himself to be sweet-talked by Sabrina into getting involved in all this? He should have known it would never be anything other than a cliquish drag. Hell, the only ones enjoying themselves were that bunch of worthies at the bar. Yeah, but when did you ever see unhappy herons in a trout farm? One thing that did puzzle Jigger, though, was the fuss the worthies were making of old Archibald Gormlie-Crighton. They were treating him like a bosom pal — all laughs, back-slaps and handshakes. Yet those were the very men that the whole village knew had been taken to the cleaners by Archie during his bent poker game in the pub only a few nights before. Strange.

"What's the score here?" Jigger murmured to one of the wags. "How come there's all this buddy-buddy stuff with old Archie all of a sudden?"

The wag nodded in the direction of the door. "There's Hamish Glenkinchie comin' in now. Ask him. He'll give ye all the crack."

In a way, what Hamish divulged came as no real surprise. The worthies' miraculous mateyness towards Archie was all down to young Ludo. The bit of "family business" he'd cleared up at the Cuddy's Rest with his bingo money that afternoon had been the repayment of all Archie's misbegotten winnings, with clear instructions to Hamish to redistribute it to the appropriate losers without delay.

Well, he'd be buggered, Jigger said to himself, if that young Ludo wasn't turning out to be a right wily one after all! Even though he'd told Hamish to let the worthies believe that the repayment had come from Archie, Ludo was crafty enough to know that the truth would eventually out, and that he himself would become the true hero of the piece. *And*, in all probability, in good time for the forthcoming parliamentary by-election, at that!

Be that as it may, it was patently clear that Archie was more than willing to accept the immediate kudos for this unexpected gesture of penitent benevolence. He

233

was the one who was being treated like a lord now, and he was loving every minute of it.

Suddenly, a strange hush descended on the room. As one, everybody had stopped speaking, and all eyes were drawn towards the entrance, where two footmen were standing mincingly to attention and holding open the double doors with white-gloved hands. At some unseen signal, the piano player broke off from his funereal tinklings and cued his trio into a cod-burlesque version of "I Left My Heart In San Francisco". To Jigger's jazzy ears, this sounded about as hip as a rap version of the National Anthem.

He felt a dig in the ribs and glanced round to see Bertola, staring at the doorway, his eyes popping like bloodshot ping-pong balls, his jaw level with his collar bone.

"Jesus wept, man," he drooled, "check the hooters on *that*!"

The centre of attraction was, as Jigger had anticipated from the stage-managed build-up, Sabrina Ng. She was making the grand entrance in a black Lurex sheath, which, if any tighter, would have called for her own skin to be worn on the outside. As it happened, a lot of her own skin already was, one leg being given total freedom of exposure with each step via a side slash that ran from hem to hip. And her hooters, as Bertola so poetically referred to them, were bobbing about like two blancmanges to the distress of a ring-pull zipper that appeared to be heading for refuge somewhere in the region of her navel.

234

Sabrina chasséd in time to the music, bumping and grinding to the beat, and kicking a polar bear rug contemptuously in its gold teeth as she slunk relentlessly across the floor. She was like a doe-eyed panther, slowly stalking, closing ruthlessly on her prey.

"So, Jigger," she purred in her quarry's face, "what *is* worn under the true Scotsman's kilt, as the old question goes?"

Jigger arched his eyebrows and held onto his sporran. "As the old answer goes," he Conneried, "there's nothing worn under *this* Scotsman's kilt. On the contrary, madam, everything is in mint condition and, although I say it myself, in *perfect* working order."

Sabrina gave him the slow once-over, then whispered in a voice of shameless seduction, "It had better be, honey. Oo-ooh, but it had better be . . ."

Painfully aware that all eyes, including some of the most mischievous that ever God gave sight to, were now focused squarely on them, Jigger took a deep breath, a tactful step backwards, jerked his head in the direction of the wall painting and said by way of diversion, "Tidy Muriel. Nice likeness an' all."

When this failed to halt Sabrina's advance, he ventured, "Why all the "I Left My Heart in San Francisco" bit? I mean, what was all *that* about?"

"'Frisco's my favourite city, that's all, so I kinda think of that song as my theme tune. Hmm, of all the places in the world we have houses, Frisco has gotta be the place that I call home."

"Funny, I had you tagged as the "I Love Paris In The Springtime" type."

"Paris?" Sabrina shook her head. "Strictly passé, honey — ever since they opened that Channel Tunnel. Fulla goddam Brit day-trippers now."

"So, what about your house there?"

"A house in *Paris*? You gotta be kidding me! Milan, Geneva, New York, sure. But Paris?" She shook her head again. "Uh-uh, not my kinda town, baby."

Having recovered from their initial stupefaction at the entrance of Sabrina, and their ensuing mass nosiness having subsided, the guests had now reverted to their clannish mumblings. The only glances in Sabrina's direction now were cast by covertly lecherous husbands and their jealously scandalized wives. For their own conflicting reasons, they seemed quite incapable of keeping their eyes off this extraordinary creature for more than a minute or two at a stretch.

"On the subject of music," Jigger said, "no offence, but where the hell did you get that trio? Rent-a-zombie?"

The trio, like the five footmen, replied Sabrina with a blasé batting of eyelashes, had been hired by her husband from some London agency or other.

Jigger couldn't resist making a sardonic dig. "And this is their night off on a nationwide tour of gay wakes, is it? Your old man got a bargain deal for them to turn up at this bash, did he?"

Sabrina heaved the enticing curves of her bare shoulders into a disinterested shrug. Babu had had them flown up from London specially for her party, she said. That was all she knew. Apart from the fact that the musicians were minge-cringingly crap, of course.

Although he could only take Sabrina's word for the accuracy of her adjective modifier, Jigger had to agree wholeheartedly that the musicians were, indeed, crap. Painfully so. And a quick burst of mental arithmetic brought him to the conclusion — even more painfully — that the air fares alone for that lot of fakes added up to about double the fee he would have charged for his own band to do the gig. And they would have had the joint jumping in one minute flat! He told Sabrina so in no uncertain terms.

Well, she retaliated, why hadn't he suggested his own outfit when he was helping her with the invites, for Chrisakes? How was she supposed to know he had his own bleedin' band? And on the subject of invites, she went on — no offence, but where the hell had he found all these deadbeats? Rent-a-corpse? Take a look! They were nothing but a collection of Palookaville hicks and boring mortgage monkeys. She'd asked for fun people, Goddammit!

Gripping his broad kilt belt with both thumbs, Jigger set about informing her — in even less uncertain terms — that most of these local people, these "hicks", were capable of having more down-to-earth fun in one night at a barn dance than she'd probably had in the whole of her flash, mink-coated life. What's more, although he didn't know the track record of any of the incomers in the jollity stakes, this party would have been an ideal chance for them to show what they were worth. It *would* have been, that is, if Sabrina and her mega-rich husband had paid more attention to laying on the simple basics of a good ceilidh instead of trying to

237

impress — unsuccessfully as it had turned out — the hicks and mortgage monkeys with an imported trio of survivors from the golden age of Harrods tea dances, and those resting luvvies dressed up like poncy pantomime transvestites. Maybe, he pointedly suggested, her heart wasn't the only thing she'd left in San Francisco!

The look on Sabrina's face, Jigger figured, would have curdled cream. She was livid. Cracks were beginning to show in her veneer, and he guessed, from her unexpected use of the word *bleedin'* a moment ago, that the lingo about to be released from between those narrowed, snarling lips would owe more to London's Isle of Dogs than New York's island of Manhattan. He wasn't wrong.

"'Ere! Ooja fink ye're talkin' to? Ooja fink ye're callin' brainless, 'aggis? Bleedin' sauce!"

The sophisticated, mid-Atlantic drawl had made a rapid and raucous diversion eastwards.

Jigger was sorely tempted to get a dig in that he wasn't sure who he was talking to — Mrs Ng, Madame Chan or any of several other aliases that he suspected she and her husband used, but he decided to bite his lip . . . for the present. Given enough rope, the Ngs would surely trip over it, or perhaps even hang themselves.

"I'm sorry, Sabrina," Jigger lied with an 007 lisp, giving her the full licensed-to-kiss pout. He moved closer, his eyes half-closed beneath suggestively-raised brows, his hand slipping audaciously around her waist, the cool, silky pelt of his sealskin sporran touching the warm, exposed flesh of her thigh. He felt her body shudder — ever so slightly. She wasn't in the Tabetha Spriggs class of knee-tremblers yet, but, Jigger was pleased to note, his effect on her was a marked improvement on their last liaison all the same. The gear must have done it. Sabrina was obviously a kilt freak. He gazed deeply into the inviting pools of her eyes. "Please forgive my bluntness . . . uhm, Sabrina." he crooned. "Hmm?"

He felt a hand at the small of his back, eager fingers exploring the deep folds of his kilt, working their way slowly downwards, their touch growing bolder, their movement more intense as they reached the firm roundness of his buttocks.

"Turned on by tartan-draped buns, are you?" he asked Sabrina with a knowing, lopsided smile, his voice growing hoarse. His brain was fighting to control his rising pulse rate, but the battle was being lost.

The confused look in Sabrina's eyes belied the confident work that her hand was busy with. Jigger felt the cheeks of his bum tighten involuntarily as the fondling fingers ventured ever farther into the pleats of his kilt.

Perhaps it was the surging sound of the blood pumping in his ears, or perhaps it was the intoxicating spell that this fascinating witch was casting upon his senses that made Jigger unaware of the startled buzz that had run through the room, causing heads to turn, eyes to gawp, voices to drop to tattling whispers. All that existed for him was the feel of Sabrina's skilful fingers, insolently exploring, illicitly creeping their mind-blowing way like an erotic tarantula.

Then, as if struck by some invisible force, Sabrina suddenly stood back — one step, two steps, then a third. Yet, somehow, her tormenting hand remained, wandering and groping almost frantically now in Jigger's tartan-shrouded nether regions. My God! he screamed inwardly, how long was this woman's arm?

Without warning, the tarantula struck, snatching like a sneak thief in the night at Jigger's family jewels and, once located, squeezing them in an ever-tightening grip. He felt the blood drain from his face, tears welling in his eyes. His lust-lulled brain exploded back into action and set alarm bells ringing round his nervous system. Agony! Some sadistic perv was trying to wrench his Christmas crackers off, and he realised now that it couldn't be Sabrina. He immediately thought of that big Jessie of a doorman. No fury like a woofter scorned, or whatever the saying was. But, on taking a panic-stricken glance over his shoulder, he saw that the heavily made-up eyes that were glaring at him were not those of the peacock Pimpernel. No, they were the eyes of none other than his own dear wife Nessie. And well nettled they looked, too!

"Having a nice time, lover boy?" she asked, spitting acid with every syllable, but mercifully releasing her vice-like hold on her husband's palpitating privates. Having made her presence felt, she wasn't about to cut off her nose to spite her face, so to speak.

The stunned buzz that had permeated the gathering of guests on Nessie's arrival changed now to a ripple of congregated titters, interspersed with delighted asides of:

"You could see that coming!" and "Serves the randy bugger right!"

Jigger fought to regain his composure — never easy when you're standing like a half-shut knife with your knees bent and tears dripping down your jabot.

"Honest, Nessie," he pleaded while leading her with decidedly short steps to a quiet corner of the room, "it wasn't what it seemed, all that phoney canoodling with Sabrina. It was all part of the master plan. Just a bit of a con. Just setting snares, if you see what I'm saying."

"Mm-hmm," hummed Nessie, with an I'll-believe-you-though-thousands-wouldn't twist to her mouth. "But just be careful you don't get caught in one of your own snares, if you see what *I'm* saying."

Jigger discreetly fanned his lap with his sporran. "I see what you're saying, Nessie," he grimaced, his teeth still tightly clenched. "Oh aye, I see what you're saying, all right."

As he blinked the last tears of pain from his eyes, Jigger suddenly found himself looking at a Nessie he had never seen before. Only now did it dawn on him why she'd been keen for him to come to the party ahead of her. Only now could he see why Sabrina Ng had slunk off like a submissive vixen when confronted by Nessie just a moment ago. And only then would he have realised, if he had not been otherwise engaged at the time, why Nessie's arrival in the room had created such a stir. She looked absolutely ravishing!

Not since he first set eyes on her in that most unlikely setting of the pits at the Edinburgh Speedway more than twenty years before had Jigger been so stunned by Nessie's dazzling looks.

"But — but you're beautiful," he stuttered. He feasted his eyes on her every detail, from the luxuriant, copper sheen of her hair to the teasing glimpse of varnished toenails peeping from her little gilt mules.

Nessie flicked a glorious billow of hair from her shoulder with an almost haughty air of self-confidence that fairly set Jigger back on his heels. "Of course I am," she stated matter-of-factly.

"B — but your dress is so — so glamorous, so — so — ehm —"

"Sexy?"

"Well, yes. That's to say — I mean, I don't know if you should be out in such a . . ."

"It's sexy *and* classy, dear." Nessie smoothed the shiny satin over her hips in a way that rang a vague bell in Jigger's memory. "That's what's known as style — a commodity your friend Sabrina isn't too familiar with, by the looks of things."

Jigger was all of a fluster. "But why? What I mean is where? That is, what I'm saying is, I've never seen you in —"

"Yes you have. Yesterday. I tried it on in front of you in the bedroom after your set-to with Babu Ng. I asked you whether you preferred this one or the flared one, remember?"

"No — ehm, maybe. I can't exactly —"

"Anyway, I decided to wear this one. The slinky number. More suitable for the occasion, I thought."

Jigger smirked knowingly. "Battledress, in other words."

"That depends. But I'll tell you this for nothing, I took a good gander at the lovely Sabrina parading through the village in her leopard-skin cat-suit and black thigh boots when I was down there on Granny's moped yesterday, and I decided there and then that I wouldn't be coming here unprepared tonight."

"So, *that's* why you nipped off to Jenners' sale so smartly, eh?"

"You got it. And if Sabrina's looking for competition, *she's* got it too!"

"And that goes for me, as well!"

This latter declaration was resolutely uttered by a young woman, a gorgeous young woman, who had been standing near Nessie during the foregoing contretemps, but of whose presence Jigger had only been marginally aware, so pressing had been the nature of his immediate undertakings. It now took him but an instant to survey and evaluate the heavenly quality, the sheer knock-'em-dead good looks of this nubile goddess. She was a right wee stotter! It then took him but a skipped heartbeat to realise who this divine creature was. It was his own daughter — young Maggie!

Jigger was dumbstruck. Her hair had been released from the severity of its French-roll imprisonment and was celebrating its freedom in luxuriant cascades of bouncing auburn. Softly framed by those magnificent tresses, her face seemed suddenly to have exchanged its former girlish prettiness for the full-blossomed beauty of womanhood. Gone were the huge tinted spectacles that she had almost sinfully worn to conceal the allure of her emerald green eyes, shining now in a glow that was a mixture of gritty defiance and sophisticated, feminine poise. Gone, too, were the prudish, schoolmarmish clothes. All Maggie's previously-hidden assets were displayed now through the cling-wrapping of a mini-length, scarlet boob tube.

Jigger had anticipated, had hoped even, that dropping the tactical incendiary bomb of Lord Ludovic's "frump" remark might have fired her into swapping her frigid librarian's image for something a bit more tepid. But the resultant transformation had turned out to be spontaneously combustible. It would take the entire resources of the Horseburghshire Fire Brigade to douse the flames that Maggie's reformed image would be likely to kindle in the loins of the local blades.

That, at least, was Jigger's considered opinion, and verification of its accuracy was instantly to hand in the drooling form of young Ludovic Gormlie-Crighton.

"Oh yay! Oh yay!" he ejaculated, a polite bow serving as ideal cover for the meandering of his eyes over Maggie's mesmerising hills and glens. "From whence cometh this daughter of Aphrodite?" He nudged Jigger with his elbow. "Come on, my old mate — introductions, s'il vous plaît!"

Maggie cast a sideways glance at her suitor's outstretched hand in a way that suggested its pores were exuding the whiff of a fresh dog turd. "Bog off, Ludo!" she snapped.

"Cripes!" gasped his Lordship, recognising those same chastening tones that had so recently thwarted his budding literary aspirations. "It's young Miss McCloud, the librarian, right? Wow! One would never have recog —"

"If one is a Pekingese," Maggie interrupted, "why try to look like a greyhound? — as Edith Sitwell might have said under similar circumstances!"

"Greyhound? Oh yah — greyhound, right," Ludo bumbled, clueless.

"Try not to overtax your brain, Ludo, but for greyhound read frump, OK? And don't ever forget, frump or greyhound, I'm way too fast for you."

Ludo made a feeble attempt at an apology, but failed.

"And what's more," Maggie barked from atop her high horse, "for a Pekingese, I've got a bite like a bloody Rottweiller!"

Ludo was demolished, a crumpled heap of embarrassment, floundering hopelessly in the morass of Maggie's metaphors.

Any twinges of pity that Jigger might have felt for Ludo's public humiliation were amply ameliorated, however, by Maggie's display of dogged self-assurance. He wasn't too sure what all that greyhound, Pekingese and Rottweiller doggerel had been about either, but one thing *was* for sure — Maggie could be a right wee terrier when it suited her. She'd be all right — boob tube an' all!

The uncomfortable conversational hiatus in which the little group now found itself was mercifully penetrated by an outburst of good-natured hollering and hand-clapping from the direction of the main entrance. Jigger could hardly believe his eyes. For there, standing in the threshold at little more than waist height to most of her applauding audience, was Granny. Her head was encased in a Greta Garbo cloche circa 1925, her aged body draped in an ostrich-feathered flapper dress that ended in a tasselled fringe just above the knee. There, support hose met flannel bloomers. Her feet had been coaxed into a pair of button-down evening pumps that hadn't enjoyed a shuffle over a dance floor since the halcyon days of the Charleston.

In a flurry of feather boas and mothball fumes, she stepped as jauntily as her rheumatism would permit into the bosom of her astounded family. "Ah came on ma moped," she casually announced.

"But you were adamant you weren't coming," Nessie said, doing her best to suppress a giggle as she viewed this diminutive throwback to the Roaring Twenties.

"Aye," Granny agreed, "but a lassie's surely entitled to change her mind, is she no? So, after I saw you two goin' out all tarted up like a dog's breakfast, I decided I was comin', too. I just thought to maself, what's the point in sittin' mumpin' in front o' that old range with nothin' but that manky mutt Bert for company? Ye've hid yer candle under a bushel for too long, says I to me, so here I am!"

"That's the spirit, Gran!" Maggie laughed. She gave the old woman a hug. "'Tis better to be in good company than alone, as George Washington might have said under similar circumstances. United we stand!"

Jigger stroked his chin uneasily. Any normal man would have been delighted to be seen in the company of three generations of such breathtaking women (literally breathtaking, in Granny's case). But these were not *normal* women. They were McCloud women, and Jigger felt a headache coming on.

The flutter of excitement caused by Granny's entrance had now subsided, and an ominous quiet filled the room once more, broken only by the occasional crude guffaw from the seriously-imbibing brigade over at the bar. This party was on the skids, Jigger decided, and it was about time something was done about it.

"Where's Bertola?" he asked Nessie.

"Over there, talking to young Davie."

"OK, you keep the wolves from Maggie's door — *and* your own — for half an hour or so. I've got things to do."

"You're jivin' my socks off, man!" wailed an incredulous Bertola. As was his wont, he leaned back to pull a better focus on Jigger's face. "Like, we haven't got enough musos here to shanghai this gig."

"No sweat. We only need a rhythm section and me on the fiddle out front. So, it's you on bass, Davie here on drums —"

Bertola cut him off in mid-team-selection. "But no piano player, pops. That's the drag." A panic-making thought then staggered into his sherry-and-dope-befuddled mind. He took a sideways glance at the Richard Clayderman version of Dracula tinkling away in the Busby Berkeley area. "Hey, cool it, daddy," he said to Jigger. "Don't even *think* about it. We can't play with that old Rubick Cube on the keys. He's just *too* square, man!"

Jigger gave him a calming pat on the arm. "Don't blow a gasket, Bertola. Leave the pianist problem to me. Just you go and tell the trio to take a break in five minutes." He turned to Davie. "And you go and fetch my fiddle out of the pick-up. This party needs a good boot up the backside, so let's give it one!"

Jigger didn't need to ask his chosen stand-in pianist twice.

"Of course I can still busk with the best of 'em! Your grandfather always said I was the best damned piany player the Cuddyford Cornkisters ever had." Granny was confidence personified. "Aye, and piany-playin's like fallin' off a bike — once learned, never forgotten." She took Jigger's arm. "Just accompany me to those ivories, sonny!"

And so it was, despite undisguised looks of misgiving from Bertola, that Jigger called out to his little pick-up group, once assembled within and around the giant alabaster shell:

"OK! Four bars drums into *Sweet Georgia Brown*! A-one, two, a-one, two, three, four!"

Young Davie hurled himself into a drum break that could have wakened the dead, then, with a keyboard-crunching glissando from Granny, the makeshift combo was up and swinging.

Before even one chorus was complete, even the doubting Bertola had been converted, leaning his commandeered bull fiddle toward the piano and shouting phrases of musical acclaim to Granny like:

"Crazy left hand, man! Yeah, sock it to 'em, digits!"

Granny merely smiled modestly up at him and punished the keys with another merciless flourish. "This young bass-playin' Muppet," she muttered smugly to herself, "ain't heard nothin' yet!"

And neither had the old manse. Nor, it appeared, had many of the invited guests. Natives and settlers alike quickly shed their inhibitions and were on the floor bopping and jiving away merrily — though still, it has to be said, in strictly tribal pairings. Anyway, Jigger concluded, it was a start. The party was coming alive at last, but no thanks to the host or hostess.

In fact, he couldn't help but notice as he weaved some hot improvisations on his fiddle strings that Sabrina had now become decidedly conspicuous by her absence. Surely the brief confrontation with Nessie hadn't frightened her off completely. She was too much of a hard nut for that. No, it was much more likely that she was merely saving her reappearance for the most favourable moment. Jigger quaked at the prospect.

Of more immediate concern, however, was the fact that Sabrina's husband had zeroed in on the corner which Nessie and Maggie were occupying. It was obvious that Ng was subjecting them both to what Jigger fancied would be a right load of lecherous baloney. His dusky hands were sculpting the air expressively, reminding Jigger of a slave-trader spinning women an ensnaring yarn in some sweaty North African souk.

Jigger and Bertola looked at each other, then at Babu Ng, then at each other once again. No words were necessary. They both knew what they were witnessing. It was a re-enactment of a drama they'd both seen many times before. It was a scene straight out of *The Blues Brothers* movie; that one where John Belushi barges into the restaurant and confronts the bewildered family man at his table. "How much for your women?" Belushi says blatantly. "I want to buy your women! How much for the little girl?"

Granny had noticed these unsavoury goings-on in the corner as well. She shot Jigger a warning glance.

Jigger kept fiddling like fury. He felt a bit like Nero, but what else could he do? He had hijacked the music-making for the most community-minded of reasons after all, so Nessie and Maggie would just have to man their own fire hoses for a while.

The audience's response at the end of the first number was little short of rapturous. Jigger deftly seized upon their euphoric mood to inveigle them into a wee dance that, like it or not, would have them all changing partners every so often. If ever there was a social equivalent of an electric food processor, it was the good old *Dashing White Sergeant*, and even the most obstinate of Cuddyford's apartheid disciples proved to be defenceless against it. Perhaps the more pernickety doyens of the Royal Scottish Country Dance Society would have looked down their prim noses at the unorthodox steps and patterns being practiced by this unlikely mix of participants. But so what? Their adlib antics were a sight for Jigger's sore eyes.

Who, before this, would have contemplated the sight of starchy Commander Plimsoll-Pompey "birling" Camshaft McClung's burly wife like a top; or of mousey little Tabetha Spriggs being "wheeched" from one strapping tractorman's crooked arm to another's; or of stuck-up Mrs Littleton-Nimby's staunchly middle-class, whale-boned bosoms shuttling up and down like common knockers as she set to her enthralled partner, the intellectually-challenged wee Eck "Napoleon" McClarty?

The Cuddyford social barriers were crumbling like the Berlin Wall. But, glad as Jigger was of that, he was less than pleased to note that Nessie and Maggie hadn't managed to escape into the comparative safety of this merry mayhem. They were still cornered by Babu Ng, who was now being provided with ogling back-up from the persistent Ludo. Talk about flies round a midden, thought Jigger!

To give everyone, not least himself, a well-deserved breather, Jigger announced a slow one for the next dance. And while not every local plucked up the courage to couple with an incomer, the number of mixed pairings was a marked improvement on what had previously seemed a compulsory form of self-imposed segregation. Even among those choosing to sit this one out, there were isolated pockets of conversational intercourse being established between the two factions. If music be the food of integration . . .

Jigger played on.

One of the peculiarities of his playing style was a tendency to close his eyes for lengthy periods during slow pieces, caught up, as he often became, in the mood of the music. Although he'd resolved to keep his eyes wide open in this instance, the dreamy effect of the melody eventually lulled his eyelids shut as usual. He opened them with a start, though, when Bertola elbowed him in the back and nodded, frowning, towards the far side of the swimming pool. There, in the broken shadows of the potted palms, was the unmistakably-sinister silhouette of Babu Ng. He was dancing with Nessie! *And*, Jigger reckoned, a bit too bloody smoochified-like at that! A quick scan round the room revealed that at least Maggie had escaped the attentions of Ludo. She was indulging herself in a bit of slow-tempo heart-breaking at the expense of a blushing young sheep farmer, whose plodding footwork appeared more suited to the heather hill than the dance floor.

Granny, meanwhile, had become quite oblivious to all such goings-on, totally lost, as she now was, in her rediscovered love affair with the piano. Tricky arpeggios which, when attempted at the start of this romantic medley, had sounded not unlike someone rolling an orange up and down the keys, were now falling effortlessly from her fingertips. Sure enough, piany-playin' was just like fallin' off a bike. But the gentle reverie that had transported her back to village hall dances of yore, when she would play the night away with the sweet strains of her Tam's fiddle singing in her ears, was abruptly disturbed by a shouted command from Jigger.

"Right!" he yelled to his musicians. "Cut it at the end of this chorus!"

"Just when I was startin' to enjoy maself, too," Granny grumbled, ending the tune with a grandiose, two-handed sweep up the keyboard, and only just managing to apply the brakes before she toppled sideways off the piano stool.

"Hey, play it cool, man," Bertola advised her with a lugubrious shake of his head. "At your age, that kinda flash jazz could prove fatal!"

"Away an' air yer G-string!" Granny growled at him. "And never mind yer fatal stuff. I'm only just comin' alive!"

"OK," said Jigger, wasting no time, "we'll hit them with that Charlie Daniels number, *The Devil Went Down To Georgia*. You take the vocals, Bertola. All set?"

"But, Dad," Davie objected, "nobody can dance to *that*. It's far too fast."

"Good for you, son. You've read my thoughts precisely." Jigger then asked Granny, "Think you can keep up with us on this one?"

"Keep up? Just you rosin yer bow, laddie, and stand back from the piany if ye don't want yer kilt to catch fire!"

253

Jigger took her at her word and counted the band in at an even quicker tempo than usual. From the first frantic torrent of notes from his fiddle, a crowd began to gather below the marble-balustraded dais that was serving as the bandstand. Jigger was right in the groove, sawing away like fury at the strings, the forefinger of his left hand pointing skyward as stiff as a poker, while its neighbours raced over the fingerboard like a three-legged spider with St Vitus' Dance.

Granny gave a chuckle of delight, her old hands pounding away on the keys in a blur of knobbly knuckles. The heat of the rhythm seemed to lend temporary flexibility to her rheumatic joints, even spurring her feet into a time-keeping stomp that caused the tasselled hem of her flapper dress to ride upwards and reveal an unseemly expanse of pink bloomers. But Granny couldn't have cared less. This session was taking her right back to that magic night when four-year-old Jigger made his sensational debut with old Tam's band. The years were rolling away, Granny was having a ball, and if anybody wanted to have a peep at her breeks in the meantime, they were more than welcome.

Just at that climactic point in the tune, where the arrangement called for him to thrash the strings with his bow using the fingerboard as a rack on which to rend tortured wails and screeches from his fiddle as though it were the Devil incarnate playing, Jigger threw himself like a whirling dervish into one of his famous jigs. The crowd roared their approval. This was what those who knew him had been waiting for, and it was something that those who didn't know him would be unlikely to forget.

He'd performed this wild dance of his a thousand times before, but there was something different, something more exhilarating, more abandoned about it tonight. He could feel it. It seemed like Satan himself had possessed his prancing feet, had injected his fingers and elbow with the fires of hell. And right there inside the old manse of all places an' all!

With eyes closed, Jigger redoubled the ferocity of his playing, spurred on by the driving rhythm of Davie's drums. The thundering beat penetrated the very marrow of his bones as chorus followed torrid chorus. Then, little by little, he became conscious of the crowd's chants increasing in volume, their excitement rising towards fever pitch. He half opened his eyes and, through the misty haze, could just make out the curvaceous shape of a woman dancing. She was twisting and turning, bending and stretching her bared limbs, arching her back, tossing her shiny black mane as she cut a sensuous swathe through the audience. She snaked her way Salome-style towards Jigger, her dark eyes burning his.

Sabrina was back!

Thunderstruck, Jigger stopped playing. Next, Bertola dropped out, then Granny. All that remained was the pulsating beat of the drums, vibrating through the steamy air like jungle tom-toms, reaching out to Sabrina and goading her into ever more sensuous gyrations of her body.

"I don't know what this chick's on, man," a goggle-eyed Bertola yelled at Jigger through the din, "but whatever it is, I could do with a piece!"

What Jigger saw next made him wish that this was all a bad dream, that a devouring hole would open up beneath his feet, or, better still, that he had never been born. For there, emerging from the leafy concealment of a clump of banana plants away to his left, were his wife and daughter, still fully clothed (if that was a reasonable description of what Jigger judged to be their somewhat risqué party attire), but doing a fair simulation of the Dance of the Seven Veils, nonetheless. They flaunted their natural attributes slinkily over the floor, until they caught up with Sabrina and joined her in a free-for-all belly dance slap in front of the band.

Jigger was gutted. He was all for competition, right enough, but this was taking female rivalry a bit *too* far. What would people think? My God, and he'd reckoned Nessie's Hogmanay motorbike wheelie up the High Street in her skirt had been the height of mortification! He fired an advice-seeking glance in Granny's direction, but all he got in return was a flat look that said, "Your problem, laddie!"

The drums played on, and the men in the crowd cheered, while scandalised women gaped slack-jawed at the three objects of their husbands' leering.

Instinct, more than inspiration, lifted the fiddle back under Jigger's chin. Necessity, more than ingenuity, laid his trembling bow on the strings, which, as if taking on a life of their own, instantly emitted a strident trill. This triggered another nailbusting glissando from Granny's piano, automatically propelling the band into a storming reprise of *The Devil Went Down To Georgia*.

A great roar went up, and the three war-dancing women wiggled and strutted their stuff with renewed zip. Their antics suggested to Granny that somebody must have surreptitiously slipped a handful of itchy barley awns down their knickers in the ladies' loo.

Jigger had no choice but to play on, transfixed and red-faced. Bertola's half-spoken vocals droned on narcotically, while the sound of his leader's fiddling filled the air. And whether Jigger liked it or not, his wild musical outpourings were soon provoking Nessie, Maggie and Sabrina into even more daring contortions. Then, for no apparent reason and followed by the milling crowd, they began to slink and slither off poolwards, Nessie and Maggie circling their adversary like a pair of wildcats stalking a distinctly uncowed mouse.

Suddenly, though, just as the final cadenza of notes poured from Jigger's fiddle, a scream and a loud splash reverberated round the conservatory. An outburst of laughter and applause rose from the poolside scrummage, which then parted to reveal the solitary figures of Nessie and Maggie. They were standing side-by-side, grinning triumphantly and dusting off their hands.

Granny winked at Jigger. "Takes the McCloud women," she smirked. "Aye, that'll cool the hotarsed bitch down a bit!"

CHAPTER
TWELVE

A Case of Hidden Identities

The Cuddyford Community Association's letter was delivered to Craigcuddy Castle at eight o'clock in the morning, and by three minutes past eight the Duke was on the phone to Jigger.

Who the Dickens did this Plimsoll-Pompey fellow think he was? That was what the Duke wanted to know. "Damned impertinence," he fumed, "— demandin' this, objectin' to that! None of his damned business what happens to Craigcuddy Estate! Damned seafarin' types — no damned respect for the landsman! Typical! He should be rowed out to the middle of the Forrit Firth and scuttled, that's what!"

Jigger had never known the old boy get so worked up. "Hold your horses, Duke," he said when he finally managed to get a word in. "You're getting way ahead of yourself there. Just calm down. I'll be right over, OK?"

After listening to the brief low-down on the proceedings of the Community Association meeting that Nessie had given him, Jigger would have anticipated a resentful reaction from the Duke when the Commander put his presumptuous proposals to him, but this was something else! When Jigger pulled up at the castle, Old Horace was already prancing up and down outside, his face like a beetroot, the offending letter brandished aloft like Exhibit "A" at a murder trial.

"Take a look at that, m'boy, and tell me if it isn't the most outrageous piece of impudence you've ever set eyes upon. Bad enough havin' that Murphy fellow's pigeons and his cronies' hounds let loose about the place, but *this*? Over my dead body, I tell you!"

Jigger let him rant on while he read the letter. By the look of the veins standing out on the old bloke's forehead, it would do him some good to let off a bit of steam, anyway.

"If you want my opinion, Duke," he announced at length, "this is good news. Just what we've been waiting for."

He thought old Horace really *was* going to burst a blood vessel now.

"No, just think about it for a minute," he said while the Duke was still attempting to get the first tongue-tied word of objection out. "The only way you're going to be able to hold onto the estate is by generating income, and what old Popeye's suggesting here fits in quite nicely with what I've had in mind all along. Another piece of the jigsaw, sort o' style."

The Duke was at a loss for words.

If the people the Commander purported to represent wanted more access to the Craigcuddy lands, then they should be given it, Jigger said — but on the Duke's terms *and* at a price. Access was one thing, but *free* access? No chance. There were plenty of things that could be organised on the estate that people would pay sweetly to get in on. To the Duke's further mystification, Jigger added that even one of Babu Ng's alleged plans was worth nicking. A tidy little earner it would be, too. Golf courses usually were, if they were in the right place, and the Cuddyford area was screaming out for one. Even the financing of schemes like that wouldn't necessarily be an insurmountable problem, Jigger suggested, what with diversification grants and advance membership fees and everything. No need to use up any of the good agricultural land on the Home Farm, either. The parklands around the castle were more than big enough, and they didn't bring in a penny at present in any case.

The Duke was still patently confused, but, Jigger noticed, a glimmer of interest *was* beginning to twinkle in his eyes.

"Look at it this way," said Jigger. "At the moment, you keep all the sporting amenities on Craigcuddy to yourself. And, with all due respect to the shooting and fishing abilities of the few old aristo chums you invite to join you from time to time, most of the pheasants and trout on this place die of old age. Apart from the ones the poachers swipe, of course."

Jigger could see that old Horace was winding himself up for an umbrage outburst after that comment, so he briskly proceeded . . .

"Take Italians, for example. They're so shotgun-happy they say they even blast butterflies out of the sky in their own country. Nothing else left to shoot. They'd pay a fortune to come on shooting parties over a spread like this. Americans an' all. Yeah, all it takes is a bit of organisation. Travel arrangements, accommodation, food — there's bags o' money to be made outa all o' that." The interested glimmer was glinting in the Duke's eyes again, so Jigger moved up a gear. "Hey," he said, with what he hoped would be infectious enthusiasm, "if you wanted to, you could even join in the action with the customers yourself. You know, shoot along with the Duke of Gormlie — that kind of thing? Tidy gimmick, and more money in the pocket for you."

The Duke was beginning to look quite groggy under this barrage of ideas, so Jigger thought he'd hit him with the knock-out punch while he had him on the ropes.

There was now the very real prospect, he disclosed, of a small but highly exclusive housing estate (something the Duke had been unsuccessfully angling after for ages) being built on Craigcuddy land — on the outskirts of the village, but down in the little valley behind the Dower House, where it wouldn't be seen from the outside. Not even the not-in-my-back-yard settlers could seriously object to that. It was still all very hush-hush, of course, and although young Ludo himself didn't know about it yet, it was all tied in with his new political relationship with Mick Murphy. Mick, Jigger explained, was both chairman of the County Council planning committee and some sort of cousin of the potential developer, who was based over in the west of the country. "A slightly knocked-down price for the land would be part of the deal, of course," he said, giving the Duke a conspiratorial wink. "The unofficial price of obtaining planning permission, you might say."

It all sounded a mite corrupt to him, the Duke muttered after a moment or two of scowling contemplation. "It all seems a bit dodgy, m'boy, and somethin' I'd rather not get involved in, thank you very much. And anyway, I've always been told by those socialist chappies on the Council that they're agin luxury private housing and that sort of thing."

"Not any more," Jigger was quick to point out. "All part of the modern socialist doctrine, you see. It's still all that old redistribution-of-wealth stuff, like, but with an up-to-date slant, if you see what I'm saying."

The Duke snorted one of his assured dukely snorts and said that he didn't understand what the blazes Jigger was talkin' about.

Jigger heaved a long-suffering sigh. "OK, let me put it this way, Duke. Mick Murphy and his comrades on the Horseburghshire Council have a policy of big civic spending in the areas they represent — building new swimming pools, community centres, widening pavements for the pedestrians, narrowing the roads for the car-owners, that sort of thing. That's how they get their votes. Trouble is, a lot of the voters in those places aren't too keen on paying their Council Tax, and the money has to come from somewhere. So, every now and then the Council encourage a few select, private housing developments in pretty locations like Cuddyford, with every executive villa in a high Council Tax band and every purchaser the type who'll cough up faithfully to the Council whenever the tax is due. Simple — the

262

redistribution of wealth. And if Mick can redistribute a bit of it in his own direction while he's at it . . ."

He certainly didn't take to the sound of that, grunted the Duke. All much too money-grabbing for his liking. And what's more, he firmly added, he didn't like the idea of being offered knock-down prices for his land either. Damned cheek!

"And how much does that wee valley earn for you just now?" Jigger asked outright. "A few hundred pounds a year in rent for sheep grazing because it's too steep to cultivate, correct?"

The Duke nodded confidently, which just went to show how much he knew, for it was Jigger himself who had the grazing let and he hadn't paid a penny for it in years. Anyway, that was by the way. More importantly, it now looked as if a bigger carrot would have to be dangled in front of the Duke if he was to come around to Jigger's way of thinking about this housing development caper.

"Mind you," he said, "you *could* stick out for a higher selling price for the land from another builder. I'll grant you that." He cocked his head inquisitively. "But then, another builder wouldn't get planning permission, would he?"

A vacant stare was the Duke's reply.

The moment was clearly right for Jigger's *coup de grâce*. "So," he said, "what if I were to tell you that even this slightly knocked-down price from Mick's cousin would bring you in the best part of five million quid?"

The Duke wore a stunned expression. He also wore a deerstalker hat, which he now removed in order to scratch his puzzled head.

"Five mil — mil — mil —"

"Million!" Jigger stated emphatically, by way of the usual stylus-nudging. "Now then," he said, rubbing his hands together, "that should keep the bank happy 'til we get the other earners going. Yeah, and with Ludo soon to be off your back, your troubles would appear to be over, wouldn't they?"

Jigger was starting to feel well pleased with himself — and justifiably so an' all, he reckoned. My God, it had taken every last scrap of his wheeling-and-dealing know-how to get this one sorted out, and there had been a few times when even he thought he might not be able to get all the pieces to fit. But they had in the end, and things were beginning to look bloody tidy. And they were going to get even tidier, because part of this executive housing lark involved a bit of the wee valley that was on Jigger's land, and that would put a nice earner his way when everything clicked. He'd be keeping well shtum about that in the meantime, of course. No point in counting chickens and all that stuff. He treated himself to a self-satisfied smile all the same. For some reason that he just could *not* comprehend, though, the old Duke didn't appear to be sharing his feelings of good cheer.

"Ever read a book called *Legends of Lowland Scottish Castles*?" Jigger asked chirpily.

The Duke indicated glumly that he had not.

"No? Well, there's a bit in it that tells you all about a fair they used to hold every May in the olden days here at Craigcuddy Castle. All the village folk would turn up and get stuck in for a right good time, it says. All sorts o' fun and games — feasting, music, dancing, everything like that. Could be a good idea to revive it, eh? Do the whole bit — fairground attractions, marching bands, sports competitions, horse races. Could even tie it in with that Hunt Ball of yours and charge everybody plenty. People would come from all over." Jigger's persuasion engine was now in overdrive. "Just think," he grinned, "at a fiver a time, the car park tickets alone would bring in a bundle!"

But even this jubilant prospect failed to lift the look of gloom from the Duke's face. "It's no good, m'boy," he mumbled into his chest. "I'm truly sorry to have put you to so much trouble in vain, but there is nothing else for it. I shall still have to sell up — lock, stock and barrel." He raised his head and looked at Jigger through doleful eyes. "Cousin Archie, you see, will not be denied."

Jigger could scarcely believe his ears. "Stuff Archie!" he retorted. "Once we get everything going, you can pay him off by instalments. He surely can't complain about that, for heaven's sake!"

Looking forlornly at Plimsoll-Pompey's folded letter, the Duke shook his head with an air of total despondency. "Why did I bother to become so infuriated by this?" he muttered. He thought for a moment, then said, "Just because Craigcuddy is in my bones — that's why, I suppose. And although I can hardly bring myself to think about it, soon the castle and the estate and everything to do with them will be the concern of that Ng fellow, and no one else."

"But you're not making any sense!" Jigger exclaimed. "I've just handed you solutions to your problems on a plate, and you're turning me down!" He was beside himself with frustration. "What the hell's wrong with you, Duke?"

The Duke didn't reply. With one final look of helplessness at Jigger, he turned and trudged stoop-shouldered away.

Nessie and Granny sat silently at the breakfast table while Jigger poured out the astonishing account of his conversation with the Duke. He was fiddling nervously with a slice of toast, his customary morning fry-up lying cold and untouched in front of him.

"I mean, I just don't get it," he said. "It's perfectly obvious that the very idea of losing the estate is breaking the old boy's heart, yet he seems hell-bent on selling it. But *only* to Babu Ng, and all because old Archie says so. It's just weird." He stirred the umpteenth spoonful of sugar into his coffee. "I bust my gut figuring out a way to raise enough money to keep the place in his hands, and now what? I mean, it's going to knacker the whole MP stunt for Ludo as well, and there's a helluva lot riding on that for all of us, believe me. Mick Murphy will do his bloody nut, and I can't blame him." He shook his head. "God, what a damned mess!"

Nessie took Jigger's plate away and scraped the sausage, bacon and eggs into Bert's dish. "You know, when you mention Archie," she said pensively, while pouring Jigger a fresh coffee from the jug on the range, "it brings to mind something Babu Ng was bumming to me about at the party."

"Uh-huh?"

"He was only interested in blowing his own trumpet, of course, but there was *something* he said. What was it again?" She thought hard. "Ah, yes, it comes back to me now. The power of money, it was. Something along the lines of, if you can get a man in debt to you for enough money, your castles need no longer remain in the air. Something like that. Even a duke, he said, has no defence against the power of a wealthy creditor."

Jigger rested his head on his hand and thought for a bit. "The only thing wrong with all that," he eventually said, "is that *our* Duke isn't in debt to Babu Ng. To just about everybody else that you can imagine, maybe, but not to Ng."

Nessie sat back down at the table. "I know, but the odd thing was that he kept glancing over towards old Archie at the bar when he was saying these things."

"Could be that Archie's in debt to him all right," Jigger shrugged. "I certainly overheard them discussing the tail-end of some bit of business or other that same night." He scratched his head. "But Archie isn't a duke, so it still doesn't make any sense. Did Ng say anything else, by any chance?"

Nessie pursed her lips, thinking hard. "Nothing of much interest, as far as I can remember. No, I think he just thanked me for the dance and said I was a lady, that's all."

Jigger pulled a wry face. "Aye, and from what I could see of his dancing technique, the main reason he asked you up in the first place was to find out whether you were or not!"

Nessie let that one go without comment.

Granny, whose brows had been gathering into deep furrows of agitation during all of this, supped the dregs of tea from her saucer and growled, "Well, what that Ali Baboon man said makes sense to me." She rose from the table and shuffled over to the door. "For I told ye, didn't I, that Archie Gormlie-Crighton would bring us nothing but trouble!"

Jigger and Nessie were left looking blankly across the table at each other, while Granny disappeared muttering upstairs. She was soon back, though, but now carrying a bulky parcel under her arm, with a look on her face that was a curious mix of bitterness and melancholy. She placed the package in front of Jigger.

"This would have come to ye when I kicked the bucket anyway," she panted, "but your grandfather always said I should give it to ye early, if ever I thought the time was right." There was a slight tremble in her voice as she added quietly, "And I think that time is now." She gave Jigger a nudge. "Go on — open it."

She then wandered over to the kitchen window and gazed out into the yard, her back to the table, the tears that were gathering in her eyes hidden from view.

Without speaking, Jigger untied the string and carefully pulled back the crumpled brown paper to reveal the scuffed leather object inside. He swallowed hard. It was old Tam's fiddle case — a cherished memento that Granny had kept hidden away in her room for the ten years since his passing.

"Open it," Granny repeated, still staring out of the window, her voice a throaty whisper.

Jigger released the brass catches with his thumbs. His hands trembled as he raised the lid and gingerly lifted the old instrument from its musty cradle of crushed velvet. He ran his fingers lovingly over the contours of the mellow wood, allowing them to linger lightly on the fingerboard. Its silky black surface was still dulled by the warmth of old Tam's touch, the prints of his fingertips on the little pegs still as clear as the last time he tuned the strings to play Christmas carols for wee Maggie and Davie on the very night he died. Even after all those years, Jigger could still hear the strains of *Silent Night* floating from the old fiddle.

Somehow, his grandfather seemed so near again. Even the almost-forgotten aroma of his favourite pipe tobacco rising faintly from the faded lining of the case brought his presence so much closer. It was all Jigger could do to hold back the tears.

He drew in a deep breath. "But why, Granny? Why now?" he asked.

Granny sniffed, then blew her nose. Without turning round, she replied softly, "In the fiddle case. You'll find your answer there."

Laying old Tam's fiddle gently on the table, Jigger reached into the case and took out the dog-eared Manila envelope that was lying in the bottom, half hidden under a yellow duster. Inside were two folded sheets of paper and, between them, an old sepia photograph. Nessie moved her chair nearer to Jigger's. With bated breath, he opened the first piece of paper and placed it on the table between them.

It was a birth certificate. His own birth certificate. The first time he had seen it. He felt numb, almost afraid to look at what it would reveal.

Her hand resting on Jigger's, Nessie began to read, her voice little more than a murmur:

"Name of Child — Thomas McCloud. Name of Mother — Nell Margaret McCloud. Name of Father — James Thomson . . ."

Jigger caught his breath. James Thomson . . . Hearing the true identity of his father for the first time in his life was traumatic enough, yet he still didn't know who his father was. James Thomson . . . It was a name totally unknown to Jigger, and one towards which he was already beginning to feel a deep resentment. At once, in a way that he couldn't explain, he felt strangely isolated, almost as if he had suddenly become outcast, not even a member of his own family any more. Also, this revelation had completely shattered his long-harboured suspicion — his belief, truth to tell — that he shared the blood of the Gormlie-Crightons. His feelings were in turmoil.

Granny had moved away from the window and was now standing by Jigger's shoulder. "He was a fine young man," she said, struggling to control her own emotions. "They were at university together, ye see. At St Andrews. Always together, Nell and Jimmy.

Inseparable, everybody said." She took off her glasses and rubbed her eyes. "Damned pollen at this time o' year!"

All three remained silent with their own thoughts for a while, each of them staring wistfully at the names on the page.

Nessie was the first to speak. "So, where was he from?" she asked, saying the words that Jigger couldn't yet bring himself to.

"From Perth, I think," said Granny. "No family of his own, though. Brought up in an orphanage, the wee soul. He used to come here to Acredales and spend all the university holidays after he met Nell. A grand hand he was for Tam and me about the place, too. A fine, strong lad. Oh aye, he would have made a good farmer, mind," she smiled. "But — well, it was never to be . . ." Her voice trailed off and she slumped into a chair next to Jigger, gulping down little silent sobs, and wiping the effects of that damned April pollen from her eyes.

Jigger still said nothing, but ran a finger slowly over the yellowing paper, drawing an invisible line over and over again between the names of his mother and father, as though trying to find something of them that he could recognise, something of them that he could feel through the fading strokes of the registrar's pen.

"Young Jimmy," Granny went on after a while, "had been called up to do his National Service in the army when he graduated from university. The troubles in Northern Ireland were brewing at the time, of course, and everyone who had a son or a boyfriend in the armed forces used to pray that he wouldn't be sent

271

there. For eighteen months, it certainly seemed as if Nell's prayers for Jimmy were being answered. So far, he had seen service nowhere more dangerous than in Catterick or Aldershot. But then had come that fateful day when he arrived in this very kitchen and announced that he was on a long weekend's leave before being flown out to Belfast for the remainder of his stretch.

"Well, it would only be six months, Nell and Jimmy had said, trying to cheer each other up. And for all anybody knew, the troubles might be over before then. It wouldn't be so bad. They had got engaged the very next day. It was at Edinburgh Zoo, of all the daft places," Granny remembered with a sad smile. "And they were to be married just as soon as he returned home in the new year," she said. "What plans they had for the future . . ." She savoured the memory for a while, then hesitantly continued, "He was shot by a sniper's bullet on 20th July — less than a month after he arrived over there. He was still only 22. After that," she said, looking fondly at Jigger, "the only thing that kept Nell going was the news that you were on the way. Her Jimmy would never be dead as long as she had you, she would say. There would always be a part of him that would live on in you." She paused and sighed. "Those eyes of yours, Jigger — your father's eyes. Aye, Nell would have seen her Jimmy every time she looked into them." Granny fell silent again. "But she never did, the poor lassie," she eventually murmured. "She never did . . ."

Jigger touched the names of his mother and father one final time before folding the birth certificate and returning it to the envelope.

"I know we should have told you before," Granny said, a touch of remorse complicating her already troubled feelings, "but your grandfather and I, well, we always thought it would be too difficult for you — and for us — when you were young. Then the years just passed by and we —"

Jigger gave her hand a little squeeze.

Granny then reached over for the photograph and handed it to him. "Mrs McCurdy, the old cook at the castle, took that on her wee Box Brownie. Recognise anybody in it?"

He looked at the three coyly-grinning figures standing stiffly side-by-side in the old snapshot. They were young boys of between eight and ten, maybe — stepping up in height from left to right, and dressed in knee pants, belted jackets and floppy caps. The clothes were typical of those worn by the children of well-to-do families in the era between the two World Wars. Jigger had seen kids just like that in those ancient gangster movies on TV. He peered more closely at the faces, the details of their boyish features blurred by time. Shaking his head, he showed the snap to Nessie, but she was unable to detect any clues as to the identity of the youngsters either.

"Turn it over, then," Granny said. There was a note of apprehension in her voice.

On the reverse, printed studiously in pencil along the bottom edge, was the simple inscription: "Horace,

Thomas and Archibald — Craigcuddy Castle, Summer 1929".

A little shiver ran through Jigger's body, almost as if a long-locked door had blown suddenly open, hitting him with a blast of ghostly air. His fingers shaking, he turned the photograph to look at the faces once more.

"It's Granpa," he gasped. He held the picture up to the light. "It's him — the stocky lad in the middle! And the wee fellow on the left — that can't be . . .?"

"That's Horace," said Granny, still distinctly ill-at-ease, "the present Duke himself. He sprouted fast after that, mind you. Well, ye know the kind of gangly gowk he is now."

"So, the boy on the right —"

"Is Archie!" Granny was making no attempt to disguise the venom in the way she spoke the name. "And a long, useless drip o' a creature he was, even then!"

Jigger's mind, striving to make sense of all the information being hurled at it, was becoming more confused by the moment. He pointed at the photograph. "But look at their clothes," he said. "It looks as if the three boys are dressed in identical suits, and not what you'd say cheap-looking gear, either. How could Granpa's parents afford that? I mean, his father was only a horseman."

Granny gave his hand a soothing pat while gesturing towards the second piece of paper from the envelope.

Jigger took the brittle, discoloured document in his hands, his pulse racing, his brain trying to impart some calm to his fingers as they fumbled with the folds of parchment. Inside, the formal, copperplate lettering read:

"AN EXTRACT FROM THE REGISTER OF BIRTHS IN THE PARISH OF CUDDYFORD, THE COUNTY OF HORSEBURGHSHIRE, THIS YEAR OF OUR LORD, NINETEEN HUNDRED AND NINETEEN".

Below, a bit unusually, Jigger thought, was the hand-written note of not one birth, but two — of male twins, it said. "Born to one Eliza McCloud, Maidservant and Spinster of This Parish".

His heart was in his mouth as his eyes searched further over the page. The stark legal details had been copied in the precise, unhurried hand of the time, the blue-brown tint of the ink, though softened with age, still somehow affording a harsh, dispassionate edge to the tale of human fallibility that the curt particulars recorded:

Christian Name of Child (1) . . . Thomas
Christian Name of Child (2) . . . Archibald
Name and Profession of Father . . . Ludovic
Gormlie-Crighton, Peer of the Realm.
Signed: William G Borthwick,
Registrar of Births, Marriages & Deaths,
Horseburgh.
This Twentieth Day of August, 1919.

It was several minutes before Jigger, thunderstruck as he was by these starling revelations, could bring himself to ask Granny to fill in some of the missing details. How was it, for instance, that old Tam and Archie, although brothers, had been brought up separately — Tam by the mother's poor family, Archie by the rich father's?

Oh well, that had been the pernickety way of the old Duke Ludovic, she explained. Forever playing the part of the domineering, arrogant, even eccentric nobleman to the full, he had displayed, nevertheless, an innate sense of honour — quite untypical of many of his social order in those days — by admitting his paternity of, and by accepting his responsibility for, the two illegitimate boys. Old Ludovic had decreed that the most equitable solution to what he regarded as an unfortunate mishap would be for one of the offspring to be reared by him, the other by the mother. The twins being in no way identical, even at birth, the Duke had merely selected the larger of the two, Archibald, for himself. "The pick of the litter" was how he'd flippantly described him. That aside, he'd still insisted that every assistance be afforded the McCloud family towards the wholesome upbringing of the other.

"Hence Granpa's fancy suit in this old photograph," said Jigger.

That was right, Granny replied. Of course, as soon as old Ludovic (who was still very much young Ludovic then) had married, the infant Archibald had been dispatched forthwith from Craigcuddy Castle to be brought up by the uncle who looked after the

Gormlie-Crighton affairs back in the industrial towns that bore the family name. Archie would often come back for school holidays, though, and it must have been during one of those that Mrs McCurdy had taken the snapshot. She had eventually given it to Tam, and no one else except Granny had known of its existence, until this day.

"Are you saying that Horace and Archie were never told that Granpa was the brother of one and half-brother of the other?" Nessie asked.

"Oh, they were told, all right," said Granny. "That was another thing about old Ludovic — he'd rather they heard the truth from him than from some clatter-jawed busybody in the village. He was thoughtful enough in that way."

"And yet Archie seems to have got a better deal in life from him than Granpa did," Jigger remarked. "You know, being brought up in the big house, then living a life of ease in America with a big allowance to fritter away. Meanwhile, Granpa had to work damned hard as a hand on the Craigcuddy lands until such time as he had scrimped and saved enough to put a down-payment on Acredales here when the estate started flogging off its tenanted farms."

Shaking her head, Granny stated that, while that was the way it had looked, it wasn't the way it had actually happened . . .

When both boys had reached the age of 21, the old Duke had arranged for their respective futures to be taken care of, in the most appropriate ways, naturally, that he himself saw fit. It was then that the absolute ownership of Acredales of Cuddyford had been passed over to Tam, and a lifelong annuity from Craigcuddy Estate funds allotted to Archie. All that Duke Ludovic had asked in return was the twins' word that neither would demand any further favour nor lay claim to anything from him or his heirs for as long as they lived. This agreement had been honoured by Tam until his dying day. He had neither asked for, nor had he received, one iota more from the Gormlie-Crighton family.

For his part, Archie had kept turning up like a bad penny at the castle from time to time. Whether or not his purpose had been to sponge more money from the Duke, Granny had no way of telling. All she did know was that he'd made himself universally unpopular around the Cuddyford area, roaring about the narrow country roads in his silly, wee MG sports car, frightening cart horses and cattle and so on. He'd also nurtured the habit of carousing until all hours at the hotel with the other upper-class nitwits he used to hang around with, before waking up half the village with idiotic yelling, laughing and horn-tooting as they drove off to God knows where in the middle of the night. And no girl for miles around had been safe from Archie's lecherous advances, either. It wasn't the first time that some irate father or jealous boyfriend had kicked his aristocratic arse for him.

Archibald Gormlie-Crighton and trouble, in Granny's experience, were one and the same. She'd been glad to see the back of him forty years ago when he finally disappeared to America, where, she stated categorically, he should bloody well have stayed!

"It's funny," Jigger reflected, still mulling over poignant aspects of the secrets that had now come so unexpectedly to light, "how both old Horace and Archie talked about my mother. The dear, sweet girl, they both called her. It made me think that — well, what I mean to say is that it almost seemed to me as if they both sort of —"

"Loved her?" said Granny, her eyes melting into tears again. "But they did. She was their niece, you see — the only one they ever had. Oh, they loved Nell all right. Everyone did, because she truly was a dear, sweet girl."

"One thing I still can't figure out, though," Jigger said purposefully, hoping to guide Granny's thoughts away from those heart-rending memories of her lost daughter, "is how Archie has managed to browbeat old Horace into selling up after all, especially after I'd fixed everything really nicely for him."

Granny's eyes lit up. "Aha!" she said, "but Nessie had the clue to that when that Baboon bloke half referred to Archie as a duke."

Jigger scratched his head again. "I'm still not with you," he frowned.

"Mmm, but I think *I* am," Nessie chipped in, "and it's all to do with the date of old Duke Ludovic's wedding, isn't it?"

Aye, she was getting warm, Granny confirmed as she lifted her cup and poured a fresh measure of tea into her saucer.

"Wedding?" Jigger asked, still puzzled.

Nessie was warming to the subject now. "Look, it's like this, Jigger," she said. "We presume that Horace was not born out of wedlock, right?"

"Right . . ."

"And as we know old Ludovic married after the twins were born, it follows that Horace is younger than his half-brothers."

Jigger's eyes opened wide, as did his mouth. "Well, I'll be . . ." he quietly exclaimed, expletive omitted in the presence of ladies. "So that was what old Horace meant when he said Archie had a document. He was talking about this, Archie's birth certificate!"

"That'll be it precisely," Nessie concurred, feeling a bit like Agatha Christie. "And that'll be what Babu Ng was getting at as well. As the older brother, Archie actually *is* the Duke of Gormlie."

"And, as Ng has somehow got him over a financial barrel," Jigger continued, feeling a bit like Hercule Poirot now himself, "Archie has decided to dump his promise to his old man and put the squeeze on Horace. Step aside, brother, says Archie to Horace — I'm taking over now because I need to get my mitts on Craigcuddy Castle and Estate to pay off the loan shark, sort o' style."

"Something like that," Nessie said in confident inconclusion. "You can bet it'll maybe be something like that."

Jigger nibbled at his lower lip, wrinkles of anxiety creasing his brow. "You can also bet, if that's the case, that my arse is right in a sling."

280

"Meaning?"

"Meaning, Nessie, that if Archie really has got a claim to the Dukedom, none of the strokes that I've been planning to pull in order to save Craigcuddy for old Horace — and to safeguard our own interests — will be worth a snail's fart!"

Granny, who had been listening quietly to these deliberations while softly blowing over the steaming tea in her saucer, suddenly uttered a little cough — as dramatically timed as any coughed by the celebrated Miss Marple herself — and pronounced:

"Ah, but ye overlook one thing."

Jigger and Nessie pricked up their ears.

Granny picked up the birth certificate and laid it on the table in front of them. "What this copy doesn't tell you," she said, "and what old Archie's copy won't tell him either, is the actual time that each twin was born."

Nessie gripped Jigger's sleeve, took a faltering breath and whispered to Granny, "You're not going to tell us that — that Granpa was actually — that, in fact, he was . . .?"

"Born twenty minutes earlier than Archie," Granny stated flatly, her expression not exactly one of comfort. "It's all there in the archives at Register House in Edinburgh, if you want to see it. I have." She gave them both a stern look. "But it's something your grandfather and I swore we'd never divulge, except in the direst of straits — which, thanks to Archie, is what we appear to be getting into now!"

"So, what this all adds up to," Jigger said, "is that, if Granpa was still around, *he*'d have the claim to the Dukedom, not Archie. Is that what you're saying?"

Granny sucked up a slurp of tea and nodded her head.

"And when Granpa passed away," Jigger reasoned, "his birthright would have passed on to his only child — my mother. But as she'd already passed away herself, her birthright would have passed on to her only child — me."

"Heavens above, darlin'," Nessie warbled, going all a-wobble as the true significance of these genetic unravellings began to sink in, "that means *you*'re the rightful young pretender to the title. You're actually Duke Jigger of Cuddyford!"

CHAPTER
THIRTEEN

If In Doubt, Celebrate!

"Ye can pretend all ye want!" That was all Granny had to say to Jigger. "And so can that old pretender Archie, because that's the nearest either of ye will ever get to being the Duke of Gormlie!"

Hell's teeth! He'd be damned if that Granny of his didn't have a right knack of setting you up just so she could knock you down again, Jigger said to himself. "You've lost me again," he muttered, his thoughts spinning. "I mean, why put us through all that birth certificate ordeal just to arrive back where we started?"

Surely he didn't *really* think the Duke would be daft enough to hand his title over to any of his born-on-the-wrong-side-of-the-blanket kin just like that, Granny scoffed. "Old Horace would need to be a *real* gormless cretin to do a glaikit thing like that, wouldn't he?"

"That would be because, in a dispute, the hand-me-down-a-title laws would probably come down in favour of the legit sprog, right?" Nessie said, as much by way of making a statement as asking a question. "Even if the challenger with the whodunnit pedigree happened to be the older of the two."

"Aw, now I get it," Jigger smiled, the dawn of comprehension finally shedding its kindly light. "Any claim of Archie's to the title — or any claim of mine, for that matter — would likely be regarded by the courts as illegitimate, if you'll pardon the pun. All a question of whose blood is the bluest, like."

"Ye hardly need to be a Frillydelphia lawyer to work that one out," Granny jibed.

"Anyhow, who cares what the law says?" Jigger declared. "As far as I'm concerned, Horace is welcome to his bloody title. I'm happy the way I am."

Nessie wholeheartedly agreed. "Mind you," she thought aloud, her lips spreading into a wistful little smile, "the Duchess Agnes *does* have a nice sort of ring to it . . ."

"Aye, nice ring to it. And so did the bells of Notry Damn," Granny countered, "but that never did much for old Karzimodo, did it?"

Jigger didn't even bother to try and work out the relevance of that quip. His powers of reason were still too busy attempting to make sense of why Granny had outed their family skeletons in the first place, if doing so wasn't going to make any difference to the Duke's way of thinking. Whatever Archie was or wasn't entitled to in the eyes of the law, he'd certainly managed to put the frighteners up old Horace, and that was all Jigger was bothered about at this particular moment in time.

"Why doesn't the Duke just tell Archie to bugger off, then?" he asked Granny. "I mean, why let himself be stuffed down the tubes by Archie if the old git hasn't got a legal leg to stand on?"

Nessie, meanwhile, was nodding her head meditatively. "Hmm," she said, "I think I know what Granny's getting at now. Pride may lurk under a threadbare coat, as Maggie might have put it if she'd been here."

Jigger stroked his chin while he let that one sink in. "Pride comes before a fall, more like. I mean, are you really suggesting, Nessie, that old Horace's pride would be less hurt if he let Archie ruin him, rather than playing things my way and holding onto nearly everything he's got? Nah, don't think so."

The trouble with Jigger, Granny rounded sharply, was that any true blue blood in his veins was too damned diluted by now to make him capable of thinking the way the likes of old Horace did. Saving the estate and the castle for himself wasn't the most important thing in the Duke's mind. It was saving the good name of the Dukedom that counted most. Nessie was right, she said. Pride in the Gormlie-Crighton heritage was all that mattered to the Duke, however crap the circumstances his pride might land him in. For remember, she stressed, without their high and mighty sense of family dignity (no matter how unjustified), what else of any real worth would that lot be left with at the end of the day?

The cogs of comprehension were beginning to mesh in Jigger's mind at last. "According to Bertola," he said, "old Archie says he's come back to sort out his inheritance, so maybe he really does think he's in with a chance of copping the title off old Horace. He seems to have convinced Babu Ng that he can at any rate."

For all she knew, Granny conceded, maybe Archie *had* told the Duke that he would press his claim to the title through the courts, and whether he believed he could succeed or not was beside the point. The mere thought of having the Gormlie-Crighton's dirty washing hung out in public could well have been enough to prompt old Horace to throw in the towel.

"But why the hell didn't the spineless old bugger just come clean about all this from the word go?" Jigger asked.

"That's easy," Granny replied. "He obviously didn't want you to know the truth about Tam and Archie . . . or yourself."

"The devious old bastard, if you'll pardon another pun! Listen, I'm really gonna let him have it for this, and I kid you not!"

"Now, just take a minute to think before you fly completely off the handle," said Nessie, pouring her calming oils on Jigger's increasingly troubled waters. "It could just be that the reason the Duke didn't tell you the truth about his half brothers was as much to protect *your* feelings as anything else. And, if that is the case, it puts an entirely different complexion on the whole affair."

"Nessie's right again," Granny agreed, a note of melancholy returning to her voice. "Ye see, although he could never show it openly, Horace was devoted to your grandfather. Tam *was* his big brother, when all's said and done. And in many ways I honestly believe that Horace was envious of Tam's life — a simple, country upbringing with a simple, happy family, instead of the lonely childhood existence he must have led at the castle, with nobody but a governess and the domestic staff for company. And, all the time, having to put up with the dictatorial tantrums of his bampot of a father, old Ludovic I, as well." Granny lowered her eyes. "Then there's the memory of Nell, and I know the Duke would never do anything to taint that. Never."

Jigger sat and looked down at his hands, his thoughts beset now with pangs of humility as he pondered the implications of Granny's words.

"Then there's you," she went on, her voice dropping to an emotional whisper. "Ye're not just his nephew, ye see. Since Tam died, you're the one person in the world he feels he can really trust in times of trouble." Granny gave a little laugh. "Which has been just about all the time in recent years. And last but not least, of course, there's this little family of ours — the three of us, and young Maggie and wee Davie. Oh aye, for all his faults and weaknesses, I'm fairly sure old Horace would never hurt any of us on purpose. Deep down, this is still the family he always wanted for himself, don't forget."

"Well, throwing us and our way of life to the mercy of Babu Ng and his crazy plans seems a queer way of showing it," Jigger blurted out, then instantly wished that he hadn't.

Sensing this, Granny simply shook her head and said, "Leave him with his pride. It's about all the silly old bugger's got left. And anyway, he'll likely believe that *you'll* survive OK, no matter how many sleekit, foreign bandits ye have to deal wi'." She gave Jigger a knowing wink. "That's the difference between being a McCloud and a Gormlie-Crighton, see!"

It was now beginning to seem to Jigger that, for every piece of this damned jigsaw he managed to put in place, another couple of bits were being knocked out. Painful though it had been to him, at least Granny's disclosure of his and his grandfather's paternal origins appeared to have explained the Duke's hitherto-unfathomable insistence on yielding to old Archie's will, and he was grateful for that. It now presented him with the dilemma, however, of whether to inform the Duke of his new-found knowledge of the shadier boughs of the Gormlie-Crighton family tree in the hope that it might take some weight off the old boy's shoulders, or whether to leave him, as Granny had advised, with what little remained of his precious family pride. Also, would it be wise, perhaps, to confront Archie with those same facts, stressing the vital significance of who was the elder twin, in the hope that it might discourage him from proceeding with any threatened claim on the Duke's title?

On both counts, he ultimately decided to stick with the status quo, at least for the present. If Granny had been right in what she said (and she doubtless would have been), spilling the birth-certificate beans to the Duke would only serve to upset him, yet do nothing to alter his resolve. Whereas, cornering Archie might make matters in that quarter even more complicated, if his situation with Ng turned out to be as desperate as it appeared.

288

Yes, continuing to act the daft laddie to Ng was still the best policy, Jigger reckoned. Just take it easy, and keep giving the creep plenty of rope. Conversely, a new, more positive approach was needed in the Duke's case. And that approach, he decided, had to be implemented without delay.

Jigger had nothing to lose now. He knew what had to be done, so he would go right ahead and do it without resorting to further shilly-shallying with the Duke. That would only be a waste of time, and time was a commodity of which he guessed he now had precious little. What he did have in abundance, though, was imagination, and this would be the staple component of a combined vehicle of defence and attack — namely a detailed, five-year business plan for the Duke's bankers, complete with precisely-concocted cash-flow projections. Such things would relate, of course, to ideas along the lines of those he had sketched out for the Duke regarding the transformation of the estate from a loss-making dump into an ecologically-sensitive, neighbourhood-friendly, spick-and-span, profit-generating dynamo.

Fair enough, maybe he was allowing his imagination to run a smidgen wild there, but modest indecision, no matter how honest, had never been known to implant the seeds of courage into a banker's heart. So, from now on, corporate confidence and actuarial audacity would be flowing from Craigcuddy like the Cuddy Burn in spate.

The small problem of just who had the professional smarts required to convert Jigger's flights of creative fancy into sober and convincing documentary form was immediately solved by Maggie. There were, she informed her father, a couple of her young intellectual admirers well qualified to formulate such works of mathematical invention in a way that would have the most cagey of bankers gladly loosening the old purse strings in a flush of confused daring. Why, Maggie even had a quotation to fit the bill:

"Remember that a banker, according to Mark Twain, is a person who lends you his umbrella when the sun is shining, and wants it back the minute it rains." And the only way to solve that commercial conundrum, according to Maggie, was to give the hydrophobic Shylock a pair of Ray-Bans and a sunbed — which, metaphorically speaking, was precisely what her two egg-headed suitors would be falling over themselves to do.

Jigger truly admired his daughter's wonderful, literary turn-of-phrase. Much more cultured, more couth-like, than "Bullshit baffles brains", he felt.

While Maggie's wooers were competitively grappling on the business-plan front, Jigger wasted no time in launching the second phase of his last-ditch campaign, which would have to involve having a quiet chat with the Duke . . .

Old Horace was sitting on the bank of the burn, absentmindedly twitching his fishing rod. Jigger propped himself against the stooped trunk of a nearby aspen tree. "It's like this, Duke," he said, "I don't know what the situation is between you and your cousin

Archie, and it's none of my business anyway. But all I say is this — whatever pressure he's putting on you to sell to Ng, just do me one more favour and hold him off a bit longer. I'll level with you — I haven't a clue how I'm going to do it yet, but the chance to stymie that pair will come. And soon. I feel it in my water."

The Duke cast his line again and sighed. "That Ng chappie's threatenin' to withdraw his buffer funds from the bank if I don't settle soon," he droned. "Time's runnin' out, m'boy."

"Don't listen to him, Duke. It's a bluff. I'm telling you, there's more to all this than Ng simply wanting to turn Craigcuddy into a theme park. He's got bigger fish to fry, I reckon, so there's no way he's gonna whip his bait out of the bank as fast as that. And don't worry too much about the bankers either. I've got a couple of things cooking that'll make their greedy mouths water. But," he swiftly tagged, "I won't bother you with the details until it's all set up, if it's all the same to you. Are you with me?"

Raising his lugubrious face, the Duke blinked his rheumy, pickled-onion eyes in a way that made him appear to Jigger like an aged bloodhound that was sitting on a prickly thistle but had lost the will to stand up. "It's Archie," he moaned. "The blighter's got me beat, and he knows it. The document, y'know. Threatenin' to go public with it. Wouldn't look too good, y'see."

Suddenly Jigger wondered if, because of all the stress, the old boy might have decided to make a clean breast of everything to him after all. "The, eh, document?" he fished.

But the Duke merely looked away and shook his head forlornly. "Not somethin' to burden you with, m'boy. A cross for me to bear alone, y'might say."

A wave of pity mingled with frustration swept over Jigger. He longed to tell old Horace that he knew all about the birth certificate, and that, instead of allowing Archie to blackmail him with it, he should use its contents to his own advantage. He wanted to assure the Duke that it would be all right. Jigger's family — *his* family — would stand by him, no matter how much scandal Archie stirred up.

But, as Granny had so shrewdly observed, he was thinking like a McCloud, and the Duke was a Gormlie-Crighton. Jigger left his feelings unspoken.

"Maybe I know the weight of that cross better than you think," were the words that eventually came out. The Duke didn't seem to notice, though. Jigger ambled over and sat down on the bank beside the disconsolate figure of the uncle who, for the sake of his own pride, could not be acknowledged, could not even be comforted by the little gesture of a reassuring arm round his shoulder. Instead, Jigger decided to adopt a positive, encouraging approach.

"Come on now, Duke," he said as cheerfully as he could, "you haven't lost Craigcuddy yet, so why don't we lighten things up a bit, eh?" In the absence of any discernible reaction from the Duke, he then elected to increase the buoying-up voltage. "Look," he breezed, "remember the bit in that old book I told you about?

You know, that stuff about the May Fair they used to hold here in the castle grounds in bygone times?"

The Duke nodded one of his glum, faraway nods.

"Well, I honestly think we should bring it back. Show 'em all that there's life in the old place yet. Mind you, it'll take one helluva lot of hard graft to get it organised in time to coincide with your Hunt Ball, but it's just what's needed to get everybody around here mucking in together." The Duke still didn't respond, so Jigger hit the enthusiasm button even harder. "Which gives me another great idea!" he beamed. "We could dream up some charitable-sounding caper to get old Plimsoll-Pompey and his crew busy with the fund-raising tins. A wheeze along the lines of, let's say . . . the Craigcuddy Castle Preservation Fund, or something like that. Yeah, that's it! All the May Fair profits would go to that, and it could be a right tidy earner an' all!" Jigger was getting well fired-up already. "So, come on — are you game for it?"

"If you think it'll do any good, old boy," the Duke sighed, more concerned with releasing an old welly boot that had become caught on his fishing hook than thinking positively about the more serious predicaments facing him. "If you really think it'll do any good."

CHAPTER
FOURTEEN

In Vino Veritas?

Offering Commander Plimsoll-Pompey the position of Captain Elect of the proposed Cuddyford Golf Club was the smartest bit of carrot-dangling Jigger had done in a long while. The Commander breathed in deeply at the very prospect, devouring great lungfuls of air as he gazed, head held high, over his garden hedge in the general direction of Craigcuddy Estate — the master on the bridge of a newly-launched ship bound for glory.

"A golf course!" he boomed. "Ah yes, that was the one aspect of the Ng fellow's outrageous proposals of which I thoroughly approved. Dashed fine thing it will be for the community, too!"

If, though, the golf course were to be created under the benign auspices of the Duke, Jigger promptly pointed out, it was imperative that the community's potential beneficiaries should do, as a matter of urgency, all that they could to support the Duke in his quest to see off the predatorial advances of Babu Ng. And that meant raising money. Fast. In that respect, Jigger revealed poker-faced, an energetic person of impeccable integrity, with proven qualities of leadership and organisational experience at the highest level, was being sought to take up the post of Executive Community Co-ordinator of the Craigcuddy Castle Preservation Fund.

"Tell the Duke to look no further, McCloud," the Commander commanded. "Plimsoll-Pompey to the fore!"

"But just one wee point I should maybe mention in the passing, like," Jigger coyly cautioned. "I'm afraid that even if, with your help, the Duke does manage to hold on to Craigcuddy Estate, any notion of extensive free access to his lands for ramblers' clubs and the like still won't be on."

"An attitude with which I most heartily concur. Admission to a modest nature trail or something of the sort would be more than generous enough a response to the selfish demands of that Spon fellow and his motley crew of Greens. And, uhm, with the strictest proviso that they do *not* trespass on the golf course, of course."

"Of course!"

Mission accomplished. With the Commander in the vanguard of fund-raising activities, a plethora of car boot sales, raffles, whist drives, car treasure hunts, coffee mornings and soirees ranging in kind from pub trivia quizzes to swank cocktail parties were soon going strong in Cuddyford and then surrounding area.

"Cast your net wide to maximise the catch!" was Plimsoll-Pompey's seafaring motto. And, by the Pole Star, he meant to see to it that it was followed to the letter!

The pigtailed and pink-bespectacled Nigel Spriggs, because of his standing (albeit nebulous) in the advertising business, was expressly seconded by the Commander as Convener of Publicity for the campaign. Despite most of his slogans being rubbished by Bertola Harvey, claiming in the Cuddy's Rest that he could eat a tin of spaghetti alphabets and shit a better line than that, hardly a garden fence, telegraph pole, sweetie shop window, tree trunk or domestic letterbox in the district escaped one or other of the Spriggs posters or flyers. And even his summary sheriff court appearance to answer a charge of illegal bill-posting did nothing to detract from the cause. Quite the reverse. Thanks to the *Horseburghshire Courier*'s routine report on the case, a couple of national dailies were soon sniffing about and keeping a nostril open for an angle on what might just shape up to be a nice little human interest story.

Spriggs' £250 fine, paid for out of the rapidly-multiplying campaign funds, was cheap at the price, in Jigger's view. However, the altruistic Bertola wasn't slow to point out that it would have been cheaper still if they'd let the freaky little twonk cop for the alternative rap of five days in the fuckin' slammer at Horseburgh nick.

Meanwhile, not to be left in port, so to speak, by her actively-serving husband, Mrs Plimsoll-Pompey had zealously offered her energies to Jigger, to be employed in whatever capacity he deemed would be most constructive in the run-up to his "fabulously exciting May Fair project".

"It's all yours, darlin'," was the equally zealous response from Jigger. In a trice, he listed for her the hundred-and-one things that would have to be seen to in order to make Craigcuddy Castle and its surrounding parkland ready for the big day. One of the most daunting challenges, he underlined, would be the tarting-up of the dilapidated Great Hall to a standard fit for staging the grande finale of the whole jingbang — the new-style, cobwebs-off, come-all-ye Hunt Ball.

None of that would pose her the slightest problem, Mrs Plimsoll-Pompey was eager to emphasise. After all, her vast knowledge of such undertakings had been gleaned from a lifetime of organising all manner of public occasions, from the annual Poole Sea Scouts Jamboree to many a breathtakingly-opulent Admiralty Gala (royal patronage *de rigueur*) from Greenwich to Gib and from Plymouth Hoe to Honkers.

"Permission to recruit local auxiliaries, Mr McCloud?" she asked, shoulders back.

"Aye, aye, permission granted, darlin'!"

Jigger was immediately troubled, however, by a worrisome inkling that, his or anyone else's permission notwithstanding, any attempt by Mrs Popeye to chivvy the dour matrons of Cuddyford into taking orders from her would be met with a concerted volley of:

"AWAY AN' BOIL YER SASSENACH HEID!"

But he inkled wrongly.

Not one of the austerely-parochial members of the SWRI, the Church Flower Volunteers, or even the highly xenophobic Cuddyford Village Knitting, Embroidery and Scone-Baking Guild failed to respond to Mrs

297

Plimsoll-Pompey's call to duty. The irresistible attraction turned out to be, as Jigger had so remissly failed to anticipate, the open-sesame to a good old rummage through the hitherto-forbidden corridors of Craigcuddy Castle, and an equally socially-elevating rake around its previously-private, upper-class grounds.

What Babu Ng may have thought of this sudden upsurge in local unity was beyond Jigger's ken. In fact, Jigger had been so busy fixing up attractions, laying on facilities, and generally doing his impresario bit for the forthcoming May Fair that he had put the enemy (the unwitting instigator of all this rare co-operative activity) almost completely out of his mind. But not for long . . .

"Ah, Mr McCloud," said the sinister-sounding telephone caller just as Jigger was enjoying a well-deserved afternoon cuppa in the kitchen, "it is I, Babu Ng."

Jigger gave Nessie a sly wink and faked a covering cough as he pressed the record button on the answering machine.

"Sorry, could you repeat that?"

"It is I, Babu Ng."

"Yeah, Babu, and what can I do you for today?"

"The, uhm, small item of business which we discussed regarding the doors and bath that you wish to sell?"

Another wink at Nessie. "Uh-huh?"

"The time has come to take delivery . . . my friend."

A shiver ran down Jigger's spine. There was something so cold, so terminal about the way Ng had spoken that last line. In an attempt to sound as unconcerned as possible, he came out with one of his pseudo-bumpkin chuckles and said:

"Oh aye! Tidy, Babu! Tell us all about it, then."

"Wait in your truck at the rear of my house at eight o'clock this evening. Be alone."

The phone clicked off.

Jigger drummed his fingers on the answering machine. "The crafty bugger!" he muttered. "I was hoping to get some incriminating info on tape there."

"I don't like it," Nessie said, a look of genuine concern on her face. "Those lies about his name, and the wine coming from his non-existent house in Paris and everything. It stinks, and it's bound to be dangerous. Honestly, Jigger, I think you should get out of this before you get sucked too far in. You don't know what you might be getting involved in, but whatever it is, you can bet it's illegal for a start. I mean, who's to say that Ng isn't just using you as a —"

"Patsy? That's as sure as there's fleas on a fox. But even so, this could be the best chance we'll ever get of finding out something we can nail him with."

Nessie frowned. "I still don't like it."

"I've got to do it, darlin'. There's just too much at stake for me not to."

"Well, at least take somebody with you. Two of you will have a better chance if something goes wrong. *And* you'll have a witness."

Jigger put his arms around her and gave her a hug. "Ng's already put the kibosh on that one, pet. Alone is what he said, so alone it'll have to be." He planted a reassuring peck on her forehead. "And stop worrying. It'll be all right, honest." Seeing that Nessie was far from convinced, he then said, "But I'll tell you what — if it's gonna make you feel any happier, I'll take Bert with me. OK?"

Nessie's look of anguished resignation said it all.

By the time Jigger left for the manse, the light of day was already dissolving into a fiery ribbon along the western skyline, on which stood the old farmhouse and its clustered steading. The old buildings were silhouetted against a backcloth of Scots pines and framed in the pick-up's rear-view mirror like a three-dimensional pop-up in a children's picture book. Jigger savoured this magical view of his home — serene, solid and timeless, the very embodiment of all those enduring rural qualities of Cuddyford that would be lost for ever, unless . . .

An owl hooted as Jigger swung the truck into the yew-darkened driveway of the manse. The bird's chilling cry set tiny voles and field mice dashing for cover, the merest rustle of their frantic scurrying only increasing the inevitability of their own demise. Jigger took the message to heart.

After the contrived glitz and glamour in which it had basked on the night of Sabrina's party, the manse appeared more morose and sepulchral now than ever. Its heavy front door was closed and uninviting, all its windows shuttered and deathly dark, except for one solitary light that shone dimly from what used to be the old wash house at the rear of the building. Jigger stopped the pick-up there and waited, engine off, headlights out. Bert growled nervously and shuffled over the seat until he felt the confidence-bolstering touch of Jigger's hip against his own. Then he barked, only once (and more of a whistling-in-the-dark yelp than a proper macho "woof" it was at that), before curling up close by Jigger's side. The whites of his eyes were exposed like canine flags of surrender. The beginnings of a snarl rumbled quietly in the depths of his throat, but ventured no farther.

Jigger started to hum a cheerful tune. This place, and Bert, were giving him the bloody heebie-jeebies!

The last crimson slivers had now melted from the twilight sky, transforming the back yard of the manse into a quadrangle of creepy shadows. Jigger's eyes were drawn to the towering presence of ghostly oaks surrounding him, their boughs moaning mournfully in the night breeze, their outer branches appearing like spidery fingers clawing menacingly downwards. Despite himself, he suddenly felt threatened by these spooky, almost-humanoid shapes.

"Bugger this!" he exclaimed an octave higher than usual, causing Bert to leap whimpering into his lap. Bert's undisguised terror jolted Jigger into trying to get a grip of his own jumpiness. It'd be bad form, he figured, to let the dog think his master was as shit-scared as he was. Pulling himself together, he gave his little chum a reassuring pat on the head.

"I know what you're thinking, Bert," he said in a voice exuding fake confidence. "You're thinking I should've listened to Nessie after all, aren't you?

Should've brought proper backup instead of just you, eh?" Not wanting to risk hurting Bert's feelings, he then added under his breath, "Yeah, thanks, wee pal. In a situation like this, you're worse than a man short."

Once he was sure that this cascade of incomprehensible verbals had dried up, Bert's look clearly stated: "Whatever you're trying to tell me, boss, just cut the long-winded claptrap and let's get the hell out of here!" But his ESP message didn't get through on this occasion.

"Nah, what the hell, boy," Jigger confidently declared, an upsurge of vanity-induced bravado suddenly doing its best to fight off his natural instinct for self-preservation. "In for a penny, in for —"

"A thousand pounds, Mr McCloud?"

If Bert had had a big enough lap, Jigger would have jumped whimpering into it. As it was, he truly feared for the integrity of his underpants as he struggled to identify the dark eyes staring at him through his open driver's window.

"Holy shit, Babu! Where the bloody hell did you spring from?"

"Ah, but I have been here all along, my friend — watching you from the shadows — waiting for darkness."

"Right! It's as dark as it's ever gonna get now," Jigger snapped, his nerves a-jangle, "so let's bloody well get on with it! Come on," he said, the shock of Ng's sudden appearance flicking his adrenalin pump into overdrive, "I don't want to be up all night. I've got a lot on my plate tomorrow!"

Ng was as stone-faced as a Mississippi gambler. "Please, do not allow yourself to become so excited," he crooned. His voice was oozing menace. "A cool, clear mind is required for the task ahead. My wine, and perhaps your life, will depend upon it."

Jigger didn't like the sound of that one little bit. It was time to wick up the bravado again. "Yeah, yeah, so just give me the instructions, OK?"

Ng was unimpressed. "Why so nervous, Mr McCloud?" His voice was dripping derision now. "The thought of earning a thousand pounds for one hour's work too much for you?"

"Aye, right, that *will* be the day!"

Moving closer, Ng spoke in a solemn drone. "Perhaps so. But now to business." He narrowed his eyes into a stare that brought the Jack Palance cobra correlation back to Jigger. "Are you familiar, my friend, with a small inlet on the coast known as Cavey Cove?"

Jigger raised his shoulders. "Sure, but there's no way into it, except by boat — unless you go cross-country from the old radar station where I keep my pigs, that is."

"Precisely."

"But that land's been planted with spuds." Jigger gave a dismissive little chuckle. "And I'm telling you, old Watty the farmer isn't gonna be too chuffed if I go churning through his tatties with —"

"Farmers and their miserable potatoes are of no consequence!" Ng interrupted, discharging his words like bullets. "Now, listen carefully to *me!*" He pointed a forefinger directly at Jigger's face. "You will head for

303

your pigsty, but you will extinguish the lights of your vehicle as soon as you turn off the main road. You will leave them extinguished until you have reached the cove, where you will flash them twice and then wait with your engine turned off. Is that perfectly clear?"

Suppressing an urge to bite the end of Ng's offensive finger, Jigger nodded the affirmative.

"A dinghy carrying one man will then come ashore from a vessel which will be moored in the cove. You will approach this man and give him the password 'Lafite', whereupon he will assist you to transfer two wooden crates to your vehicle."

"Then I bring the crates back here, right?"

Ng brushed that question aside. "Then you will follow the same route away from the cove, again with your vehicle's lights extinguished. As you approach the main road, stop. Another vehicle will be waiting for you there. The driver will give you the same password, and you will hand the crates over to him."

Jigger cursed inwardly. Even if he was beginning to sound like he was reading the script of a corny old spy movie, this sly bastard had thought of everything.

Ng leaned closer still — close enough for Jigger to make out the vicious sneer contorting his face. "I expect you back at this very place within the hour to report that all has gone to plan. And I warn you that you must tell no one of this little errand that you will have run for me tonight." He fluttered a wad of money in Jigger's face. "You have much to gain, my friend, but you have much more to lose." Then, lest there be any doubt in Jigger's mind as to what exactly he meant by that last remark, he added, "I trust that your enchanting wife and beautiful daughter are well?"

Jigger was instantly stung by a feeling of alarm at the stark realisation that the game he was playing with this character wasn't just potentially risky for him, but could also end by putting the safety of his family at risk.

With a smug laugh, Ng turned and receded back into the shadows.

"You have one hour, Mr McCloud. No more . . ."

The moon was already rising through drifting clouds when Jigger entered the field beyond the old radar station. Dim and intermittent as they were, those moonbeams were all he'd have to light his way from now on. Taking care not to drive over them, he steered the truck between two ranks of meticulously-drawn potato drills, then followed their line to the far headland, where a belt of wind-bowed thorn trees marked the boundary between cultivated land and coast. There, he turned into a narrow gap in the undergrowth, at a point where a ditch collected the outfall of field drains from the neighbouring land. With its wheels straddling this shallow channel, Jigger inched the pick-up over the rough ground until it entered a narrow gulley cut by a stream. The moon was now obscured by trees overhanging the steeply-rising terrain on either side, so following the rocky course of the burn in the near pitch darkness became more hazardous by the yard. Without warning, great boulders would loom out of the murk dead ahead, forcing Jigger to suddenly jerk the steering this way or that, and throwing the

305

understandably perplexed Bert off his seat and over the floor of the cab like a drunken rag doll.

"I hope Ng's wine travels well, boy," Jigger grunted, wrestling with the steering wheel as the truck lurched and bucked along the bed of the stream. "It's got a rough ride ahead of it. That's if we ever get to the end of this bloody obstacle course to pick it up."

After stomach-churning minutes that seemed like hours, the buffeting and slithering gradually diminished, until the feel of truck's tyres ploughing through sand told Jigger that they'd reached their destination.

He breathed a whistle of relief. "God knows how, Bert, but at least we've made it *one* way. Now, let's just hope Ng's boat's here an' all."

Pulling up at the edge of the sea, he switched off the pick-up's engine according to Babu Ng's instructions and peered out over the water. But he could see nothing. The cove and its encircling horseshoe of vertical cliffs were lost in an impenetrable blackness.

"I wish I could whistle the moon out from behind those clouds, Bert boy, 'cos I can see bugger all out there. Anyway, flick the lights twice was what the man said, so here goes . . ."

The momentary flashes revealed nothing but darkness beyond the ripples of tiny waves gently lapping the shore immediately in front of the truck. Jigger stepped out and listened to the silence that filled the bay beyond the sough of miniature surf breaking at his feet. Blindly, he gazed around the cove.

Although it was many years since he'd been there, he could remember well the summer treks that he and his school chums had made on foot along that same route he'd driven tonight. Smiling, he recalled the adventures they used to get up to; diving from the rocks to swim in the still, deep pools; imagining that they were smugglers, whom local legend claimed had once made use of this hidden place to land their casks of untaxed brandy from France; recklessly accepting dares to climb (though always in vain) the sheer rock face that protected the entrance to Smugglers' Cave, a mysterious lair that it was said could only be reached from the sea, and even then, only from a steady boat at high tide. In his mind's eye, Jigger could still see, hanging above the mouth of the cave, the rusty iron ring that, as boys, they had fancied must have been used by the smugglers to haul up precious cargoes of contraband.

Just then, the moon began to steal from behind its veil of cloud. Jigger's attention was drawn back to the dense blackness of the bay by the sound of a muted splash. It was almost as if some unseen creature of the sea had taken advantage of the moment to surface fleetingly, then to submerge once more into the deep. He squinted into the gloom, his eyes straining to catch sight of something, anything. Another muffled splash — this time nearer. Bert growled courageously from his seat in the truck, then slunk out of sight onto the floor.

A trailing wisp of cloud drifted past the moon, allowing its pallid glow to wash for a moment over the cove, picking out ashen highlights on the ledges of the surrounding cliffs and scattering flickering shreds of silver over the surface of the water.

Jigger looked again, and exhaled a faint, whispering note between his lips. It was there! Although only just visible for those few seconds, it *was* there. He had caught the merest glimpse of the sleek shape, lurking soundless and motionless, with not a glimmer of light piercing the brooding bulk of its hull. It was a shape exuding power, and as menacingly-beautiful as the fastest gunboat . . . or coastguard cutter.

"A bit like having your milk delivered by a Centurion tank, Bert," he muttered through the pick-up window. "Still, not for us to reason why."

The muted splashing grew closer. Jigger now recognised it as the sound of oars entering and exiting the water with infinite stealth as a rubber dinghy slipped its way commando-style to shore. He waited until the lone rower had pulled his little inflatable onto the sand, then stepped tentatively over to meet him. As he drew near, he could see that the shadowy figure's body was sheathed in a wet suit the colour of shark skin, his head and face covered by a black ski mask.

"And all because the lady loves Milk Tray?" Jigger enquired, unable to resist the obvious wisecrack, then prudently pronouncing the password just as the cagey courier's hand grabbed for the bowie knife strapped to his thigh.

All Jigger's premeditated attempts to elicit morsels of "incriminating info" from the maritime deliveryman proved to be even less than successful than they were subtle. Such cryptic probes as "This the vino for Babu Ng, then?" and "Good trip over from France, was it?" met with a stony wall of silence. After helping lug the two crates over the sand to Jigger's truck, the spectral oarsman simply slipped back into the watery shadows as inscrutably, and as anonymously, as he had arrived.

Having once more gained the cover of the rocky ravine, Jigger quickly set in motion the first part of the ploy he hoped might lead to Ng's undoing. With the minutes ticking rapidly past, and in the knowledge that one of Ng's henchmen was probably already waiting for him back at the main road, he knew it had to be now or never.

He halted the pick-up in mid stream, unceremoniously tucked Bert under one arm and scrambled onto the back of the truck, a flashlight in one hand, a jemmy in the other.

"Right, Bert," he panted, "whatever dodgy gear is stashed in these crates, we're gonna find out exactly what it is right now!"

Bert adopted his most pathetic shivering pose on the truck's deck, wishing he was anywhere else but there, and letting Jigger know it via his full repertoire of whines and whimpers.

"For God's sake, shut your face, Bert, or I'll stick you back in the cab on your own," Jigger hissed. "For all we know, the Creature from the Black Lagoon back there could still come wading up the burn and spike us with his dagger, so just belt up, OK!"

Bert retreated into a profound huff, firing every known telepathic bolt from his pathos arsenal at his master's sympathy sensor. But all to no avail. Jigger was much too busy trying to prize open the wine cases without inflicting terminal damage on the splintery wood to be bothered with Bert's wimpy performance. The creaks and squeaks of levered slats and pulled nails echoed off the walls of the gorge, amplified to the volume — in Jigger's jittery ears — of the death groans of a giant tree being felled.

"Fine, that's one o' them open!" he puffed at last. Wasting not a second, he picked up the torch and shone it into the case. "Now then . . . what have we here?"

He pulled out one object, then another and another, until he had a round dozen standing in neat formation on the flatbed of the truck. Nothing untoward there, he thought — just bottles of wine, right enough. He started on the second case, extracting first one bottle, then the next, swiftly inspecting each one in the torchlight, then setting it down carefully beside its partners. His exasperation escalated through despair to near panic as his sacking of the crates revealed nothing more sinister than what Babu Ng had said they would contain — a collection of dusty, old bottles of wine.

"Well, that's that theory down the Swannee, Bert," Jigger sighed. He glanced at his watch. "Bugger! We'd better put this lot back the way it was and get it to Ng's flunky up at the main road before he smells a rat and shoots the crow!"

No matter how meaningless most of that outpouring must have sounded to Bert, the one phrase that he most surely did comprehend was the final one, "shoot the crow". This was the best news he'd heard since being conned out of lying in his cosy kip to come on this harebrained mystery tour in the first place. Tail erect and quivering like a newly-landed arrow, tongue set to work overtime on his master's face, he fairly leapt out of his sulking corner and bounded over to where Jigger was kneeling.

"Gerroff, Bert! You'll knock the bottle out of my hand, you bloody idiot!"

To Jigger's great astonishment, Bert did "gerroff"! He stood back, ears pricked, one front paw on Jigger's knee, the other pointing gun-dog-style (Jigger could have sworn!) at the bottle in his hand. Bert then barked, over and over again. But there was none of his timorous yipping this time. Now it was the full fox-terrier macho bit.

Jigger was almost hysterical, doing his best to muzzle Bert with his free hand. "Hey, take it easy, boy!" he urged. "You'll give the game away, for Pete's —"

At that, Bert lunged forward, clamped his teeth round the neck of the bottle and tried his utmost to wrench it from Jigger's grip.

"Give us a break, Bert! You're a greedy little bastard, I know, but eating bottles . . ."

Much to Jigger's relief, Bert did then ease up on his tugging. He didn't let go of the bottle, though. He just stood there, as is a terrier's way, jaws locked on his prey, eyes staring rabidly ahead, a constant growl gurgling in the depths of his chest, all fours firmly set to renew the struggle at the drop of a hat.

In this instance, however, it wasn't a hat but the torch that dropped — from the crook of Jigger's elbow, where it had been conveniently wedged, and onto his lap, where it settled against the object of this unlikely tug o' war. Jigger looked down to where the beam of light now shone directly onto the bottle, its brilliance piercing the shroud of dust clinging to the glass.

"Christ!" he gulped, his eyes on stalks. "*Now* I see what's driving you bonkers, Bert. The bottle's full of bloody hamburgers!"

CHAPTER
FIFTEEN

The Spider and The Fly

When Sergeant Brown arrived in his Panda car, he found Jigger's truck slewed across the radar station access track just a few yards short of the main road. Jigger was sitting crouched on the pickup's front bumper, his head and shirt covered in blood.

"What's up here, then?" the policeman asked. "I got a phone call from somebody who said he was drivin' past the road end and witnessed some kind o' disturbance takin' place here." He shone his flashlight on Jigger. "Bugger me! You need an ambulance, lad!"

"Nah, it's not as bad as it looks. Just a bump on the nut. I'll live."

"But what the hell happened?" The sergeant cleared his throat, took out his notebook and adopted a policemanly stance. "I'll be needin' a full statement, of course."

Jigger took a deep breath. "OK, I was driving up here after checking the pigs, and then — blank! I remember nothing." He tentatively touched the back of his head, then winced. "Sorry, but that's as full a statement as I can give you."

While visually appraising the evidence, Sergeant Brown chewed on his pencil for a moment or two. "Hmm," he hummed conclusively, "from my long experience o' the criminal mind, I'd say that ye've been the victim of a muggin', son."

"Funny you should say that, Sarge" said Jigger, poker-faced. "Yeah, I took a wild guess and came up with that exact conclusion myself. Anyway, what about your phone-caller. How much info did you get from him?"

"No that much. Just said he was ringin' from a phone box. Wouldnae even leave his name. I mean, I ask ye! How can the bloody public expect the fuckin' polis to solve —"

"Ehm, 'scuse me, Sarge," Jigger butted in. Ng had given him a strict time limit and the deadline was rapidly approaching, so he couldn't afford to let Sergeant Brown indulge himself in one of his windy diatribes. "You're the expert, of course," he said as nonchalantly as he could, "but don't you want to know if anything's been stolen here?"

The sergeant coughed into his notebook. "Oh aye . . . good point, lad. I, eh I was just comin' to that." He shone his torch into the back of the pick-up and confidently enquired, "Any evidence of robbery bein' the motive here, by any chance?"

"Search me. I can't even remember if I was carrying anything."

"Well, there's nothin' in your wee truck now."

"So, what does that tell us?"

The sergeant gave that one some thought, then answered positively: "Nothin'!"

"Fine," Jigger sighed. He stood up and climbed into his cab. "That'll be the end of my statement, then."

Sergeant Brown turned over another page of his pad. "Do ye wish to press charges, sir?"

Funny, Jigger reflected, how old Brown always called people he'd been on familiar terms with for years "sir" when he was in investigative mode. "Charges?" he yawned. "Who against and for what?"

"Aye, and that's exactly what I'll be puttin' in my report," the Sarge muttered, scribbling laboriously. "Victim . . . concussed . . . and . . . suffering . . . from . . . severe . . . ambrosia."

Jigger stifled a snigger. "Could I ask you one wee favour?" he said. "Any chance of you dropping by the old manse and telling Babu Ng all about this when you get back to Cuddyford? You know, in the course of your enquiries, like."

"Enquiries?"

"Yeah, you could say that, in the course of your enquiries, somebody reported seeing me driving away from the manse earlier tonight, and you just wondered if he could throw any light on the case — if you see what I'm saying."

"Case?"

"It'll all become clear to you once I get my memory back, I promise," Jigger said. He stretched across the cab and producing a bottle of his "Home Brew" from the glove compartment. "Here, take this. Maybe it'll help to lubricate the course of your enquiries in the direction of the manse."

"Is that you?" Nessie called from the kitchen on hearing the familiar footsteps clomping along the back lobby. "I've been worried stiff. It's past midnight and you said you'd only be —"

She let out a blood-curdling scream to greet Jigger's gory entrance.

"Don't get yer breeks in a fankle," he said as he stripped off his blood-splattered shirt. "It's not my blood, it's Johnny Ardonski's."

"Johnny Ardonski's? Oh, the poor man! An accident, was it? Drunk, was he?" Nessie was in a right tizzy. "Is he going to be all right?"

Jigger was the epitome of indifference. "Well, he'll be a black puddin' or two light, but he'll struggle by, I'm sure." He stuck his head under the taps in the kitchen sink. "Squirt some Fairy Liquid on my hair — there's a good lass."

Once Nessie had recovered sufficiently from the shock of seeing him coming in looking like one of the Texas Chainsaw Massacred, Jigger gave her a debriefing on the evening's events . . .

He revealed that, but for Bert's one-track mind, he would never have rumbled Ng's scam of filling his wine bottles with hamburgers — or, more specifically, with hamburger-shaped packets of dope. Heroin, Jigger reckoned it was, although he couldn't be sure, not being an expert on that lousy habit. Anyhow, one thing he *was* sure about was that it wasn't sherbet — not

316

after all that cloak-and-dagger palaver Ng had organised for smuggling the stuff into the country. Yet for all that, Jigger continued, the really crafty bit was how the bottles had been made with screw-off bottoms, with the join simply waxed over and covered in dust. It was a tidy trick that could have fooled anybody. Except a hamburger freak like Bert, of course.

So what the blazes had Jigger done with the stuff? Nessie demanded to know, her voice warbling with worry. She hoped he hadn't brought any of it home with him. Heavens above, there was no saying what Ng might do if he found out that Jigger was trying to double-cross him!

No need to worry, Jigger assured her. Sergeant Brown had already been drafted in as a red herring carrier, so they were safe enough in that respect . . . for the moment. Now, if she'd kindly stop interrupting and jumping the gun, he'd get on with the story.

Jigger went on to explain that, once he'd discovered what was really inside the wine crates, his first port of call had been the piggery.

But that would surely be the first place Ng would look, Nessie exclaimed, unable to hide her anxiety. Jigger had really pointed the gun at his own head if he'd dumped the dope there, for goodness' sake. She pointed to the phone. "Right, you'd better contact the CID or somebody straight away!"

Electing, in his exhausted state, to ignore all this twittery female flapping, Jigger suggested with deliberate calm that, if Nessie would be good enough to pretend, just for the present, that he wasn't a complete bloody numpty, she might be able to button her lip for long enough to learn a thing or two. He resumed his narrative . . .

On the day of young Ludo's candidature interview at Cowdenbings Miners' Club, he told her, Johnny Ardonski, while trying to trace the source of some minor flooding in the basement of the old radar station, had made a startling discovery behind a steel door that, as far as anyone knew, had never been unlocked since the last war. That door opened into a tunnel, which, in one direction, led to the coast — straight into the Smugglers' Cave at Cavey Cove, in fact. The reason for the flooding had turned out to be nothing more troublesome than the unusually high spring tide that had occurred the previous night. This, combined with a strong onshore wind, had merely caused the spray from the breakers to enter the cave, from where the gathered water had eventually trickled down the gradient of the tunnel to the piggery.

Whether or not that tunnel to the sea had been used for some secret purpose by the military during the war was neither known, nor was it of any real importance now. What was significant, on the other hand, was the fact that the tunnel had obviously been there for many centuries before radar was ever dreamed of. But of even greater significance, had been the discovery that, in the other direction, the tunnel led directly to the dungeons of Craigcuddy Castle.

Nessie was dumbstruck.

Jigger was grateful.

He proceeded . . .

In the light of these revelations, therefore, Ng was welcome to poke about the piggery to his heart's content. Why not? He wouldn't even find the concealed trap door to the basement. Jigger's obvious requirement to camouflage the entrance to his little distillery had covered such potentially tricky eventualities years ago.

So, where precisely were the bottles of hamburgered heroin now? Nessie finally ventured to ask.

"In a place where nobody will dream of looking for them tonight," Jigger proudly confided. They'd been wheelbarrowed, he smirked, through the tunnel and were now stacked in the racks of the Craigcuddy Castle wine cellar. And, OK, the cellar-raiding habits of young Ludo might have posed a problem in the long term, he was promptly willing to concede, but if all now went according to plan, there would be no long term to worry about anyway.

So far so good, Nessie said, only marginally less confused than before, but he still hadn't told her how he got covered in Johnny Ardonski's blood. And that was what she was worried about in the *short* term.

Ah well, it was only Johnny Ardonski's blood in kind, Jigger explained. In other words, it was pig's blood, saved in a bucket for Ukrainian black pudding purposes from a porker whose throat the old bugger had cut that afternoon.

Nessie squirmed.

Jigger continued . . .

With the wine cases temporarily hidden down in the wee distillery, he had hung about until such time as Ng's man waiting up at the main road had lost his bottle and buzzed off. He'd then phoned Sergeant Brown on his mobile, giving him the spiel that he was a passer-by who'd witnessed a kafuffle on the track to the piggery. After that, it had just been a matter of parking the pick-up across the track up near the road, splattering himself with blood, then sitting on the bumper and waiting. Once Sergeant Brown had come and gone, he'd returned to the piggery to get on with lugging the wine cases through the tunnel to the castle. Jigger nodded his head, a self-satisfied little smile tugging at the corner of his mouth. It had been a nerve-wracking night right enough, he admitted, but worth it — so far.

"But wouldn't it have been a good idea to have gone back to the manse to let Ng see all the blood and everything?" Nessie suggested. "You know, as sort of proof that you *had* been mugged or whatever."

"No way," said Jigger. "I'm still suffering from loss of memory, remember, so I've forgotten that Ng has anything to do with this. Anyway, if he puts two and two together, he'll be pointing his finger of suspicion at the guy who was supposed to pick the crates up from me at the main road. And, with any luck, Ng'll be nicked before he finally puts four and four together and points the finger at me."

"But why not just get Ng arrested right away, this very night? I mean, you've got the drugs as evidence now."

"As evidence of what? I haven't got one bit of proof that Babu Ng was involved in this at all, remember. He's been cute enough to see to that." Jigger shook his head. "No, no, Nessie, I've got to catch him in a trap." He looked her resolutely in the eye. "And that'll be set in the morning, never you fear."

Nessie was becoming as confused as she was anxious. "That's all very well, but tomorrow's the day of the fair, don't forget. So, how are you going to cope with running that *and* find time to chase around after Babu Ng?"

Jigger chortled in that over-confident way of his that Nessie knew he always did when he was biting off more than he could chew. It made her nervous. "Don't worry, darlin'," he grinned, "Ng will be the one doing the chasing, I promise you. Commander Popeye has already played on Ng's conceit by inveigling him into giving kids free rides in his helicopter from the castle grounds tomorrow, you see. Of course, Ng likely thinks that'll help get the locals on his side. But who cares?" He gave Nessie a confidence-boosting wink. "The main thing is that he'll be right there on Craigcuddy Estate when I spring the trap."

Nessie gave the embers in the grate a final rake with the poker, then sat down beside the range and mulled over all this fantastic stuff that Jigger had just told her. It was late, but her mind was reeling with things that she needed to get straight before she could even think about sleep.

"From what you say," she recapped after a while, "Ng's real reason for wanting to buy the estate is to get access to the castle from Cavey Cove through the tunnel, right?"

"That's how I see it. Perfect set-up for drug running, see." Jigger was thoroughly convinced now. "That's why all this theme park stuff is balderdash. It's just a cover. Yeah, and maybe a tidy way o' laundering some o' his dirty gains an' all. You never know."

"But I've never heard any of the local folk — even the oldest ones — ever mention that tunnel. So, I mean, how did Ng get to know about it? That's what's puzzling me."

Jigger wrapped a towel round his shoulders and sat down opposite her. "For your answer to that, look no further than Archibald Gormlie-Crighton."

"How d'you mean?"

"That old library book, *Legends of Lowland Scottish Castles*, remember? Well, the tunnel's mentioned in that, and every detail it describes is spot on, as far as I've seen so far."

"So, where does old Archie come in?"

"Inside the front cover of the book. His initials are written there, dated nineteen-forty-something. Matter of fact, I wouldn't be surprised if that book originally belonged in the castle and was only bought by the library at the big Sotheby's sale a while back."

"Even so, it still wouldn't prove that Archie knew about the tunnel."

"Maybe not, but if you tie it in with what he told Bertola about Babu Ng's theme park caper . . ."

"Which was?"

"That nothing's what it seems on the *surface*. That's what he said, and for me it adds up to a fair likelihood that he's known all about that tunnel since long before he went to the States."

Nessie's eyes lit up. "Right, now I see how all the pieces could fit." She let out a little laugh. "Maggie would say it's all a bit Agatha Christie-ish, but I see how you're thinking. Archie the gambler gets himself in hock to Ng, sweet talks Ng with all the bull about being the rightful Duke with the collateral of Craigcuddy his for the claiming, then he spins the yarn about the tunnel, maybe knowing how useful this could all be to somebody in Ng's line of business."

"You're getting there."

"So, Ng lets him get deeper and deeper in debt, and then snatch! The spider catches the fly."

"Yeah, then Ng and Archie go to work on the Duke from both sides, and bingo! We arrive back at the present. That's how it all looks to me, anyway. But tomorrow will tell us for sure." Jigger's mouth opened into one of those have-to-yawn yawns of the truly knackered, then he said, "Which reminds me — tomorrow's another day, and it's tomorrow already. Let's hit the sack, darlin'!"

CHAPTER
SIXTEEN

The Big Showdown

In all probability, Craigcuddy Castle hadn't seen so much restless activity in its grounds since Oliver Cromwell laid siege to it in 1650, for when Jigger and young Davie arrived on site in the pickup at just after 7.30 in the morning, Mrs Plimsoll-Pompey and her volunteer army were already swarming all over the place. They were busy putting the finishing touches to all their hard work, which, cosmetically at least, had transformed the run-down old pile into something more worthy of its baronial station.

Stirred by a warm morning breeze, flags and banners proudly waved above the castle's towers and turrets, and seemingly endless garlands of multi-hued bunting fluttered cheerfully along castellated rampart and sunbasking battlement. Even the little tented village, which housed every service and facility from bars, coffee shops and craft stalls to the ladies' and gents' toilets, added a definite festive air to proceedings. They weren't unlike the pennanted pavilions surrounding the lists of a mediaeval jousting tournament, Jigger fancied. He blinked, almost unbelievingly, when he noticed that Bertola (in what was still the middle of the night for him) had also been cajoled into getting involved, and was doing a final circuit on his trusty lawnmower, adding the essential aroma of freshly-cut grass to the garden-party atmosphere.

Completing what Jigger liked to call the fixed attractions, a small funfair of roundabouts, Dodgems, a Ferris wheel and an assortment of sideshows were huddled in a fairy-lit encampment away in one corner of the east lawn. High above, from his whistling post atop an ancient chestnut tree, a blackbird poured out a gloriously tuneful matinal to the farthest boundaries of his curiously-bustling territory.

The stage was set for the Cuddyford May Fair.

If only the spectre of Babu Ng hadn't been hanging threateningly in the background like some dark thundercloud, the outlook for the day would have been near perfect, Jigger contemplated. But then, without Ng's presence in the village, this forgotten gala day of bygone times would most likely never have been revived at all. Be that as it may, however, the vitally important task of putting a stop to Ng's foul objectives would still have to be tackled — *and* concluded successfully — today. Jigger's stomach was churning at the thought.

He drove on, shouting cheery words of encouragement to Mrs Plimsoll-Pompey and her troops as he passed by. He continued through the grass paddock that had been roped off to act as the main arena for the horse jumping, children's races, farm animal and pet shows, sheepdog trials, marching band parades, five-a-side football competitions and the like, then on into the south meadow. There, he recognised the officious figure of the Commander, already briefing a white-coated crew of village youths on the essential prerequisites of the efficient car park attendant.

"Welcome aboard, McCloud!" Plimsoll-Pompey hollered, dispersing his sniggering trainees to their allotted posts with much semaphoric waving of his arms. "Everything shipshape and Bristol-fashion enough for you?"

Jigger replied that he had never seen the old place looking so shipshape. Nor, for that matter, had he seen the young local skivers looking so Bristol-fashion — if the simultaneous wearing of pristine white coats and manky trainers could be so described.

"All a matter of discipline, sir! One does not aspire to the captaincy of an association such as Cuddyford Golf Club without first commanding the respect of the indigenous deck hands, if you will."

Jigger nodded and said he reckoned that would be right enough, too — although he'd never thought about it in that way himself, like.

"I have, nonetheless, taken the precaution of charging Littleton-Nimby with the responsibility of supervising the financial exactitude of all car parking operations. Officer i/c harbour fees, you might say." He ruffled up his white whiskers and straightened his shoulders. "Never trust a swab with the purser's key. That has always been my motto!"

"So, that would be what you actually meant by commanding the respect of the indigenous deck hands, then?" Jigger enquired with an impish smile. "Keep 'em firmly in their place, eh?"

"Precisely!" the Commander replied, apparently unaware of the satirical undertone of Jigger's question. "Stalwart fellow, McCloud! Glad to have you aboard, sir!"

Espying a couple of early-arriving horse boxes and a lumbering beer-delivery wagon entering the field on his starboard bow, Commander Plimsoll-Pompey then veered off and headed like a galleon in full sail to direct the approaching flotilla to their respective moorings. His crew of white-coated, indigenous swabs, meantime, merely stood taking the muttering-micky and left him to it. If the loud-mouthed, bombastic old balloon was daft enough to do all the work himself, he was fuckin' welcome to. And that had always been *their* motto!

It was Jigger's an' all.

The slow thud of rotors carrying on the still air from the direction of the old manse told him that Babu Ng was preparing for the short hop over to the castle esplanade, which had been designated by the Commander as the start/finish point of the free helicopter rides for the duration of the Fair.

Jigger turned to Davie. "Got the Polaroid ready?"

"Yep. All set."

"OK, you know the routine." He handbrake-turned the pick-up and started back for the castle, divots flying from the truck's wheels. "As soon as he comes out of the chopper, I'll walk up to him and try to keep him facing in your direction for as long as possible. Take as many snaps as you can, then shoot off back home through the woods in the pick-up. Your mother will have the fax machine all set for firing off the best of the pictures to Police HQ in Edinburgh. The Chief Constable's expecting them, so there should be no problems. All right?"

"Right, got all that, Dad."

Jigger pulled the peak of his baseball cap down to a businesslike tilt over his eyes and growled, "OK! As they say in the movies, let's kick ass!"

"YEE-EE-EE-HA-AH-AH!" Davie yelled, planting his feet on the dashboard for maximum purchase, as the truck broadsided and leapt at full speed over the undulating turf. He'd watched these sort of stunts in *The Dukes of Hazard* often enough on telly when he was a nipper, but the real thing was, well . . . WOW!

Babu Ng's expression on alighting from his helicopter was, to say the least, one of extreme disaffection. He stood and stared icily at Jigger, while the beat of the slowing rotor blades struck Jigger as being a bit too similar to the slashing of a cut-throat's knife for his liking.

"So, Mr McCloud," Ng said at last, his features and entire bearing a chilling marriage of cobra and vulture, "you appear to have made an amazingly speedy recovery from the effects of your unfortunate accident last night, no?"

Sidling round a bit so that Ng was standing full-face to the pick-up, Jigger touched the back of his head with accentuated caution and sucked in sharply through his teeth. "Oo-ya! Still hurts somethin' terrible!"

Ng's eyes narrowed to cynical slits. "And have you recovered anything of your power of memory yet?" he asked dryly.

Jigger scratched his chin, gave a short burst of hillbilly laughter, shook his head and replied, "Nah, not that I can remember, anyhow."

"Your quaint, boorish act does not impress me, my friend. Already one person has met with the fate common to all who are suspected of betraying me. You know, of course, to whom I refer?"

His mouth gaping in the expectant grin of the innocent yokel, Jigger asked in reply, "The band agent that flogged you that crap trio for your wife's party?"

The screech of the pick-up burning rubber behind him confirmed to Jigger that Davie had done the Polaroid business and was on his way. All he hoped now was that the quality of the faxed photographs would be sharp enough for the police to run a check on Ng through Interpol.

Ng eyed the departing truck with undisguised suspicion. "You will recall," he snapped at Jigger, "that on our first meeting I advised you — to the sound of your invisible poultry — not to play your fraudulent little games with me, for you would always be the loser, yes?"

"Eh, no! My memory seems to have let me down there as well, if you see what I'm sayin', like."

Ng stepped forward and punched Jigger on the shoulder with a leather-gloved fist. His chin was quivering with pent-up fury. "Permit me to warn you, Mr Jigger Hillbilly McCloud, that if my stolen property has not been returned to me intact by the end of this day, you will not live to see the start of another!"

By mid-morning, there was a tailback of traffic stretching all the way from the estate gates through Cuddyford Village and almost a mile down the Horseburgh road. Sergeant Brown had never seen nothin' like it. Bloody frightenin', he said it was, and a damned good job it was, too, that he'd had the perspexacity to draft in a few extra polis for point duty and that. He himself was directing operations by two-way radio from his Panda car, which he'd strategically stationed behind the main beer tent at Craigcuddy Castle.

The Duke, despite the resounding apathy with which he had greeted Jigger's initial suggestion of resurrecting the Cuddyford Fair, was now absolutely revelling in the atmosphere. He was strolling in his kilt among the milling crowds, doffing his deerstalker to pretty face after pretty face, and even allowing the occasional toddler to pat his dogs. Of course, these dogs, being labs, were totally at a loss as to what to make of it all, but were grateful, nevertheless, for being offered the previously unexplored opportunity of enjoying a quick slobber at the occasional lab-high, ice-cream-covered face.

The Duke had now had a couple of days in which to make what he could (which wasn't much) of the contents of the comprehensive Five-year Plan for Craigcuddy Estate that young Maggie's brace of anonymous academic admirers had rustled up. Jigger, therefore, had as much confidence as was realistically possible (which wasn't much either) that old Horace would be capable of presenting the document with some authority to the group of high-ranking officials of the Royal Scottish Commerce Bank, who, with their wives, were to be his guests at a private alfresco luncheon on a castle balcony overlooking the delightful setting of the Fair. It was, however, an even bet, Jigger calculated, that the bankers wouldn't be able to make much savvy of the intentionally-complex details of the plan either. And this, in the presence of the money men's ambitiously-vying wives, would be all to the good.

Jigger's main concern in that regard was to ensure that the eavesdropping ears of Archibald Gormlie-Crighton were kept well away from the Duke's informal, though life-or-death, financial conference. To this end, Bertola Harvey had been primed to lure old Archie away at the appropriate moment to the arena, where it had been carefully timed that the professional five-a-side football tournament would then be commencing. Representative sides from several of Scotland's premier clubs, including Rangers and Celtic, had accepted invitations to take part, so the bookies would be out in force. And that would be right up Archie's street.

Since most of the kids would be temporarily more interested in watching their football heroes than taking a free helicopter ride, Jigger had also chosen this hour as the one for springing his trap on Babu Ng. For the purpose, odd as it may seem, he required to call upon

331

the assistance of young Lord Ludovic. With this in mind, he had noted that, at about the same time, Nessie would be competing in a motocross event in the upper glen of Craigcuddy Wood. So it was there that he'd picked as the most secure and, being well away from the booze tents, the least distracting location in which to explain the relevant details of his plan to Ludo . . .

"As long as you remember to stress that it's Château Lafite 1961, the rest'll be a doddle, I guarantee it."

Ludo's jaw dropped and he gazed heavenward as if searching for some sort of celestial autocue. "Yah, now, uh, just let me run all of this past myself one more time, Jigger mate. Keep me right, right?"

"Right."

"Right — I nobble Ng at the snack bar or wherever, and casually bring the conversation round to the subject of wine."

"That's it."

"OK, then I drop the old bombshell — still casually, of course — that one's old man has this very morning taken delivery of a couple of cases of, wait for it, Château Lafite 1961 — arf, arf, arf! — and would he be interested in quaffing a gargle of same with one's good self? Right, mate?"

"Right, so far."

They paused, fingers in ears, while three motorbikes flew past, line abreast, at an altitude of fifteen feet. Jigger recognised Nessie as the meat in the sandwich by her distinctive red leathers and, lest there be a modicum of doubt, by her loopy caper of raising one hand high off the handlebars to wave merrily at him as she roared hell-for-leather through the air.

He shook his head. "The mother of my children," he muttered to himself in resigned disbelief.

Ludo took a deep breath and continued his parrot-like recitation of his instructions . . .

Once he had led Ng down to the cellar, he would guide him over to the claret racks and point out the bottles of the jolly old '61. Then he'd make the excuse that he'd forgotten to bring a corkscrew and wine glasses, and would, accordingly, nip back up to the kitchens to fetch them, leaving Ng to his own devices.

"Bull's eye, Ludo. That's it in a nutshell."

"Ah . . . righty-ho," smiled Ludo, apparently quite surprised that he'd got it right. His smile quickly faded into a customary frown of puzzlement, however. "But tell me, old mate," he said, "what the fuck is all this about?"

"Best that you don't know too much at this stage, Ludo. Too dangerous. But just bear in mind, the future of your father, the estate, your entrance into Her Majesty's Government, and maybe even the very future of the Gormlie-Crighton name will depend on you not ballsing this up. Got me?"

"Wow, no pressure there, then," Ludo yodelled, blanching by the second. "But, yah, you — you can rely on me, mate." His eyes darted furtively from side to side, then he whispered hopefully, "But, uhm, what say we toddle back down to the jolly old hooch marquee for a quick belt before zero hour, OK?"

"Toddle away," Jigger replied with a shrug. "But you're toddling on your tod. I'm off to check a snare."

"Aye, fine that, then, Mr McCloud," the Chief Constable lilted in his sing-song Highland brogue, his booming voice skilfully lowered for the occasion to the stealthy tones of the highly-trained, on-the-case sleuth. "Your laddie has made a fine job of installing yon video camera. Yes, chust fine." He took a closer look. "Michty me, the lens looks chust like the top of a bottle hidden away in the wine rack there, so it does."

"Yeah, Davie's a dab hand at the electronics, right enough," Jigger replied. "So, you see, all we have to do now is hit the remote control button here at the crucial moment, and Bob's yer uncle."

"And after that you'll leave everything to me, mind, laddie." The Chief Constable was not mincing his words. "The apprehension of a desperate suspect," he cautioned, "is not a job for a amachoor."

"Whatever you say, Chief. It's your show from now on. Which reminds me — thanks for sending down your mounted bobbies to put on a display here today. Much appreciated."

"Och, but it's good for them, Mr McCloud — a nice day in the country like this. Aye, a big change from having cigarettes stubbed out on their rear ends by the hooligans in Edinburgh every Saturday during the football season, so it is."

Jigger was aghast. "Talk about cruelty to animals!"

The Chief allowed himself a quiet wee chuckle. "Well now, city hooligans they may be, but they're no that daft. No, no — it's the polismen's arses they stub their fags out on, laddie, no the horses'!"

Jigger put a finger to his lips. "Shoosht! Voices!"

Cocking an educated ear, the Chief promptly deduccd: "Aye, there's somebody coming!" Then, stepping lightly on the balls of his Doc Marten-shod feet, he shepherded Jigger into a low, arched alcove that reeked of mould and mouse droppings. They crouched behind a cobweb-curtained wine rack, listening in the gloom as the voices and their affiliated footsteps descended the stone staircase and entered the cellar to the creaking of its stout oak door.

Jigger pressed the camcorder's remote button and mouthed a silent prayer that Davie was really as dab a hand at this sparks caper as he had boasted.

"Yah, absolutely spot on, Babu mate," young Ludo's voice enthused. "Indeed, it may well have been Jigger who fixed one's old boy up with the Lafite. One can't say for sure, OK — but old Jigger, well, he *is* always flogging something, right? Arf, arf!"

Ng stood inside the door. He scrupulously surveyed the vaulted expanse of the cellar, his dark eyes glinting in the glow of naked light bulbs as he satisfied himself, like a panther entering a jungle clearing, that no danger lurked ahead.

"OK, claret, right?" mumbled Ludo, while strolling down the ranks of near-empty racks that stood ceiling-high like the deserted combs of giant bees, the best of whose bottled honey had been systematically filched over the years by none other than the mumbling stroller himself. "Now, where would old Elephant Bollocks be hiding the claret these days?"

Ng followed noiselessly behind, his face a sphinx-like mask, his darting eyes everywhere.

"Jackpot! Yah, here we are, Babu — the Bordeaux department. Now to locate the jolly old Lafite!"

But Ng's attentions were already concentrated elsewhere. As if guided by some strange sixth sense, he had homed directly in on the rack immediately opposite the alcove in which the two trappers lay in wait. It was the very rack in which Jigger had placed the bait the night before. Ng gently extracted a bottle and held it up to a light bulb dangling above.

The Chief Constable gave Jigger a dig in the ribs, followed by a confident thumbs-up. The stakeout was coming good.

"Hey, don't tell me!" Ludo exclaimed in mock shock, while loping over to join Ng. "Old Elephant Bollocks has stashed the latest Bordeaux batch in the Burgundy department, right? Sly old creep. Still, a claret by any other name . . ."

Ng replaced the first bottle and pulled out another, though this time taking particular care not to hold it too close to the light.

Ludo leaned over his shoulder. "What say, mate? Fancy a glug? Come on — one's old boy will never miss an Aristotle or two." His exhortations were clearly falling on deaf ears, but Ludo kept to Jigger's script all the same. "Hey, tell you what, Babu," he said, "you hang about here for a mo while I dive up aloft and fetch an opener and a couple of jars, what!"

Even before the echo of Ludo's decamping footsteps had died away, Ng was scraping frantically with a penknife around the base of the bottle, twisting off the bottom and shaking out the first "burger". Quickly opening the covering of brown wax paper, he poked a forefinger into the packet's powdery contents, then dabbed it gingerly onto the tip of his tongue.

"I have it!" he cried, his triumphant declaration the first words he had uttered since entering the cellar. "I have it!"

"Correction!" thundered the Chief Constable as he stepped out from the shadows of the alcove. "You've *had* it! Aye, you're nicked, laddie, and it is my jooty to caution you in front of this here witness that —"

"Get back from me!" Ng yelled, that same scared-stiff look on his face that Jigger had seen back in the Acredales farmyard when Granny offered to air-condition the seat of his pants with her shotgun. "Get back, or you are both dead men. I mean it!"

They knew he meant it. The revolver that had suddenly appeared in his right hand convinced them.

"Are you packin'?" Jigger muttered in the Chief's ear.

"What's the point? We'll not be going anywhere, by the looks of things."

"No — I mean are you carrying a shooter? You know, packin' a rod, like they say in the gangster movies."

The Chief Constable chose to remain silent, but Jigger noticed a look of deep concern spreading over his craggy features.

337

"Face that wall with your hands high and pressed against it!" Ng rasped. "Quickly!"

They complied. *Very* quickly.

"Now, if you move a muscle, I will blow your thick heads off your shoulders!"

They heard the pad of his feet hurrying away down the rows of wine racks, the groaning thud of the door slamming to, the rusty grind of the lock turning, and then the spine-chilling rattle of the key being removed. They were trapped!

"We're trapped," the Chief Constable confirmed, red-faced and gasping for breath after making his umpteenth shoulder charge at the door. "Ach, I'll never knock this thing down in a month of dry Stornoway Sundays, Mr McCloud."

Jigger was leaning cross-legged against the wall, thinking hard. "Hmm, I kinda suspected that myself — eh, in my own amateurish way, like," he muttered. "Yeah, and don't bank on Lord Ludovic coming to our rescue. He was well-and-truly told to keep right away from here once he'd delivered Ng, so he'll now be busy celebrating the delivery by propping up the bar in the nearest bevvy tent."

"Well now, we're entombed down here in the bowels of the earth sure enough, then," the Chief concluded. He pushed his silver-braided cap back and scratched his head. "Aye, aye, maybe I should have put my wee two-way handset in my pocket after all." He looked squarely at Jigger and raised a confidential eyebrow. "But I'll be honest with you, laddie — I was feart in case some thick-heided polisman might have broke radio silence and would have blew the whole rickmatick."

"Mmm," Jigger droned absentmindedly, eyes down, still deep in thought. "God spare us from thick-heided polismen, right enough."

Jigger was trying to recall something that the Duke had said when they met for that confab in the Great Hall; his answer to Jigger's question about where the secret passage led from and to. What was it the old boy had said? Something about nowhere but everywhere . . . if you do it right. Yeah, that was it! And that would tie in with the stuff he'd read about these dungeons in the old "Legends" book. He took up position with his back against the concealed door that he already knew was the exit from the tunnel, and pointed his right hand to the corner of the cellar diagonally opposite.

"Let's take a look behind that wine rack over there, Chief. If there's a door there, our bums may not be completely out of the window yet."

That seemed logical enough for the Chief Constable. Or so he claimed. In the wink of a Highland cow's eye, he had applied his considerable weight to the bulky framework and had moved it sufficiently to confirm that Jigger's interpretation of the Duke's conundrum was correct. What's more, the ancient door opened — not without putting up a struggle, but ultimately yielding to the force of the Chief's expert shoulder, nonetheless. And it *did* open into a passage, just as Jigger had hoped.

By the trusty light of the Chief Constable's rubber truncheon-torch, they passed through the doorway, then groped their way through a maze of dank passageways, always taking the right fork whenever there was a choice. And sure enough, the cackling chatter of women at work eventually beckoned them to a chink of light in a wooden partition up ahead.

Remembering how the Duke had made his entrance on the day of the Ludo-for-Labour-Candidate meeting, Jigger put his fingers to the sliver of light and effortlessly slid the oak panel aside. Unfortunately, though, he hadn't acted quickly enough to forestall the Chief Constable's instinctive shoulder charge straight through the now-open secret entrance. He staggered at the gallop into the Great Hall, where teams of Mrs Plimsoll-Pompey's helpers could only stand gaping in shocked disbelief as the cobwebbed copper crashed headlong through ranks of stepladders and trestles, shouting:

"Stand back in the name of the law, the lot of ye! This is polis business!"

Shrugging his apologies to all concerned, Jigger followed in his leader's wake, onwards and outwards until they reached the castle's main entrance. There, however, the scene that greeted him made the chaos which had just been created in the Great Hall look like a harmless game of musical chairs in comparison.

Women and children were running screaming in all directions, causing their confused menfolk to desert the beer tents in droves — some even without their drinks. Panic reigned.

"He's got a gun!" was the concerted cry. "Run for your life!"

Jigger made a beeline for the pie stall, where Granny had been doing a roaring trade selling her home-bakes.

"It's Maggie," she shouted as soon as she saw Jigger fighting his way through the scattering crowds. "That dirty Baboon bastard — he's taken Maggie!"

"What do you mean, he's taken Maggie? She was told not to leave the stall here, and you were supposed to be looking after her, for God's sake!"

The old woman's normally unflappable temperament was in tatters. "He — he just barged in and grabbed her," she stammered. "And — and he put a pistol to her head. He was raving like a madman. Honest, there was nothing I could do . . ."

"It's all right, Granny," Jigger said, giving her a reassuring pat on the hand while trying to gather his thoughts. "Sorry — I shouldn't have got on at you like that."

Suddenly, there was a cacophonous thwacking of air and the roaring whine of an aero engine. Ng's helicopter rose from the other side of the castle and swept low and fast over the site of the Fair. The turbulence from its rotors was sucking up great vortexes of dust and buffeting the canvas of the tents like sails in a hurricane.

"What's happening?" yelled Nessie, her arrival on her motorbike having gone unnoticed in the pandemonium.

Jigger pointed upwards to where their daughter's terrified eyes were staring at them from inside the helicopter. "Look!" he shouted. "He's heading north." Then, as the chopper roared away at speed, the realisation of what Ng was up to struck him like a thunderbolt. "The bugger's heading straight for the coast at Cavey Cove!" he growled. "That motor launch of his — it must still be there. Quick!" he called to Nessie. "He's gonna use Maggie as a hostage for his getaway. Let's get hold of a fast car!"

"Not a chance, lad." It was the sombre voice of Sergeant Brown, standing with his two-way radio held firmly to his ear. "The road out o' here is jammed solid for half a mile or more. Cars comin' and goin' all at once now. Gridlock. Bloody shambles."

"OK, Sarge," Jigger said, "get word to the Chief Constable — wherever he's got to — and tell him to get some back-up down to Cavey Cove by whatever way he can. We're off there right now, cross country!" He turned to Granny and gave her as reassuring a wink as he could. "It'll be OK," he told her. "Don't you worry."

With that, he leapt onto the big Honda behind Nessie, and in a shower of flying gravel and a rasping belch of exhaust smoke they were away.

"Hold on tight," Nessie yelled over her shoulder. "We'll have to cut through the woods and jump the burn at the far side!"

Jigger didn't need to be told twice. Both hands were already clinging like limpets to the most conveniently clingable parts of Nessie's anatomy — a sensation which, even under the prevailing stressful and perilous circumstances, he found distinctly pleasurable. If they were fortunate enough to get out of this madcap chase alive, he'd have to suggest to Nessie that it might be an interesting bedtime idea to swap slinky black nightie for kinky red leathers once in a while. The impact of landing splay-legged on the motorbike's unyielding back mudguard after being propelled into a lengthy trajectory over the Cuddy Burn rapidly cooled his ardour, however. He promptly re-focused his thoughts on the serious mission in hand.

"Take a look at Ng's chopper," he shouted in Nessie's helmeted ear. "If I didn't know better, I'd swear he was pissed!"

Sure enough, although still a good half mile ahead of them, the helicopter had reduced speed noticeably and was dipping and slewing wildly.

Once out of the woods, Nessie twisted the throttle wide open and, front wheel pawing the air like a rearing stallion, the big red Honda took off through a field of spring barley with its pilot and passenger holding on for dear life.

Jigger pointed frantically ahead. "Look at the chopper now!" he yelled. "The damned thing's coming down. Bloody hell, he's gonna crash land in the piggery!"

Using a handily-placed knoll as a launching ramp, Nessie cleared the main road in one giant leap and made a perfect one-point landing in the track leading down to the old radar station. She slid her machine to a sideways halt in a cloud of dust about fifty yards from where the helicopter had come to earth on the edge of the little wood by the piggery.

"At least he's got it down in one piece," she panted, pulling off her crash helmet. "Let's rush him before he gets his wits together!"

But before they had taken a single step, the helicopter door flew open and Maggie was unceremoniously bundled out, landing in a sprawling heap on the ground, with Ng following immediately after. He stood towering over her, revolver in hand. Even from where they stood, Jigger and Nessie could make out the crazed look in his eyes, his body swaying as he took unsteady aim at Maggie's head.

Without thinking, they both started to run towards him, shouting in a desperate attempt to make themselves heard above the clatter of the helicopter's still-whirling rotors.

Ng raised his head and, catching sight of them, fired a couple of wild shots in their direction. One bullet ricocheted off a fence post away to Jigger's left. The other thudded into the ground inches in front of their feet, stopping them cold in their tracks.

Realising that his only means of escape would be by using Maggie as a shield, Ng hauled her to her feet and held her in a neck-lock from behind, his revolver pressed to her cheek. Nessie and Jigger could only stand there watching helplessly as Ng staggered backwards towards the wood, dragging Maggie with him. Suddenly he stumbled, seeming to lose the power of his legs, as if hit behind the knees by some unseen force. He fell to one side, pulling Maggie down with him, but letting the gun slip from his grasp as his elbow smashed heavily into the ground.

Maggie seized the opportunity to wriggle half free of Ng's restraining arm. She reached for the gun, only for Ng to throw himself clumsily on top of her. He grabbed

344

her wrist in both hands as her outstretched fingers closed round the barrel.

Yelling their encouragement, Jigger and Nessie charged forward, but were abruptly halted by Ng screaming incoherent threats at them while he wrestled Maggie onto her back and locked one hand around her throat.

"The gun!" Jigger shouted. "Get rid of the gun, Maggie!"

Desperately summoning up every last dreg of her strength, Maggie responded by wriggling a leg free of Ng's lunging weight and ramming her knee into his groin. During the ensuing split second that his grip slackened on her wrist, Maggie flicked her hand backwards, lobbing the revolver in the direction of a thick tangle of brambles at the edge of the wood. But it fell agonisingly short. Ng grabbed it and gave Maggie's a sickening blow to the side of her head for her efforts.

"The bastard!" Jigger growled and started instinctively forward.

Nessie took hold of his arm. "Stay where you are! It'll only make it worse for Maggie."

Ng heaved himself back onto his feet, yanking Maggie up by the hair then brutally forcing one of her arms up her back.

"If you wish her to live, you will come no further!" he bellowed at Jigger and Nessie, his speech strangely slurred. "I warn you, she will be dead before you have taken two paces." He crooked his arm around her throat again, forcing her head backwards, straining her neck to the point of breaking.

Nessie had to physically restrain Jigger yet again. "Please, Jigger, don't move," she pleaded. "He's not only desperate, he's flipped, and he'll snap Maggie's neck without a second thought."

"This is when we need the US Cavalry to come cantering over the horizon," Jigger muttered stonily, never more wishful that one of his movie fantasies might actually come true.

But there was no spirit-rousing bugle call to be heard, only the tense hush that followed the final thrashes of the helicopter's dying motor. Yet there *was* a far-off sound that did resemble the faint rumble of galloping hooves. Jigger and Nessie exchanged puzzled glances. They could hear it plainly now. It was the unmistakable sound of horses approaching at speed, but superimposed with a frenzied nasal buzzing, as if they were being chased by a swarm of horseflies.

Ng had heard it too, and he redoubled his struggle to drag Maggie into the cover of the wood. But he stopped short as the source of this curious clamour became apparent.

There, bursting into view at the top of the track, was the entire mounted force of Edinburgh City Police, the Chief Constable himself riding point immediately behind the most unlikely of trailblazers. It was Granny. She was crouched over the handlebars of her moped, her long skirts billowing around her waist as she careered full-throttle down the lane.

"I brung 'em across the fields," she yelled triumphantly as soon as she was within earshot. But Granny's elation was summarily deflated as soon as she became aware of the mortal danger young Maggie was now facing.

With raised hand, the Chief Constable signalled his troops to halt close to where Granny had already joined Jigger and Nessie. "Dismount!" he shouted. "And prepare to advance! Truncheons at the ready!"

However, a warning shot from Ng's revolver saw the Chief promptly reassessing the situation from an astute position in the lee of his horse's rump. "Take cover and await my command, men," he grunted, a measure of prudence suddenly tempering the veteran lawman's sense of duty.

His rapid approach obscured until now by the clouds of dust that had been raised by the galloping horses, young Davie, with a visibly shaken Bertola by his side, skidded the pick-up to a stop at the side of the track. He kicked open the little truck's badly-battered door, which seemed to have half the hedgerows of Horseburghshire hanging from it, ducked low and scurried over to join his distraught parents and great-grandmother.

Jigger tried to put a brave face on things for him. "Talk about yer Mexican stand-offs, eh! Welcome to John Wayne country, son."

But Davie wasn't in the mood for platitudes. He stared in horror at his sister's plight. "If I get my hands on that swine over there," he snarled, "I'll tear him limb from limb!"

"Aye, but ye'll have to get in line, sonny," Granny muttered. "I'll leave ye a leg, though."

Out of the blue, a commotion resembling a distinctly one-sided dog fight started up inside the pick-up.

"Cool it!" Bertola was heard to shout. "Don't lose the place, daddy! Hey, too many heroes end up stiff, man!"

But there was no stopping Bert. He was out of the cab in a flash. In a burst of speed that belied his girth, he scampered across the no-man's-land that separated the stationary combatants and sunk his teeth deep into Babu Ng's ankle. Screaming in agony, Ng released his stranglehold on Maggie, dropped the gun again and launched a frantic attempt to shake Bert off his leg.

Like a portly will-o'-the-wisp, a hunched figure then appeared through the door of the piggery, slightly behind and just out of sight of the writhing and hopping Babu Ng. Then, before any of the others had fully realised what was happening, a one-litre bottle of whisky was smashed down on the Ng's head, felling him like a tree.

"Jesus Christ, Ardonski," Jigger shouted angrily as Maggie threw herself sobbing into her rescuer's arms, "you might have bloody well used an empty one!"

EPILOGUE

Of Burgers and Baths

"Cuff him!" commanded the Chief Constable after a perfunctory check with one of his Size 13 Doc Martens had confirmed that there was still a groan of life in the prostrate body of Babu Ng. "And then fling him in yon pigsty. When he comes to, he'll feel at home in there until the Black Maria gets here." Then, turning to Jigger, he said in all seriousness, "No offence to your pigs intended, Mr McCloud."

"None taken, Chief."

"Fine that, then, laddie." The Chief Constable then cleared his throat with a force befitting his rank, lowered his voice to a confidential level and said, "My, it was stoorie work riding all the way down here like that, Mr McCloud. Aye, and the smell of yon spilt whisky makes a man fair thirsty, so it does."

Jigger tipped the wink to Johnny Ardonski, who repaired to the sanctum of the old radar station and returned with a jam jar containing a hospitable helping of Jigger's "Home Brew".

This the Chief accepted gratefully. "Michty me, is that the time already?" he asked, glancing at the pocket watch he'd conspicuously produced. "Well now, that'll be me off jooty, so it will." He took a sizeable slurp of whisky. "Good health!"

"My wery best respecks," said Johnny, returning the compliment and treating himself to a sociable slug from a half bottle of vodka that had materialised from his inside jacket pocket.

With a wag of his forefinger, Jigger declined Johnny's kind invitation to join him in a nip from his bottle. He still had the Duke's Hunt Ball gig to play tonight, after all.

So, for that matter, had Bertola, who also elected not to imbibe just yet, but proceeded to roll himself a nerve-settling spliff instead.

The Chief Constable, dewy eyed, started to hum a plaintive Hebridean air as the smoke from Bertola's ignited joint wafted over his jam jar. "Losh, laddie," he said, a warble of emotion contorting the deep drone of his voice into something akin to a tuneless Highland yodel, "the whiff of yon herbal tobacco fair takes me back to the Skye of my youth. Aye, the smoke o' the peat fire flame in the wee but an' ben, the smell o' the burning heather on the far Cuillins . . ."

"Whatever turns you on, man," Bertola mumbled in a wheezy monotone. "But I'll stick with the Lowland grass."

The Chief was oblivious to Bertola's thinly-veiled reference to his narcotic preference. His nostrils flared luxuriantly as he savoured the heady nose of Jigger's "Home Brew". "Aye, and this single malt reminds me of something as well. Let me see now . . ." He sipped another goodly nip and swilled it expertly around his mouth, making a hollow sloshing sound not dissimilar to that of an old stirrup pump being primed. "Well, well," he continued, pausing to smack his lips, "at first I was tempted to say that it reminded me of my very favourite, the twelve-year-old Glenreckie. But damn me, Mr McCloud, if anything, this stuff is even better!"

Jigger nervously massaged the lobe of his ear. "Yeah, well let's just say there's some truth in what you say there, Chief," he said, paying cryptic homage to the purloined Glenreekie malted barley from which his much-praised moonshine was made. "But, ehm, we're both men o' the world, I daresay, and some things are even better when there's a wee shroud of mystery about them — if you see what I'm saying, like."

The Chief tapped the side of his nose and slowly lowered one bushy eyebrow into a wink of masonic intensity. "Say no more, laddie. Say no more." He sniffed the jam jar again and leaned closer to Jigger, whispering, "A braw dram, mind you. Aye, a braw dram. Eh, I don't suppose, Mr McCloud, that there would be . . .?"

Jigger nodded the almost imperceptible nod of the practised auction bidder, then confirmed out of the corner of his mouth, "Next hay delivery — six bottles — tidy price."

Nessie came over from the pick-up, where she had been busy comforting her distressed daughter. "I was just asking Maggie why Ng lost control of the helicopter and set it down here, half a mile short of Cavey Cove."

351

"That's right," said Jigger, "if he hadn't done that, he'd likely have escaped dead easy. What did Maggie say?"

"She says he just came over all funny — eyes rolling, foaming at the mouth and talking gibberish and everything. Honest, she really thought he was going to crash the blooming thing."

Jigger stroked his chin. "Weird."

"Och, don't even concern yourselfs about it. One of my bobbies will breathalyse him when he wakes up," the Chief Constable assured them, then swallowed another swig of his new-found favourite. "On top of everything that Interpol has told us about him, we'll be nicking him for being drunk in charge of a helicopter, if I'm any judge of the evidence."

Bertola edged over to Jigger's side. "The fuzz is talkin' crap, man," he muttered.

Jigger cast him a what-the-hell-are-you-on-about? sort of scowl.

"It was the vol-au-vents, pops."

"The *vol-au-vents*?"

"Yeah, the Ng cat was scoffing a plateful of them back in the snack tent. Mushroom ones, dig?"

Jigger shook his head. "Nope. Don't dig."

"Get with it, man! He was all ears listenin' to Ludo's wine cellar spiel, OK, so I like sprinkled a few slices of my titanic toadstools onto his vol-au-vents when he wasn't lookin'. Just kinda figured it might slow his tempo down a bit if it came to a jam session."

"Now I do dig," Jigger beamed. He slapped Bertola's back. "And that means it's really you we've got to thank for helping save Maggie. Well, you and your magic mushrooms, at any rate," he added in a guarded whisper.

"Yeah, well, such so-called *illegal* substances do have their uses, man," Bertola shrugged, then exhaled a cloud of herbal smoke which drifted off under the nostalgia-steeped nostrils of the Chief Constable.

Jigger said a silent amen to that and poured the Chief another dram of "Home Brew".

The Hunt Ball — or the Cuddyford Fair Charity Ball, as it had now been officially dubbed — seemed to pass unusually quickly for Jigger. So many incredible things had happened in the previous twenty-four hours, yet many unresolved matters were still left spinning round and round in his mind. Not that he didn't enjoy the gig. In truth, he had rarely had such a ball. It was the first time that his full band had played together for a while, so spirits were high and they made music to match, much to the unbridled enjoyment of the rare social mix of revellers who had packed into the cleverly made-up Great Hall for the big event.

Those hesitant seeds of cross-community harmony that had been sown on the night of Sabrina Ng's party germinated and sprouted sufficiently during the Ball to suggest that, while it might take some time (if at all) for their shoots to blossom and fully flower, an acceptable enough show of seedling camaraderie could be relied upon when the occasion warranted. Babu Ng had done Cuddyford a favour.

But it was a month or so later, when most of the dust of that eventful spring had finally settled and life at Acredales of Cuddyford had returned to uncomplicated, unhurried normality, that Jigger and his little family at last got round to taking stock of things. And all in all, they agreed, things could have turned out a lot worse.

The law having frozen the assets of the incarcerated Babu Ng, the Royal Scottish Commerce Bank — with the endorsement of those officials (and their wives) who had graced the castle balcony for the May Fair luncheon — consented to lend the Duke an umbrella just as soon as the sun began to shine on the proposed executive housing development in the wee valley behind the Dower House. And if Mick Murphy had his way (which he invariably did), an early sunrise was virtually guaranteed. Consequently, the golf course and other mooted money-making schemes for Craigcuddy Estate all started to appear more feasible, and Commander Plimsoll-Pompey and his band of "community-minded" citizens stiffened their resolve to convert such feasibilities into realities.

As for another of the Duke's problems, namely Cousin Archie, all that anyone knew was that he had disappeared as quickly as he had arrived. In Jigger's opinion, he would probably have decided to put his Machiavellian ploys aside and make a timely return to where there were more opportunities for bent poker games than he'd ever find around Cuddyford, secure in the knowledge that his principal creditor would be spending the next few years behind bars. And although Granny was adamant that Archie would turn up again like the proverbial bad penny one day, Jigger reckoned it would be time enough to worry about that if, or when, that day ever came. For the present, the Duke (and, therefore, the McClouds) were safe from Archie's machinations, and that was all that mattered.

Meanwhile, young Lord Ludovic was also looking less of a future problem for his father by the day. As Jigger had so shrewdly recognised, the lad was a natural politician; all smiles, balderdash and bonhomie. As the weeks flew past in the run-up to the local by-election, Ludo became the bookies' favourite to increase even further his party's already sizeable majority in the Horseburghshire constituency, so popular had he become with all the nouveau rustique yuppies who had settled in the area. Luckily for Ludo, they were found to be keen converts to fondue-set socialism after just one glad-handing session with a real blue-blooded, red-rosetted lord right there on their own heavily-mortgaged front door steps.

Yet, busy canvassing for votes as he was, Ludo still found time to pay regular visits to Acredales, ostensibly to confer with his "agent" Jigger, but in truth to pursue his growing infatuation with young Maggie, who, it must be said, continued to lead him a right merry dance. She was one yuppie who was *not* for converting. Or so she would have it appear . . .

After one hot and thirsty June day of turning and baling hay over at the Home Farm, Jigger and young Davie were happy to be sitting in the pleasant evening sunshine outside their own kitchen door, enjoying a bottle of ice cold beer, lazily swatting midges, and listening to two thrushes gushing out their full-throated songs from the Scots pine windbreak behind the steading.

"Bonny that," Davie remarked sleepily.

"Mmm, tidy. Ye'll never hear anything bonnier than a thrush singing, son — except maybe two, like."

"And just hear how they repeat their favourite wee phrases! Amazing that. I've never noticed it before."

"Yeah, two cock thrushes singing away like that in the mating season never fails to amaze me either, Davie. Even more amazing when you think what it is that they're actually saying to each other in these bonny wee songs."

"Uh-huh? And what's that, Dad?"

"Get the hell out o' my territory, ye spotty bastard!"

"Here! That's no way to speak to yer own son!" Granny scolded, shuffling out of the kitchen carrying a tray of food. "He can be a right pain in the arse at times, right enough, but so were you at his age, and yer grandfather never told *you* to leave home!"

Jigger leaned back in his chair, closed his eyes and chortled away quietly to himself. "Aye, aye, Granny. Whatever you say . . . whatever you say . . ."

Nessie and Maggie appeared from the kitchen next, a selection of plates and cutlery in their hands.

"Come on, grab your own," Nessie said. "We're having our tea out here tonight. Too nice to sit inside."

The aroma of hot food lingering on the still evening air soon had the predictable effect on Bert. In accordance with his habit at this time of day, he'd been having a quiet kip over by the barn door. Stirring from his dreams, he ambled over to the table and, with an expectant grin on his upturned face, sat down, rather surprisingly, at Granny's feet.

"Heavens above!" Nessie gasped. "What's come over Bert?"

"Never mind, Gran. Better to have a dog fawn on you than bite you," Maggie quipped, "as Babu Ng would doubtless now say."

"Aye, and that's why I've made the smelly wee tyke this," said Granny, while placing a dish in front of Bert and giving him an unprecedented pat on his head. "It's a hamburger! 'Cos remember, one way or another, it was him and his burgers that saved everybody's bacon."

"Absolutely," said Jigger, his face a picture of unashamed pride as he watched his little pal wolfing into the scrumptious treat that he'd waited for so long to taste. "Forget yer Lassies and Greyfriars Bobbies, boy. Some day Hollywood will make a movie about you. You're a real wee star."

Bert momentarily interrupted his eager gobbling to bark his acknowledgement of that compliment.

"See," Jigger said to the others, "the wee bugger knows every word ye say!"

And maybe he did at that. But words or no words, what Bert certainly did know was that all was well in his little world, and that was a feeling affectionately shared by the whole family. Bert knew that, too.

"I'll tell you this for nothing," said Nessie, preparing to clear the table when the sun setting behind the pines had begun to dapple the yard with shadows, "if there's

357

anything to be learned from all the goings-on of late, it must be that we should just be thankful for what we've got."

"How true," agreed Maggie. "Catch not the shadow and lose the substance, as the old proverb goes."

Jigger stood up, stretched his arms and yawned. "I couldn't have put it better myself. But anyway — no rest for the wicked. I'm away down to the old manse before it gets too dark."

"What on earth for?" said Nessie, a mischievous glint in her eye. "I thought Sabrina had flown the coop."

"Yeah, and it's a pity if she has," said Jigger. He winked at Nessie, then looked her up and down with a critical eye. "But, as you so truly put it, we just have to be thankful for what we've got, eh?"

Granny gathered her brows into a scowl of suspicion. "Why go over there at this time of night, then?"

"To get the old doors and bath back, of course," Jigger called over his shoulder as he lifted Bert into the pick-up. "Yeah, I know just the man who'll pay me a right tidy price for that stuff!"

No Suspicious Circumstances

The Mulgray Twins

It can be tough working undercover for HM Revenue & Customs, but DJ Smith has more than a little help from her trained sniffer cat, Gorgonzola, a moth-eaten Persian with gourmet tastes and a mind of her own.

This first investigation finds DJ and Gorgonzola on the trail of a heroin smuggling ring operation in and around Edinburgh. Their first port of call is the White Heather Hotel, owned by the formidable Morag Mackenzie.

Beneath the innocent surface of the country house hotel eddies a sinister undercurrent. One death follows another. Who among the guests specialises in making murder look like accident? As sea mists gather, the killer awaits a chance to strike. A deadly game of cat and mouse is played — but who will survive to fight another day?

ISBN 978-0-7531-7978-9 (hb)
ISBN 978-0-7531-7979-6 (pb)

The Sporran Connection

Peter Kerr

The droll Scottish detective, Bob Burns, is once again aided by his game-for-anything forensic scientist lady friend, Julie Bryson, and abetted by keener-than-smart rookie detective, Andy Green.

When Andy becomes the unwitting recipient of a drop of £100,000 in used notes, the trio become enmeshed in a web of murder, intrigue and Caledonian skulduggery, as the action shifts to Sicily, New York and a remote Hebridean island. The arrival of a Sicilian blacksmith as the island's new laird leads to some hilarious misunderstandings as the line between the good and bad guys becomes increasingly blurred.

After many a Highland shenanigan, including a vital kilt-raising stunt by Andy Green, the mystery is finally solved . . . or is it?

ISBN 978-0-7531-8028-0 (hb)
ISBN 978-0-7531-8029-7 (pb)

Mr Henry Mulligan

Vernon Coleman

Mr Henry Mulligan is an old man who is dying. He disappears from the geriatric ward of a large hospital in the English midlands. His wife, suffering from Alzheimer's disease, disappears with him. Where have they gone? And why?

A young, newly qualified doctor working in hospital has made friends with the couple and decides to try and find them. His search proves more of a challenge than he had expected, and he discovers that he didn't know as much about Henry Mulligan as he thought he did. Only by uncovering some well-hidden secrets can the young doctor find the missing couple.

ISBN 978-0-7531-7930-7 (hb)
ISBN 978-0-7531-7931-4 (pb)

A Boy of Good Breeding

Miriam Toews

Life in Winnipeg hasn't worked out so well for Knute and her daughter. But living with her parents back in her hometown of Algren and working for the longtime mayor, Hosea Funk, has its own challenges. Knute finds herself mixed up in Hosea's attempts to achieve his dream of meeting the Prime Minister — even though that means keeping the town's population at an even 1500. It's not an easy task, with citizens threatening to move back, and one Algrenian on the verge of giving birth to twins — or possibly triplets.

Full of humour and larger-than-life characters, A Boy of Good Breeding is a warm-hearted novel about families that have been split up but are inexorably drawn back together.

ISBN 978-0-7531-7860-7 (hb)
ISBN 978-0-7531-7861-4 (pb)

The Mallorca Connection

Peter Kerr

A rare combination of suspense and humour, with a real twist in the tale

Bob Burns is an old-fashioned kind of Scottish sleuth, more interested in catching villains than creeping to get promotion. So, when his enquiries into a brutal and bizarre murder are blocked by his bosses, should he risk losing his career by carrying on his investigations?

Encouraged by an attractive, though maverick, forensic scientist and assisted by a keener-than-bright young constable, Bob does it his way. The trail leads the trio from Scotland to Mallorca, where intrigue and mayhem mingle with the crowds at a fishermen's fiesta.

ISBN 978-0-7531-7844-7 (hb)
ISBN 978-0-7531-7845-4 (pb)

ISIS publish a wide range of books in large print, from fiction to biography. Any suggestions for books you would like to see in large print or audio are always welcome. Please send to the Editorial Department at:

ISIS Publishing Limited
7 Centremead
Osney Mead
Oxford OX2 0ES

A full list of titles is available free of charge from:

Ulverscroft Large Print Books Limited

(UK)
The Green
Bradgate Road, Anstey
Leicester LE7 7FU
Tel: (0116) 236 4325

(Australia)
P.O. Box 314
St Leonards
NSW 1590
Tel: (02) 9436 2622

(USA)
P.O. Box 1230
West Seneca
N.Y. 14224-1230
Tel: (716) 674 4270

(Canada)
P.O. Box 80038
Burlington
Ontario L7L 6B1
Tel: (905) 637 8734

(New Zealand)
P.O. Box 456
Feilding
Tel: (06) 323 6828

Details of **ISIS** complete and unabridged audio books are also available from these offices. Alternatively, contact your local library for details of their collection of **ISIS** large print and unabridged audio books.